Demon Soul

by
Christine Ashworth

Christine Ashworth
March 22, 2013

www.crescentmoonpress.com

Demon Soul
Christine Ashworth

ISBN: 978-0-984805-9-2
E-ISBN: 978-0-9846394-5-8

© Copyright Christine Ashworth 2011. All rights reserved
Cover Art: Ash Arceneaux
Editor: Liz Pelletier
Layout/Typesetting: jimandzetta.com

Crescent Moon Press
1385 Highway 35
Box 269
Middletown, NJ 07748

Ebooks/Books are not transferable. They cannot be sold, shared or given away as it is an infringement on the copyright of this work.

All Rights Are Reserved. No part of this book may be used or reproduced in any manner whatsoever without written permission, except in the case of brief quotations embodied in critical articles and reviews.

This book is a work of fiction. The names, characters, places and incidents are products of the writer's imagination or have been used fictitiously and are not to be construed as real. Any resemblance to persons, living or dead, actual events, locale or organizations is entirely coincidental.

Crescent Moon Press electronic publication/print publication: March 2011 www.crescentmoonpress.com

*For my husband, Tom Ashworth, who knew it all along.
And for my father, Chet Cunningham, who set the example of what a working writer did all day. I love you both so very much!*

Chapter One

"Where the hell are you?" It took all of Rose's concentration to keep walking, one throbbing foot in front of the other, down the length of the empty outdoor shopping mall in Santa Monica. The long night had finally tumbled into a dawn cloaked in shadow and fog and the cry of seagulls.

After walking west for more hours than she cared to remember, at last she'd ended up at her destination, cold and miserable. With no purse, no money, and no wish to return to her previous life. All she had to cling to was a name.

Gabriel Caine.

She stood on one foot and eased the tennis shoe off the other one, wincing at the sight of crimson blood on the heel of her white sock. Blisters. Perfect. Add that to being cold, ready to drop from exhaustion, miserable and without a penny to her name, and the day was starting out just great.

"Freaking *perfect.*" Rose sat heavily on the curb of the empty mall and rested her head on her knees. She wasn't going to give up. Not now, not after all she'd been through to get here. Yet it would be so nice to sleep...her head slipped off her knees and she jerked awake.

Damn it Gabriel Caine, I need to talk to you. Please.

Rose chewed on her thumbnail. He had to be close, *had* to be here somewhere. She refused to give in to panic.

"Gabriel. Gabriel. Gabriel." His name fell like a litany on the cold air, as it had in her mind for the last three months.

When she'd been stuck in a coma, wandering the gray between-place, she'd been offered a chance to come back. *Rescue Gabriel Caine.* She'd accepted the task, grabbed for it eagerly. When she finally woke up, she'd worked her ass off

~ ☾ ~

getting healthy again. If saving this Gabriel dude meant she'd begin to atone for all her past sins and achieve some sort of redemption, then she was all for it.

She winced and walled out thoughts of her muddy past, refocusing on Gabriel. Guided to this place, at this time and in fighting shape despite the blisters and the exhaustion, the only missing ingredient was the man himself. As she waited for him, doubts crept in.

"I'm clear on the saving part. But from what? And how?" Her words fell flat in the thickness of the mist. "Especially since I can barely stand. I'm not exactly Marines material, people. And would it have hurt the lesson to add some aspirins to my pockets?"

The cry of a gull brought goose bumps. "Sorry. No disrespect meant, you know that, right?" Rose rubbed her chilled arms. *Gabriel Caine. Gabriel Caine. Gabriel Caine.* "Come on. I don't have all day. Where the hell *are* you?"

Shut up, woman. Let a man think. His voice was like velvet brushed with impatience in her mind.

Rose's muscles locked. *Gabriel?* Excitement rushed through her body, giving her the energy to stand and stare wildly into the mist. She cursed her racing heart. A dark shape came striding toward her through the fog and her breath caught. *Gabriel Caine?*

You've been yammering at me for hours. Shut up, would you? You're giving me a headache.

His long black coat flared out as his legs ate up the space between them. Even from a distance he exuded a sexual magnetism that made Rose's knees weak, a cliché she'd never believed before now. She stared down the mall as he came toward her, the fog alternately hiding and revealing him with every step.

What the hell were you thinking, projecting my name out there for anyone with any telepathic abilities to overhear. Are you trying *to get me killed?*

Rose put her hands to her head in wonder, dug her fingers into her hair and tugged. The new pain assured her she was awake. His exasperated sigh in her mind had her wincing.

~ ☽ ~

"Sorry, but we need to talk. Out loud." She was still wrapping her mind around the whole telepathic thing.

He was closer now. Gabriel Caine in person was bigger, stronger, sexier than any man she'd ever met, with an energy she could feel charging the air and brushing up against her skin. He had to be six five, if not taller.

She took a step back both mentally and physically. She was supposed to save *this* man? Rescue *him*? This muscled guy in leather, black jeans and a dangerous aura blended in perfectly with the misty, deserted mall. He didn't need her help. There wasn't anything he couldn't handle, she was quite sure of it.

Rose swallowed her disappointment. She'd been so sure she could save him. But with each step bringing him closer, she had the overwhelming urge to curl up and cry.

Or curl up in his arms. A surge of longing for him shocked her. She'd never been so strongly attracted to anyone, but she could think about little else than the two of them, naked. Heat lit her cheeks. Talk about bad timing.

Gabriel snorted. *Bad timing doesn't begin to cover it. You don't want me too close to you.* His mental tone was dry and unamused.

Rose flushed. "I can't believe this," she said, and crossed her arms protectively. "People shouldn't go around reading other people's minds." *Arrogant ass.*

When they broadcast, it happens. Your mind is broadcasting on a wide band. You have no shield, no barrier of any kind to keep me out. And I'm not an arrogant ass. As he came closer, he slowed down, finally stopping a couple yards away.

Surprise crossed his face before it hardened. "This is no time for games, Satine. You're not welcome here. You will never be welcome here."

"Excuse me? I'm not – whoever. My name is Rose," she protested. "I'm supposed to be here. I've been sent here to help you. Though now that I see you, I'm not exactly sure what the hell it is I'm supposed to do for you."

He took a couple more steps toward her and they stared at each other.

~ ☾ ~

The picture she'd seen didn't do him justice. He looked dark-angel, messed-up beautiful. His gray eyes were a study in intensity. White skin covered a classical bone structure made more approachable by a crooked nose. A thick, shiny scar on his left cheek stretched down his throat and continued below the neck of his shirt. His hair, the color of ebony, brushed his shoulders without a hint of curl.

She glanced up and noticed him looking *her* up and down, interest gleaming in his half-open eyes. Heat washed over her body.

Power radiated from him. She fought to stand straight, to appear strong in the face of his strength. Inwardly she quailed. He really didn't need her. What was she supposed to do now?

"Are you done staring?" His physical voice sounded much like his mental voice, a rough velvet. The interest she'd seen was masked now.

"Yeah. You?" Rose bit out the words. She looked around, anywhere but at him, and saw her shoe on the ground. She bent and slipped it on, wincing as the canvas hit her blister. "It's important that we talk."

He studied her for a moment. "Through there." He pointed to an easily overlooked door beside an imports shop. "If I know my brother, it'll be open."

The glass door led to a staircase. Doing her best not to limp, Rose went first, flushing again as his scent seemed to surround her, an earthy, greenish-brown scent, elemental. She totally had to get a grip or she'd start stripping for him right on the staircase.

I wouldn't mind, but the staircase isn't my preferred place to make love to a woman. She could hear the faint mocking tone in his words and flushed even hotter.

"Would you stop that?" she snapped.

"Sorry." But he didn't sound it. "When you project such clear and detailed images, it's very hard to ignore." They got to the bare landing and Gabriel reached around her to try the doorknob of the door to the left.

Rose stopped breathing as his arm brushed her breast. *Ye*

~ ☾ ~

gods, woman, get a grip. He is so not for you. And yet, what they could do...*Hell! He can hear me!* Biting her lip, she focused on the tiny pain, working hard to keep her thoughts to herself.

Gabriel rattled the doorknob again.

But the door remained stubbornly closed. Rose backed toward the staircase to get some breathing room. Standing so close made her entirely too aware of him, his scent, his implacable strength. Retreat seemed like a good idea.

Gabriel frowned at the door, then knocked hard enough to rattle the glass. "Damn it, Justin, open up."

Something in the air shifted slightly and she shivered. Even Gabriel tensed and faced her, muttering beneath his breath. A noxious smell drifted toward them. She sneezed and looked down the staircase.

A small, misshapen creature in a brown cloak flowed up the stairs, showing glistening teeth. Its thin, long arms ended in stubby fingers with wicked claws that reached for her.

Fear and panic tumbled in her head. *Protect Gabriel. Save Gabriel. I can do this.* A cry built deep inside her as the nightmare came closer.

Heedless of her battered body, her energy surged as the nightmare came closer and she let loose a warrior's cry. Grabbing both hand rails of the staircase, she kicked out at the thing with her feet, knocking it back a few steps. A sharp red pain radiated up her legs and she yelped. *Mother of God that hurt! Is it made of cement?*

* * *

Gabriel plucked her off the stairway and shoved her behind him with a little too much force. He winced at her cry of pain when she landed against the far wall, but kept his focus on the demon coming at him.

He should have known better than to come home. He shows up here, and of course there's some girl reaching out to him telepathically. A girl, moreover, whose power drew demons to her without effort.

Even he felt the draw of her power, every bit as much as this lesser demon coming toward him. Gabriel hungered for her, his demon blood yearning to taste her.

"Stay back, as far as you can go," he ordered her. If the demon got past him, she was dead. An old memory, better left buried, was jarred loose, and his breath caught. *No.* He wouldn't be the unwitting cause of yet another girl's death.

Gabriel swung but the demon evaded his punch. It sprang at him, striking with surprising speed, sinking its teeth into Gabriel's upper arm and winding its long arms around his torso. With an oath, he wrapped his good arm around the demon's head and gave it a sharp jerk, snapping its neck and ripping the teeth from his flesh. Poison sped its way through his system. He dropped the demon and staggered back to lean against the wall.

Lifeless, the creature tumbled back down the stairs to land in a pile of rags and bone at the bottom of the stairway. Great. He'd have to dispose of the carcass before the place opened or there'd be mass hysteria.

Gabriel turned to check on the woman. She lay sprawled against the far wall where his shove had landed her. Her summer-blue eyes were big in a classic oval face, coppery curls surrounded her pearly skin. Her eyes and her mind were clouded with pain and questions.

Her power pulled at him, and yet she looked so much like Satine that a part of him wanted to recoil. Energy crackled in the air between them. Did she know that she called to his kind?

"What the hell *was* that?" she demanded. "Aw, man. You're bleeding."

Gabriel checked his arm and grimaced at the blood flow.

"It was a demon." He went to her side and scooped her up in his arms. "I know you're in pain," he said before she could object, and going to the door he knocked again.

"Demon? Yeah, pull my other leg."

Gabriel frowned at the visceral tug brought about by the feel of her body against his. Holding her gave him a jolt of energy, clean and pure, a hit straight to the veins. No, she wasn't like Satine. That didn't mean he trusted her.

He took a deep breath and her scent clouded his mind.

~ ☾ ~

Yeah, okay, so his mating instincts were now jumping up and down like crazy. His attraction to her didn't matter. The sooner he put her in his brother's care, the better. He shifted her weight to his good arm and pounded again on the glass. "Damn it, Justin."

"Put me down." She squirmed in his arms. "Oh come on. Enough. Put me down."

"As I saved your ass, you can damn well be gracious about me taking care of you."

"You killed it, didn't you?"

"Yeah."

"I should have protected you. I'll do a better job, I promise. You can count on me. Now put me down." She actually seemed to believe what she was saying.

"No one has protected me in years." He read the trust on her face with dismay. He'd much rather she was scared of him.

She shrugged and looked away.

Gabriel eyed her warily. "Why are you here?" He slid into her mind and met a maelstrom of thought, a snake pit of pain and fear that bit at him.

She sighed. "You're in danger. I'm here to save you. And yeah, totally aware how stupid that sounds, considering you're carrying me and all."

"Just—don't talk. Keep your thoughts to yourself and do not talk. Justin, I know you're in there. I can smell you."

The door opened abruptly. Gabriel tensed. It had been years. What would he say? How could he begin to explain such a long absence?

After one comprehensive glance at both Gabriel and the woman, Justin yawned and opened the door wider, letting the sound of reggae music out into the hallway. "You're early. Or is it late? At any rate, you sure know how to make an entrance."

Gabriel looked at his brother and didn't move. "Still dressing in bayou chic, I see. I don't think I could have found an uglier Hawaiian shirt if I'd looked with both hands."

Justin glanced down at his purple and orange flowered

~ ☾ ~

shirt with the green monkeys and sniffed. "This is the So Cal Surfer Dude Dress Code, man, Hawaiian shirt and board shorts. Some of us prefer color, unlike your assassin chic." He gestured to his brother's clothing and shook his head, his brown dreadlocks bouncing.

"So Cal by way of Jamaica, mon," Gabriel retorted. "The worst of both worlds."

"Yeah yeah. You waiting for an engraved invitation? Come on in." He gestured toward the woman in his arms. "Who is she?"

Gabriel walked into the office. "I don't know."

"Would you put me down? I can walk. With help," she amended. "Not to mention, hello. Here and listening."

He ignored her and looked around the sparse reception area. "You got a couch in this place?" The walls were white, the carpet industrial gray. The office felt chilly, and not just due to air conditioning. "Gregor chose the color scheme. Am I right? "

Justin led the way down a narrow corridor. "Well, you know our brother. Cool and controlled. Watch your head," he warned, ducking into the first office on the left. "This place wasn't built for people as tall as us. Go on, all the way down the hall to the left." The island music came to an abrupt stop.

Gabriel found the right room and, ducking under the doorway, went directly to the black leather couch in the corner of what looked like a conference room. He bent and put the girl down gently.

Her fiery hair curled madly to her shoulders and her tee shirt and jeans blended into the black leather, leaving her arms and face a contrast of startling white.

His brother joined him by the couch.

Gabriel frowned as he looked at the girl. He reached for her chin, studied her, ignoring her startled "Hey!"

The superficial resemblance to Satine still made him leery. Red hair, blue eyes, yes, but life shone from this one. Satine was death. This one – Rose, she'd said – had a completely different energy signature. Still...he sighed and turned at last to face Justin. "Well?" He waited for his brother's judgment.

~ ☾ ~

"Damn it to hell. Blood?" Justin took his brother's arm. "Give me a minute."

Gabriel turned so the girl couldn't watch. "Do it."

Warmth emanated from Justin's hands, closing the wounds with a dance of blue light. "There's poison at work."

"I've handled worse." It hurt like a sonofabitch, but he'd live.

"Damn it, Gabriel. What's going on? Tell me everything," Justin ordered, and sank down into a chair.

"That's it? No recriminations, no yelling, no telling me how I broke Dad's heart?" Gabriel kept to his feet, not yet able to relax.

Justin shrugged. "Guilt trips? Not my style. Fill me in. Ten years is a lot to catch up on. Start with her."

"Yeah, start with me." The redhead wrapped her arms around her knees. Her wary gaze darted from Gabriel to Justin. "I'm Rose Walters. I've been sent back from the dead to save Mr. Studly there." She gestured to Gabriel.

Justin smothered a startled laugh.

"Not that I did a good job just now," she added. "Some warrior chick I'm turning out to be. Oh, and there's this thing at the bottom of your staircase. It was really smelly."

"Smelly?" Justin's eyebrows rose.

"It was an Uupka demon." His brother didn't look impressed with the foul addition to his stairwell. "Should I have let it kill her? Fine. Tell me where you want me to dump the demon, and I'll do it." He felt ten again, after batting a baseball through the kitchen window.

"You don't have to dump the demon. I just asked."

"And I told you." Gabriel paced the length of the conference room and back, trying to catch his breath. There were too many people in the room, damn it. Family and togetherness had all been left behind years ago. He never should have come home. Not after all this time.

"Tell me why you two are here. If you want me to help, I'll need some details."

"I don't know why she's here," Gabriel declared. "I've been headed this way for a while. Two nights ago it became

~ ☾ ~

imperative that I come home." He turned back to Rose. "Don't change the subject. You're here to save me from what, exactly? It's time to explain."

* * *

Rose licked her suddenly dry lips. "I'm to prevent your death, I guess." She looked from Gabriel-the-arrogant to the other man, just as devastatingly attractive in his colorful wardrobe. They had to believe her. She had nowhere to go, nothing else to do in this world.

"You *guess?*"

She glared at him. "Looking at you, yeah I'm kind of wondering what the hell I'm doing here, too. In the meantime, my ankle hurts. Hell, my whole body hurts. I've been walking for hours. Can I get some aspirin or something?" She looked from one man to the other. "Well?" These big guys talked about demons as if it were *normal*. What's wrong with this picture?

"I'll take care of it." Justin knelt at her feet and took her injured ankle in both his hands. "So tell me, what will happen if Gabriel here ups and dies?" His hand warmed against her foot. "This shouldn't hurt, but if it does, give a holler."

Rose bit her lip and struggled to keep still. A pale blue light flowed from Justin's hands into her ankle, soothing the throbbing there as energy tingled along her skin and sank deep. She sighed in surprised relief as the pain disappeared.

He picked up her other foot. "I smell blood."

"Yeah. Blisters."

Justin's eyebrows rose. Soon the throbbing in her heel subsided, and the lack of immediate pain had Rose melting into the couch.

"Those are some hands. Thanks. All better." She tucked one leg under her. Her gaze flickered over Gabriel, but she couldn't find open wounds. "Did you heal him the way you healed me?"

"Yes. Sort of." Justin winked and stood easily, his hands in his pockets. "The only thing to do for the exhaustion you feel is sleep. So before you pass out, if Gabriel dies, what will happen?"

~ ☾ ~

She eyed him, trying to keep her thoughts in a tiny black box so they couldn't be overheard. If she told them everything, they'd just pat her on the head and send her away. At least, that's what she'd do. Close ranks. Why should they believe her? Then again, they *did* believe in demons...

"Okay. If he dies? I don't know." Rose took a breath and turned from Justin's open face to Gabriel's closed, suspicious one. "I made a deal, okay? I get to live, and the only thing I have to do in return is to save you."

"What are you supposed to save me *from*, and who did you make a deal with?"

She shrugged. "It seemed like the right thing to do under the circumstances."

Gabriel shook his head, clearly exasperated. "I don't have time for this. Justin, you take care of her, see her home. I've got a job to do."

"No!" Both Justin and Rose spoke at the same time.

"I have to stick with you." Rose stood. "Anywhere you go, I'm going, too. No offense," she said to Justin.

"None taken. What kind of job?" Justin turned back to his brother. "What's more important than family? Stay. It's been too long for you to just leave."

Gabriel turned on him with a snarl. "I can't. I'm tracking my soul."

Rose swallowed. "You – you're *what*? No. No way. This can't be happening." He lost his soul? Demons weren't bad enough? Talk about hopping into the fire.

"Explain. Now." Justin pointed his brother to a chair. "Sit." He slammed the chair into the conference table and faced them both.

"Some chick on the beach ripped most of my soul out of my chest. Happy now?"

"How?" Bewildered, Rose watched as Gabriel prowled the room like a tiger in its cage. "I'm not saying I don't believe you, I just don't understand."

Justin folded his arms across his chest. "Details."

"Two days ago, while I slept, this vampire I once knew dug into my chest with magic and her hands and pulled out my

~ ☾ ~

soul. I fought her for it, managed to keep a part of it but she got the lion's share. Can't get clearer than that."

"Vampires don't steal souls. That's a legend. It's not real, Gabriel." But Justin's voice held more than a bit of doubt.

Vampires? Rose rubbed her arms as the tension in the room rose. Demons, stolen souls, and now vampires. Terrific. What's next, flying monkeys?

"If that's a legend, then I'm fucking crazy. Do I look crazy?" Gabriel demanded. "What else could possibly bring me back here? I tracked Satine back to L.A. I want my soul back, and I'm counting on you to help."

"Okay. Okay, let's just be calm, okay?" Rose jumped up. "Maybe this is all the same puzzle. If Gabriel's soul is missing, then maybe I'm the person who needs to find it for him. I can do that, I know that much. It was part of what they told me while I was in the waiting room. Not that I believed it, because, hey, how do you lose a soul? It didn't make sense to me until now. Not that it makes sense, really, and okay, shutting up now." Rose sat back down as the two Caines stared at her.

"What, just in the nick of time we get a Soul Chalice?" Justin frowned. "Isn't that a huge coincidence?"

"Soul Chalices don't exist," Gabriel protested.

"You can't have it both ways. If Soul Stealers exist, which you say they do, then so do Soul Chalices. But still, big coincidence."

"Maybe too much of a coincidence." Gabriel scowled at Rose. "I'm beginning to understand. You made a deal, all right. But you made it with Satine. You're here for the rest of my soul. Well, you're not going to get it."

"Gabriel, I swear I'm here for you. I've been sent back to help you. I spent a lot of time in the waiting room and I was sent back here, instead of forward to death, for only one reason, and that's to help you in any way possible."

"Forget it. Don't say another word, because who knows when the next thing out of your mouth will be a spell? Justin, do you have anything to bind her with?"

"Like truth-silk? Nope. Take a couple steps back, Gabriel.

~ ☾ ~

Don't accuse the child—she's shaking," he chided.

Gabriel rounded on his brother. "She's in league with Satine. That's the only explanation that makes sense. She wants to destroy me. You want me to trust her?"

"I didn't say that. I said to step back. She's obviously exhausted, and you're obviously not thinking clearly."

A healthy dose of anger surged through Rose and cleared her head. "Stop it, both of you, and listen to me." They looked at her, Justin with annoyance and Gabriel with hostility. "I'm sorry, but I don't know what a Soul Chalice is. I don't know who Satine is, and to my knowledge I've never killed anything except myself and that was technically an accident. I don't know how I'm supposed to save you, Gabriel, but you don't seem to care that you might be in serious danger."

She took an unsteady breath. "I asked you for a few minutes, and you gave that to me. But you don't believe in me or in my mission. So unless you tell me to stay, I'll go now, and if I'm lucky I won't die right away since I'm not upholding my part of the bargain. But pushing me away will be most likely the last mistake you make. Well? What's it gonna be?" Rose locked gazes with Gabriel.

Justin moved and would have said something, but a quick wave of her hand shut him up as she kept her gaze on the man she was sent to save for a full minute.

Rose gave him a brief smile. "You've made your choice. Good luck with getting your soul back." She left before she began pleading with him. She didn't have much any more, but she still had her dignity.

Beyond the conference room door, Rose broke into a run, a wild pain deep in her heart. She gave it a shot. Not her fault. It's not like the world needed someone like her. Death would be a relief, after all. So she never had true love. So she never had a child. Big deal. *Her* family was nothing to brag about.

Rose shut the door of Caine Investigations with a sense of utter failure.

~ ☾ ~

Chapter Two

Gabriel let out a breath. "She's gone." His hostility evaporated. "Hell."

"Yeah. And you did nothing to stop her."

"Neither did you," he retorted. "Besides, she looked like the vamp that stole my soul. I'm supposed to cozy up to her? Get real." Doubt twisted through him.

"She didn't want me to ask her to stay, she wanted you to ask." Justin shrugged. "But she didn't smell like a vamp to me. Hey, it's your soul. I don't think I'd let a surface resemblance bother me if she could help. But I'm not you. Hell, it's been so long I don't even know you anymore." He settled on the couch and leaned his head back.

Gabriel moved to the window and brooded. "She didn't smell totally human, you know. You're right, she didn't smell like a vamp, but there was something extra about her."

"Wondered if you'd caught that. Demon, perhaps?" Justin shrugged. "Or something else? Maybe she's a hybrid."

"Maybe. Or maybe she really is a Soul Chalice. Did you feel her pull?"

"Yeah. But for me it was more of a protective pull. You?"

Justin's knowing gaze made Gabriel shrug and turn away. "It's pretty strong, whatever it is." Movement in the misty mall below caught his eye and he watched as Rose dropped to her knees. He tensed. Was she hurt? Without thinking, he reached for her mind, slipped in, and listened.

Oh God. I'm sorry I failed you. Can you take me quickly? Without pain? I'd even be happy to sit around the waiting room again, if that's what's needed. I just – I can't do this. Okay, I can, I know that. I'm not sure he's worth it, though.

~ ☾ ~

Oh, what the hell. Oops, sorry. I mean, I really don't want to die just yet. I like feeling healthy, you know? Forgive me for screwing this up.

Gabriel shut down the connection with her and left the conference room at a run. He had to get to her before she left. If she was right and she died it would be his fault. If she was wrong, well. He'd deal. His pulse pounding, he took the stairs three at a time and leaped over the dead demon at the bottom, catapulting to the outside.

She was still there, still on her knees, her arms wrapped around her stomach. He noticed for the first time how thin she was, and began to wonder about her past.

"Rose?."

She scrambled to her feet. "What do you want?"

"You." He crowded her. "I mean – hell, I'm not good with words." She didn't respond, so he tried again. "Don't leave."

"Why shouldn't I? You don't want me here. You don't trust me."

"I changed my mind."

"Why?"

"Why?" The question threw him. "Does it matter why?"

"Yes, it matters. If you're just pretending to believe in me, then we're both gonna die."

Gabriel stared into her eyes. "I snooped, okay? In your mind, I mean. And now I believe. More or less. So don't leave."

Her eyes cleared. "You believe I've been sent here to save you?"

"Yeah." Not that he was all warm and fuzzy about it, but he believed. "Somehow."

"You'll work with me to find your soul?" she pressed.

His fist tightened. Everything deep inside him argued against that course of action, but she held the cards. If he wanted the rest of his soul back, he'd need to concede. "Yes. I'll work with you." *But I don't have to like it.* He saw, with some satisfaction, the shock on her face when she heard him in her mind.

Rose narrowed her eyes at him. "The first thing I need to

~ ☾ ~

learn is how to create a barrier to my thoughts."

He rocked back on his heels and pretended to consider. "I need to see if I can mentally locate the bitch-vamp that has my soul. Somewhere in there, I need to learn exactly what happened to you in the waiting room while your life hung in the balance. Then I'll teach you to barrier."

She stared him down. "I won't go back to my old life. I have no home, no clothing other than what I've got on my back, and no living relatives I care to claim. If you truly believe, then you'll know we need to stick together."

From the way she looked ready to bolt, he understood it was an either/or situation. "We'll take care of you. No worries." He held out his hand. "Come back upstairs."

Rose let out a breath and wiped her eyes. She closed the distance between them, but put her hands behind her back. "The minute I feel used, I'm gone."

Her eyes met his and he saw her determination. "I understand." He did, too. More than she'd expect him to understand. For one moment, an overwhelming need filled him to crush whoever had abused her in the past. He led the way back to Caine Investigations, his headache now approaching massive proportions.

Justin greeted them cheerfully as they filed back into the conference room. "I found an old sweatshirt for you. Saw you were cold. Hope you like UCLA." He pushed the faded blue sweatshirt toward her.

Rose took it. "Go, Bruins." Gabriel watched as she headed back to the couch. She curled up on one end. "Now what?"

"Think we could get some coffee up here?" Gabriel met Justin's curious gaze. "Probably safer here than going out."

"Sure. CaféGo is just down the mall a bit. I'll go pick up." Justin left the room, leaving Rose and Gabriel alone.

He sighed and turned to the girl. "Tell me about the waiting room."

"This big black woman came in and pitched a fit about me being there."

"Would you let me see what happened? Take me there, in your mind?"

~ ☾ ~

"I thought you said my mind was wide open?"

"It is. I thought I'd ask this time." It was the closest thing he could get to an apology.

Rose bit her bottom lip. "If you have to."

"Thanks." Gabriel sat on the coffee table across from her. "Now close your eyes and relax. I don't think you'll fight me, but if the instinct to fight is there, try to ignore it for now. We'll get to that part later. Ready?"

She gave him a wan smile. "As ready as I'll ever be."

Gabriel slid into her mind and smiled at her wonderment. He sifted through her most recent memories of their first meeting, re-living the sexual reaction she'd had to him. Reliving his reaction to her, and her burning need to save him from the demon in the stairwell.

He moved past that quickly, bringing to light the last few hours. A nurse had dropped her off at a restaurant in Culver City. Rose had looked into the window of the restaurant, then turned and headed west. She walked the eight miles of city streets all the way to Santa Monica and the Third Street Promenade.

The picture jumped, and he saw her long recovery in the hospital. Before that, there was darkness, full of waiting and a sense of...happiness? The picture changed again and there she stood, looking down at her body as a medical team frantically worked over her.

Time seemed to pass. She spent what felt to him like a long time in the waiting room. Colorful lights zipped by her in the gray room, souls not confined to any human body. She was the only human there. Constantly looking down at her body, lonely in the hospital bed. Her only visitors were medical staff.

Then a big black woman with a clipboard came up to her and started furiously gesticulating. The two talked, but he couldn't hear a word. A shadowy female figure hovered just out of his vision.

Another step had them up against a mental blank wall that didn't feel organic. It was almost as if someone else had put that barrier up, walled out her past. But why?

Gabriel slid out of her mind. The scent of coffee filled the

~ ☾ ~

air. "God, I need coffee."

"On the table. You okay, little brother?"

"Good. Tired." Gabriel moved to the conference table.

Rose joined them, a frown pulling her lips down. "Didn't find much, did you? Didn't really think you would."

"You did fine." Justin handed her a cup of coffee, and passed one to Gabriel. "Drink up. It's a girly drink, just for you. Lots of chocolate."

"How long did that take?"

"Thirty minutes. No big deal. But you'll need the caffeine and the sugar, so drink up," said Gabriel. She believed, completely and totally, that she was there to rescue him. He knew it from the way she'd approached the demon, from the way she'd thought about it. But why?

"Why do I need the caffeine and the sugar?"

"Memory reads can be very draining. Caffeine and sugar help. Sleep helps more, but we're a bit away from letting you sleep." Gabriel shrugged, dragged his gaze from her. "I don't know the science behind it. Sorry."

He turned to Justin. "She's telling the truth about all of it. As far as she knows, at any rate." He turned, caught her staring at his mouth. She flushed.

He lifted a brow, a smile twitching at his lips. *Thinking about kissing me, are you?*

"Stop it," she hissed.

Justin looked from one to the other. "What did I miss?"

"She needs a barrier, a shield. Doesn't have one now, and tends to broadcast everything she thinks," he explained. "I'll work with her on that."

"Not everything," she protested. "And it's not like I knew I was broadcasting my thoughts."

"A barrier is a good idea." Laughter glinted in Justin's green eyes. "I didn't hear anything, though. Maybe you're just tuned to her? Or she's just tuned in to you?"

"Okay, let's change the subject." Rose fanned her face. "I need something clarified for me."

"Name it."

"You talked about demons and vampires. I thought those

didn't exist."

Gabriel snorted. "You came back from the dead with a mission to give me my soul back, and *you* can't believe? Do you think I'm human? That Justin is? What about you? Are you human? Because I'm not so sure about that."

* * *

She stared at him. "What the *hell*? Of course I'm human." Irritated, Rose swirled the last of the mocha around, getting as much of the chocolate from the bottom as possible. Her energy had come back with every sip and now she almost felt well rested. "Jeez. Of course I'm human. You're human, too. You've got a soul that's okay, currently missing, but still. You've got one. Somewhere." If he'd told her the truth. But he didn't have a reason to lie, did he?

Gabriel leaned toward her, his smile chased away by darkly slanting brows. "If you're going to hang out with us, you need to get this straight. Vampires are *real*. Like demons and the Fae and humans are real," he said. "And everything else that goes bump in the night. Truthfully? You don't smell any more human than I do."

"What? I don't smell human? Is that man-speak for saying I need a shower?" She eyed the two men.

"No. We're not sure why you carry the scent. But we're, well..." Justin exchanged a glance with Gabriel. "We're not exactly, totally, human. But we are on your side," he added.

"Justin," Gabriel warned. He crossed his arms.

"Come on guys, don't tease."

"Not teasing. And Gabriel, it's okay. Like you said, if she's hanging around us she'll need to know what we are sooner or later." Justin smiled as he turned back to Rose.

"What are you?" They were big men, she realized. Very big men, and didn't Gabriel kill the thing in the stairwell? Rose swallowed.

Justin leaned forward. "You need to know that Demons and the Fae have been roaming the earth almost as long as men have, crossing over from their own planes of existence. Over time, they've crossbred with humans. Most of the crossbreeds don't live, but a handful of clans have thrived over the last few centuries."

Gabriel groaned and stalked off to the other end of the conference room.

Rose stared. "You're a cross-breed of demons, humans and fairies?" She tested the thought and found herself fascinated. *Wow. Good morning, Rosie!*

"The Caine clan is - we call ourselves tribreds." He shrugged. "It seems to fit. Our gene pool has all the various Fae characteristics, as well as all the various human characteristics in it. The demon part of us tends to be more, um, specialized."

"That's why you guys look so different from each other. That's...that's absolutely fascinating." Rose looked from Gabriel to Justin, her eyes wide with interest.

Justin coughed. "That's genetics. Now. Can you give us any more details on the saving of Gabriel?" He sat on the edge of the conference table, his body loose, an interesting contrast to the tightly wound Gabriel.

"Just that it has to do specifically with him. I was in the waiting room. Well, you saw that," she added, sneaking a look at Gabriel. His face still like stone, she turned back to his brother. "Apparently I wasn't supposed to be there. This big black woman got really irritated at me, and finally she gave me a choice. If I could save Gabriel, I'd obtain redemption and I'd get to live out my natural life span. If I don't succeed then I die anyway. But he looks disgustingly healthy. The only thing wrong with him is most of his soul is missing."

"She didn't tell you how to save Gabriel?"

Rose shrugged. "I have to believe I'm to find his soul and return it to him. They mentioned something about that, briefly, but come on. The whole thing was pretty unbelievable. I agreed because what did I have to lose?"

Justin nodded. "Interesting." He looked to Gabriel. "Any sense as to how long she was there?"

Gabriel shook his head. "Longer than I'd originally suspected, that's all I can tell you. If she had any family, any friends, I didn't see them in the hospital room."

Her hand tightened on the paper coffee cup. "No family.

~ ☾ ~

No friends. Not going back."

"We'll need to find a place for her to stay," Gabriel said.

"Right. We'll get on that. How are you feeling, health-wise?"

"Exhausted and hungry. Why are you asking?"

Justin smiled. "We're trying to fill in the gaps. Making sure you're safe while you're in our care. Any help you can give me would be appreciated."

"All right. It took me three months to recover from the coma. I had weight to gain, rehab for weak muscles, that kind of thing. I don't know exactly when I was in the waiting room – apparently I was in a coma for quite awhile, or maybe a couple of different times. But once I'd had that experience with the big black woman, I got better very fast. My doctors were surprised at how fast I healed up. I guess I was anxious to find you, to keep you safe." She looked over at Gabriel and a part of her yearned.

"The block on her memory could have come from the waiting room," mused Gabriel.

"It's possible." Justin shrugged. "How old are you?"

"Twenty-three." She chewed on her bottom lip and decided they didn't need to know she asked for that block on her memory. "My turn. Tell me about Satine."

"Satine's a vampire. She's the one who ripped a good hunk of my soul out of me the other night," Gabriel said. "You and she could be related, only she's dark and you - you're light. I'm not exactly thrilled with the resemblance, however surface it may be."

Justin broke in. "Rose, did you ever get your drivers license?"

"No. I know how to drive but I never bothered with a license as I've never had a car. I was...you don't need to know what I was. I'm not that person any more, and that's all you need to know." She shuddered in revulsion.

"Drugs." Gabriel's gentle voice broke into her memories. "You're broadcasting again." He came around the table and helped her sit.

Rose gasped. She remembered the craving, the sexual rush

~ ☾ ~

as the drugs – any drugs - hit her system, the hallucinations and paranoia that came all too quickly after the rush. "I did a lot of different drugs. It made the empty parts of me go away. But I'm clean now. I'm not that empty person anymore." She looked up, from Gabriel to Justin, sure of her ground on this point.

"No," Justin agreed. "You're right, you aren't that person. You're a bit on the thin side, but I'm a good cook, I'll soon fatten you up." He winked at her.

She turned with hope to Gabriel, and at the disbelief in his eyes she reached out and gripped his bare forearm, focusing all her energies on him. Heat flashed down her arm and into her fingers. "I'm clean. I swear it."

"I believe you," he soothed. "You need to let go now, Rose. Let me go, or we're going to have a situation."

"What?" Startled, Rose looked at her hand gripping his arm.

Justin swore and reached for his cell phone.

Rose saw the tiny flickers of flame licking at his skin, coming off her fingers. Horrified, she pulled her hand away. The flickers died, leaving scorched fingerprints behind on his forearm. She put her hand up to her cheek, felt the heat lingering there.

"What am I?" Panic blurred her vision as she looked at Gabriel. "Tell me, what the hell happened to me when I died?"

Gabriel held her by the shoulders, his big hands warm and comforting. "I don't know. Breathe now, Rose. Be calm." His own breaths were slow and even.

"I'm calling in reinforcements," declared Justin.

"And who would that be, exactly?"

"A sorcerer I know slightly named Kendall Sorbis. Hopefully he'll take my call. Don't start with me," Justin ordered, frowning as Gabriel opened his mouth to object. "We need help. This just got too big for us to handle on our own."

Rose shuddered at the memory of fire shooting out of her fingers. *God oh God oh God, what has happened to me?*

Gabriel rubbed her arms gently, bringing her a measure of comfort. *We'll figure it out, Rose. I swear it.*

~ ☾ ~

Chapter Three

Rose wiped her mouth. "Good pizza. Thanks."
"You're welcome." Gabriel had watched Rose devour almost a whole medium pepperoni mushroom pizza. He hadn't wanted any himself, but watching her eat had been a revelation.

Each bite looked like ambrosia from her reactions. Those sexy, low moans of appreciation she gave, her tongue sweeping her lush lower lip swiping up any remaining sauce, almost undid him. Gabriel hadn't had this much temptation in front of him since high school. Not to mention the pull she had on his demon blood.

"Tell me, what was that? With the fire, I mean. I didn't mean to hurt you, you know that, right?"

"It might be something you brought back with you from the waiting room." Like a fire demon, which could mean he was doomed to repeat his past. Morose, he watched her lick her fingers.

Had food ever tasted as good as she made it look? He'd been eating just to survive for too many years to count.

"Brought back with me? I don't understand."

Gabriel shifted in his conference chair and desperately wished for Justin. He didn't do conversation well. Right now his mind didn't want to talk, and his body had its own agenda. "You said you watched a medical team work on your body. That you were above yourself, which I saw as well."

"Yeah. Pretty much." Rose shrugged. "Why?"

"The waiting room is a kind of holding tank, a place for souls between places. Call it Purgatory, for want of a better word. Your body was on earth, hovering between life and

~ ☾ ~

death. Your consciousness, your soul, was elsewhere, in-between."

"In-between what?"

Gabriel shook his head. "I'm not sure. Between this life and whatever is next, I suppose." Hell, if she would just stop asking questions that he had no answers for. Talking to her brought his past too close.

Brought *her* too close.

He didn't dare do what his body ached for, even if she'd allow it. He didn't trust himself enough. Gabriel jumped up and stalked to the window. Where in hell was Justin?

"So...I brought something back with me? Like a virus or something?"

"That's the current theory."

The door opened and Gabriel turned in relief. "Any luck finding your sorcerer?"

Justin shook his head. "Not so far, but I've left a few messages. Any luck on your end with finding Satine?"

"Not yet. If you can take care of Rose, then I'll get back to it." His morning search of the mountain ranges near the coast had left him veering out of control. He kept refocusing on Rose, on the need for her building inside him, instead of on Satine. It had been a frustrating and wearying exercise. "I need to be alone this time."

"Sure, I can do that. I've got some filing that needs to be done."

"Uh, no. I'm not going anywhere without Gabriel. I'm feeling a whole lot better now, and I'm sticking." She glared at them both.

"You can't. Not this time." Cut and dried. No slack. He had to break this fascination with her, starting right now. "Absolutely not. I need to concentrate, and I can't do that with you here."

"Don't care. Not budging," she said, and settled further down into the chair. "Not one bit. I'm not moving, I promise you that."

Gabriel looked at her, firmly planted in the chair on the far side of the conference table. He'd take the loophole she gave

~ ☾ ~

him. "Oh. Good. Enjoy." He left the conference room and walked down the back hallway. Another office sat at the very end. He slipped in and closed the door, allowing himself a deep breath of relief.

Alone. *Finally.* He hadn't been around people this much in months and he'd started to feel suffocated around Justin and Rose. Here he could breathe, at least. It wasn't his hideout in the mountains, but at least he was alone.

He walked to the far windows and stared out at the slim band of the sea. Rose. What was he supposed to do about her? She'd wormed herself into his life and she scared him to death. He'd known her for what, a handful of hours? Whatever she was drew him. He'd locked onto her when he first saw her, just like that lesser demon had. The demon wanted to devour her. So did he, but in a completely different way.

Rose was too *much* for him. She didn't know what she was, and that put everyone else in the dark. Maybe put them in danger. His fingers brushed the burns on his forearm and he sighed. A fire demon, at least partially was his guess.

The drug thing – well, she *looked* clean, if a bit too pared down. And, he had to admit, she *felt* clean, too. The pure energy she'd given him every time they touched attested to it. Yet he'd seen into her memories, seen her as an addict, a girl with a big, gaping hole inside her.

Poor kid. At least she wasn't a killer. She hadn't crossed that line, no matter what else she may have done. But if she's a Soul Chalice, he didn't have a clue how to handle a myth come to life.

Settling on the wide window ledge, he let the sun warm him as he closed his eyes. He'd look for Satine in closer areas than the mountains, start at the sea, and work east. The vampire had to be in L.A. somewhere. He'd tracked her to this area, and all he had to do was find her.

Rose's image filled his thoughts, interfering with his search. He cursed and cleared his mind once more. Focusing on Satine's signature vamp aura, he searched carefully, touching minds along the beach cities ten miles north and ten

~ ☾ ~

miles south. Slowly he worked outward, lost to the sun as he filled his mind with thousands of other people's thoughts.

Finally he found Satine. He lurked, hoping to escape her notice as she stirred in the dark, naked on her silken bed. He watched as she ran her hands through her dark red hair and over her full, naked breasts. Her eyes remained closed, but her smile turned feral.

Gabriel. You have come to me. Where are you, my love? Oh, did you think I wouldn't know you were there? Silly man.

Her voice in his head brought knives of pain. *You have something that belongs to me, Satine. I want it back.*

Lover. It pains me to refuse you. Her mental voice was slurry, as though she'd had too much blood. *Come to me tonight, though, and we shall discuss it.*

Gabriel didn't hesitate. *Where?*

Twisted. My new nightclub in Santa Monica. You'll find it, I'm sure. Three in the morning, and don't be late. She sent him images of the two of them, naked and coupled together, using each other like animals.

He shuddered and began the tedious task of walling her out of his mind again.

* * *

Rose watched as Gabriel sat, unmoving, on the window ledge with his eyes closed. After an hour of Justin's questions and delays, she'd finally just left the room to find Gabriel. She poked along all the offices in the suite. There were five, not counting the front reception desk and the conference room. She'd found Gabriel in the very last one.

Moving quietly, she curled up on the ledge next to him, her attention veering between the man and the glorious horizon.

Never in her life had she wanted a man the way she wanted him. That alone made her suspicious. Trust didn't come easily to her.

Gabriel and Justin were good people. Tribreds. Whatever. She could *feel* it inside them, just knew that their souls were good. She knew she couldn't be anything but safe in their company. Rose frowned. Safe. *God.* This was the first time in she didn't know how long that she felt *safe*.

~ ☾ ~

Demon Soul

She studied him, her fingers fisted tight. The need to touch him had been building since early that morning. She reached out and laid her hand on Gabriel's forearm. He held an energy that sparked inside her.

She let out her breath in relief. Just touching him, skin to skin, made all the difference in the world. Here was stability and goodness. Here was eroticism. Here was l...

That part of her that had been so empty for so long opened to him in a rush of sweet pain that skimmed her entire body. A shimmering light came from him and spilled into her, went up her arm and into her chest. It dissolved there, a golden warmth that made her giddy. *At last, at last!* Her body exulted in the feel of him inside her even as she felt the taint of evil edging his soul.

"What did you just do?" Surprise filled Gabriel's voice, breaking the silence around them. He pulled away from her and backed up, staring. "I'm... Something's different. Something's different with you, too. You're glowing."

Rose blinked as the exalted feelings faded with his disapproval. "I touched you. I needed that physical connection to you. I don't know why. I just knew that I had to touch you." She reached for him again but he shifted away.

Rose brushed away the hurt.

"What the hell did you do to me?" Gabriel wiped the sweat off his face and frowned back. "I'm off balance and you're glowing. This feels bad. Really bad."

"Like I said, I touched you. Then I felt this rush, and you were staring at me like I had three heads." Those golden feelings swept through Rose again, clearing away all her small aches and pains, disintegrating her exhaustion. "I feel great."

Understanding dawned on Gabriel's face. "Of course you do, damn it. You took the only thing of value I had left."

"What? I don't understand what you mean."

"You took what was left of my soul." Bitterness dripped off his words. "I should have known. You are just as bad as Satine." Gabriel pulled her off the window ledge. "Come on. You're going to fix this."

"Hey, wait a minute," she protested, and twisted around to

~ ☾ ~

look at Gabriel. He kept his hands on her shoulders, moving her inexorably forward.

"Don't talk to me. Right now I need Justin's help."

Sounds of shouting came from down the hall. They both stopped dead and looked at each other. "I don't know," he said. "Come on." He shackled one of her wrists in his hand and towed her along behind him, her glow not a bit diminished. "I'm not sure what's going on here, but trust me, you're not going anywhere."

Rose sighed, exasperated.

Gabriel shoved the door open to his brother's office.

Justin and a tall, voluptuous woman, her body poured into jeans and some sort of flowy, gypsy-like top, were standing toe-to-toe and snarling at each other. A big purple leather bag sat on the desk. Rose envied her both the bag and the curvy body.

"Just tell me where Kendall Sorbis is. I need the real deal, not a floozy who'll wave sage in the air and do a few chants," Justin sneered at the woman in front of him.

She crossed her arms tightly over her ample chest. "Kendall's on his anniversary trip," she retorted, her voice a whiskey rasp. "I really don't think whatever emergency you've cooked up to embarrass him this time is going to pull him away from his wife and their celebration. Wasn't the last time you manipulated information bad enough? It took almost three years for him to repair his reputation."

At their entrance, the two turned to look at the door. "Busy here," Justin barked.

"So am I. Look." Gabriel pushed Rose in front of him. She stood there, her head held high. Gabriel might hate her, but it's not like she'd had any control over what had happened.

The woman had eyes only for Rose. "Oh." Her voice was faint.

"See? I didn't make it up. She's real, she's here, and she's, she's..." Justin looked harder at Rose. He sat against the desk, stunned. "Wow."

"She's an angel?" The woman took a step back. "No..."

Justin shook his head doubtfully. "Probably not. They

~ ☾ ~

aren't usually found this far south." He sighed, turned to Gabriel. "Gabriel, Rose, meet Magdalena de la Cruz. Magdalena, this is my brother Gabriel, and Rose Walters. Magdalena is here because she thinks she's as good as her boss."

"He's not my boss," she snapped. "You can call me Maggie," she said to the newcomers.

"She *glows*," Gabriel said, gesturing to Rose.

Maggie laughed. "I noticed."

"She didn't earlier," Justin muttered.

"I take back almost everything I said about you, Justin." Maggie circled Rose, fascinated.

"Oh, it gets better. She just took what was left of my soul." Gabriel leaned against the wall, his palms flat against it.

Justin stiffened and even Maggie's eyes turned cold.

Rose caught her breath. "I didn't know it until it happened. I didn't mean to. It was an accident, I guess you could call it. I'm sorry."

"Yeah, right," Gabriel muttered.

"Who really sent you?" Justin crossed his arms, looking much more formidable without his signature smile.

"I've already told you everything. Gabriel's been in my head, he knows what I know. I didn't mean to hurt him, I didn't mean to take his soul." She turned to Gabriel, her hands reaching for him. "I'll give it back to you. Here, let me give it back," she pleaded, and walked toward him.

Maggie put a hand on Rose's arm. "Wait." She turned to Justin. "She's a Soul Chalice? You weren't joking?"

"I don't usually joke about things like this."

"I've never met a Soul Chalice before. I don't even know how they work." Maggie narrowed her eyes as she studied Rose.

Frustration flowed through her. "I'm a human. I work the same way every other human works." Rose shook off Maggie's hand, her confusion flipping into irritation. "I eat, I sleep, I dream, I love, I hate, I have nightmares. This, right now, has turned into a nightmare that I can't wake up from. Just let me give him his soul back, and I'll leave."

~ ☾ ~

"You can't leave." Gabriel looked at her accusingly. "You can't. If you really are a Soul Chalice then you're my only hope of getting my soul, the majority of it, back from Satine."

Maggie tilted her head toward Gabriel. "How does it feel, having your soul in two places?"

"Not now, Magdalena."

Maggie flushed at Justin's reproof. "Sorry."

Rose barely heard them talking, she was so focused on Gabriel. "Will you let me try to return it to you? Please. I'd do anything to help you. You must know that."

Gabriel winced. "You can try." He flicked a glance at Justin. "My demon is unstable. I had problems, the past two days, of turning into my demon without being aware of it. Now that my soul is entirely gone?" He shook his head and flexed his hands. They fluctuated between human and demon, quick and sharp visual changes that blurred under Rose's eyes. Maggie sucked in a breath and Gabriel looked to Rose. "I just don't know."

Justin moved to Gabriel's side and put a hand on his shoulder. "I've got you. Go ahead, Rose."

She took a couple of steps toward him, but his ferocious concentration unnerved her. "Would you, um, close your eyes?"

Anger flared, but he shut them. Rose took another two steps and held her hand out to him, unsure. Finally she pressed her hand to his broad chest. She glanced over to Justin. He'd reverted to neutral, but stood ready to help his brother.

Rose closed her eyes and with all her heart, she willed his soul out of her and back into him.

* * *

Gabriel felt her touch go through him, soothing him. His demon reluctantly receded. As they stood there, connected through her hand, he could breathe easier. His vision, too, had cleared. It was as though she were containing his demon, somehow.

But his soul stayed stubbornly within the girl in front of him.

~ ☾ ~

He opened his eyes and looked to his brother. "Nothing."

"I'm trying. I swear it, I really am trying." Pure determination rang in Rose's voice.

Justin frowned. "Nothing? I felt something. You didn't feel anything?"

Gabriel gave a slight shake of his head. He put his hand over hers. "You tried," he said to Rose. He'd revised his opinion of her so many times in the past few hours that he didn't know what to think anymore.

"Damn." Rose freed her hand, wrapped her arms around her waist and turned toward the windows.

Gabriel took a deep breath and bent his head to Justin. "I did feel something," he said softly.

"I know. Your demon is quiet now."

"I don't know how to explain it." Gabriel glanced at Rose now on the far end of the small office and lowered his voice again. "Maybe it's because she does have my soul? Maybe that's why my demon subsides when she touches me?"

"That makes as much sense as any other explanation."

Magdalena stepped closer. "So she really is a Soul Chalice?"

"I think we have to make that assumption. Which means, Gabriel, you need to stick close to her."

"She spent time in Purgatory. Anything could have happened to her there." He looked over at Rose and sighed. "She fills me."

Maggie looked at him sharply. "She what?"

"You know we're tribreds?" At her impatient nod, he continued. "When I'm running low on energy, I can feed off other people's fear. Pain. Panic. It's a desperation move on my part, and it doesn't feel good. A bracing tonic that energizes you, but at the same time turns your stomach."

"Okay."

"But this is different - she *fills* me. A touch from her is pure energy, clean, light. Similar to what you do, Justin, but different. It's not a healing. It doesn't feel like a Fae power. But it makes me whole."

Maggie looked to the girl in the window thoughtfully. "Maybe I wasn't far off. Maybe she *is* an angel of some sort.

~ ☾ ~

Soul Chalice, huh?"

"Her aura grew solid and shimmery like that after I contacted Satine. Her scent is tainted with a splash of demon and something else I can't quite identify." Gabriel leaned against the doorjamb. He held out his forearm, brushed at the burn marks there. "And her fingers carry fire. I thought maybe she'd picked up a fire demon, or was part fire demon herself, but now I don't know."

"We need to know more about Soul Chalices," mused Justin. "I just don't know where to go for that kind of information."

Gabriel rubbed his chest absently. "With an aura that strong, coupled with that pull she has, demons will come out of the woodwork after her."

Rose approached them again. "I've been thinking. I'm here to save you, Gabriel. If I'm not supposed to have your soul right now, I don't think I could. I don't think it would have been possible to take it from you if it weren't meant to be."

Maggie nodded. "So what's your theory?"

"That I'm meant to hold his soul for now. He's not supposed to have it, not right now. I am. It makes sense when you think about it." She turned toward Gabriel. "I mean, it didn't hurt you, did it? It didn't hurt the same way as it did when Satine stole most of your soul."

He frowned, aware that his initial panic at missing his soul had subsided. The gaping hole was there, but no panic. "You're right. It didn't hurt at all. But that might have been the magic she used."

"Maybe. But I didn't use any magic. So just maybe I'm right." Hope shone in her eyes.

Maggie turned to the men. "Hey, guys. Can you give us girls some alone time? We won't go anywhere, I promise."

Gabriel looked to Rose. "Okay?"

"It's fine by me."

"Right, then, off you go," and before he knew it, Gabriel found himself and Justin herded out and the door closed behind them with an audible 'click'.

~ ☾ ~

Chapter Four

"I can't believe you have to do this twice in one day."
"I used to do it more than twice a day on you, remember?"
Gabriel remembered. He sat motionless while Justin did his Fae healing thing on him. That's how he used to think about it when they were kids, the "Fae healing thing". Justin would practice whenever one of them got a black eye or a skinned knee.
Gabriel had tried to do it once but ended up giving his brother an even bigger bruise. He never bothered again, figuring he didn't have enough Fae blood in him to get the healing gene the others had. Oh, he could do some small Fae things, like tapping into the power of all plant life; but he couldn't heal.
It just confirmed what he already knew. He was a killer.
"So. Did you find Satine?"
"Yeah. She's local – owns a nightclub called Twisted. I'm meeting her late tonight."
Justin's hand moved up one arm to where scorch marks from Rose's fingers showed. The cool healing flowed, erasing the marks. He hovered his hand over Gabriel's heart, then up and down Gabriel's body, side to side.
"I can feel the place where your soul should be," Justin said. "I've never felt that before, that emptiness."
"Does it feel wrong?"
"Yeah, it does. But I believe in that girl, I believe she'll help. I know, that sounds weird."
"You always sound weird."
"Ha ha." He moved his hand up Gabriel's neck to the scarred cheek.

~ ☾ ~

Gabriel felt a cool tingling against his scar and hit his brother's hand aside. "Don't waste the energy." The words came out harsh. "I know how it drains you."

Justin sat back, concern in his moss-green eyes. "What happened to you? You didn't have that ten years ago."

"Demon fire, a very long time ago." He shrugged. "A lot of things happened to me. Nothing you could have fixed, so drop it. Okay?"

"Gabriel!" Rose's scream cut through the thin walls of the office.

Gabriel was up and halfway down the hall before she'd finished his name, the terrors in her voice a surprising prod to his protective instincts.

He shoved open the door to the conference room to see Maggie frozen by the couch and Rose plastered against a window, flames licking at her right arm. Shadows of tiny horns graced her temples and her skin had an orange cast.

Rose shot him a defiant look out of whirling yellow eyes. "Help me, damn it!"

Gabriel cursed under his breath and brought lessons back to mind he'd thought forgotten long ago. "Close your eyes and breathe slowly. No one is going to hurt you. We're here to help." He kept his voice low and even as he took measured steps toward her.

"You're fine, Rose. You call the fire and it responds to your call. Now thank it and send it back to its source. Send it away."

The flames shrank, disappeared as he reached her. Gabriel brushed his hand along her arm, cooling the heat there. Rose opened her eyes and wrapped her arms around herself. "Okay, scared now. Really."

Justin started in on Maggie, but Gabriel ignored them as his past and present merged and dread settled in his belly. He closed his eyes. Not another innocent woman harboring a fire demon, not another killing. He barely survived the fight last time. What made him think it would be any different this time?

"You must have done something to upset her," Justin pointed out to Maggie, who kept shaking her head in denial.

~ ☾ ~

"I told you, I didn't do anything. We were just talking, that's all. I got caught by surprise. Let me check her over." Maggie moved to her purple bag. "I've been working with Doc Cavanaugh."

"No." Gabriel sensed both of them turn his way in surprise, but he couldn't take his eyes off Rose now. "She'll be okay. I've seen this before. It's proof that she's got a fire demon inside her, but by my guess, it hasn't been there very long." Gabriel shot a quick glance to Justin, who turned to Maggie.

"What did you guys talk about that so upset her?"

"Stuff. Nothing of any importance, until the demon she's harboring spoke to me. He said that what was left of Gabriel's soul was safe with her. He said he wouldn't touch it." Maggie spread her hands when the men turned to look at her. "Don't ask me why. It wasn't that chatty."

"And yet, it spoke to you. Fascinating. What about motive? Why would any self-respecting, talkative fire demon latch on to *her*?"

"I don't know, but I'm staying with her until we get this figured out. No arguments," Gabriel said to Rose, who shivered. "You're getting what you wanted."

Justin raised an eyebrow. "Is that wise? Besides, you don't have a place to stay."

"We're moving in with you. When I go out tonight, you'll take over watching her. You're here in the area?"

"Yes." Justin's unvoiced protest hung in the air.

"You have a better idea?" Gabriel sent him a challenging look.

"No. I just have to change my plans for tonight," Justin said. "You remember where Dad used to keep the spare key?"

"Yeah."

"It's in a similar place at my house. I'll leave you directions on my desk." Justin looked at Rose, now staring unblinking out the window. "Magdalena and I have some research to do, and I've got some people to see." He gripped Maggie by the arm and hustled her along, talking over her protests. "So we'll say goodbye for now. Just lock the door when you leave," he instructed Gabriel. "I don't know when I'll be home tonight,

~ ☾ ~

but I've got my cell on me. The number will be on the desk, along with the address."

"Get your hands off me," Maggie hissed. She sent a narrow-eyed glare at Justin before turning to Gabriel and Rose. "I look forward to seeing you both again. I promise I'll do everything in my power to help you." The door closed behind them.

"Now what? What else will go wrong?" Rose turned away from him to walk in circles.

"So, this being host to a demon isn't something you already knew about? They didn't tell you that part while you were in the waiting room?" Gabriel leaned against the desk and watched her.

"No. They didn't say a word about demons. I don't know if I'd have gone along with that, seeing as how I didn't believe in demons then. I'm just a normal person. How can they expect me to handle this?"

"I know you're scared, but I can't go along with the normal bit. Not now, when you can use a fire demon's powers. Do you know how rare that is, how dangerous?" He never knew Marianne had been a host to a fire demon. At least with Rose, he knew in advance. He'd do everything in his power to help her control the demon.

"Great. Just great. I'll never have a normal life." She threw herself on the couch and stared at the ceiling.

Gabriel eyed her uncertainly. "I'm not an expert on demon possession, but I do know that handling demon powers is mostly a matter of control. Do you remember what you were talking about before this last manifestation?"

"Maggie wanted to separate us." Unexpectedly she blushed, a fiery wash of color over her pale cheeks.

His lips twitched. "Okay, so you felt strongly about it. You and me, staying together, is important to you? I'm trying to stay out of your head now," he added.

"Right," she mumbled. "I've told you that part, though. I need to be with you to protect you. Plus, you feel better when we're together."

He skated over that issue. "You were trying to make

~ ☾ ~

Maggie see your point?"

"Yes."

"Demons respond to strong surges of emotion, especially when they have a new host. When your emotions engage, you need to be careful about where you put your energy."

Her gaze met his, her eyes forlorn. "So in the meantime, I've just got to live with it?"

"Something like that. Are you scared of the demon?"

"Yes. No. I mean, I went from watching myself die to having been dropped into a fantasy world. Now I find I'm one of the fantastical creatures. How would you feel?"

Remembering his adolescence and grappling with coming into his own demon powers, he understood exactly how she felt. Still, Gabriel picked his words carefully. "Disoriented. Unsure who to trust and unaware of how powerful you could be. I've been there, Rose. I can help you."

"Really?"

"Demon blood, remember?"

Rose rubbed at her eyes. "My life has taken a very 'Alice in Wonderland' turn." She sighed. "So what do we do now?"

"You need rest before we train at Justin's house. Later tonight, I'll go hunting for Satine."

Rose shuddered. "Hunting vampires? Are you freaking insane?"

"Maybe. But the damn bitch has a good chunk of my soul. What else can I do?"

"You really don't have a choice, do you?" Rose looked down at her fingers. "It would help you if I could, what, protect my mind?"

"It's the best thing you can do to keep yourself safe."

Rose took a deep breath. Her eyes met Gabriel's, full of determination. "Okay. Train me."

* * *

Sweat rolled down Rose's throat and soaked into her tee shirt. They had found Justin's house and she'd rested. The past couple hours had been spent training in the backyard, sitting on a perfectly groomed lawn surrounded by tropical plants. Palm trees stood motionless in the hot summer night.

~ ☾ ~

A koi pond shimmered, the waterfall adding to the island feel of the place. The pool, at the other end of the yard, beckoned.

Gabriel had lit incense and the smoke curled upward, adding a sharp, exotic spice to the air. "I'm going to slip into your mind again. I want you to stop me."

"I'm exhausted. How am I supposed to stop you?" Rose lay flat on her back and closed her eyes. "You're a slave driver. Can't you give me a better explanation than 'keep me out'?"

"My teaching skills are non-existent. I should have left you with Justin."

Remorse filled Rose. She sat up, caught his arm. "I'm sorry, I don't mean to complain. I'll try harder."

"Control, Rose," he cautioned, and the fire in her fingers backed off at the reminder before she dropped her hand. "Think of it like a game of hide and seek. When you sense me in your mind, just drift away. Okay?"

Rose bit her lip. "Let's try it again."

It felt strange, but not unpleasant. The scent of earth rose up as he slipped into her mind. He shared a vision of a hallway with a ton of doors off it.

She smiled.

Don't smile. Stop me instead, he chastised. He opened a door. Abruptly they were in a small, sticky-hot bedroom that reeked of drugs and urine. A woman huddled up against a wall, her eyes closed, a pipe clutched to her naked chest, recognizable only by the color of her hair, lank and plastered to her head. Rose.

Gabriel had them out of there before she could protest. He headed for another door, but she slammed it before he could get it open all the way.

Better.

I don't like this game.

It's not a game, Rose.

Her heart hammered hard in her body. She opened her eyes to see him glaring at her.

"Get it through your head. You're not alone any more. You've got a demon roaming around inside you. Plus, you've got a part of my soul in there. The vampire with the other part

~ ☾ ~

of my soul is a master at mind manipulation. You really want to wander around without any mental protection?" he demanded. "Not to mention the whole Soul Chalice thing you've got going."

"I don't know what I want," she said. "My life was so ugly. I don't want you to see it. Can you blame me?" Shame beat against her mind, filled with images she'd just as soon forget. "God, I'm tired."

"I won't hold your past against you if you don't hold mine against me. Deal?" At her nod, he continued. "If you can hold a barrier when you're tired, the rest will be easy. Come on. Work to keep me out of your mind entirely. Unless you're wimping out on me," he prodded.

Rose stiffened her spine. "I'm not wimping out. Try to get into my mind, and I'll try to keep you out."

It was like a damned sword fight, Rose thought as she wiped the sweat from her forehead. He poked at her mind, looking for the hallway of doors. She learned to parry his pokes, and even managed to prevent him from slipping in some of the time.

Barrier. Barrier. The only things that came to mind were the cement barriers between freeways. She kept searching and evading, looking inside her mind for a good barrier.

God she was hot. All she wanted was to cool off and rest. Or, alternatively, get hotter and naked with Gabriel in the pool. Her body, healthy for the first time in a long time, was itchy with the need for release. The pool called to her, distracting her long enough for Gabriel to slip into her head once again.

You can swim when we're done. Focus now. Be a good girl.

Get out, damn it! Tired of being caught thinking about him, Rose reacted instinctively, the thought accompanied by a hefty mental shove and a slammed door. At a muffled curse by Gabriel, Rose opened her eyes to find him sprawled backward on the grass.

"Are you okay?" Horrified, she flew to his side and touched his cheek. "I didn't mean to hurt you."

~ ☾ ~

In one swift move he had her on her back, staring up at him while he leaned over her. Rose saw the need, the loneliness in his eyes. As she sensed him drawing away, she reached up to his shoulders. "Oh, come on. What do we have to lose?"

With a muffled oath, he covered her mouth with his.

She'd expected the flash and heat, and gave as much back to him. But she got so much more. He tasted of darkness and need, and both twined themselves around her, left her aching with him. Lonely, he'd been so lonely...she caught those glimpses of his past as he ravaged her mouth, his guard lowered.

Surrounded by his strength, his hard length pressing her into the warmth of the grass, she gloried in the taste of him, in the darkness. She pushed at one side and he rolled, taking her with him, easing her on top of him.

Rose broke their kiss to pass her fingers over the hard planes of his face, the shiny-smooth ridges of scarring on his cheek and neck. She met his gaze, saw the wariness in them and shook her head. "It doesn't matter," she said, and kissed along his scars before taking his mouth with her own, pressing her body close, her hips moving against him.

***

Gabriel grabbed for the reins of his control even as he ached to let loose his desire. Her body moved against his in a long-remembered dance. He ran his hand down her side to the gentle curve of her ass. He pressed her hard against him, thrust his tongue deep into her mouth, and sent Rose an image of her writhing in ecstasy, naked and straddling him, her hair streaming down her back as she arched back, shuddering in completion.

The image tipped the scale and the woman sprawled on him stiffened and screamed into his mouth as she came.

Gabriel wrapped an arm around her as she found her way back to her body. She melted against him, making him reluctant to move. The warmth of her cuddled next to him opened long-closed parts of his heart, bringing with it a jolt of joy.

~ ☾ ~

He held her gingerly, as if she were a priceless piece of art that would shatter at the flick of his careless fingers. His mating instincts were clamoring for him to lay his claim to her but fear froze him. He'd kill her if she got too close, and he wasn't about to risk her.

As she pressed tiny kisses to his chest, Gabriel steeled himself to do what he knew must be done. He shifted, moved her to his side and put some distance between the two of them. He'd held her longer than he should have. His arms were empty now without her, and yet he had to pretend it didn't matter. *But it did. Oh God, it mattered more than he'd thought possible.*

"You caught me by surprise." He sat up and winced as more than just his head throbbed. "The bronze door, now that was a good touch." He could feel her gaze on his face and strove to keep it neutral.

"Glad you liked it." Her voice was flat.

"Yes, well." He took a careful breath. "That door will keep your thoughts to yourself, help keep your mind impenetrable. After you get used to keeping it shut, it'll become second nature."

"What the hell are you playing at?"

Gabriel looked at her. "If you work daily on your barrier, you'll be able to call it without thought. It'll be ever-present in your life, a psychic insurance policy, so to speak.

"You - that was mutual. You wanted me just as much as I wanted you," she accused.

"Have I ever said differently?" He kept his voice bored. "Let's work on your fire demon capabilities."

"You can go to hell." Rose wrapped her arms around her knees.

Gabriel ignored her hostility. "For you, it seems to be an emotional tie. You need something badly, and the flame comes to you in response. Go ahead, try to summon it."

"Why are you shutting me out? Why don't you want to talk about what just happened? Damn it, Gabriel. You're not playing fair."

"I'm not playing." Gabriel grabbed her by the shoulders

~ ☾ ~

and shook her lightly. "The demons are real, not fueled by drugs and imagination. Sex is just a need, a distraction. I helped you with that need so you could focus on what's next. Nothing more, nothing less."

Gabriel felt his words slice into her, slashing at the tinker-toy structure of her self-image. It teetered and then - nothing. She'd slammed that door shut on her mind again. Approval raced through him, but he was careful to keep it from her. Anger in those blue eyes was easier to deal with than hurt. "Now come on. Bring the fire. You know how." He let go of her and moved back. "Do it."

* * *

Rose shut her eyes and drew the hurt deep inside, checking to make sure her mental door was firmly shut and locked. She'd been stupid, thinking even for a second that he'd want her. She wouldn't make that mistake again.

Now she focused on bringing the fire. She knew the warmth, could feel it running through her veins, but couldn't bring it forth. Frustrated, she opened her eyes and scraped her hair back from her hot face. "I can't do it on purpose. I got nothing." Resentfully, she looked at him sitting across from her. He was cool in the heat of the night despite the leather coat he still wore.

"Focus on your need. What do you need, so badly, that you can't live without? Take your time and think about it." His voice was a soothing rumble.

Rose closed her eyes but she didn't need any time. She needed him. She needed his trust. She just didn't want him to know all about her past. How awful she had been, how empty. Fate had brought her here. Surely Fate wouldn't send her away?

Her hands grew hot. Carefully, Rose opened her eyes to see flame dancing along the back of her hands. She laughed a little, still not sure how to feel about this external sign of being a demon-carrier. Her gaze met Gabriel's. "Look! Isn't that amazing?"

"Remember, fire carries inside it both life and death. If you let yourself accept the fire's inherent contradictions, then it

~ ☾ ~

shouldn't be a problem - as long as you stay in control. But once it controls you, once the need for it outweighs your common sense, then it could kill you."

"It's not going to kill me." Rose could feel the source of the fire inside her. The demon was amused at her attempts to draw it out, but she didn't feel any ill will from it. She watched, fascinated, as fire danced along her fingers.

"You can't possibly know that," Gabriel said. "Put the fire out, and then call it again. See if you can do it faster this time."

Rose sent the fire away. It flickered out reluctantly. This time, she left her eyes open and focused on heat, flame, and Gabriel. Sensation stroked the air, made her shudder in distaste. "That didn't feel right. It felt like this morning, remember?"

The air changed, a displacement on a molecular level that was its own warning. Before she knew what was happening, Gabriel had scooped Rose up and tossed her toward the patio door, where she hit with a crash. She lay, huddled against the door, dazed. "Now, see, you've really got to stop doing that," she grumbled as she got to her feet, wincing at a few new bruises.

"Get inside! Now!" Gabriel barely had time to turn around before a streak in the air solidified. Rose watched the very deadly dance from the safety of the porch, both repulsed and fascinated.

A short creature with shiny brown fur and a mouth like an alien predator cat crouched before Gabriel, its three rows of vicious teeth gleaming in the night. The demon snarled slightly and jumped toward Gabriel. Rose's heart raced as she watched, praying that Gabriel would start punching or kicking soon.

But Gabriel slid out of the way and the demon didn't have time to correct. He landed where Gabriel had been, slightly off balance. Gabriel moved behind the demon with lightning speed and sent him flying with a foot against his back. The creature smashed against a palm tree with a grunt, bounced off it and turned around, its lips curled back in a snarl that

~ ☾ ~

filled the air, teeth snapping back and forth.

Rose grew hot, knew the fire inside her was close. All she had to do was call it, and it would be there. The fight was so tempting. She wanted to hear the demon's heart stop. She wanted to *cause* the demon's heart to stop. Bloodlust rose in her eyes and she blinked. Her body shook briefly as that emotion took over.

Gabriel and the demon circled each other. Rose heard Gabriel cursing under his breath. Then it lunged at him and took a swipe. Gabriel jumped back but not far enough. The claws grazed his stomach. "Shit."

"No!" Outrage pulsed through Rose and she sped past Gabriel, jumping to land on the demon's back. "Not him," she growled. Flexing her flaming hands with sharp claws, she dug them both into the demon's neck. The demon howled – and so did Rose, in victory, until pain flared down her arm. She vaulted off the demon's back and whirled around, ready to attack again. Wanting to kill the demon she recognized as "enemy".

Gabriel moved in front of her before she could engage the demon again and kicked it hard in the face. The creature roared, shook its head, and sprang at him. Rose stepped back as Gabriel jumped straight up. He landed with one foot on the demon's neck and the other on its lower back. Gabriel rode it down to the grass.

Rose watched in horror as the weight of Gabriel audibly cracked the creature's spine. The heat and the anger that had propelled her into such bloodlust had left her. Now she leaned against the palm tree, shaken. Neither the pain in her belly or the pain in her arm could cover the fear she felt inside as the demon in front of her let out a loud wail.

Cursing again, Gabriel leaned over and snapped its neck, putting the creature out of its misery. Rose watched Gabriel as he let the body drop and shuddered hard, cold in the heat. What did he feel? Did he love the kill?

* * *

Silence shivered through the yard. Gabriel looked to Rose, huddled against a palm tree. She'd shifted back and looked pale. He grimaced. Not exactly the way he'd wanted her training to go, but at least they'd confirmed her ability to use all the fire demon's powers. When she'd launched herself at the demon, when he'd seen that sexy body covered in a pale orange fur, he'd almost had a heart attack. He never remembered Marianne actually *becoming* the demon she carried.

Gabriel looked to the sky, opened that thoughtway he'd worked so hard to block earlier. *Satine. Come and get your pet while he's still fresh. Dinner time.*

You bastard, she hissed. *How dare you!*

Your stink is all over him. Pick up your trash. He closed the link, took a deep breath. His head throbbed with the brief contact. He knew death shadowed him. What made him think he could protect Rose?

A sound came out of Rose then, a half-whimper. "It hurts. Gabriel, it hurts."

"What hurts?" He turned to her, shocked to see three claw marks deep on her left shoulder, ripping her tee shirt and reaching to her elbow. Blood dripped from her arm down into the grass. "Damn it. Let's get inside, I'll fix you up."

"What? Oh, my shoulder." She winced. "Yeah. But that's not what hurts." Rose put her right hand just above her hipbone. "There. It hurts there."

Frowning, Gabriel knelt in front of her and gently lifted her hand away. He tugged at her damp black tee shirt, bared the pale skin of her flat belly. A spiral of runes rippled and moved there, a mesmerizing magical dance. Made of colored ink, and yet not ink...a tattoo, but no human hands had a part in its creation. Gabriel narrowed his eyes. If he looked closely, he could see flickers of flame and a familiar pair of eyes sliding through the runes, not quite daring to meet his gaze.

A shudder of recognition went through him as his fear came true.

The demon scent, the fire, the runes. *Mephisto.*

The last time all three had been in front of him, he'd killed Marianne, the girl he'd loved, while trying to kill the demon Mephisto. Ten long years ago.

~ ☾ ~

Now here he was, full circle, back home with as much bad hanging around him as the last time. Mephisto was back, loaning Rose his powers. Satine was somewhere near, coming to kick his ass. And Rose, the sexy little redhead in front of him, not only carried Mephisto, but she also held part of his soul.

Gabriel had always suspected Los Angeles would be the death of him. He just hadn't expected it to be quite so soon.

Chapter Five

Gabriel looked up at Rose, regret in his eyes. "It's a demon spiral. The fire demon is living there, providing you with power when you need it."

"Wow. Even though I saw it, felt the fire, I didn't really believe." Rose swallowed hard as she leaned against the palm tree, ignoring the prick of the trunk against her back. That was nothing compared to the acid of the claws in her arm or the burn of the demon mark on her belly. The heat of the flame, the life and death of it, the sheer *power* still raged through her blood and held her.

Gabriel put his hand on her belly, the coolness of it soothing the burn. Her hands came up to cover his. She pushed both hands against his to keep him there. "Are you okay?"

She resisted the urge to roll her eyes. "No. Yes. I was terrified that it was going to kill you. I needed to do something rather than just be a bystander, and then..." Rose shook her head. "Then I grew so angry. I wanted its death. That's not like me, honestly."

The fire burned hotter on her belly, like acid seeping through her pores. Gabriel still knelt before her, his hand cooling the burn, his eyes grave. "I had it under control. You should have had more faith in me."

She shook her head. "You don't understand. I wanted its death. I wanted it, so desperately." Rose didn't recognize the voice that came out of her. She put a hand up to her throat and kept her eyes fixed on Gabriel. "A part of me thrilled to hear the crack of the neck breaking. Kind of a dark glee, you know? And that totally shocked me."

~ ☾ ~

"That's being a demon for you." Gabriel smoothed her shirt down and stood, a frown darkening his eyes to slate. "You need to go inside before Satine gets here. Get some witch-hazel, Justin's bound to have some, and wash those wounds down. I'll be in as soon as it's safe to help you."

"I would have killed him to protect you." Rose tilted her head to keep the eye contact between them. "I would have done anything to protect you. You are why I'm alive at this point. But you killed him for me. Again."

Impatience and regret passed over Gabriel's face. "Yeah. Had to. You shouldn't have watched. Now, would you go inside before all hell breaks loose out here? Again?"

Rose considered it. Shook her head. "No. Not unless you come with me. Come inside, bandage my wounds, and tell me all about Satine. Please."

"This isn't the time for a chat."

The scent of lilies washed over them.

"Do tell the little girl all about Satine," the vampire purred, startling them both.

Gabriel and Rose shared a glance. He shook his head, his mouth set in a grim line. *Trust me, you don't want to know.*

Then he shut down. *Gabriel? Don't shut me out.* "Gabriel?"

"Rose. Go inside, now. For once." Gabriel grabbed her good arm and tugged her to the patio. "Go."

"You do like to manhandle me," she grumbled, but Rose backed toward the glass doors. Prudence had her opening them and stepping into the house, but still she protested. "I need to meet the bitch who has the bigger part of your soul. You need to let me." The thought brought a scowl to her face.

He gave a bark of laughter. "She's nobody," he said as Satine appeared at the foot of the fallen demon. Rose watched, fascinated, as he corrected to keep Satine in front of him and Rose to his back. "She stole my soul because she doesn't have one of her own."

"You are being less than polite, Gabriel," Satine chided him, but her interest had focused, laser-like, on the girl. "Come out, come out little girl. Let's see what you're made of."

~ ☾ ~

The voice was familiar. Rose frowned, trying to remember. Gabriel's voice rumbled, interrupting her concentration. "Don't do it, Rose. Stay where you are. She can't get in unless you invite her, and trust me, that never ends well."

"I've read vampire books, Gabriel. Don't treat me like a child," she snapped. Rose took a step away from the safety of the house, then another one.

"Not all the books get it right," he murmured. "Artistic license."

Rose shrugged. How could she help him if she didn't face what she'd be up against? "I need to see her. If this is the day for fairy tales to come true, then the nightmares should come true, too." She moved to one side of Gabriel and studied the vampire.

Satine stood on the grass by the pool dressed in four-inch gladiator heels, a bustier in stark black framing her full breasts, and lace boy shorts riding low on her pale hips. Her blood-red hair fell in a curling mass to her waist and her makeup was Hollywood perfect. She exuded a pale red light, and underneath the cloying scent of lilies Rose could smell death.

By contrast Rose felt too thin, too plain to play in Satine's sandbox. Rose's eyes narrowed. She took another small step toward Satine, battle-ready even as horrified recognition balled in her belly.

"That's right, little girl. Come on out and let's play, shall we?" Satine cooed.

Rose touched Gabriel briefly; the coolness of his skin, or perhaps it was the energy that passed between them, sparked the golden aura around her.

"Oooh, don't you look tasty with your angelic armor." Anticipation brightened her eyes. Satine licked her lips and reached out a pale hand. "Come closer."

"I don't think so," Rose said, her voice calm. "I know you, Sara. You've seen me before. Look into my eyes, and remember."

Satine looked. Her normally pale face went stark white with recognition, the blush she'd applied appearing garish

~ ☾ ~

now on her marble skin. She snarled. "You don't stand a chance. You didn't then, and you don't now. But this time, when I kick you in the teeth, I'll be snapping your neck. Then I'll drink your blood."

"You'll never control me. Not again. I do have a chance, more than just a chance. I will win. I've been chosen to stand against you." Rose stood as tall as she could at a mere five-feet-five-no-spike-heels, and faced her enemy. The air around her seemed to pulse.

"Chosen," spat the vampire. "It's all very well and good to be *chosen*. You have to actually be able to resist all you are in order to win. Can you resist?"

Rose held her gaze steady. "I ran away from Kevin. I won that round."

"Oh yeah. But what happened after that? Oops, you died." Satine tossed her head in contempt. "You can't run away from yourself. Look at me and remember your past. For we are alike, you and I. *Look* at me."

Rose looked into the vampire's deep blue eyes and fell into memories of drugs, emptiness, and reckless behavior. Her very being became weighed down with longing for the drugs, the alcohol, and the anonymous sex. Kevin. She should find Kevin, beg his forgiveness. She should…her body fell into trembling; hard, jerking shakes of crystal meth need. The spiral on her belly burned and the energy she'd received from Gabriel dissolved as though written in vapor.

"No!" Gabriel shoved Rose to the patio door and moved between them, and faced Satine. "Grab your trash and go. This isn't the time or the place. We're meeting later tonight, remember?"

Satine's lip curled. "You really think that I'm going to just hand over your soul? Hmmm. Well. Maybe I will. Trade. Your soul for the girl." She smirked and put a hand on one hip, flipped her hair over her shoulder.

Rose huddled against the door. Even wallowing in remembered pain, Rose understood. Of course. It was the only solution. Whatever she was supposed to do didn't necessarily mean she'd survive it. They hadn't promised her survival.

~ ☾ ~

Inside, she trembled as she waited for Gabriel to seal the deal. But his answer was as incomprehensible as it was straightforward. "No."

"So, you give her your protection. Do you really think she's strong enough to do the job of satisfying you, Gabriel?" Satine laughed, a high, sharp sound that hurt Rose's ears. "Ah, you are too funny. She's a suicide and a drug addict. Look at her, caught in the web of an addict's need. Watch your wallet around her, because she'll steal from you. Anything to get her next fix."

Rose paled at the vampire's vicious words, so familiar, rendering her unable to move, to defend herself against them. How many times had she been accused of stealing, when all the time it had been Sara? Now Gabriel would make the trade. He'd have to, and she wouldn't blame him.

Gabriel exploded in a rush of movement and caught Satine by surprise with a foot to her ribcage. She flew backwards, hitting the block wall at the rear of the property and causing it to bulge outwards. Foul curses streamed out of her mouth.

Before Satine could regain her feet, Rose felt herself gathered up in Gabriel's arms and they'd moved through the patio door. He shut and locked it, then headed to the basement.

In Gabriel's arms, Rose grew hot with shame as she replayed Satine's words in her mind. True, all true, and the heat of her addiction fed a gnawing emptiness in her belly. Gabriel's coolness, a delicious contrast to her own heat, didn't penetrate the doubt that swamped her. She'd never win. She'd never fulfill her mission, and as a result, she'd die. Gabriel would go demon without his soul. And the world will become a sadder, messier place without him.

Despair took her over. The spiral on her belly burned, writhed. Tears streamed down her face. She should just kill herself all over again. She'd really messed up there with the vampire. She was worthless, where was her vodka, her pipe? Deep shudders wracked her body as Gabriel laid her down on a big bed.

"Here. Just – stay here."

~ ☾ ~

Rose turned her face into the pillow and listened as Gabriel moved around. She heard a splash of a faucet and then Gabriel was beside her again. He used a wet washcloth to clean the jagged wounds on her arm.

"Damn it. I'm sorry you were hurt. I can't—okay, I've got to put some stuff on there that will make the demon venom seem like water. Take a breath."

She squeezed her eyes shut tight as liquid fire seemed to travel the same path as her wounds. She let out a quick gasp of breath and heard Gabriel swear quietly. "I'll be right back." Abruptly he left the room.

Rose seethed with pain, both from her shoulder and in her heart. A tear trickled down her cheek. As if she was worth his time. *As if.*

"Rose?"

She started, wiped her eyes. "It still hurts."

"I know. I'm almost done here." With a gentle hand, he smoothed a cooling cream deep into the long scratches. "There. Now just some gauze, and frozen peas." He wrapped her arm gently and laid the cold bag against her wound. "To cool the burn," he said, and sat back on his haunches and looked at her. "You want to tell me what all that was about?"

Rose turned her head away from him, shame heating her cheeks. "All what?"

"You know Satine." His voice was flat, daring her to contradict him.

"She's right. I can't win. You were right not to trust me. I'm an addict," she whispered, and her eyes filled again.

"Bullshit. I've smelled you. You're not an addict, not anymore. You're clean, pure."

"I'm not. I'm not! I'm nothing, a nuisance, a burden." Rose trembled.

Gabriel moved, found a knitted blanket, and wrapped it around Rose. He sat next to her. "Tell me." He reached for her hand and held it.

"My mother was an alcoholic and a junkie and a whore, and we rarely lived in the same place more than a few months at a time. Crayons, chalk, and paints kept me sane. I could

~ ☾ ~

lose myself in the pictures I created." Memories flooded back, the good and the bad. Rose cleared her tight throat. "When she died, I was only sixteen. I became her in some weird way. The only difference between us is I never got paid money for sex." She faced Gabriel, but saw no judgment there, only a waiting. She continued, his hand her lifeline.

"Sara - Satine and I are cousins. You were right about the family connection. After mom died, I worked, stayed with a friend's family. Got raped by my boss so I quit, and then my life fell apart. Like there was a part of me missing. I stole from the people who'd taken me in. They threw me out, so I got a new job. I hooked up with a co-worker who was both married and hooked on drugs. I took drugs to make the ugliness of my life just go away."

She stared over Gabriel's head. "As long as I never sobered up I was fine. I lost weight. Lost strength. Then I left my lover, tried to get clean. A week went by, then two. Then a month, and I was still clean. So I went by his place to prove something to myself – stupid. I got sucked back in, overdosed on my lover's lawn just as she drove up with his kids." Gabriel made a sound and she looked toward him, but he just shook his head, so she continued.

"The paramedics came and revived me on the lawn. Somebody gave me something that accidentally put me into a coma. And I had that experience in Purgatory that I already told you about. Like I said, now it's like the hole inside me is filled. But I was a fool to think it could last." Her eyes squeezed shut against his judgment.

"Look at me."

Rose shook her head. "Don't pretend this doesn't bother you. It has to bother you. I am no saint, Gabriel." She moved the bag of peas down a little bit. Finally she opened her eyes.

Gabriel turned her hand over in his, traced the lifeline in her palm. It was broken in two places, she'd known that for years. "Rose, I'm not a saint. I've been a mercenary, a messenger, a hired hand. I've traveled the world, helping out where I could but more often being muscle for people who paid well. I'm good at menacing people, but I don't often kill.

~ ☾ ~

Today I killed twice."

The loathing in his voice had her struggling to sit, clutching at his hand. "Wait a minute. You were protecting me," she protested. "If you hadn't done what you did, I'd be the dead one right now. And we don't know what would happen to the part of your soul I carry if I died." They were face to face now.

"Look. I didn't save you because you have a part of my soul," he began.

"I don't care why you saved me," she cut in. "I'm just glad you did. I'm not ready to die again. Not yet." They fell silent, each one taking the other's measure.

"Do you trust me?" His voice was gruff and low.

"With my life." Her eyes searched his. The slate gray had gone misty, and she couldn't see in. "Do you trust me?"

"With my soul, obviously. Do me a favor. Lie down again, and keep looking at me," he said, his voice soft. "I need to try something."

Curious, Rose lay back down. The hand that wasn't holding hers moved over her body, an inch or so away, as if he were testing her aura. A pale blue light shone from his hand and she remembered Justin and his healing. It was like a film was being stripped from her mental state as he proceeded. The confidence she'd felt since she first left the hospital came back. How could she possibly think she'd return to drugs?

Rose watched, astonished, as a quick pain showed in his eyes when he moved across her hurt arm. The sting eased within her and she broke into an awed smile. He ended the connection between them and breathed heavily, sweat sheening his forehead as though he'd been running.

"That was awesome. I feel good. Real good. What was that?"

Gabriel stood, walked to the door and back, shaking out his arms. "The most basic Fae healing. A baby could do it. Are you okay? I'm not very good at it."

Admiration filled her. "I'm fine, now. But how did you do that?"

"It was mostly illusion. Satine is very, very good at illusion. I managed to break through it." He sat again next to her. "You

~ ☾ ~

know what happened to her." It wasn't a question.

"Sara." She sighed, pulled her knees up to her chin. "We were camping, me and a bunch of family from my Dad's side. She left in the middle of the night with a man. She wanted to go with him. I'd seen her earlier that night with him.

"Something in me knew enough to be afraid for her. I held on to her, screamed, fought hard, and she kicked me in the face for my pains. I was only thirteen. She was eighteen. Her mother never forgave me for "losing" Sara, and I never saw that side of my family again. That was the real beginning of all my troubles."

"Has she ever tried to contact you before? Either mentally or physically?"

"No. Never." She looked up at him, startled. "Do you think she could, mentally I mean?"

Gabriel frowned. "You shared blood, but through family ties. I don't think it's possible for her to contact you mind to mind, but you must not let her bite you. That would be—bad."

Rose took a breath. "Thank you."

"For what? I've done nothing except put you in danger. I'm not exactly dancing at the thought," he growled. "I'll have to hang around to protect you until Justin comes home."

"I thought you wanted to face down Satine?"

His eyes bled to iridescent green. "I do. But I can't do anything until I know you're protected. I'm not having her come here after you, not before we're ready."

Rose shifted uneasily. She wished she could just reach out and take his hand, soothe whatever bothered him. Gabriel was definitely bothered, she could tell.

Abruptly he stood. "I suppose you're hungry again."

Her stomach rumbled at the thought of food. "I ate a ton of pizza just a few hours ago," she protested. "I can't be hungry."

"Spending time in demonic form is traumatic to your system. You need food. Fuel. I'll see what Justin has upstairs." Gabriel headed to the door.

"I'll come with you." Rose flung off the blanket and swung her feet over the side of the bed. "I'm perfectly fine. I'll come up and keep you company."

~ ☾ ~

"You should stay down here," he cautioned. "I'll bring food down to you."

"Don't be ridiculous. No one has ever brought me a meal in bed," she said, following him up the stairs. "There's no reason to start now. I'll eat up here with you."

He let out an exasperated sigh. "Are you going to argue with me the rest of the night?"

"Probably, if you continue to be overprotective. You're just going to have to deal, Gabriel."

"Huh."

~ ☾ ~

Chapter Six

Deep below the club levels of Twisted, Satine paced in the office of her private lair and smoked her tenth cigarette of the night. Her ribcage still hurt where Gabriel had kicked her though the bruise had already faded. She'd changed into a negligee of frothy pear-green lace that stopped just short of her bare crotch in front, down to her knees in the back. Angry and humiliated, she paced in front of the naked were tiger lounging on her couch, aware of his gaze on her. "Stupid bitch," she growled between puffs. "Stupid, stupid bitch."

"Family. You can't get away from them. Ignore her. Or, better yet, give her to Vlad." Chazz rose from the couch and caught her hips in his hands. He moved up behind her, nestled his hard and ready cock against her.

She rolled her hips against his heat in an almost automatic response. "She'll ruin everything. I need him, Chazz. I can't continue like this," she whined.

"What do you want with a part-demon when you have the master of the city eating out of your hand? Not to mention me, ready and waiting to take you at a moment's notice," he added with another grin.

"Vladimir scares me. But Gabriel, now..." Her voice trailed off, but she finished the sentence in her head. *With all of his soul, I could win my freedom...*

"Vlad loves you," murmured Chazz. He reached around and pulled hard on her nipples. "Doesn't he turn you on?" His mouth found her throat and licked.

Not one to let opportunity pass, Satine moaned her pleasure. "Vlad owns me, he doesn't love me." Satine basked in the were tiger's warmth. "Nothing feels as good as you do."

~ ☾ ~

Except for Gabriel, she thought, but, uncharacteristically, kept that to herself.

Impatient, Satine turned in his arms, circled hers around his neck. She met his gaze and smiled slowly, rubbed her bare crotch against his. "I need you to do something for me." She heard his heartbeat speed up in anticipation.

He held her by the ass and squeezed hard. "Anything, you know that." Chazz bent to kiss her. She placed a hand between their mouths.

"I need you to take care of the girl. Keep her occupied for, oh, several hours. Several days," she corrected, baring her throat to his nips. "She's in the way of my... project." She felt his cock grow even harder between them, felt her desire finally stir.

"Dead or alive?"

"The longer you keep her, the less it matters whether she survives," Satine murmured. "Come here." She reached up, tugged his head to one side, and licked his throat like he had hers. Beneath her tongue his vein pulsed, and she could scent the sweetness of his blood. It called to her. "Now," she murmured and his hands gripped her ass, lifted her, and impaled her on his cock as she wrapped her legs around him. He slid in, all the way home, just as she struck, her teeth piercing deep.

Chazz cried out. Three hard thrusts and he came, again and again as she drank. He sank to the couch, with her wrapped around him. Finally she pulled away from his neck, licking her lips. She knew her eyes whirled red as she looked at him, lifted away, and stood.

She sighed, hands on her hips. This time, he didn't even come close to satisfying her. What a disappointment. Too bad she needed him. "Go to bed. Your job starts whenever you wake up. The longer you keep her occupied, the happier I'll be. Do anything you like with her. Kill her if you want."

"'Kay." Chazz's head lolled against the back of the couch. "That was great, babe." His eyes closed and Satine left, shaking her head.

She needed a dominant, someone who could help her get

~ ☾ ~

rid of Vladimir. Once that was done, her life would be so much easier. Gabriel would help run her business and keep the weres and vampires in line. Chazz just wouldn't do. She needed *all* of Gabriel Caine's soul and she needed it yesterday. With the rest of his soul inside her, she'd have more power than Vlad. Gabriel would be hers. He wouldn't be able to break free of her, nor would he want to.

That had been the plan, until it all went wrong on the beach. She hadn't expected him to deny her sexually. She really hadn't expected him to fight her, had thought the spell she'd used would have immobilized him. But no. He had to fight, and her strength had waned too fast. She'd fled with only part of her prize.

Satine slipped into her private apartment, slumped at her desk, and brooded. Kendall Sorbis, Hollywood's local go-to sorcerer, had given her a bad spell. He needed punishing, a swift retribution.

A knock on her door had her growling. "Come in."

Kendall Sorbis walked in, and Satine shook her head. This was almost too easy.

"Kendall," she purred. "What can I do for you?"

Tall and on the Nordic side, Kendall inclined his head to her, an affectation she hated. "Satine, my gorgeous one. I have come for what you owe me."

"I owe you nothing." Her lips twisted. "The spell was flawed. It didn't work."

"I can see his soul in you. It flares brightly. How can you say it didn't work?"

"He fought me for it!" She spread her hands out on her desktop and stood, keeping her gaze fixed on him. "He fought and kept a part of it. His soul is damaged, incomplete, and unusable in its current state. The spell didn't work."

Kendall's eyes remained unconcerned, his body relaxed. Inwardly, Satine frowned. He should be quaking in his Italian loafers at her anger. "Therefore, I owe you nothing."

His dark eyes flickered at that. "You have more than you had. It isn't my fault you can't figure out how to use the part of his soul you stole."

~ ☾ ~

"I claimed it, I didn't steal it," she flared. She caught her anger back. Keep calm, she cautioned herself. Calm, but prepared. Straightening, she sauntered around the desk and leaned against it, never taking her eyes off the sorcerer. "Tell me how to use it, then."

One pale eyebrow rose as their gazes locked. "It will cost you more."

"I will give you what you require. After I have what I want."

He seemed to consider that. A half-smile curved his lips. "I don't think so," he said cryptically.

She charged him then, enraged enough to take his life, but her arms closed around air. Satine turned wildly, looking from one end of the office to the other, but Kendall had disappeared. If he'd ever been there at all. She sniffed the air, but smelled only herself in the room.

Her rage cooled as fear set in. She'd known better than to deal with a sorcerer. But now she'd need to carefully set her course of action, or Vladimir would discover her secrets.

Vlad had sought her out, turned her into a vampire because she was a Soul-Stealer. The very first soul she'd taken had been Rose's, and wasn't that sweet?

He'd allowed her to keep that one. The other souls she'd brought to him he'd used and grown stronger in the process, keeping her ignorant. When she had killed a Soul Stealer without Vlad's knowledge, she'd absorbed all of the souls that one had amassed, growing ever stronger. But as her strength grew, so did her fear.

Eternal death stalked her. It breathed down her neck in her daytime sleep, lurked in shadows in the depths of night. Vlad controlled her; the others only tolerated her because of him. They'd moved in on the old Master of the city and had prevailed, the war short and bloody and unnoticed by the humans. Three of their vampires had gone missing, the only ones she'd counted as friends. Vlad had said it was due to discipline problems.

Satine moved from her frozen position in the middle of the room and turned to a dresser. She unlocked a drawer and pulled out a photo album, flipping the pages until she found

~ ☾ ~

the photo she'd wanted.

There. Sara and Rose. Sexy Sara and Rose the Cootie Carrier. Satine had swiped the photo from her parent's album, needing the reminder to find Rose, to take care of her. Her parents had much-preferred Rose for a daughter. Quiet, obedient, bookworm Rose was more to her staid parents' taste than their wild daughter.

But Satine had decided not to kill her. Stealing her soul, then setting Rose up with the drug dealer had been much more to her taste, a delicious revenge; and yet her cousin was still alive *and* giving off the scent of the blessed. It was enough to give the most even-tempered vampire a migraine.

Satine locked the album back in its drawer and shook off the black mood. The night beckoned. Time enough to play with the stupid humans. She waited impatiently for the elevator to take her up to the club. Surely someone up there needed an ass whipping. She fluffed her hair as floors flashed past and stepped off the elevator in search of a little pick-me-up.

Satine felt the whip-touch of Vlad's gaze the minute she walked into the bar, his eyes coldly assessing.

"You've fed."

Satine pouted. "Just a bit. Chazz." She picked up the glass of his favorite red wine and sipped, watching the patrons watch them.

He sniffed. "You've had sex with him," he accused.

"Oh Vladimir, really. It just sort of happened, the way it does when I walk around half naked," she said. "It was nothing. How many women do you take a day?"

His hand moved to her right breast, squeezed cruelly. She gasped at the pain that shot through her, her eyes wide on him. Her body throbbed with need, her fear an added spice. "Yes," she whispered and moved in to lick his lower lip. "You know what I crave."

He fingered the lace. "You wear these things to entice the humans." His voice, devoid of emotion, sent a shiver of fear down her spine. Her nipples hardened further and her body ached for release.

~ ☾ ~

"I wear them because I want everyone to see what only you can have," she purred.

"And yet, you had sex with the were tiger." Vladimir motioned to the bartender who brought over another glass of red wine and set it in front of Satine.

"I would not give a human the pleasure," she snapped, and immediately lowered her head. "I'm sorry," she whispered, and shivered as the hand at her breast moved to the other one. It clamped down on her body with the force of mountains.

"You know my rules. No sex unless it's with me. You are begging to be punished, aren't you?" The words came to her ears without inflection, as though he could care less. Satine thought she knew better.

Eagerly, she pressed her crotch against the length of his erection, only his leather pants between them. "You always have the most divine punishments for me, my lord." She whispered the words against his lips, knowing those lips were hard enough to bruise even her. Her hands spread across the cold perfection of his bare chest, delighting in him, so much harder than all her other lovers with their basically human bodies.

"Divine punishments? Perhaps. Drink." Vlad released her and turned to watch the crowd, his voice dismissive of both her and the plans he had for her.

Twin licks of fear and desire slid through her. She was stronger than she had been and stronger than he knew now that she held a part of Gabriel's soul. She would find out tonight if that strength would be enough to get her what she wanted, or if she'd need the rest of Gabriel's soul to win her freedom.

Which reminded her. "I have an appointment." She bowed her head as he turned to her. "Three a.m. I will join you at four."

Vlad raised an eyebrow. "Something serious?"

She shrugged one bare shoulder and picked up her wine. "Just an irritation from my past. A family thing. I'll get it taken care of, and then I'll be yours."

Vlad's eyes hardened to bits of black stone. "Whether you

~ ☾ ~

do or not is immaterial. You already belong to me. And I will never let you go." He turned away from her. "Until it's time to unmake you."

Satine jerked, her hand convulsing on her glass. Wine spilled on her skin.

"Careless," murmured Vladimir, not bothering to turn her way. "So unsatisfactory in a mate, carelessness. Don't you think?"

Satine bit her lip until she tasted blood.

~ ☾ ~

Chapter Seven

"These are fabulous." Rose dug into the peanut butter and jelly sandwich. Gabriel had made five, two for her. He set two big glasses of milk on the kitchen table and sat across from her. The kitchen was a showplace in stainless steel and granite. The scent of garlic and onions hung faintly in the air.

"Just like mom used to make or, in my case, Dad, since my mother died giving birth to me. At any rate, they should help take care of that empty, dizzy feeling you've got going." He bit into his first sandwich.

Rose looked at the jelly oozing out between the slices of bread. "I don't know how to repay you. It's not like I'm rolling in dough. I don't even have a bank account."

Gabriel shifted in his chair. "Has anyone asked you for money?"

"No, but I feel like I should pay my way." Helpless, Rose shrugged. "It just seems fair."

"You're carrying my soul for me."

"And you're not happy about that." Rose shook her head. She watched as he ate his way steadily through the sandwiches. "Do you always eat so much?"

"I'm fueling up in case I need to resort to demonic tactics tonight. If one of us changes without being properly fueled, the aftermath is harder to shake." He gulped down the milk and went for a refill.

"I wish you didn't have to go. Confronting Satine just doesn't seem smart."

Gabriel raised an eyebrow. "How else am I supposed to get my soul back?" He poured himself a second glass and put the milk away.

~ ☾ ~

Rose rubbed her arms. "I could go with you."

"No, really." Gabriel eyed her warily. "You can't. You don't want to mess Satine again."

"I should go with you. If I'm a Soul Chalice, won't you need me? Plus you know, fire whatchamacallit here. I could help, like you said."

"Forget it. Remember how quickly she shut you down the last time?"

"I'll keep my mental walls up and my fire on hand. You know, as best as I can. And I'll carry a knife or something. I'll be fine, if you're there." She put a hand on his and smiled. "I really don't want to spend too much time away from you. Even if it means fighting."

She could read the indecision deep in his eyes, the gray clear of any evasion. He pulled away and abruptly stood. "I've got to call Justin."

Rose looked down at her hands, picked absently at a hangnail. She could feel his soul inside her, a warmth that lent her strength, though different from the fire demon. Closing her eyes, she explored it.

His soul was more than his being and yet less at the same time. A repository for memory and a welling of life, everything he had been and would be lay inside her. His years away had been lonely ones as he struggled with the girl's death. He'd never forgiven himself, never forgotten. Self-hatred burned inside him. A longing for the mother he never knew. He'd been consumed by a bone-deep need to be alone.

She saw herself there in his soul, too, the picture of the two of them stopped in time as they'd first met, the mist billowing. Now she saw what she hadn't seen then, the twin strands of color that circled him. How startled he'd been when they'd first met, and how some ice had cracked off his frozen heart as the morning progressed.

Gabriel came back into the kitchen, startling her out of her reverie. She looked at him with new eyes and a heart that wondered.

He frowned down at her. "I had to leave Justin a message. Couldn't get through."

~ ☾ ~

"You need me." She grimaced as she wished the impulsive words unspoken. "I mean, you need to take me with you. I'm not staying here by myself."

Gabriel sighed. "I can't promise to keep you safe, though I'll keep you as safe as I can. You've got to agree to do exactly what I tell you to do, or no dice. And if you die while we're there, I'll never forgive myself. Or you," he added, his arms crossed.

"So don't let me die. That's pretty simple. And I guess I'll do whatever you tell me, as long as I don't think it's a stupid order."

He eyed her. "You're not making this easy."

"Look." Rose met his gaze straight on. "I'm pretty sure I know how to get your soul back. Satine craves the rest of it. If you fight her, and I'm not there, how are you going to get your soul back? If you kill her, what then? Does your soul know to return to you?" Rose shook her head. "I don't think so."

"You couldn't give me my soul back earlier," he pointed out.

"Because I wasn't supposed to, obviously. I have to believe I'll know what to do when the time comes, since I wasn't sent here with a how-to manual."

The kitchen clock ticked the seconds off as Rose continued to eat while he thought.

"I don't know how to get my soul from her," he finally admitted. "And there's no time right now to see if Maggie can give me a spell to use."

"You need me." Pleased with the way she put the issue, Rose licked at the peanut butter on her fingers.

Gabriel's left eye twitched. "Fine."

"Don't sound so happy about it."

"Not likely when I'm putting your life in danger," he pointed out.

"We just need to get your soul back before she takes you out," she soothed. "Then we can all move on."

"I'm an idiot. Just stay alive. Okay?"

Elation pumped through her. "O*kay*. Let's go. I'm fueled up and ready for anything."

~ ☾ ~

Gabriel stood and picked up their plates. "This is gonna get ugly." He put the dishes in the sink.

Rose turned to him, one eyebrow cocked. "No, really? I thought taking a vampire out would just mean a stake and a poof of dust," she said wryly.

He just looked at her, his face set. "Do as I tell you. It's going to be hard enough keeping you alive; if you go rogue on me, it'll be damned near impossible."

"Gee, thanks." She studied him, searched his eyes. Something in their gray depths made her uneasy. "You want to fight her by yourself. Are you nuts? What if she has more demons with her?"

"She probably will."

"Then ask for Justin's help. Don't be stubborn."

"I don't want to risk him, but my wishes have never stopped him in the past. He said he'd be here tonight. If he wants to come with us, then he will. I'm not his keeper." His face closed up.

"Yes you are, because you're his *brother*," she emphasized. "Brothers take care of each other, guard each other's backs. You don't have to keep yourself isolated, not now. Not anymore."

"It's a long-standing habit. Besides, my reasons are my own. I don't need to share them with you," he retorted. "I can't believe we're arguing about this."

"Then let's not." Rose backed down, not wanting him to change his mind about taking her with him. "Tell me your story. I want to know how you met Satine."

"Why?"

"I want the history. And if you don't want to tell me, I can always get my cousin to do so. She'd probably love to fill me in on all the details." Rose shot him a triumphant look as she played her ace. "Besides, anything I don't know can be used against me. If I know what the hell happened, then there's a greater chance of not falling into any traps. Come on, sit down and tell me."

"Fine. But don't blame me if you don't like what you hear. And don't interrupt."

~ ☾ ~

Rose crossed her legs on the kitchen chair and leaned her elbows on the table, chin on her hands, and waited.

Gabriel stared at the table between them. "Ten years ago, I killed a human. A demon had messed with her but I didn't realize it until too late. Marianne and I were up north on a short road trip. I was eighteen and in love. We'd gone to the same high school, and had hooked up right before graduation. We were on the beach one night and I showed her how fast I could run. Then she turned into a demon in front of me, a male demon. I didn't know what to think. Was she really a male demon, and not a female human? He challenged me and we fought. I killed it. Broke it's spine against the rocks at the beaches of Carpinteria.

"But to my shock I didn't kill *it*, I killed *her*. When she died, the demon possessing her laughed at me as he appeared next to her broken body. I fought him like a madman. He was hurt bad when he disappeared in front of me." He touched the scar on his cheek. "I was hurt pretty bad, too. I thought I'd killed him.

"I was left with Marianne, dead on the beach, and nothing to prove that she'd been possessed except a spiral tattoo on her stomach."

Rose clenched her hands together at the mention of the tattoo. She swallowed hard. "What happened next?"

"My first instinct was to go to the police and confess. But I was a coward. I couldn't make myself do that, even though it was the right thing to do. So I took off. I crashed my car against a tree, left her purse and my wallet after taking the money out of them. And I disappeared, into the desert, hoping the world would think we'd both been killed."

Her heart ached. "You were just a boy, Gabriel. He tricked you, used you."

"It doesn't matter. You had to know that part before I could tell you the rest. The first time I met Satine, it was like a dream. I'd been living in an empty shack along the highway. There are a lot of them, if you know where to look. One night, she—Satine—was just there, hovering above my pallet, her outfit porn chic, something a lonely man might conjure. She

~ ☾ ~

came to me, offered herself, and I took her without thought, without care. She was a dream, not a woman. Just someone who wanted my punishment, who needed to be used. A mindless fucking, that's all she wanted. Hell, that's what I wanted.

"Demons can get rough without knowing it, and apparently I got rough. She loved it, wrung me out, had me, or I had her, again and again that night. And two, three, four nights in a row she came to me to be...used.

"I'd wake up feeling dirty. Not rested or refreshed, but tainted. I don't know when she started taking my blood. Not a lot, not ever a lot. But finally one night, her eyes were red with need. She asked me then if I wanted to die and live forever. She...tempted me, said she would free me of my human guilt, my human existence."

Rose cleared her throat. "She didn't know you were a tribred?"

He shrugged. "Don't know. But her calling me human shook me out of that waking dream. I cursed her to hell and back. She laughed, told me I was already hers, and reached to me with her mind, implanting the suggestion of knives as she spoke. As a result, she speaks, I get the pain."

"Oh." Rose looked at him in dismay. "So when you talk to her, mind to mind..."

"Yeah. It hurts."

Rose got up from her chair and went around the table to stand behind Gabriel. She wound her arms around him; laid her head on his shoulder, and gave him what comfort she could, ignoring his discomfort. "It's not your fault. What she did was awful."

"Right. And I was a Boy Scout." Self-loathing filled his words.

She spoke softly. "You were in pain, not to mention you were very young. You distanced yourself from your family, and you handled the problem in the only way that your sense of honor would allow."

"Sense of honor." He unwound her arms gently and turned to look at her, holding her away from him. "A full demon

~ ☾ ~

raped my mother. Their blood types weren't compatible, and she died while giving premature birth to me. I don't have the full complement of human and Fae DNA in my makeup. Not like the rest of my family. I'm mostly a demon, a killer. Don't make me out to be better than I am."

Rose ached to hold him close. "I think you're probably one of the best people I know."

A flash of emotion showed in Gabriel's eyes before he let her go and turned from her. "Yeah, well. You've just come back from the dead. You're not at your best mentally right now." He stood and moved to the doorway, Rose trailing after him.

"You've got a pure soul, Gabriel. I should know. I'm carrying a part of it. You haven't lost your humanity. I'm just keeping it safe for you."

Gabriel hesitated before he said over his shoulder, "I need to get ready for later tonight. I've got some computer work to do before I head out." He left the kitchen, a restless man haunted by too many demons.

"Hey! Before *we* head out." Rose scrambled to follow. "What can I do?"

"Go take a nap, or something. Rest." Gabriel turned into Justin's office and settled himself at the computer.

Rose followed him into the office. Lined with books, it was a cozy room done in earth tones, with the desk in one corner and a couch and reading chair opposite. Perfect. She settled into a corner of the couch and picked up a book sitting there. She wasn't letting him out of her sight.

* * *

Gabriel wanted her with him as much as he wanted her safe. But he couldn't let her stay here alone, and he had no idea when Justin would be back. If she shifted in and out of her demon form again tonight, she'd be too weak to be of much use in a fight if things went bad.

Which they usually did when vampires were involved.

Gabriel frowned and looked at his search results. Twisted Sister, rock group. Twisted Pretzel Factory. Twisted Tights Dance Studio. Twist and Shout. Twist Tie Trio. Twist Off the

~ ☾ ~

Weight. Doggedly, he continued wading through the sites looking for Satine's nightclub. Three Google pages in, he found just plain Twisted and clicked on it.

A red page opened up with a black whip snaking out from one corner to lick the T in Twisted, the words By Invitation Only written in elaborate script below it. When he rolled the cursor over the word Invitation, it changed into a hand. Gabriel clicked on the word.

An address in black popped up, plus an envelope below the address. Curious, Gabriel clicked on the envelope and when it opened, he stared.

```
            Club Twisted
              welcomes
      Gabriel Caine & Rose Walters.
  Invitation good for 3:00am on this night
                 only.
```

"Hell," he said, and closed out the windows. He powered the computer down. "We got an invitation to Satine's club."

Rose looked up from her book. "That's a bad thing, I guess?"

"Yeah. Really bad." He turned in the chair to look at her and frowned. She looked good, too good for his self-control. "You should be napping."

"I will if you will." She raised a brow in challenge.

"I'm not the one who shifted this evening," he reminded her. "You really need to nap."

Rose sighed and put the book down. "I guess I need to spell it out for you. I don't feel safe anywhere without you. So I'll nap if you lie down and nap beside me."

"I don't nap." Irritated, he growled at her. "I'm a demon. Demons don't nap. It's not...seemly."

"Oh, really." She crossed her arms and raised one brow, amused.

"Really. Not ever." He rose from his chair and came to her, helped her to her feet. "You, however, really do need to rest. Regain your strength."

~ ☾ ~

He hustled her down the stairs and to a bedroom before she could protest. One glance at the bed and he felt her sigh in his bones.

"You're right. I need to rest." She climbed onto the bed, holding fast to his hand. "And you need to rest beside me." Her eyes closed and her breathing evened out.

Gabriel cursed under his breath. The last thing he should do was the thing he most wanted in the world. He took a step away from her, but her fingers tightened on his. He gave in. If nothing else, touching her kept his demon calm. Shifting her to the middle of the bed, he lay down beside her and gathered her close. If he just kept thinking of her as a child, maybe his body would behave.

Mentally taking note of the time, he set his internal alarm and allowed his mind to wander.

He woke slowly to the fresh scent he'd come to associate with her. She'd sprawled across him, a warm bundle of female, her hair tickling his nose. He turned on his side and adjusted her as he moved. She snuggled further into his arms and he just held her, allowed her light to fill him up.

She made a purring sound low in her throat, somehow a question.

"I'm awake."

Rose raised her head from his chest and smiled at him with a radiance that had him blinking. "What's the plan for tonight?"

"Recon, an hour or two before we're expected. I want to know what the place looks like and how many we'll be dealing with. Ideally, I'd like to know who's gonna fight when pushed to it, but this isn't an ideal situation."

"I suppose not." She looked down at the collar of his tee shirt and bit her lip.

"What is it? Ask. You know you're going to."

"Are you going in armed?"

"Yes."

"Will you arm me?"

The question brought Gabriel up short. He shifted away from her and sat up. Rose followed suit. "Well?"

~ ☾ ~

Gabriel looked at her coolly. "Can you shoot? Use a knife? Can you stake a vampire in the heart and not miss?"

"No, yes somewhat, and I don't know. I've never tried. But if you give me lessons," she began.

"There's no time for lessons. You use the weapons you have. Right now, all you have is the ability to shield your mind and the demon on your body."

"I'd rather use my wits and a gun. Or a knife. Anything. I just – I don't think I'm ready to be the demon again just yet."

Gabriel sympathized. "I know. But if you're coming with me, you'd better be prepared to use what you've got. I can give you a knife, but that's all," he added grudgingly. "I must be crazy. I should really leave you behind."

"No, you shouldn't. You should keep your soul close to you." And Rose blinded him again with her smile.

* * *

"We can do this the easy way, or the hard way." Gabriel stood across the street from the club, his arm around Rose. He tried hard to ignore her tight little body pressed up against him. The midnight hour had a surprising amount of foot traffic in this area of town, so they didn't look out of place.

"Which is which?" she whispered. They'd walked from where they'd parked Justin's car four blocks away and had stumbled into a pool of light from a flickering streetlight, giggling and pretending to be drunk. It had been her idea, and to his chagrin Gabriel hadn't come back with a better one.

Gabriel buried his face in her hair, breathed deep. Her scent sank into him, reminding him of the wild sun-filled days of his youth. It was enough to make him drunk. He struggled to answer her. "Easy is just observing from the outside." He nuzzled her neck and felt a tremor go through her. Where her pelvis pressed, her heat seared him.

"But that won't give you the information you need, will it?" She pressed her nose into his chest and breathed deeply. "Mmmmm."

She fit in his arms. Felt far too good there. Gabriel yanked on his libido and refocused on her question. "No. So it's the hard way, after all." He took a deep breath and, one finger

~ ☾ ~

under her chin, tilted her face up to his. "Promise me you'll run if I tell you to." He kissed her, keeping it light.

"Yeah. Sure." She licked her lips. "Anything you say." She reached up for another kiss, and this time he couldn't resist her temptation

Her lips were soft, purposeful, searching as she reached up to him. She tasted of the night and secrets and sorrow, a dark, addictive flavor that he'd craved since their last kiss.

Heat flared between them. Not flame this time, just old-fashioned sexual heat. Gabriel's arms tightened, holding her closer even as his growing need for her scared him. Pulling away, he murmured, "What am I going to do with you? You don't belong in my world."

"Neither of us knows where we belong," she said, and kissed his throat. "Maybe together, we could find out."

Gabriel's heart sank. "It's safer for everyone if I walk alone." He eased away from her, brushed her hair off her cheek. "Let's focus here. We've got a job to do."

"It's more than just that I'm carrying a part of your soul, Gabriel. You don't have to be alone." She fiddled with his coat buttons, her head bowed.

His lips twisted. "You have no idea," he said under his breath and turned away, motioning with his shoulder towards the club. "I'd rather avoid the bouncers at the front door. From what I learned off the Internet, our best bet is to go in through the back. There's a balcony, two doors and a set of windows on the second floor, which is where the legitimate business offices are. If we can get in there, we have a chance to do some real recon. I'll go in and let you know if it's safe."

"Oh, no you don't," she whispered, her tone no less steely for its softness. "I'm not letting you go in alone."

Gabriel grimaced over her head. He really didn't want her turning demon. She'd be far safer outside of the club, so he'd leave her there, unable to follow the route he'd planned. But she won't know that until he was up on the second floor balcony, leaving her safe below. "The guards aren't watching us any more. Let's go."

They wandered back the way they had arrived, arms

~ ☾ ~

around each other, giggling. Once out of sight, Gabriel was quick to step aside, refusing to acknowledge the chill left by her absence. "Come on." He set off down the street at a jog.

"I'll be there in a bit. Shorter legs and all," she called after him.

Guilt had him slowing until she finally caught up with him.

"We can do this, you know," she panted.

"If we get caught, just run, okay? Get gone. Don't wait for me."

They had gone around the block and now came up to the back of the building, a dark, unkempt parking lot butting into an alley lined in oleander bushes ten feet tall. Two lights burned dim at either corner, creating more shadows than light in the lot. He looked up to where the balcony circled the second story. Yeah, that would work just fine.

"Now what?" She hissed as they moved forward. "What's the plan?"

Gabriel frowned. Her energy was all over the place, amped up somehow, and her aura glowed golden again. How did she *do* that? Where did it come from? What the hell was she? He could feel her sexual pull on him, stronger now that he'd imprinted the feel of her body on his. He gave a quick look around, grateful that the parking lot remained empty.

"The plan?" Gabriel gauged the height, the rail of the balcony. "I'll see you in a bit. Stay out of sight, and keep watch. Hide in the bushes. Keep my soul safe." Unable to resist, Gabriel kissed her once, hard, before jumping straight up. He caught the rail and swung over. A quick jimmy of a window and he was in.

Gabriel followed the scent of demon, opened his senses to see how many were in the building. The upper story was clean, which is why he'd gone in that way. The first floor was mostly human, but beyond that...he caught the mingling scents of blood, sex, and death—the stench of vampire, as well as an energy signature not to be missed.

Weres.

Damn it all to hell. He headed toward the emergency stairwell and sped down on silent feet. The scents of sex, of

~ ☾ ~

death grew stronger as he descended below street level three floors and counting until the stairs just stopped at a door. He went through it and found himself in a dimly lit, cement hallway.

They hadn't bothered with paint down here. The long hallway, less than hospitable, had drains spaced five feet apart down the middle. The rooms lining the hallway were empty but he could scent death down here. Despair. Not sex, not here. A part of him drank down the fear that lingered in the air, even as it disgusted him. He hated that part of himself, hated the need that drove him to feed off the fear of others. Yet another reason he'd spent so much time alone.

Gabriel! Where are you?

Shocked, Gabriel recognized Rose's mental voice. Holy hell. *Where are you?*

I had to come inside. Demons were patrolling. I'm in the stairwell – Gabriel!

Damn it to hell. He headed back to the door and pulled.

All thoughts of Rose fled as the door flew open and three J'aadt demons, looking more like badgers with semi-automatics than humans, aimed straight for his heart.

"Oh hey guys. I think I'm lost. Is this where I can get some werewolf pussy? That purty gal up front said something about that the last time I was here." He put on a western drawl and looked around, wide-eyed, and noted the close quarters of the hallway landing. It'd do. "Hey, you guys aren't all human, are ya? I'm kinda fucked up myself, ya know. Too much to drink upstairs."

Gabriel weaved a bit, slapped one of the demons on the shoulder and used him as leverage to kick the far one in the jaw, ripping the gun out of the demon's hands as he turned to look. The one in the middle got a funny look on his face and he went down, his eyes wide with confusion, revealing Rose behind him, jerking her knife out of his back.

"Hey there," she said, and as one they turned to the demon still alive. Gabriel turned the semi on the demon and shot him, once between the eyes, even as he opened his mouth, showing off all his sharp, pointy teeth and snapping toward

~ ☾ ~

Rose's face. He went down with a grunt of surprise.

Damn it. Guns hadn't been in his plan. Killing again *really* hadn't been in his plan. "What the hell are you doing here?" Gabriel hissed the words at Rose, motioning her up the stairway.

"Get away now. Explanations later," she said as she took the stairs, two at a time. Exhilaration and a strength Gabriel hadn't expected poured off her as they raced up the stairs.

So far, all remained quiet.

They had gotten to just below the first floor when Rose stopped, swerved out of the stairwell.

"Hell." He followed her. "Rose! What the hell?"

She waved at him to be quiet and stood outside a door three doors in. She leaned against it, closed her eyes and sighed. "We have to help her out." Rose looked at Gabriel, her determination clear. "She's being held prisoner. We've got to rescue her."

"We'll come back. I promise. There's no time now." All his senses were humming on high alert. "Come on," he urged, and turning, headed back to the stairwell, relieved when she followed him.

"She's angry," Rose whispered as they continued their race up the stairwell. "She's a werewolf. I think she might be pregnant, too. We've got to contact someone."

"We will. I promise. Just keep moving." Gabriel never saw the fist that came out of the darkness, catching him in the temple, and dropping him like a stone.

Rose screamed, shades of white-hot anger and fear aimed at the looming shadow between them and safety. She launched herself over Gabriel, her fists at the ready, but before she connected, a shadow came down and she crumpled at the vampire's feet.

~ ☾ ~

Chapter Eight

Rose sucked on the pipe, cradled it like a lover. She flicked the lighter again and took another hit deep into her lungs. The rush took her by surprise as it always did, the one-two punch of sexual heat and euphoria as the drug spread. She dropped the lighter and giggled. Saw herself in the mirror opposite the toilet and giggled again. She'd gotten her hair cut short like a boy's. The guys liked it. She ruffled her hand over her head and reached for the glass of vodka, missed the glass, and sent it shattering into the sink. The smell rose, tantalizing her, and with a cry for the lost drink, she shoved her hands into the glass, digging for the alcohol, uncaring of the shards slicing her hands. She licked the vodka off her fingers and spit the glass out, the cuts stinging, still craving more. She'd have to go get the bottle, go into the rest of the house.

Shhh. Rose giggled quietly, opened the door, and lurched out of the bathroom. Now where was the kitchen? Or did they keep the good stuff in the living room? Which house was she in? Rose looked around, frowning, and looked down at herself. She was naked. Naked, and her hands were wet. She dried them on her stomach, ignoring the pinpricks of pain, and thought hard.

Shit. Was she supposed to be fucking someone? But no, the house seemed quiet. No music, no smell of weed, no one vomiting in a corner. No one banging anyone else. Must be early morning, then.

Wobbly, she made her way to the kitchen. Stopped when she saw a man sitting at the table smoking a cigarette. He looked at her with soft grey eyes. She knew him. Knew his

~ ☾ ~

broken profile, hair like silk, the scar that dripped down his neck. Memory jabbed, sent a spear of pain just behind her eyes.

"Oh no," she moaned, and turned away, embarrassed and ashamed that he should see her that way.

"Come on, honey. Let's go home." His voice rasped like velvet against her ears. She put her hands up to block it, felt wetness against her scalp. A cigarette in his hand flamed, glowed in his eyes, and he turned into the whip-thin, weaselly-eyed Kevin.

"No! You can't make me. You can't make me!" She flung her hands out toward him, and the power in her gesture had him splayed against the kitchen wall. Fire licked at his feet, followed the outline of his body. She panted with the effort, felt alive. Felt strong.

He held his hands out to her as he changed back into the dark haired, broken angel. "Come, Rose. We need you. We love you. Come home."

Rose shook her head but dropped her hands. The man settled lightly on his feet and the flames faded. Memory scrolled through her, a future she'd yet to see. A face...

"Gabriel? Where are you?" She crumpled into a ball on the kitchen floor, sobbing as he dissolved in front of her eyes.

But then strong arms came around her. "I'm here. I'm right here. Come on. Let's go home." She sighed, nestled against him.

* * *

Gabriel opened his eyes, hoping this time he'd managed to pull her from the nightmare, but Rose still slumped against the wall across from him, her eyes tightly shut. Her arms were stretched out to either side and manacled to iron rings low in the walls. Her head hung to the left, her legs splayed out like a doll's, making her look forgotten and alone.

"Gabriel, help me." She twisted, pulled at the manacles chaining her, moaned as the iron cut into her wrists. Blood seeped around the metal, but she didn't wake up.

His heart aching for her, Gabriel looked away. He'd been chained standing up, his legs locked down, too. His arms ached, having had to take all his body weight until he woke up and he could hold himself upright. He didn't know how long they'd been in the dark. The chamber was small and barren, with another handy drain in the floor. Calling upon his demon heritage, he could see well enough in the black, could see the tears on her cheeks.

"She has terrible memories." The male voice came to him out of the darkness, jolting him.

"Why are you having her relive them? Getting your jollies from it, are you?" Gabriel sneered.

The hand came out of nowhere, the force of the slap banging his head against the cement wall. Gabriel tasted blood on the inside of his cheek and moved his jaw to make sure it wasn't broken.

"She killed one of my demons."

"Yeah. A lesser demon. You don't seem the type to get bent about it."

"No demon is without worth. You should understand that, being one yourself."

Gabriel gritted his teeth as a fist plowed into his face, breaking his nose again. He felt the blood spurt out then settle to a slow flow down his lip.

"Such...restraint. Why haven't you changed, broken free of the manacles?" He came within Gabriel's eyesight, looked him over. "You could have."

Gabriel struggled not to respond. The voice flowed over his body like a thousand feathers whispering, caressing him beneath his clothes. He forced himself to keep his focus on Rose. "I haven't exactly been thinking straight. Getting cold-cocked tends to have that effect on me." Gabriel stuck to the truth. This guy spooked him. He could usually feel out vampires, but this big bad? Nothing. Not even a ping on the vampdar.

"Why are you here? What were you hoping to do here?" The big blond moved to kneel down at Rose's side. He lifted her face with an immaculately manicured hand and studied her. "And why did you bring her? She's not much."

Nausea threatened Gabriel as the vampire's hands trailed

Demon Soul

over Rose. "Don't touch her."

"Oh, does this bother you? Sorry. Tell me, what is your tie to Satine?" He turned to Gabriel, one hand smoothing down the front of Rose's body. She shuddered in reaction, but didn't wake up.

Gabriel stiffened in outrage but kept the anger out of his voice with effort. "She came to me years ago, several times. We had sex. She took my blood. Offered to make me one of you. I said no, thanks anyway, and un-invited her." He shrugged. "Pissed her off some, I guess. That's pretty much it. Where is she?"

"Out. Did you think she would rescue you?"

"I expected her to be here, gloating. Besides, if she's your lover, why would she rescue me?" he countered.

"Good question." The big blond studied Gabriel, looked from him to Rose. "Are you soul-bound to this one?"

Shock had him jerking against his restraints. "Hell, no. I just met her a few hours ago."

"And yet here you are," he mused. "Both of you. Surprising." He moved to Gabriel and put a cold hand against his cheek. "What I don't understand is your refusal to turn demon and save the both of you. Why haven't you? She's in a dark place, and you can't help her unless you change."

"I can be there for her, in her mind. It doesn't hurt her to see me there."

"Ah. You think you might hurt her. Kill her, perhaps?"

Gabriel kept silent.

The vampire chuckled, a sound that held no humor. He moved in closer on silent feet, licked the blood off Gabriel's chin. "Mmmm. Tasty. Simply magnificent." His cold hand stroked down Gabriel's chest. "You just need incentive. Maybe this will help you change your mind. You will be kept here until one of my wolves needs a snack. Then I'll toss her in with the two of you. Which do you think will be safer for your pitiful human? A hungry werewolf, or an angry demon?"

Gabriel could feel the vampire study him, his blond head to one side. He didn't move a muscle.

The blond heaved a dramatic sigh. "Ah well. I guess only

~ ☾ ~

time will tell. I should leave. The scent of your blood is...almost irresistible. If I weren't trying to give up men, I might even keep you for myself."

Gabriel shut his eyes. "It's always the same with your kind, isn't it? Sex and blood. Is that why you started the club? Playing with your food before you eat it?"

"And demons are the epitome of restraint," scoffed the vampire, quite close to his left ear, and Gabriel jerked in surprise.

"I guess the answer is boredom," he replied. "After a couple hundred years, there's not much new to keep my interest. Humans, though, continue to be stubborn, stupid, endlessly fascinating in their quest for the ultimate fulfillment." He shrugged. "It'll do for a distraction. For now, anyway."

"If you ever touch Rose again, I'll rip you into a thousand pieces and burn each one, slowly."

"Like I said. Stubborn and stupid. Bored."

Gabriel didn't answer, and the silence that held heaviness slowly became empty. Minutes passed. Hours. Gabriel thought the vamp had left. Hoped so, anyway. He reached for the thread that connected him to Satine, but it was like wading through a river of mud and never getting to the other side. He slumped against the wall and focused, sweat trickling down his neck, and kept the picture of Satine in his head.

The door to their cell crashed open. "All right, all right. What the hell is the matter with you?" Satine, irritated, stood just inside the door. She wore a trench coat and spike heels and brought the scent of lilies and the night with her. "Oh, my. You have gotten yourself in trouble, haven't you?" She shut the door behind her. "You're here early," she scolded, sauntering to where he stood manacled. "What did Vlad do to you?" She reached for his face, to lick off the rest of the congealed blood, but he turned away in disgust.

"Is that his name? Figures." He shrugged. "There was a...disagreement," he said. "Open these cuffs."

Satine looked at him with amusement. "You can't honestly think I'll free you when I've got you where I want you?"

Anger surged through Gabriel. "You don't want to piss me

~ ☾ ~

off," he warned. His demon prowled close to the surface and he shook with the effort of keeping it controlled.

"Don't I?"

A low moan came from Rose. Glee brightened Satine's face as she crossed to the girl. "You brought me a present! How thoughtful."

"Stay away from her."

"Oh, I don't think so. I really don't think I can do that." Satine knelt and broke open the manacles and lifted Rose. "Such a pretty plaything."

Rose stirred in Satine's arms. "Mama?"

Satine looked down and bared her teeth. "Your mama never loved you, brat. She never knew your daddy. Your side of the family has always been white trash, and you always will be."

Rose moaned.

With difficulty, Gabriel held in the rage bursting to be set free. Seeing Rose in Satine's arms beat out killing Marianne Farlane as his worst nightmare. "You like talking trash to an unconscious woman?"

Satine moved so Rose's back was against her front, her arms wrapped around Rose's torso. "I like doing a lot of things to unconscious women," she crowed, and licked the spot where Rose's vein throbbed in her throat. "Mmmm. She's so sweet." Satine sent a sly grin toward Gabriel. "You had her yet? Word has it, everyone in the San Fernando Valley has." She sniffed the air, frowned. "But you haven't touched her, not really. Have you?"

Anger and fear snapped his control and his demon surged against the restraints, snapping all four of them at once. Gabriel lunged for Satine as she dodged. He roared in anger. "Give her to me."

"You can't have her." Satine's eyes grew wild with cunning. "Unless – give me the rest of your soul, and I'll give her to you."

A part of Gabriel stilled–Satine didn't know Rose held the rest of his soul. If she knew...he shuddered and lunged again.

Satine zipped past him and hovered by the door. "I like my

~ ☾ ~

life the way it is. I like bleeding humans and fucking were animals." She licked Rose's throat again as if in comfort. Her voice brightened as she looked at him again. "But I'll be much more powerful with all of your soul. Give it to me, and then, after we kill Vlad, maybe we can be friends. You're right, you know. I don't need to bring you over in order for you to be helpful." She stroked Rose's breasts. "And we can share her. Keep her as a slave, or have sex with her until her heart stops. What do you say?"

"My soul first."

Her eyes glittered. "Never."

He roared again, a large, guttural cry that sounded as if it were ripped from the very earth. The walls trembled. Satine bit down on Rose's neck and he lunged, grabbing the vampire.

* * *

Rose's eyes popped open at the searing heat in her neck and on her belly. She cried out in confusion and pain, caught in arms of marble crushing her chest. A breath later, huge hands had torn her away. Air rushed into her lungs and fire speared the juncture of her neck and shoulder as she was slammed hard against the concrete wall.

She got a glimpse of a huge creature the color of oak as she struggled to steady herself. She saw the manacles, knew suddenly where the sting around her wrists came from. She turned and watched as Satine dodged his blows.

Gabriel was massive in the small room. His clothes hung in tatters, his back had ridges along the spine, and his hands ended in claws. Fighting Satine, he kept Rose between his back and the wall.

Emotions welled up in her. He cared, at least. If he hadn't cared, she'd be dead.

Gabriel?

Busy here, he answered, swatting Satine out of the air like a bat hitting a baseball. She flew against the back wall with a sickening crack. Gabriel lifted Rose over his shoulder. *Let's get out of here.* She hung on tight.

The door burst open and vampires poured into the tiny room, one of them with a sword. The vamp slashed,

~ ☾ ~

advancing, and Gabriel howled as the sword caught him in the side as he turned to protect Rose. He swung a whip and two vampires were suddenly headless, their corpses falling where they stood. Rose wished desperately for a gun, a spear, even a knife. Any weapon to use against these creatures would be better than no weapon.

As Gabriel fought his way to the door, Rose hung on and kicked out at the faces around her, connecting with more than one snarling mouth until both her shoes were covered in blood. Gabriel's roars, and the whip he wielded, kept the others at bay long enough for them to reach the stairwell. Then they really began to move.

The world sped by nauseatingly fast once they gained the street. Rose shut her eyes tightly and took deep breaths of the fresh, untainted air.

Though he carried her, Rose had never felt so strong. She'd fought back. For the first time in her entire life, when it counted she'd fought back. Exhilaration poured through her. Maybe this second chance at life had a lot of good things in store.

Gabriel slowed down and changed back to his human shape in front of the house. He hustled her inside, keeping her in front of him. "I'll just go get some pants."

Rose turned in time to see his well-muscled backside disappearing down the hallway. Grinning to herself, she went to the powder room and stared. Blood had caked down her neck. She swallowed hard, reached for a washcloth, and stared at the blood around her wrists.

Rose met the curious gaze of her reflection. She could do this. Carefully cleaning her wrists, Rose thought back to the nightmare. To the spot after lights-out and before Sara–Satine–bit her. She relived every minute of it, watching as though it were a movie.

She finally noticed Gabriel had been there, trying to protect her even in her nightmares.

When he appeared in the doorway, she'd dealt with her wrists and most of the blood on her neck and shoulder, leaving a wad of toilet paper layered against the slow ooze.

~ ☾ ~

"You okay?"

"Yes." She fluffed her hair over the wound on her neck and turned to look at him. He'd found a pair of his brother's blue jeans and a white tee shirt. "Looking good. Thank you for getting me out of there."

Color washed across his face. "I never should have taken you there."

"It's not like I gave you much choice. Did you clean the cuts you got during the fight?"

"Yeah. I'm good."

Rose led the way back to the living room. The couches were the color of chocolate, deep and plush, piled with jewel-toned pillows. She sank down onto one with a sigh of relief. "Vampires are fucking *monsters*. Her bite hurt, Gabriel. It didn't feel good. Why do the books say it feels good? Tortured souls, my ass," she mocked.

Gabriel remained standing, shifting from one foot to the other as if he didn't quite know what to do.

She looked at him, really looked, and caught her breath. "It hurt you, didn't it? I can see it." She could, too. Pain swirled around him in shades of purples and reds and grays. She blinked and the image faded, but it was a sight she wouldn't soon forget.

"The transitions hurt, yes. I never want to get comfortable as my demon. I don't want to give it too much power over me."

His restlessness confused her. "Are...are you all right?"

"You saw my demon form. The bronze skin. The claws. The...tail." He looked at her from the corner of his eyes. "It didn't bother you?"

"No. Did you really think it would? Gabriel." She looked at him, at his uncertainty, and a part of her melted. "You are still you, even in your demon form. You were guarding me. You prevented Sara, I mean Satine, from getting to me again. She would have killed me. You, in demon form, stopped her." Tears pricked her eyes and she rubbed them. "Besides, I turned into a fire demon earlier. It didn't seem to bother you."

He sighed then and leaned against a chair.

~ ☾ ~

"Oh for goodness sake, sit down before you fall down." She waited until he sat. "I've got to talk, I hope you don't mind. I'm totally amped. I have so much energy from the fight. Do you change into your demon a lot?"

"Yes. No." Gabriel wiped his face with both hands. "No, not a lot. I've experimented in the past. But it was the first time I'd changed in public. I don't recommend it."

"There's the whole shredding clothes thing," she teased. "What else can you do as a demon? I mean, you were amazing in there, beheading demons with your tail and tossing them into walls."

"I already know I'm a killer." His voice hardened with self-loathing. "I don't need to do any further exploration."

"I think it's fascinating. Why don't you want to explore what you are? What about it scares you?" Rose leaned forward, curiosity eating at her.

"This is no time for Dr. Phil, Rose." Abruptly he stood and strode to the door. "I can't stay."

"Are you kidding? It's the perfect time to talk, while we're both hopped up from the fight. Come on, Gabriel. Stay and talk to me. You can't walk out now," she protested, jumping to her feet. "Besides, Justin's not back yet."

Gabriel turned to her and the look in his eyes broke her heart. "I can't stay here. I almost got you killed again. Trust me. You're better off without me hanging around." And he turned and walked through the door.

Rose waited a heartbeat before following him, but even as she opened the front door, she knew. Gabriel was gone.

She trembled for him. She knew he wouldn't be found if he didn't want to be. Her frustration died and with it, the late-spurt adrenalin rush that had been holding her together.

Abruptly her vision blurred and the wound in her neck throbbed. She touched her neck gingerly. The toilet paper she'd put there fell apart under her fingers, wet with blood.

Her mouth set in a tight line as her vision continued to go fuzzy. Sweat gathered on her forehead, trickled down her face. Shit. Maybe she *had* danced with the meth pipe, after all.

Help. She really needed help. She moved with care to the

~ ☾ ~

phone and dialed. An efficient recorded voice spoke. She took a deep breath, struggled to stay calm. "Los Angeles. Magdalena de la Cruz." The number came in a blur. She pressed the right number to have the call directly connected, and listened to it ring again, ridiculously relieved when she heard a sleepy voice.

"Maggie? It's Rose. Yeah. I'm at Justin's house, but he's not here and Gabriel has gone. I need help." To her horror, Rose burst into tears. "Please come."

* * *

Head down, hands in his pockets and with unfamiliar emotions bombarding him, Gabriel trudged the streets of Santa Monica, determined for once in his life to do the right thing. He'd had to leave her before he grew too comfortable. Rose wasn't for him. If he wanted to keep her alive, he had to keep her at an emotional distance. It was just that simple. He had the history to prove it, didn't he?

He scowled and a street bum moved hastily out of his way. And then tonight, there'd been too many personalities, too much fighting. He hadn't had that many conversations in one night in years. Plus, she reminded him he'd been responsible for way too many deaths in less than twenty-four hours.

Gabriel kicked at a rock in the street. She scared him. That's the real reason he left. She carried Mephisto, yes, but also because she tugged at him. Whatever she was—demon carrier, Soul Chalice, or something else they didn't know to look for—she'd made him care. So fast, so very fast.

Was it any wonder she had him reeling? Emotions he'd thought safely burned out of him were springing up like tree seeds the spring after a wildfire. He'd spent more time with her in the last twenty-four hours than he'd spent with any one person in over a decade, and he'd certainly talked more than he had in a decade. He'd tried to keep his distance from her, but how could you protect yourself against a sunbeam?

He sighed. If he never retrieved his soul, he'd build a cabin somewhere in the middle of nowhere. He'd have the wide open spaces, the wildlife, mother nature at her best. A place where he couldn't reach out and kill someone.

~ ☾ ~

Funny how little appeal his long-cherished dream now held.

Anxious and yearning for something he couldn't put his finger on, Gabriel stopped on the sidewalk, not too far from Justin's house, and searched for Rose in his mind. Just a double check, he assured himself. Just so he could make sure she was safe.

A tall, shiny brass door firmly shut against him blocked his access to her mind.

~ ☾ ~

Chapter Nine

"You want to tell me about it?" Maggie flipped through her doctor's bag, searching for the tools she'd need. One look at Rose had her nerves strung tight. Doc Cavanaugh had taught her well, though. She could do this. She *would* do this.

Rose curled up on the kitchen table, unable to stop crying. "I'm so cold. I don't know why. I've been hot most of the night, but now I'm so cold. We went to this sleazy club to find Satine, and I was helping with recon. I kept bugging him to let me help. Oh hey, I leaped onto a balcony!" Rose smiled through her tears. "It took me a couple tries, but I managed to follow him. Thought he was so smart," she sniffed, and wiped her eyes. "This demon stuff is amazing."

"Where was the club? And why the recon?"

"In the not-so-good part where Santa Monica and West L.A. meet. Gabriel wanted to check it out before he met with Satine. At any rate, he didn't get his soul back." She shivered as memory took over. "It's a sick place. They have torture rooms." Rose shivered again. "I could smell it."

Maggie felt her forehead and frowned. "You're running some fever, girl."

"We killed a couple demons in the club, I remember that. There was something about a werewolf, too, and I think she was pregnant. And then he left, and I was somewhere dark and cold, doing drugs again. I killed Kevin." She shook her head in confusion. "Though I'm pretty sure that part was a dream. But then, bam! Satine's biting me. Then he's protecting me, and we're fighting more vampires, and then we're free and moving fast through the city."

"Sounds like a nightmare," Maggie said. "Unreal."

~ ☾ ~

"It was real, all right. The kitchen keeps twirling around," she complained.

"You just close your eyes, then. I'm almost ready." Maggie cast a worried glance at Rose. Her face had lost every drop of color, leaving her freckles to stand out against the pallor. The bite marks on her body seemed to pulse even as blood welled thick in the holes. Not good. The vamp didn't have time to seal off the wound like they normally would. She poked at Rose's neck, noted the jagged edges of the bite, and sighed.

"Are you sure this was a vampire, and not a werewolf?" Maggie measured Rose's pulse. It was slow and sluggish, her skin hot as well as pale. Rose shivered under her hand.

"Satine did this. Family always knows how to make you hurt. Gabriel rescued me. Then he left. I don't understand, Maggie. I don't get it."

Maggie silently cursed all men. "I don't know. From what Justin has said, Gabriel has always lacked the social graces."

"He hurts. I hurt, too."

"I know." Maggie clucked her tongue as she prepped the vials.

"He rescued me. He didn't have to." Her voice had dropped to a mumble. "Well, yes I guess he did have to, since I hold part of his soul. I shouldn't have pushed him to talk about his demon powers. I just wanted to know."

"I'll be right back." Maggie hurried out of the kitchen to the living room, grabbed the plaid stadium blanket tossed over the couch. Back in the kitchen, she draped it around Rose and took a deep breath. "Okay now, let's get you down on the floor, chica," Maggie said, and took out an eyedropper. "I don't want you passing out sitting up."

Maggie helped the shivering girl down to the floor, wrapped her body as warmly as she could. "Now, this will hurt. Are you sure you don't want anything? I can put you into a really pleasant dream while we get this taken care of," she added, and brushed strands of damp hair gently away from her forehead. "I'm really good at that."

"No, no drugs, please. Let's just do this." Shivering violently, Rose turned her face to the floor, leaving the marred

~ ☾ ~

side of her neck open to Maggie's gaze.

"Here, then," and Maggie put a towel in Rose's hand. "Twist that up and bite down on it. Unless you want to scream."

Rose took the towel without a word, twisted it and closed her eyes. "Just do it."

Maggie dipped the dropper into her small vial of holy water, and drew some up. "Here we go." Carefully, she dropped two drops of holy water on the jagged wounds in Rose's neck. The water hissed and bubbled, drew blood, and she saw Rose's eyes squinch tight as she bit down onto the towel.

Maggie wiped away the blood and water, and dropped two more drops onto the wounds with the same results. She knew the cleansing of the wound could take hours and many vials of holy water. After the third set of drops, however, the bubbling lessened. Rose's body relaxed. Maggie sighed in relief. It wasn't going to be a bad recovery.

The scream took her by surprise. Rose screamed again, stiffened in pain and clutched her belly. The wound in her neck gushed.

Swearing a blue streak in Italian, Maggie grabbed the towel from where it had fallen and pressed it against the vampire bite. In all her years as a witch, she'd never seen anything like it. Rose screamed again and curled around Maggie in a half-moon shape, sobbing and writhing.

Maggie struggled to stay calm. She stroked Rose's back, her legs, anywhere she could reach, alarmed at how cold she felt when not even a minute before she'd been on fire. "Rose. Talk to me. What hurts? Why are you screaming? Come on, honey," she pleaded.

"Fire, it's on fire, Maggie, oh God," Rose panted, her strength waning. "Thirsty," she said. "So thirsty."

"What's on fire? Rose, damn it, don't pass out on me now," she warned. "You've got to help me. Find the strength, Rose. Find the strength to help me help you."

Rose fought out of the blanket, grabbed the hem of her tee shirt and raised it a bit. "Here," she said on a sigh. "Damn,

~ ☾ ~

Maggie. It's bad. The demon's moving and it hurts." Cold sweat beaded on her forehead.

Still holding the towel against the neck wound, Maggie stared at the design on the girl's stomach. The red, yellow and black runes swirled and glowed in a spiral pattern, rippled beneath the skin as if it were alive. Flickers of flame dodged through the runes.

Maggie sucked in a shocked breath. "Demon." Carefully, she traced the spiral of the inked skin with a finger, trying to make sense of the design. She frowned. It looked familiar, but wrong, somehow—as though the symbolism had been...reversed? "Uh oh."

"What? Why uh oh? Maggie - I - I don't - feel so good," Rose said, and with another sigh her head rolled to one side, her eyes blank, staring at the ceiling.

Maggie swore and checked her neck. The bleeding had almost stopped, but the towel was soaked and Rose's pulse was weakening. She only wavered for a moment before jumping to her feet and making two phone calls. One to Dr. Cavanaugh and the other to Justin Caine.

Sighing, Maggie punched in the number to his cell, counted the rings until he answered, his deep voice sending shivers through her.

"Justin? It's Maggie. You need to get home right away." She looked down at Rose, abnormally still on the floor in the kitchen. "It's Rose. Satine bit her, and Gabriel's gone. I need help getting Rose to Doc Cavanaugh." Maggie flinched when Justin let loose with invective. She hung up, pushed her cell phone in her pocket, and sat once more with Rose.

"Stay strong, Rose. You can do it."

* * *

Guilt consumed Justin. He sat at one end of the small waiting room, watching as Maggie paced. He should have been at the house the night before. Instead, he'd gone surfing. The ocean always soothed him and his last encounter with Magdalena had left him anything but. Not that he'd tell the witch the truth.

He cleared his throat. "I don't believe Gabriel would

willingly put her in danger."

"People change, Justin." Her face had a remote, waiting look to it. With her hair pulled back into a knot on her head, her profile caught his breath.

"No. Not my brother."

The door to the waiting room opened and Dr. Cavanaugh came in still in her baby-pink surgical scrubs.

She was a small woman in her thirties, her white-blonde hair pulled back and hidden underneath a paper cap. She reached for Justin with both hands, her eyes twinkling.

"Justin. It's good to see you." They kissed, both cheeks, before the doctor turned to Maggie. She put a hand out, rubbed Maggie's arm. "You did everything you were supposed to, Magdalena. If she hadn't called you, she probably would have bled out."

Maggie visibly relaxed. "Thank you. How is she?"

The doctor gave them a weary half smile. "Intriguing. I haven't seen skin art like that...well, ever."

"Rose seemed to think it was the demon, and I believe she's right. I keep thinking the spiral is something I know, but subverted in some way. I can't grasp the significance of it. Irritating," Maggie added.

"The spiral could very well be housing the demon. There's something about the design. It's common, but not so common, and not in the ordinary way." The doctor shrugged.

Justin broke in, impatient. "But she'll be fine, right? She's getting better?"

Dr. Cavanaugh turned to him. "Yes. She's getting better, but if she's bitten again, don't use holy water on her."

Maggie frowned. "Why not?"

"She's not totally human."

"But holy water shouldn't hurt her. It doesn't hurt us tribreds, as a rule anyway."

The doctor shot a surprised look toward Justin. "Oh, no. That's not it. She's a Soul Chalice. Holy water doesn't do anything for or against the tribreds, but a Soul Chalice—llet's just say it's almost an overdose of holy. You can get a reverse reaction, which is what happened to Rose. Plus, she's not a

~ ☾ ~

demon by blood. She's a demon by possession, so toss that into the equation, and you get a double bad reaction." She turned to Maggie. "I never taught you about Soul Chalices. I didn't know you'd need it, and I'm so sorry."

Maggie and Justin both stared at the doctor. Justin finally got the words out. "Damn it. We had thought she might be, but it didn't seem...how...it's a myth, Megan. A myth." His heart thumped hard.

"It *is* a myth. Like a Soul Stealer." The words burst out of Maggie in protest.

Doc Cavanaugh shook her head. "No myth. A Soul Chalice is a carrier of souls. They are the opposite of a Soul Stealer." The doctor rubbed her lower back and gave them a tired smile. "Very few people are Soul Stealers. The numbers have dwindled in the past centuries. But wherever there's a Soul Stealer, you'll find a Soul Chalice, doing whatever she can to rescue the stolen souls. Balance. Good and evil or yin and yang, if you wish. Usually the two Soul Entities end up killing each other."

Justin frowned. "So the marking on her stomach is that of a Soul Chalice?"

"No. I think Maggie is on the right track, that it's a house of some sort for the demon. I have some research to do on this."

"I'll help," interjected Maggie.

"Then you'll need copies of the digitals we took. I'll email them to you before I go home."

"Thanks, Megan. I appreciate it."

The doctor continued, "There is a lot we don't know. But I do know that the cells in her body are mutating. I just don't know why, whether it's the demon or the Soul Chalice kicking in. I have textbook knowledge of Soul Chalices, not practical knowledge. All I know is she'll definitely be coming into her own powers, and soon. She'll need to be watched."

"Rose was a drug and alcohol addict but recently clean." Justin shoved his hands in his pockets.

Doc Cavanaugh stifled a yawn. "Her exam shows her as perfectly healthy, no organ deterioration that would be typical of a drug addict. But that brings out another issue. Using

~ ☾ ~

demon powers can be quite a rush." She looked from Maggie to Justin. "For an addict, it can be a death sentence. Toss in whatever comes with being a Soul Chalice, and you've got the possibility for an even greater disaster."

Maggie cleared her throat. "But if we can figure out what spell was used to put the markings on her, do you think we can force the demon out of her?"

"If it's a spell, then theoretically it's possible. The question is could she survive it?" Dr. Cavanaugh shook her head. "I just don't know. I wouldn't want to take the chance, frankly."

"When can we take her home?"

The doctor turned to Justin. "Later this morning, when she wakes. I'd rather keep her here for a couple of days for observation, but I also don't have the staff." She shrugged. "We gave her a transfusion of human blood and she didn't have an adverse reaction to it, so she should be fine in a few hours. She was very dehydrated, and her blood pressure was in the basement, so she's on an IV to build up her fluids." Doc Cavanaugh frowned. "That's going to take some time. If you want to wait, feel free, but you'll be more comfortable elsewhere I'm sure." The doctor stepped back and would have disappeared down the corridor, but Justin's sharp voice stopped her.

"But what about the vampire bite? How do we rid her of its call?"

Dr. Cavanaugh turned around and grimaced. "You know the answer to that as much as I do, Justin," she said, reproof in her voice. "There is nothing we can do. She will need to learn to resist it, to wall it out for the rest of her life, or she will be at his mercy." She turned to Maggie. "I'll email those pictures to you in a few minutes."

"Thank you."

Dr. Cavanaugh waved at them on her way out.

"This is *so* not fair."

Justin took a deep breath. "Yeah. I know. Let's get to work, shall we? By the time we get to the office, you should have those photos."

Maggie turned to him with a sneer. "I'm a floozy,

~ ☾ ~

remember? A nobody in Kendall Sorbis' floozy train. I can't be trusted and I can't do anything to help you. You don't even *like* me. Why in hell would you want to work with me?"

After the guilt and strain of the morning, Justin snapped. He walked purposefully toward her, taking a dark satisfaction as she backed away from his energy. He kept coming until she pressed against the waiting room wall. He put his hands on the wall on either side of her shoulders, caging her there but not touching her. "I've made mistakes," he began through gritted teeth.

"Oh, goody, confessional time," she gibed. "Seriously?"

All thought of talking to her fled his mind. Justin bent and kissed her, a hard, punishing kiss of frustration. The softness of those pink lips, the taste of her almost undid him and he fought to keep his hands on the wall, fought not to take her in his arms and claim her. He inched closer to her heat and reveled in it.

After a momentary hesitation she softened against his chest. Her arms slipped around his waist and her lips opened, allowing him inside. Her hands stroked his back and he lost himself in her taste, in the lush curves pressing up against him.

His mouth gentled as he realized she trembled beneath his kiss. He slowly eased back from her and studied her face. Her eyes were closed, her lips parted as she struggled to take a breath. He kissed those perfect lips again once, gently, and tried not to smile when her lips clung to his.

This time he pushed himself away from the wall. He took a breath to steady his world. "See? I make mistakes. Judging you too quickly was obviously another one."

Maggie's eyes fluttered open and for a moment he saw the vulnerable side beneath the bluster. Then her brown eyes blazed in anger. "Don't you ever touch me again, or I'll knee you right in the balls and turn you into a donkey."

Justin shrugged. "Don't tempt me and we'll both be able to walk freely. Meet me at the office in half an hour."

Maggie drew herself up, her eyes frosting over. "I will check my schedule and arrive when I have some free time. Unlike

~ ☾ ~

you, I have a *real* job." She switched to Italian and let out a stream of rapidly spoken words. Her long black hair shimmered in the overhead lights as she stormed out of the hospital, hands gesticulating, still speaking in Italian.

Justin watched her go and wondered how he'd ever manage to think straight with her around. He heaved a sigh and made a mental note to pick up coffee from CaféGo.

Lots and lots of coffee.

* * *

Gabriel brooded his way across town until he made it back to Twisted. Glad to have something to take his mind off Rose, he circled the place. It was early enough for the legitimate business to be closed and light enough for the vampires to have gone to sleep for the day.

He gave a quick look around, noted the lack of an alarm system, and frowned. No alarm meant they had guards. He really didn't want to get into another fight. After changing from his demon aspect back into the human one, he'd had one hell of a headache that was just now ebbing.

But maybe... He went to the back parking lot and gave a quick look around before leaping up and over to the second floor balcony. The window he'd used the night before hadn't been re-secured. Sloppy work.

He slipped inside the building and stood, eyes closed, listening with one part of his mind to the mental rumblings beneath him. The vampires, of course, were silent, but he could feel at least a dozen of them down below. Dangerous to have a basement in the alluvial soil of Santa Monica, but he figured vampires could pretty much survive anything, claw their way out of absurd situations. If he were vampire...

Nope. Not even tempted to go there, and he never had been. His mind strayed to Rose and the bright flame of her made him smile. Every minute he spent with her set her apart from Satine, and their similarities lessened. Rose gave him something he'd never thought he would feel again. Something no one had ever thought to give him.

Hope. He rubbed his chest as the emptiness in him expanded. His demon prowled inside him, waiting for him to

~ ☾ ~

lose control.

Wrenching his brain back to the task at hand, he sorted through the scents and mindwaves of those in the building. Aside from the vampires, he counted a dozen lesser demons and no less than five weres. He couldn't tell what animal, but their energy signature flared down his skin, even from a distance.

He did another mental sweep, tensed just as the gun cocked at his forehead.

"Well, well, look at what the cat dragged in," came the soft drawl. "If it ain't Gabriel Caine. What're you doing? Don' you know the air ain't healthy here?"

Gabriel placed the voice, but didn't allow himself to relax. "Kellan. Cousin. How's it going?" Apparently it was family reunion weekend in Los Angeles.

"So far, so good."

"What are you doing here? Have you changed sides? 'Cause then I'd have to kick your ass."

"You could try," Kellan retorted. "I'm working a lead. You?"

"Came to see what we escaped from last night. These are no friends of mine." After a tense silence, Gabriel heard Kellan sigh and lower the gun, heard the whisper of metal against holster. He turned around, wary. It had been a good fifteen years since they'd seen each other.

The two men took stock of one another. Kellan had dark hair similar to his own, cut military short; but his eyes were the color of molten amber and his skin shaded toward burnished gold. He had the same build as all the Caines, big and tall.

Abruptly Kellan opened his arms and the two men did the backslap hug thing. "Let's move. The demons are starting to wake." He peered closer at his cousin. "You look terrible."

Gabriel grunted. "I thought the change had fixed all the wounds."

"Open wounds, yes. Bruises still show up. I'll bet your nose hurts."

"Shut up, Kel." He hesitated. "There's a were in here, being held against her will. She's pregnant. Any way we can rescue

~ ☾ ~

her?"

Kellan shook his head. "You do like to complicate things, don't you? Leave well enough alone, and let's get out of here."

"We need to do this. I promised." Uneasy, he looked around. "No guard? Unbelievable."

"I took out the two J'aadts when I came in. I haven't seen or heard anyone else." Kellan sighed. "You're not going to back down on this, are you?"

"No. I'm not."

"Okay. I really don't like it, but lead on."

They headed down the back stairwell, Gabriel focusing only on the scent of the female Were. Two floors down into the earth he stopped and gestured to the hallway. He held up two fingers and motioned to the left side.

Kellan nodded.

Gabriel's hand went to his holster, only to realize he'd never replaced the gun they took from him. He hadn't replaced the holster, either. Mentally swearing, he gestured to Kellan, who readied his own gun.

Gabriel laid a light hand on the door handle and moved it gently. Locked. He raised his eyebrows at Kellan, who handed him the gun and pulled out two slim tools from his back pocket. Three seconds later, the lock clicked and they were in.

Gabriel handed Kellan the gun back and motioned him to go first. The room was quiet. Kellan went in silently, Gabriel following.

The air smelled sweet. Not perfume sweet, but drug-sweet. Gabriel frowned. The female was heavily pregnant. She lay still on the raised platform of stone at the back of the small room, not moving a muscle as the men stepped in. Kellan halted when he caught sight of a man snuggled up behind her, his face turned to the ceiling, snuffling with sleep. Both blondes, it was hard to tell where her hair ended and his began.

Kellan cocked the gun and the woman's eyes flew open. Gabriel put a finger to his lips and held out his hand to her even as Kellan put the gun close to the side of the man's head.

She took Gabriel's hand, moved to stand gracefully. She

~ ☾ ~

opened her mouth and her words barely made a sound, but Gabriel heard, "He's drugged himself." She stood naked and unashamed, sweeping her long blonde hair out of her eyes. "Let's get out of here."

He shrugged off his long leather coat and handed it to her while averting his eyes. She put it on, her mouth quirking in amusement. They left the room as silently as they entered it, Gabriel locking the door behind them.

They went out the way he'd gone in, through the window and over the balcony, the pregnant woman landing easily, the coat floating around her. Once down on the asphalt, Gabriel gestured to the window. "Not secured from last night. On purpose?"

Kellan shrugged. "Who knows how vampires think. Finally grew into your potential, yeah? You have any q's, let me know. I've learned a lot."

"I'm good. So far." Gabriel knew Kellan wasn't referring to the operation at Twisted.

"Gentlemen. Thank you." The woman hooked her arms through theirs, strode between them easily, almost as tall as they were, her bare feet seemingly no problem. "My name is Chandra Roush and my mate's name is Daniel, our Alpha. We owe you a great debt."

"You look healthy. You are well?"

"Yes. One of my pack mates is very ill, though."

"And you're not home yet. No offense." Gabriel kept his eyes peeled as they walked in the early morning light. "We could get you a taxi."

She smiled. "It is almost impossible to find taxis in L.A. May I have your names?"

"Gabriel and Kellan Caine at your service." Gabriel gave her a short bow.

"I'm with the Santa Monica Preserve Wolf Pack. You are demon?"

"Tribred," answered Gabriel absently. "Human, demon, fae. Several generations now."

"Ah, of course. Gideon and Maria Therese Caine. You are their offspring."

~ ☾ ~

Gabriel and Kellan shared a glance. Shrugged. "Yeah. In a way."

Kellan cleared his throat. "Glad to help. Uh, where are we going, anyway?"

Chandra smiled again. "My mate will be here soon. I contacted him the moment I saw you."

They slowed as a black SUV pulled alongside them. Chandra stopped and turned to the car, longing and eagerness pulsing off her in waves. The passenger door burst open and she leaped to meet the dark man who wrapped her tightly in his arms.

The back door of the SUV opened and the two disappeared inside. Both doors slammed shut, and before the vehicle drove away, Gabriel's long leather coat flew out from the opened window.

Gabriel snagged the coat out of the air and slid it on before he lifted a hand to the disappearing SUV.

Kellan blew out a breath. "That was good. That was very good. Do you get to do stuff like that a lot?"

"Nah."

"Yeah. Me neither." They strode along in silence for a while. "What happened back there last night?"

Gabriel gave him a brief summary. "And then I dropped Rose off at Justin's house, I got antsy, and took off."

"You didn't know her well. Okay then."

"No, I— " Gabriel stopped in his tracks. "She's...hell. It's complicated. She's carrying a part of my soul," he confessed.

Kellan opened his eyes wide. "And you didn't take care of her? Oh man, you'd better come up with a good reason for ditching."

"This isn't high school." Gabriel turned the tables. "What were you doing there, anyway? Or have you changed that much in fifteen years?"

"I told you, I was following a lead. It didn't pan out, and wasn't part of what you guys are handling right now." He shook his head. "Not important in the scheme of things. Hey man, we really gonna walk?"

Gabriel grinned. "I'm thinking we run. You know where the

~ ☾ ~

office is?"

"Still on Third Street? Yeah. Let's go."

Running down the street, so fast human eyes couldn't track them, Kellan whooped and Gabriel grinned. It had been so long since he'd run just for the joy of it. No rescue, no fleeing danger or cops or his own heart, just running for the sheer thrill of speed and the exhilaration of wind through his hair. And after their good deed of the morning, they deserved it. They really did.

I haven't done this...in far too long...

The streets flew by as they ran toward the Caine Investigations offices.

Gabriel and Kellan pulled up to Third Street and slowed to a walk, not even panting from the four mile effort.

"So, I heard you followed in my footsteps, running away from the family."

Gabriel shrugged, stuck his hands in his pockets. "In a fashion."

Kellan stopped, gripped Gabriel's shoulder. His eyes held regret. "I'm sorry, man. Sorry I didn't stick it out for you."

Gabriel looked out at the horizon and shrugged. "Shit happens." Kellan squeezed his shoulder and let his hand drop.

Gabriel walked through the mall in silence with Kellan, marveling at how comfortable they were together. It was as if no time had passed since they'd last seen each other.

"It's this way." Gabriel led the way up the stairs and inside to the offices.

Kel looked around at the empty reception area. "Huh. Grey on white. Gregor must have done the decor."

"You know damn well Justin didn't. He's probably back in here." Gabriel walked into Justin's office. "Hey. Hi Maggie." He eyed her jeans and an old Rolling Stones tee shirt with approval. "Where's Rose?" He looked around in anticipation. He needed her energy, that clean, pure, feel-good that he got whenever he touched her.

Maggie had been looking at the monitor over Justin's shoulder. She looked up, and her eyes frosted over. "Gabriel. What the hell are you doing here? Do you realize Rose could

~ ☾ ~

have died from the vampire bite?"

"Magdalena. Cool it." Justin stood, put himself between her and Gabriel.

Gabriel's smile dissolved and his gut clenched. "Where is she? She was fine when I left. I just – I had to get away, be alone." Guilt twisted his stomach. He should have stayed. He *couldn't* have stayed.

Kellan threw him a glance. "Too many people?"

"Yeah." He faced Justin. "Look. I tried. I got her out of there, back to your place. She cleaned up. Satine didn't have her long enough for any sort of true blood bite. I swear she was fine. I had to go. Ten minutes after I left, I checked in mentally with her." His face twisted. "She had the barrier up, the one I taught her. I assumed she was fine. How could I have known?" His excuses disgusted him. He should have known. She was his responsibility, and once again he'd screwed up.

"If you followed the family pattern, you've spent most of the last ten years alone." Kellan stepped forward. "It's hard to reintegrate."

"Kellan. My God. Talk about coming out of the woodwork." Justin slapped his cousin on the back and they grinned at each other.

Maggie sighed heavily. "Not another Caine."

"You need to cut Gabe some slack, Justin."

"Only because Rose is holding her own," Justin said, frowning at Gabriel. "We're here doing some research."

Gabriel's voice got softer. "Just tell me where she is. I need to see her." Kellan was right. He wasn't used to this many people. He struggled to keep his breathing steady and his temper even.

Justin lifted an eyebrow. "All in due time. When you've got yourself under control."

"I hated that saying when your dad said it. I still hate that saying," Kellan said.

Gabriel paced to prevent panic, his thoughts in a whirl. "The two weren't together long enough for the bite to have gone deep, or gotten infected or anything. A normal person

~ ☾ ~

would have a nasty scar but would otherwise be all right. She should be all right. I don't understand how it could have gone so wrong." Except he was the champion of things going wrong, wasn't he? Everything he'd ever touched had gone wrong. He never should have forgotten that.

Maggie spoke up. "That's the thing, though, isn't it? Rose is a Soul Chalice, not a normal person. She called me. Justin and I took her to Doc Cavanaugh. She'll be all right, the bite's not the big worry."

Gabriel's heart dropped. She had a part of his soul. "What's the big worry?" His panic growing, he grabbed for Justin, shook him hard. Justin closed his hands around Gabriel's forearms with a grip like iron. "Is she dying? She's really dying, isn't she? Tell me." If she's dying, then he was as good as dead, too.

A gray light flared from Justin's hands to Gabriel's arms. Gabriel jerked from the shock, but dug in his fingers as desperation and need spread through him. "Your faerie jolts aren't going to stop me. Tell me where she is." Gabriel backed his brother up against the desk. His hands moved to Justin's throat before sanity prevailed and he went for the collarbone instead.

Justin went still beneath his hands. "Let me go, Gabriel. This isn't going to solve anything."

"You want me to beat the location out of you?" Gabriel's demon stretched inside him. The need to change throbbed through his body. If he could just get to Rose, he'd be fine. He just needed to get to her. He shook Justin again. "Tell me. Now."

Maggie cried out. "Gabriel, please. There's a tattoo on Rose that's—well, we can't figure out what it is. Let Justin go. Come here, and I'll show you the photos." Maggie hovered. "Please let Justin go. Don't make me use magic on you."

"It's not you, Gabriel. It's the demon. You need Rose, don't you? You need to touch your soul. To soothe the demon."

Justin's words penetrated the green haze over Gabriel's vision. He released his brother, aghast at what he'd done. "You're right. I need Rose. And I've seen the spiral. It's not a

~ ☾ ~

tattoo," Gabriel said. "It's a demon spiral." He swung away from Justin and moved to the window.

"What the hell is a demon spiral?" Kellan's voice came to him as he pressed his hot forehead to the cooler glass. "How do you even know about demon spirals?"

"I've seen it before. Once. It's a containment. Think of it as a way for a demon to possess a person."

"The girl you killed. She had one of these things, too?" Justin's voice had taken on a thread of sympathy.

"Marianne. Yeah."

"That sucks," remarked Kellan.

"Holy hell." Justin sounded tired.

"Since Rose is a Soul Chalice, her opposite is a Soul Stealer." Maggie recited the facts as though she were reading a grocery list. "But Doc Cavanaugh wasn't sure about the demon, or what role it's playing."

Gabriel closed his eyes against despair. "The demon is the same one who possessed Marianne. And Satine is a Soul Stealer. Now that just makes my day." Nothing in his life made any sense. To have spent ten years away, and yet come back to the very thing he ran from?

"Do you think the demon's stalking you?"

"I think it's a pretty large coincidence, that demon on that woman." Gabriel turned to face them. "Just my luck. Justin, please. Tell me where she is."

"She's in a private hospital in West L.A. She had a blood transfusion and is getting saline because she's dehydrated. You need to know that while she's fine now, according to the doc, the more she uses her borrowed demon powers, the more addicted she could get to them."

Which would be bad. Gabriel shook. Need for Rose pulsed through him. Was it more than just keeping his demon quiet? "I honestly thought I was doing the right thing by leaving." He looked toward Kellan and saw a wordless understanding there. "But leaving, running away didn't give me what I wanted or needed," he said. The realization broke over him. "I left the family for the same reasons. I left to keep you safe, and because I was ashamed."

~ ☾ ~

"It's time to get over it, Gabriel. Let it go."

Justin sighed. "Before I take you to her, let's put it together. What have we got?"

"We've got young Rose holding a part of Gabriel's soul and turning into a fire demon, which may kill her even as her Soul Chalice powers come online. And Vlad, who controls Satine," Kellan mused.

Gabriel rubbed his neck, anxious to get moving. "Then there's Satine, the Soul Stealer who has the rest of my soul and who wants me on her team, forever more."

"We've got you, Gabriel, who has no soul and whose demon is struggling to break free. We need to get you back to Rose. And we have a vamp nest that needs to be wiped clean." Justin raised his eyebrows when Gabriel frowned. "Did I forget something?"

"Yeah. I found out last night that Rose and Satine are cousins. Five years apart. Rose was there the night a vampire took a willing Satine. I guess I'm the weakest link." As usual.

"And on the positive side, we've got Kellan, Justin, Gabriel and myself." Maggie looked at the men. "Plus, Rose is a Soul Chalice and she's with us. There's some research to do there. Gentlemen, it sounds like there's a job for everyone."

"Wipe out Twisted." Gabriel looked from brother to cousin, searching for their agreement. "Take out Vlad and then Satine. Great. Can we go see Rose now, please?"

Another voice came from the doorway. "You can take out the club. Leave Satine to me."

As one, they turned to look at Rose who stood, pale but determined, swaying in the doorway. Gabriel's stomach dropped even as his hands itched to touch her.

~ ☾ ~

Chapter Ten

"I'm fine," Rose said in response to the clamor. She held out her hand to Gabriel, grabbed on and let him help her to a chair. Rose sighed in relief. It had felt like forever since he'd touched her. She kept her hand glued to his.

"You look terrible," Maggie said. "Remind me to take you clothes shopping."

Rose brushed at the black jeans and gray sweatshirt. "Hey, I'm lucky I'm not in a hospital gown."

Justin leaned over to take her free hand and squeezed it gently. "We were going to come get you when you woke up. Why didn't you wait?"

Rose leaned back with a sigh. "Nice to see you, too." She turned to Kellan. "Who're you?"

"Kellan Caine, cousin. At your service."

She smiled. "Good to meet you."

"You had us all scared," Justin said.

"Yeah, well. Apparently I'm good at that." Intensely aware of Gabriel at her side, she tugged on his hand. "Sit down, would you? Then fill me in. It sounded like I interrupted a war council." She looked at the circle of concerned faces, feeling at peace for the first time since she woke up. "It's really good to be here. What's been going on?"

"Aside from you scaring everyone?" Gabriel squeezed her hand. "Just the typical. I went back to the nightclub, found Kellan sniffing around. Oh, and we let the pregnant werewolf go."

Warmth spread through her. "You remembered? Thank you. You just made my day." Rose couldn't contain her joy and she beamed at him. She'd been cold in the hospital, but

~ ☾ ~

here warmth filled her and her smile grew wide. "Did you get the other werewolves out?"

"It's in the plan," assured Gabriel.

"So what is the plan?"

"Fire." Kellan spoke up then. "Simple. A couple firebombs set during the day, and whoomph! No more building, no more vampires, you're done."

"Not exactly," said Gabriel. "You know they've got werewolves. They'll pick up the scent of a bomb before you have it within fifty yards of the place. And even if they are on our side, they wouldn't hesitate to save themselves and make a scene."

Rose shuddered. No one could want to be there. No were animal, at any rate. "We need to free the other weres before we do any sort of bombing. I can't believe the weres are working for the vamps. The trick will be to get it done without getting caught."

Kellan straddled a chair and leaned forward against the back. "There's any number of ways. One, we take out the vamps and the demons, let the weres go, and blow up the building. Two, we let the weres go and blow up the building. I'm thinking either way—blow up the building." Kellan looked from one to another in the small office, grinning wickedly. "What?"

Rose took a quick survey and smiled at Kellan. "Maggie and I are shocked, Justin is working the angles, and Gabriel isn't sure what to make of you."

"Good read, Rose." Gabriel turned from her to Kellan. "A bit bomb happy, aren't we?" He cocked his head as he eyed his cousin.

Kellan bared his teeth in something resembling a grin. "The desert is big, my friend. Empty. I have learned a lot out there."

"It's something to consider." Justin looked around at everyone. "I'll visit the Nine Hells, see what's up. It's usually demon territory, but I should be able to find out where the weres' normal watering hole is. Hopefully Daniel Roush will be feeling generous. Willing to help."

~ ☾ ~

Gabriel's hand jerked in hers. She turned to look at him, noticed his eyes had turned molten silver. He grinned in happy anticipation. "I've never been to the Nine Hells. Legally."

"Fill me in. The Nine Hells?" Maggie asked.

"A bar in Venice Beach." Gabriel shrugged. "It's part biker bar, part demon bar. It's the kind of place where people like us tend to gather."

Gabriel had never been to a bar with his brothers. Astonished at the insight, Rose tightened her hand on his. He'd been robbed of so much. No wonder eagerness practically poured out of him. "Maybe we can all go? It sounds like the perfect place to plan." Rose sent a questioning glance to Maggie who shrugged back.

"They've got great beer on tap, and a pool room in the back. Balcony out back, too, with a nice view of the ocean. Typical fried bar food, good for what it is," added Justin. "Not many women—scratch that. Not many proper, well-groomed women go there. And they tend to stand out when they do," he added, with a meaningful look at Rose.

"All three of us will go together," said Kellan. He cracked his knuckles thoughtfully, one at a time. "We need to make up for lost time, boys."

"Maggie and I could dress down," Rose offered.

All three men turned toward her. "No."

"I can't risk you," Gabriel added, before he turned back to the other two.

Rose frowned. How could she keep Gabriel with her? How could she keep him from going to the bar?

"I guess Rose and I will do research on the spiral tattoo and the Soul Chalice while you guys are thumping your chests and grunting over beer. There's got to be something about that spiral somewhere," Maggie added.

"While you do that," Justin said, "Gabriel and Kel can open up the old homestead. It's a place to stay," he added when they groaned.

Kel and Gabriel shared a look. "Maybe so, but we're not doing all the gardening around the place," Gabriel said.

~ ☾ ~

"I'll help when I can. So will Gregor."

"Where is he, anyway?"

"Taking a break. His best friend, Tara, died a couple months ago." Justin moved restlessly in his chair. "He needed to get away. And no, I'm not calling him on this. We can handle it."

"If you say so," Kellan said.

"So, we open the homestead up. We're agreed?" said Gabriel. He looked to Kellan.

"Agreed."

"I appreciate it." He turned to Rose. "Take a short walk with me? Just down to the conference room and back." He held out a hand.

Rose struggled to keep her grin from taking over her face as she placed her hand in his. "Absolutely I'm up for a walk." She stood and smiled at everyone. "We'll be right back." So much had changed for the better in the last twenty-four hours. It felt like a miracle. Rose left the office with Gabriel in happy anticipation.

* * *

He didn't know where to start, so he didn't say anything on the walk down the hallway to the conference room. Rose didn't speak, either, which told him she was just as uncomfortable with their physical closeness.

Her hand fit his. She didn't have dainty hands. She had worker hands, big hands that fit his perfectly. He frowned over that as they settled at the conference table, side by side.

Their hands were still entwined, resting now on the table. Gabriel looked at them. It was easier than looking at her. "For tonight, you need to stay with Maggie. Tomorrow maybe we'll all be able to move to the homestead."

"What? But I thought..."

"I know. I know what you thought, and you're not wrong. I do need this," he said, lifting their hands. "I need the closeness with you." Finally he looked her in the eye. "Tonight we'll head out to the Nine Hells. If there's another fight, I want you safe. I don't know Maggie well but my guess is, she can keep you safe."

~ ☾ ~

Gabriel watched as she swallowed hard. "How long do you think you can go without us touching?"

"I don't know. Six to eight hours, maybe longer." He looked at her, bright and pretty as a sunbeam with a dark edging of cloud. She had depth. He really liked that about her. "Are you okay? I mean, really okay?"

She looked down at their joined hands. "I'm fine. But Gabriel, I'm here to rescue *you*, not the other way around. That's what Maria Therese told me," Rose said.

Gabriel stilled. "What? What's that about my mother?" Hope trembled inside him.

"I met Maria Therese, there in the waiting room. The big black woman came to talk to me, and then Maria Therese came. She begged me to come help you, to protect you, to stay by your side no matter what. She told me it was imperative. I promised her I would, Gabriel. I promised her."

Gabriel pulled his hand from hers and pushed his chair back. He didn't know what to think. His mother. He'd known her loss from the very beginning. He'd missed her from the first breath he took. "You're lying. Why didn't you say something earlier?" None of this made sense.

"I'm not lying. You are why I'm here," she shot back. "You are the only reason I'm still alive. I have a job to do where you're concerned. You want to know why I didn't mention Maria Therese earlier? You and I, we had to spend time apart before you could understand why we need to be together. Could you have believed me without our time apart? I don't think so."

"Leave my mother out of it." Gabriel pinched the bridge of his nose. There had to be a way. "I almost let you die." Options flew through his head. "Okay, look. We need to connect. A couple of times a day for a brief amount of time, or once for a longer period. With other people about, you should be safe enough. But I can't be there for you every hour of every day. I'm not good for you. Surely you can understand that."

She glared, her eyes sheening with tears. "If a demon tries to climb into my window at night and you're not there, I'm so gonna kill you."

~ ☾ ~

"Rose, I'm a demon," he said, exasperated.
"Yeah, and apparently, so am I. I'm going to need your help when I feel stronger. But Gabriel, think. You're not just a demon. You've got Fae blood in you, and human blood, and that's got to count for something. I have a part of your human soul. You are so much more than just a demon."

"And you are a Soul Chalice, something out of legend." Gabriel stared at her, feeling the ground under his feet shifting, long-held beliefs suddenly under question. "I'm more demon than the rest. I might kill you."

"You might. And I might kill you. We don't know what Soul Chalices can do. Did you ever think of that? Come *on*. You know I'm right."

"I don't know any such thing." He drew a breath through lungs that felt too tight. "We need to compromise, Rose. We'll spend the afternoon together, but you need to be with Maggie tonight. I'll see you when I can. We'll connect until the job is done, but we won't be living in each other's pockets."

"Compromise." She pursed her lips, thinking. Gabriel resisted the urge to peek inside her head and just waited. "You want me to compromise? Then go shopping with me. Spend the next few hours with me, just the two of us. If you do that, then I promise when it's time to go to Maggie's, I'll go and won't make a scene."

Gabriel narrowed his eyes. As compromises went, this one sucked. "Shopping."

"And a late lunch. Maybe dinner. I want to walk along the beach. I want to feel the heat of the day on my back and your hand in mine. I want to feel normal, just for a few hours. Fair enough trade?" She tilted her head to one side, a smile curving her lips.

He sighed. She wanted the fantasy of happy-ever-after for an afternoon. Of all the things she could have asked for, why did she pick the one that was the hardest for him to give? Her body was already imprinted on his. Growing closer to her would make his leaving worse in the end.

But he couldn't deny her, not when he wanted the same thing as she did. Time together.

~ ☾ ~

"Fair enough." Gabriel stood and reached for her hand. "Let's go tell the others."

* * *

"Here, drink this. Its just tea," Maggie said. After spending the entire afternoon and much of the evening together, Gabriel had dropped Rose off at Maggie's apartment.

Decorated in pale greens and big, bloomy pink flowers, Rose found herself relaxing in the intensely feminine living room.

Rose accepted the mug and warmed her hands. "I don't drink tea. What kind is it?"

"It's my favorite mint medley, plus some chamomile. Tastes pretty good, and it should help you sleep." Maggie perched on the arm of the couch. "How are you doing?"

Rose shrugged. "Amazingly good. Gabriel was useless in the shopping department." She giggled at the memory of him wandering, bewildered, through a woman's clothing store. "So I stuck with jeans and tees. I had the best time." She gave a happy sigh. "Great memories." They'd walked hand in hand through the mall, stopped at one restaurant for sliders and fries. At sunset, he'd picked up a to-go bowl of clam chowder and they'd walked on the beach, sharing the chowder and talking about their past. She'd loved every second of it.

"I'm glad you got your mind off this whole thing," Maggie said.

Rose sipped the tea and watched her new friend. "What do you think about it?"

"Impossible comes to mind," Maggie said dryly. "If you'd asked me two days ago if Soul Stealers existed, I'd have told you to grow up. As it is, I'm finding I have to re-think the stories and legends I learned as a child."

Rose looked into her tea pensively. "Do you think it's possible… Is there hope for Gabriel and me?"

"I believe we'll prevail, and you'll get his soul back. Beyond that, I don't know. Everything is changing shape in front of me. I'm not sure of anyone, or anything."

Rose bit her lip. That wasn't exactly what she'd hoped to hear.

~ ☾ ~

Maggie moved to sit on the floor. "I believe there's a connection between the two of you. I noticed it that first day, and then this afternoon it seemed stronger, somehow. But Rose, from what little I know about him, Gabriel has a lot to work through. He may not be capable of love right now. If you want him, you'd better be prepared to fight for him."

Rose acknowledged the worry in Maggie's eyes. "Yeah. Once we get this Satine business out of the way, that's the first thing on my to-do list."

"Good. For what it's worth, my money's on you. Now let me show you to the guest room. You must be exhausted. I know I am."

"Thank you." Rose grabbed Maggie's hand as they stood. "I'd forgotten how nice having a friend could be."

Maggie slipped an arm around Rose's shoulders and led her down a short hallway. "Welcome to La La Land, Rose Walters. Here's my office. It just happens to have a spare bed in it. Think you'll be comfortable here?"

Rose looked around the cozy room and nodded. "Perfect." Painted muted grays and greens, the room was a cool and soothing change from the floral patterns in the main room. A desk faced the window and the single bed stood opposite the desk. One bookcase held a few books. Rose looked up at her new friend and smiled. "I don't know how to thank you."

"Don't worry about it. I've got a couple of sleep shirts in the closet and a robe. Feel free to use anything you want. Now, try to get some sleep. Don't think about anything but resting. Keep your mind barrier up, too, as much as you can before you fall asleep. It should stay up automatically, but keep your focus on it for a bit. Don't want any demons smashing in the windows to get at you."

Rose laughed. "Yeah. That'll keep me from worrying."

Maggie flushed. "Sorry. The apartment is protected, of course. Nothing can get to you in here. Holler if you need me."

"I'm fine, Maggie. Get some rest." Rose smiled and waved her away. Maggie left her alone.

She checked out the closet and found a peachy silk tee shirt and a matching robe. She stripped out of her new clothes and

~ ☾ ~

slipped on the silk shirt with a shiver of appreciation.

Sliding under the covers of the bed, Rose groaned at the luxurious comfort of the softest cotton sheets and the most perfect bed ever. Before she closed her eyes, she spoke her mind to the ceiling. "Gabriel Caine, you'd better take care of yourself. I need you to come through this whole thing in one piece," she declared. "The rest will sort itself out. I hope."

* * *

"Let me do the talking. Neither of you know Little Harry," Justin advised Gabriel and Kellan as the three of them walked through the doorway of the Nine Hells just before closing time. It had the feel of a once-hip bar left over from the Seventies. Located in Venice Beach just one street away from the sand, the dark wood and monster movie posters gave the bar a goth vibe. The plants hanging in every corner were silk and dusty from neglect.

While it wasn't packed, there was still a fair-sized crowd rumbling about the place, with chaotic electronica music playing in the background. The two large-screen TVs were dark. The movies must be over for the night, mused Justin.

He nodded toward the bartender at the back. "Hey, Little Harry. How's it going?"

Harry sent them a fierce grin and slapped a beefy hand atop the bar. "Well well, if it ain't the Caines with the fairy leading the way. How ya doin', Justin? Sorry can't serve y'all, seeing as you came in after last call." As tall as he was wide, Little Harry was part demon but mostly human. Not truly a tribred, not in the Caine family's sense of the word.

Justin smiled, showing his teeth. "Not a problem, Little Harry. We're just dropping in for some information."

Gabriel and Kellan flanked him at the bar, Gabriel watching Harry and Kellan watching the crowd. Justin noted Harry paled a little bit at the show.

He sent Justin a conciliatory smile. "What can I help you with?" He wiped the thick plank of wood that served as the bar with a bit of dirty rag that had seen better days.

"Twisted. Satine. What's the scoop?"

Harry relaxed, sent a disgusted look to the three of them.

"Vampires. Jesus, Caine. You had me worried for a minute there."

Justin just stared at the big man. "What do you know?"

The big man shrugged. "She's Vlad's puppet, but she's scared. Buying protection. Word has it she's fed up with being under his thumb."

Gabriel looked at Justin and raised his eyebrows.

"You seem to know an awful lot."

Harry put on a wounded air. "You asked. I answered. Besides, yeah, I like to keep my ear to the ground. Can't afford to be caught short, right? Not in this economy."

It made sense. The Nine Hells was a demon bar much like The Crypt in Hollywood was a vampire bar. Mostly patronized by humans who didn't know any better, but often a place where the real deal would go to feel at home, get some information.

"How much more do you know?" Justin leaned in to Harry, let his eyes bleed to demon-green. "How much more should we know that you don't want to tell us?"

Harry quailed at the look in Justin's eyes. "Uh. She's got a deputy, goes by the sissy name of Chazz. His specialty is disposing of the bodies. He's a were tiger, though, so I guess names aren't everything. Oh, and Vlad has big plans for Los Angeles."

Harry got more conversational and leaned over the bar. "At Twisted, apparently a demon came in and trashed the place the other night, killed a few vampires and scared the humans shitless. Nasty mess to clean up, from what I hear," he added, his voice lowered. "The word is, Satine's out for revenge on the demon, and the girl he snatched from her. Wants them both for playmates."

Gabriel snarled. "What about the girl?" He reached across the bar and grabbed Harry's shirt. Shook him. "What have you heard about the girl?"

"Ease off, Gabriel," cautioned Justin. "As much as I'm enjoying watching Harry turn blue, let him go."

Gabriel eased his hand open. Harry slapped at Gabriel's arms, his round face contorted with fear and rage.

~ ☾ ~

"Why do you want to know? Planning on killing her?" he hissed. "I've heard talk." Kellan and Justin turned to look at Gabriel and they both froze.

Gabriel's demon snapped free. His eyes whirled electric-green and his hands had begun to change shape. With a roar, he leaned over, picked Harry up, and threw him against the back wall, a masterpiece of bottles of booze. Harry landed face down behind the bar, showered in alcohol and glass.

"Great. Just great," Justin said as Gabriel jumped over the bar and swung, catching Harry right on the chin. Harry retaliated by throwing a bottle of gin at him. Gabriel dodged the bottle, heard it shatter behind him.

A woman screamed. As though her scream had flipped a switch, fists started flying all over the bar, with four stocky young men heading toward the Caines. Justin turned to meet two of them, leaving the other two for Gabriel and Kellan. He didn't have a clue how to restrain Gabriel, to beat his demon back. As he fought, Justin thought just as furiously.

He could send more rednecks toward Gabriel. Justin blocked a blow and with his other fist, dropped the guy with a punch to the upper chest. His buddy veered away, his eyes wide.

Justin turned and saw Gabriel, his skin darkened, his hands changed and his eyes whirling electric green. Great. Justin stepped in front of a leather-clad punk that kept swinging at Gabriel and dispatched him with a well-placed kick. Gabriel didn't seem to notice, just plowed across the room, his fists swinging indiscriminately.

"Behind you, Justin!"

Turning from the leatherhead in front of him, Justin plowed his fists—one into the stomach, the other at the throat—into a guy who'd reached for something - knife, gun, he didn't know but didn't wait to find out. The guy dropped like a stone.

Justin knew they needed to wrap this up before someone called the cops. He'd never get Gabriel under control once the authorities showed up. He swung into the rhythm of the fight. His blood sang as he hit, jabbed, and kicked his way to the

~ ☾ ~

front door where Kellan deflected blows easily, making the two men trying to pound on him angrier. A flurry of blows later and the two men had fallen on top of each other scrambling to get away. They fled out the door and Kellan grinned at Justin.

Someone threw a chair into the big screen TV, but it just bounced off and fell on the floor with a clatter. A couple that had huddled up against the wall, watching the fight, chose that moment to run.

Justin kept an eye on them as the two scurried out through the billiards room to the patio beyond and saw them veering away to give someone else room to come into the bar. Weres. His senses went on full alert as a group of them headed their way.

Shit. He reached mentally for Kellan, then Gabriel. *Guys. Weres at ten o'clock.*

Both men turned to look in that direction while holding off an attack.

Justin dodged a fist, grabbed it and pushed the brawler to the front door. *I'll try to get this lot on their way, so we can get this handled. Gabriel, shake off your demon, now!*

Kellan frowned. *You sure we should work with them? It's not like we need the manpower.*

I'm sure. We need allies, trust me. Watch it, Kel!

Kellan ducked a blow, clamped his hand on his attacker's neck, and frog-marched the guy out of the bar.

Justin worked the room. A touch, a look in the eye, and the human was disoriented and apologizing. Within five minutes the place was empty of all except the Caines, the Wolf Pack, and Little Harry.

~ ☾ ~

Chapter Eleven

Gabriel pulled out of his bloodlust enough to realize just what kind of danger they were in. If this weren't the right pack, there would be hell to pay. Weres and demons weren't normally allies in any sense of the word.

The weres sauntered in, eyed the mess with no more than raised eyebrows. The first one looked solid. Pure muscle. His long chestnut hair was pulled into a plait down his back. His big yellow-gold eyes were watchful.

Gabriel looked from him to the other two. The one on the left was taller, a bleached-blond with hair maybe an inch long and standing straight up. He was bigger than the other men, bulkier. The one on the right held very still. Younger, Gabriel thought. Not as sure of himself, but definitely strong. None of these guys were ones he'd want to fight without going demon. Still, he tensed up, ready to do what he had to do. Two more weres came in and kept watch at the back door.

Harry struggled to his feet, still shaking glass out of his hair. "No more fighting, guys, please," he said, but the words lacked authority.

"No fighting," agreed the one with the plait down his back. "Gabriel Caine?"

Gabriel stepped in ahead of the others and took the hand the other man held out.

"I'm Danny Roush of the Wolf Pack in this area. That's Sig, and Favor is over there. Josh and Garrett are by the door. You rescued my mate."

Gabriel felt the signature energy rush from the were. "Justin Caine, and Kellan Caine. Demon and Fae kin."

Danny raised an eyebrow. "Brothers?"

~ ☾ ~

"Family. Kellan's a first cousin."

"We need some information."

"About?"

"Twisted. Vlad and Satine. Trouble's growing. But you know that."

At a glance from Gabriel, Justin straightened a table and motioned to Harry. "Stone Ale, Harry. Two pitchers. Lock the front door, if you will. And a clean rag for Gabriel's knuckles."

Harry bristled. Gabriel strode to the bar and dropped a couple Ben Franklins onto the wood. "Please." He sent Harry a narrow smile and accepted the damp cloth from the now docile Harry. Amazing what money could do. Gabriel went back to the table, pressing the cloth against his hand. He'd enjoyed the fight, but his skin had split and both hands were bleeding.

Sig watched as Gabriel cleaned off his knuckles, his tongue coming out to lick the corner of his mouth.

Gabriel realized the scent of blood drew them, and he hurriedly finished. Justin took his hand, concentrated, and the bleeding stopped. A thin layer of new skin lay over the wounds. Sig sighed and sat back to watch as Harry brought two full pitchers of ale.

Justin and Danny poured, and they all drank together. Gabriel wiped his mouth. "From what I could tell from my visit, Twisted is a sex club for deviants of all stripes."

Gabriel continued, "Satine or Vlad has gathered J'aadt demons, an uncounted number of weres as well as the vampires. They're all a part of the club."

Kellan spoke up. "She's put the word out, is recruiting across all fifty states. And not just vamps, either. She'll take anyone with a hint of power. Kendall Sorbis has been working with her, from what I've heard."

Justin stared. "Thanks for mentioning that."

"It hadn't come up yet." Kellan drank down his beer.

"The weres – at least, the wolves – aren't there voluntarily." Danny frowned down into his beer.

"Aside from the fact the club is a piece of depravity, apparently Vlad's got something big in the works. Satine is

~ ☾ ~

skittish about it." Gabriel met Danny's skeptical gaze.

Sig grunted. "That is not a good thing."

Gabriel leaned forward, intent on Danny. "I'm looking to take them all out. I want to wipe out Satine, Vlad, the club, the vamps, everything. Wanna play?"

Danny's eyes narrowed. "You can't do it alone. You're compromised."

Gabriel frowned. "She's taken a little of my blood. Fortunately, tribreds are no one's playthings, and she can't put me in thrall, but neither can I completely ignore her. So, yeah. Compromised. How did you know?"

"I can smell her on you." Danny shrugged.

"You could have freed the rest of the weres," blurted out the young one.

"Favor." Danny's voice went cold. "You were not to speak."

Gabriel turned to Favor. "Yeah. We could have. We made a hard choice this morning, to rescue only Chandra. But we didn't know enough about the system there. One was better than none. All of them could have gotten all of us killed." Gabriel took a breath. "But freeing the others is in our plan."

Sig hissed. Danny put a hand out as if to hold him back, and looked deep into Gabriel's eyes. "You are not lying."

"No. We'd appreciate your help."

"You've got it. Do you have any other information?"

"She also has a were tiger called Chazz. Apparently he disposes of the bodies. That information is courtesy of our host, Little Harry." The weres looked to the bar, where Harry was polishing the top and pretending not to listen.

Gabriel continued. "There were at least four more weres that I could sense the last time I was there. I don't know if they were there voluntarily or not."

Favor stiffened. Danny put his hand on Favor's arm, clamped down tight. "Two others of my wolf pack are there that we know of. They are not there voluntarily." Danny's voice tightened. "This Vlad. He has caused our pack much harm. He threatens the balance in the city, threatens us all with exposure." He hesitated. "A moment, please."

Withdrawing from the table, Sig and Favor followed Danny

~ ☾ ~

to the two weres by the door. They talked amongst themselves while Gabriel, Justin and Kellan finished off their beer.

"What do you think?" Justin murmured low at Gabriel's shoulder.

Gabriel looked thoughtfully at the group in the corner. "I think we'll make an alliance."

"There's a first time for everything," Kellan drawled.

Danny came back to the table, leaving the others waiting by the back door. "Thank you for the information. In return, we will give you this; Kendall Sorbis is planning on opening a portal to the Chaos Plane here in Los Angeles. He hasn't done too much so far; our snitch believes he needs a power boost. Perhaps through Satine?" Danny shrugged. "At any rate. We will be in touch. I need to discuss the best way to go about this with my pack. But you have my word. We will help." He stuck his hand out, and Gabriel took it.

"Good. Caine Investigations, Third Street Promenade."

"I'll be in touch within twenty-four hours. Again. Thank you. My debt to you is personal, and pack. We honor you." With a nod, and a ferocious gleam in his golden eyes, Danny left, taking his men with him.

Harry approached the trio at the table, all the fight drained out of him. "You guys done yet?"

"Yeah. Thanks, Harry." Gabriel dug in his pocket, peeled off a few more hundreds. He dropped them on the table and the three Caines stood. "Have a good night." They went out the front door, Gabriel the last to leave. He ducked his head back in, caught Harry greedily counting the bills.

"Harry. I better not hear about this meeting on the street. You know what I mean?"

Clutching the bills to his chest with one hand, Harry wiped the sweat from his forehead with the other. "Yeah, sure, Gabriel. Anything you want. You be careful out there, now."

"You too, Harry. Call us if you need anything," he said, and shut the door behind him.

The three Caines strolled down the streets of Venice Beach, Gabriel absently sucking on the healing knuckles of his right hand. "Well. That was illuminating."

~ ☾ ~

Justin frowned. "Sounds like Kendall Sorbis has, pardon the expression, turned to the dark side."

The other two groaned. Gabriel elbowed Justin. "But can we trust Maggie?"

"I don't know. I'll find out." Justin stopped at the corner. "You need to do some serious thinking, Gabriel. You were on automatic in there during the fight."

Gabriel blinked. His first reaction was to respond with a, 'yeah, so?' but knew Justin was right. But still - "Yeah, so? It got the job done. I didn't kill anyone. What does it matter?"

"You were damn lucky not to kill a were at Satine's the other night, which would have made tonight's scenario a whole different movie. You were on fucking automatic pilot in there. Get back to Rose. You need her."

"I spent hours with her," Gabriel objected. Hours that had a golden glow now in his memory. "I should be fine away from her." He missed her. The emptiness inside him grew darker without her light.

"But you aren't. Maybe it doesn't work the way we thought it did. Maybe the longer you're around her, the quicker you lose control when you aren't."

Gabriel stifled a shudder. He could feel his eyes changing. "You don't know what you're talking about."

"Maybe not. But your demon eyes tell me your control is shot. Go back to Rose. Go now, before you turn demon and we have to duke it out here in the streets."

"We just got the water, electricity and gas turned on in the homestead." Kellan grinned. "I'd really like to bunk there for the night."

"Me, too. I just want to go home. Get some rest, clean up a bit before going to see Rose. I will see her, I promise." Mentally, he needed the separation. He didn't like the notion that they were tied together by his soul.

Justin sighed. "All right, fine. You guys go on home. Let's meet back at the office in the morning, ten o'clock. We'll try to get a handle on what to do next."

"Ten o'clock," they promised, and they parted to run on swift and silent feet through the sleeping streets of Los

~ ☾ ~

Angeles.

* * *

Gabriel looked up at the home he'd grown up in, felt a bit of the peace he'd come to know as a youth. One of the last big estates still tucked deep in the San Fernando Valley, white wrought-iron gates guarded the long, narrow driveway, and the tall hedges surrounding the acreage had turned it into a haven for them all.

He trudged up the unkempt drive, Kellan silent beside him, and noted the piles of dry leaves and pine needles, leftovers from too many years of neglect. The house sat quiet in the heat of the summer moonlight. Gideon would have a fit if he could see the general state of disrepair the gardens had fallen to. The boys used to work on the gardens every weekend while Gideon reminded them all how much Maria Therese had loved them.

Maria Therese. Ever since Rose had mentioned speaking to his dead mother, a part of him wanted desperately to believe it. The other part simply could not. Growing up without her had left a hole inside him as big as the one that had held his soul. A part of him was always vividly aware that his birth had robbed his family of the woman who loved them all. He'd never called her Mom. He'd never call any woman Mom.

Gabriel pushed away the old pain and breathed deeply of the scent that had always meant home, that peculiar mash of citrus grove and eucalyptus tree. Mourning doves cooed in the night as the moon slipped toward the horizon. He took a deep breath of the air he'd known from his earliest days. He'd been happy here. Whatever he'd done, whatever he'd become, he could rest in this place. Here love lingered.

They stepped up to the wide front porch, both brothers bringing out a key. Gabriel looked at Kellan. "Gideon, right?"

Kellan put the big, old-fashioned key into the door, pushed it open. "He said I'd always be welcome here."

"Yeah." They both stepped in through the door, felt the subtle weave of contentment that hung in the air. "It's the same, isn't it?" Gabriel's voice rumbled through the empty house. He shut the door behind them.

~ ☾ ~

"Can you smell the incense that Aunt Maria always burned? Shit. I'm sorry dude." Kellan punched his cousin gently on the shoulder.

"No big. Gideon used to burn it all the time. Super Hit, wasn't it? Black and silver box? I still pick up some of that, now and then."

"Yeah. Me, too. Hey, I'm taking our old room. That okay with you?" Kellan paused at the bottom of the stair leading to the second floor.

"Yeah. Whatever. See you in the morning."

Kellan headed up the stairs.

Gabriel wandered through the downstairs rooms, memories filling him as he moved through time. He and Kellan had been a team. The older boys had a hard time with him, as they'd lost their mother because of Gabriel. Fists had flown more than once, usually in the orchards, with Kellan protecting the baby against his brothers. He'd taught Gabriel how to fight, too, and when to turn away.

The solid wood kitchen table still stood. How many times had they arm-wrestled there? How many times had they gathered around that table for a family conference? Gideon's carved armchair held pride of place at the head of the table. Gabriel could almost see him there and his heart hitched. He moved out of the kitchen, some memories too painful.

He walked into the hearth room, all the furniture sheeted and ghostly in the night. The long table where they'd done homework had been pushed into a corner. He noted the firewood stacked in the built-in box by the fireplace and, drawn toward it, knelt and built a fire more for the comfort than the warmth. Lifting a flowered sheet off one of the sofas in the living room, he settled there and stared into the flames.

Once they got this situation taken care of, he'd be gone. Setting his mind against the pang of loneliness, he closed his eyes and breathed in the atmosphere of home. He looked forward to bringing her here. Rose. She'll love the place.

He mulled over the thought of Rose and his mother, speaking together in the netherworld. It had rolled through his brain constantly and while he couldn't allow himself to

~ ☾ ~

believe it, it made Rose even more precious in his mind. She was so... Rose. That afternoon had been a revelation. Watching the delight fill her as they ate burgers. How she'd laughed at him in the clothing store. The quiet yearning that he'd felt when she leaned against him, caught in the beauty of the sunset.

Gabriel watched the flames. Running wasn't the answer. He'd learned that the hard way. But if he stayed, could he handle the fallout?

He could watch the sunlight in her hair for hours. Her top lip was just a bit fuller than the lower one, and she nibbled on it when she got nervous. She was irritating and sexy and sweet and stubborn and he'd never get over the richness of her kisses. The longer he stayed, the harder it would be to forget her.

Killer, he reminded himself harshly. He destroyed that which he loved, or that which loved him. His mother. Marianne. He was a killer. Always had been, always would be. It was in his blood, in his very nature, and not something that could be scrubbed out of him.

He didn't think he'd survive destroying Rose.

Grunting, he threw his arm over his eyes. He'd spent enough sleepless nights to know this would be another one. His mind might not get any rest, but his body would, if he could just keep himself still enough. He needed to know he could stay away a little longer, keep his demon controlled without her for just a few more hours.

He could almost feel her hand on his cheek, her sky-blue eyes full of questions, laughter. The doc said Rose was completely healthy. Yet Gabriel had recognized emptiness in her, one that mimicked his lack of a soul.

A puzzle. Rose was definitely a puzzle.

* * *

Upstairs, Kellan checked in all the rooms before claiming the one that had been theirs as kids. His itchy feet didn't seem so ready to walk away any more. He frowned, shook his head and went to shove the windows open to the warm night air, pungent with citrus and eucalyptus. The orchard remained

~ ☾ ~

the same, the trees still in the night. He dropped down on the bed. Of course he'd be going soon. That wasn't even a question. He had a horse, and a dog, and his house in the middle of fucking nowhere, Arizona. Of damn course he'd be leaving. They'd get this mess cleaned up and he'd be out of there like a shot.

Unsettled, he bent to unlace his boots, tossing them under the bed out of habit. He leaned back against the pillows and went through his sleep ritual. Midway through his mental chanting, he chanced to glance at the ceiling, the design there clear to his demonic eyes. Following it like he would a picture of a labyrinth, the painting shifted, calmed him, until his eyes grew heavy and peace soothed his restless heart.

There was something familiar about that design. Something... Breathing in the scented air, Kellan slipped into a dream where dogs barked and owls kept a watchful silence.

~ ☾ ~

Chapter Twelve

Gabriel prowled the neighborhood where Rose stayed with Maggie, waiting for dawn. He'd waited this long, he could surely wait until dawn to connect. He'd left his brother fast asleep and had run to her. The moon had set and that absolute dark before dawn settled in.

Time was growing short. With the absence of his soul, his other, less human senses were gaining in strength and his Fae instincts, few though they might be, were almost screaming with urgency.

A noise had him looking up to the balcony of Maggie's apartment. Rose came out, leaned against the railing and looked to the sea.

Gabriel knew her frustration as he knew his own. His original plan dissolved as he vaulted up to catch himself on the railing of the balcony. Joy and need both pulsed through him as he caught her scent.

Rose gasped and whirled about, pressed her hands to her mouth. Finally registering Gabriel, she wrapped her arms around the robe she wore, her eyes flashing in the dim light.

"Took you long enough. I'm going crazy here. Aren't you?"

"I stayed away longer than I'd meant." Gabriel grimaced as her shoulders tensed up. Sighing, he dropped from the railing to the balcony and held out a hand to her. "I'm not used to needing anyone. Not for years."

She twined her fingers with his. "I'm beginning to understand that." Her words were quiet in the pre-dawn. "You meant to push me away. But it doesn't matter." She turned her face up to his, her blue eyes like lasers, pinning him to the spot. "Apparently this need thing works both ways. Your soul

~ ☾ ~

has been aching for you. It's kept me awake and edgy. I've needed you. I've been calling you for hours."

"I'm here now."

"I want you to consider something very carefully. If we don't manage to get the rest of your soul back, if I can't give you your soul back, then our future is tied together. Do you understand that?"

He'd rather face a dozen J'aadt demons than this small woman with her talk of the future. "I'm too old for you. Too dangerous. I've killed. I'm not good enough for you."

Her eyes flashed again. A lesser man would have quailed. Gabriel stood there secure in the knowledge of being right, knowing that she deserved so much better than someone like him. A murderer.

"I'm a drug addict and a whore," she said succinctly. "I've done my share of stealing. I've given my body to men who never knew my name in exchange for the drugs they could put into my veins. But then I died. I changed." Rose moved toward him and put one small hand on his broad chest.

He felt that touch clear to his missing soul. Almost holding his breath, his gaze met hers. Flinched from what he saw in her eyes, even as it warmed him.

"Gabriel, I can't do anything else than protect you. I feel this is the reason I'm here, and everything that went before brought me to this place, this time. Everything else brought me to you. Whether or not we have a future together? I don't know. But I don't want to rule it out, either, just because you're scared."

"I don't want this." He searched, but words were beyond him. A helpless little sound escaped from his lips. "Rose."

She smiled a little, her eyes finally warming. "It's okay. I'm scared, too. You do what you need to do. Whatever happens with Satine, I'll be here waiting for you. We'll figure out what comes next together, okay?"

His arms came around her then, lifting her off her feet to bring their faces to the same level. Gabriel searched her eyes. They were clear, holding no secrets. Her heart shone freely, and it took his breath away.

~ ☾ ~

She wrapped her legs around his waist, took his face into her hands as he adjusted his hold. "Kiss me," she whispered. "While we have this time together."

He obeyed. Her lips were like satin beneath his, warm and alive and opening to him. His senses spun and his grip on her tightened. His control wavered.

Gabriel broke their kiss and leaned his forehead against hers, taking a deep breath. Drawing in her scent, the delicious fragrance made him yearn. Every part of him grew hard as stone.

This sprite, with her flaming red hair and Soul Chalice abilities had captured his heart like no other. Enticed him like no other. Her hands urged him to take her mouth again, and he forgot the reasons to deny her.

Her body grew warm against him. Her scent rose up to wreathe his brain, turning his thoughts muddy. He *needed*.

Urgency thrummed through him. Gabriel turned, pressed her back against the wall and, as his mouth ravaged hers, slid his hand down the front of her robe. Her skin was heated silk against the roughness of his fingers, her body wonderfully responsive.

Rose's hands spread across his chest, those strong, capable hands hot against his cool skin, sparking fires of need wherever they landed. *Gods.*

"Rose?" The door beside them opened. "Oops. Sorry." It shut. Maggie went away.

Gabriel stilled, one of his hands curved on her bottom, the other on her breast, his mouth a whisper from hers. His eyes opened and he looked into the smiling blue eyes of the woman who had captured him.

"Now there's timing for you," she said, her voice husky with need and laughter.

"Gods. Are you all right?" Carefully, he lowered her to her feet, closed her robe in front.

Rose sighed. Taking his face in her hands, she kissed him. Gabriel felt his own heart overflow, a painful burgeoning of emotion, but he kept his hands fisted at his sides. She broke the kiss and looked him in the eye, exasperated.

~ ☾ ~

"I didn't realize being a tribred meant you were slow on the uptake. I'm fine," she emphasized, "if sexually frustrated. But let's understand each other, Gabriel. I will have you. You will have me. This— you and me—was meant to be. Maybe we're only for the short term, maybe for longer. I don't know and it doesn't matter right now, but I will have you at some point." She kissed him again. "Now, come on in and have some coffee." She opened the balcony door.

Fabric fluttered above him. Going on instinct, Gabriel pushed Rose into the kitchen and whirled. A vampire. Terrific. "Stay inside!"

The male was young, thirsty. He hung on a pine tree branch that sheltered the apartment building below. "Tasty treats." The words came on a low sigh.

Gabriel roared a challenge and his demon, denied once that night, took over. His vision expanded as his skin darkened, changed as he eyed his quarry. A leap straight up, a hooking motion with his arm, and he'd ripped the vamp from the tree and tossed him through the air to land with a smashing of glass against the apartment building across the way. A burglar alarm sounded.

Gabriel leaped off the balcony to take the fight to the ground. He looked up and beckoned to the vampire.

The vamp shook free of the glass, grunted, and leaped down onto Gabriel's back. Before the vamp could latch his teeth into Gabriel's neck, another blur, this one a soft orangey-brown, leaped over the balcony railing and landed on the vamp, which took all three of them to the ground.

The vamp screamed to feel his hair on fire. He threw the demon off his back and fled on foot.

Gabriel grabbed Rose's leg before she could follow. "No."

Rose pouted. "Why not? Gabriel, he's a bad guy. We should just delete him."

He stood and took her with him. "No. Now change back, please." He did so, shook hard. "Before someone comes looking for who ruined the neighbor's window."

"Oh," she mouthed, and staggered a little as she changed form. "Oh. Ouch. Gabriel, I don't feel so good."

~ ☾ ~

He hugged her to him. "I know, baby. Come on, let's get back to Maggie's place. Think she'll have pants my size?"

Laughing, Rose led the way back to the apartment. Gabriel followed, unsettled by all that had taken place between them in such a short span of time.

* * *

When the sun stood high in the sky and he'd assured himself of Rose's well-being, Gabriel left Maggie's Montana Avenue apartment and ran the distance to the Caine Investigations office, stopping only to pick up a dozen bagels. Justin had beaten him in and the door to the office stood open.

"There's got to be a way to keep her safe." Gabriel dumped the bagels on the conference table and confronted Justin as he read the L.A. Times.

"Calm down."

"Calm down? Calm down? *Vamps* are finding her now. Demons, vampires, what the hell is going on?" A furious anxiety had taken up residence in his chest, and he didn't like it one bit.

"Stop with the freak out. If she's got the Soul Chalice thing going on, I guess it's to be expected."

"Whatever I expected when I came down here following my soul, it wasn't this," he declared. "I've spent the better part of the past decade hiding, working for the filthy rich so I could do something eventually. I finally come home and the first thing I run into is a woman who has the same freaking demon on her that made me kill Marianne. A woman, moreover, who makes me dream of the impossible. Are you surprised that I'm having trouble here?" Gabriel, his eyes hot, pushed the bag of bagels at his brother.

Justin shoved the bag aside. His strength had it spinning off the table and hitting the far wall. Bagels scattered but neither brother took notice. "You can't continue to use who you are as an excuse. Gabriel." he said, jumping up. "I hate that you were in trouble and I didn't know. I hate that you ran when we are family. We should have been by your side, helping you through it.

~ ☾ ~

"And now that you're back you son of a bitch, I'm gonna help you if it kills us both." Justin leaned on the table. "What I think about your past, what happened or how you got here, it doesn't matter. But I'd like to help."

"Hell." He'd known how it had felt to be away from the family. He hadn't realized, not really, how they would feel about his absence. "I don't blame you, Justin, for not being there."

"I don't fucking care. I blame myself, and that's what we've both got to live with." Justin blew out a breath. "Just don't forget your Fae blood, and your human blood. You're not just a demon."

"If you tell me I need to find my inner fairy, I think I'm gonna puke."

Calmer now, Justin rounded the table to pick up the scattered bagels. "I'm just saying you need balance. Right now, you're giving the demonic part of you all the power, and denying the rest of your heritage."

"Good, because I'm not down with the fairy dust, you know?" Gabriel looked out the window without seeing the clear blue sky. "You're the second person to tell me I'm not just a demon. Do you really think because I don't have balance, I'm losing myself when I fight?" Gabriel looked over his shoulder at Justin, his eyes whirling demon-electric green.

"Yeah. More and more. And the more you lose it, the harder it'll be to regain it."

"How do I... "

Kellan came through the door bearing doughnuts. "Hail, hail the gang's all here," he said. "I bring sweets to soothe the savage beast that lingers in us all." He lowered the pink box to Justin's desk, looking from one man to the other. "Oh. Did I just interrupt a moment?"

"Of a sort. But doughnuts beat bagels by a mile." Justin set the battered bag of bagels on the table and moved to the box of doughnuts. "I get the chocolate bar."

Kellan raised an eyebrow. "Who said I got you a chocolate bar?"

Justin grabbed the chocolate bar and grinned. "You

~ ☾ ~

wouldn't forget that it's my favorite, no matter how long you've been away." He bit in, closed his eyes for a moment. "Mmmm. Chocolaty, doughnutty goodness."

"Great. Now we won't get any sense out of him until he's finished it." Gabriel threw Kellan a disgusted look, sat and dug into the box for a glazed. "What put you in such a cheery mood, anyway?"

Kellan grinned. "I slept in our old room. Sorry I wasn't around when you woke up - I've been out getting supplies."

Justin blinked and reached for another doughnut.

Gabriel scowled, licking his fingers free of sugar. "I left before you, before dawn. What was so special about sleeping in our old room?"

Kellan went for the bagels. "I slept like a baby. If I dreamed, I didn't remember it, but I woke up with a smile on my face. Do you ever remember waking up and not feeling good in that room?"

"Only when I woke up sick. And even then, I wanted to get up." Gabriel frowned and took another doughnut.

"It's the perfect place for Rose. She'll feel safe there. As a matter of fact, we should all go in daylight, have a look."

"And Maggie," Justin said. "She won't want us to do anything without her. You're right; it would be a good way to get the women somewhere safe."

"I'm telling you - there's something about that house." Kellan took a chair and straddled it. "So. What's the plan for taking out the vamps?" He bit into his bagel.

"What can we do that won't have collateral damage? I'd really rather not kill any humans," said Justin.

"Or weres," added Gabriel. "Remember, we promised to get the weres to safety. We can do a quick check for humans at that point."

"No killing of humans or weres. There are demons down there, too, you know."

"Yeah, but I don't feel bad about killing demons," retorted Gabriel. "Do you?"

"Nope."

"No remorse here," said Kellan.

~ ☾ ~

"Okay then. So the demons are expendable." The three looked at each other. "Is anyone else uncomfortable with that realization?"

"Yeah."

Kellan sighed. "Yeah. Damn it."

Gabriel frowned. "Someone's gonna get killed if we take that place down. There's not a whole lot we can do about that."

"Discussion won't work, that's for sure," Justin said. "Not with a vampire."

"Not with Vlad, at any rate," amended Gabriel. "He'd be happy to kill us all." He shifted in his chair, remembering. "He's letting that place continue because it alleviates his boredom, quote unquote."

Justin shrugged. "Danny will get his people out. Weres in fighting mode will usually spook a demon, and they'll run. If not, then I guess we fight the demons and the vampires."

Gabriel looked at Justin, one eyebrow cocked. "Have you gone full demon?"

Justin shifted in his chair. "No."

"I have," offered Kellan. "And I know you have, Gabriel."

"Yeah. So you're saying that if the two of us go in, full demon, we should be able to take out the entire place?" Gabriel shook his head. "I don't think so."

"I'd rather firebomb the basement where the vampires rest. If we do it in the daytime, on a weekend, little chance of human traffic in that area of town. When the vampires scrabble to the surface to escape the fire, poof, they'll burn from the sun." What do you think, Justin?"

"Hmm," Justin mused. "That might work."

"If we think we can take the vampires out by ourselves, do we even need the weres?" Finished with his bagel, Kellan reached a long hand out and snagged a cake doughnut with white icing and multi-colored sprinkles.

"The vampires have a couple more captives. I know I'd demand to be a part of any rescue attempt if it were, say, you guys being held. We can't keep them from joining in. And frankly, the help is welcome." Justin wiped his fingers on a

~ ☾ ~

paper napkin.

A knocking at their main entrance had them looking at one another.

"Danny and his gang, already? I haven't digested yet."

"Don't snarl, Kellan. Let them in - and be nice." Justin raised his eyebrows warningly. Kellan snorted and left the conference room.

Gabriel leaned toward Justin. "What do you expect to gain from this?"

Justin shrugged. "I'm tired of being the only weirdos on the block watching out for our little corner of the world. Is there something wrong with having allies?"

Danny, Sig and Favor came into the room. Danny held himself with quiet confidence as Sig and Favor flanked him. While Gabriel knew they didn't carry guns, he also knew they had weapons much nastier than any gun.

He pushed the box of doughnuts to where they settled, their backs to the windows. "Kellan brought doughnuts."

Danny shook his head, passing the box to Sig. "There's been more demon activity lately. Signs that maybe there's more than one portal being opened to the Chaos Plane."

"Damn Kendall Sorbis."

"He's branched out from being merely the Sorcerer to the Stars, The Guru of Hollywood, or whatever you want to call him. He's definitely crossed a line. We've also got the confirmation that he's been working with the vampire Satine." Danny sighed. "We're looking for him, but he's gone underground."

Gabriel frowned. "Why would he be opening portals? What's his purpose?" He shifted uneasily.

"Demons, full blooded demons, thrive in chaos," Justin said, his eyes thoughtful. "Any number of creatures out there would love to see Earth drop into chaos." He looked to Danny. "How does this have anything to do with Twisted, Vlad or Satine?"

"We believe Sorbis has been working with both vampires, perhaps independently of each other. I'm telling you now, because we can't keep order in the city by ourselves." Danny

~ ☾ ~

steepled his fingers, looking at the three Caines slowly in turn. "I have heard mostly good things about you. And, of course, I owe you a debt beyond measure."

"Your mate continues to be healthy?"

Danny smiled. "Her unborn are fine."

"We've heard little about the were clans in general. You have kept yourselves well hidden," Justin replied.

"For good reason. We as a people have been hunted in the past. Finally our pack had found a measure of peace, until our lupa was captured." Sig bowed his head.

Danny's golden eyes grew sober. "Chandra tells me our other quickening females are in danger. We will do what we must to bring them out of that place."

Kellan stirred, drawing their attention. "What can a vampire do to a were that will keep her captive?"

Danny turned toward him. "Silver. They are bound with silver. We need your help."

Gabriel studied Danny, brushed his public mind briefly. Felt the man's grief, his fear, touched lightly on the rage that ran deep. He leaned forward and captured Danny's gaze.

"How do you guys feel about explosives?"

Chapter Thirteen

Rose paced the length of the small apartment for the umpteenth time. Her headache had receded and she felt strong, but the apartment plus the lack of Gabriel was getting on her nerves.

Maggie looked up, exasperated. "I'm working as fast as I can, Rose. Chill."

"Sorry." Rose smiled, gesturing. "You know, I think I'll take a walk. This is a good neighborhood, right?" Not that it would stop her if it weren't.

"Yeah, go ahead. We're almost out of milk. There's a small grocery on the corner if you turn right at the end of the street. Do you mind?"

"No. That's fine. I just—I'm sorry, but I don't have any money." Rose shoved her hands into her pockets, stifling any embarrassment. She didn't even want to think how much Gabriel had spent on her the previous day. "I've got to get a job."

"*I'm* sorry." Maggie jumped up and rummaged in her purse. "Here's a twenty, keep the change. And right now, you have a job. We'll figure something out for the long term, I promise."

Rose took the money without a blush. "It all depends on how this ends, right? I mean, I might not make it out alive."

Maggie's eyes sharpened. "Are you worried?"

She shrugged. "I went from a being a drug addict to being dead to being something out of a Laurel K. Hamilton novel. What's to worry about? I won't be long, I promise. Twenty minutes, max. I just – I need some air."

"No problem. Take your time."

~ ☾ ~

Rose flashed a grin. "Back soon." She made her escape.

The day had followed through on the promise of dawn. Clear and sunny, the air had a bite of heat to it that made Rose stretch like a cat before heading down the stairs to the street.

This was living. The streets here were wide and clean, the tang of the ocean lived in every breath she took. Still, the habits of a lifetime stuck with her. She checked out the street both ways before setting a foot on the sidewalk. No dark cars. No ex-lovers hanging around. No otherworldly beasty wanting her for a snack either as far as she could tell.

Rose walked slowly, savoring her solitude. For the first time since she met up with Gabriel Caine, she was alone with time to think.

Save Gabriel. How the hell was she supposed to do that? And she'd sworn to kill Satine, her long-dead cousin, yet another thing to add to the 'how the hell' column.

Not to mention, the demon on her belly would most likely kill her. That was a pretty big glitch in her happy-ever-after plans.

"Fix it? How the hell am I supposed to fix it?"

She'd just about reached the store when her instincts sharpened. She looked up and saw a couple of men standing next to a motorcycle, watching her, and she knew – she just *knew* they weren't human. Fear shot through her and she bolted the other way, ignoring the shouts behind her.

The bike roared a challenge. Panic had her dashing into the small health food store. She fled through the store, out the back and into a courtyard filled with folks having their morning coffee.

Rose bumped into a table, grimaced as hot coffee splashed on her new tee shirt. "Sorry." She edged around the table and fled, ignoring the insults the couple hurled at her retreating back.

She found an opening between two buildings and sped down it. Barely wide enough for her, she drew a breath of relief when it opened out into another courtyard, this one empty.

She stood, panting, trying to calm her wildly beating heart,

~ ☾ ~

Demon Soul

and listened hard. The motorcycle hadn't gone—she could hear its throaty rumble somewhere to her right. Try though she might, she couldn't hear any footsteps. Damn. Which way?

An alley led to the street to her left. A shopkeeper had just opened his back door, which would take her to the street to her right. He looked kindly, so she ran that way and passed him before he could finish his "good morning".

She didn't see him stick his cane out, didn't see his hand come down to push her to the ground, but her instincts had her diving for the doorway into a somersault and back on her feet, the nice man now cursing at her back. She ran through the darkened shop, sparing a quick glance behind her.

She ran right into a wall of flesh.

Rose's head jerked up as his hands closed about her arms and lifted her to his face. He was a big demon, his skin the faded color of dying grass, his eyes a snapping black with blue flares.

Rage filled her, smothering any fear. A wild energy crackled through her. Flame licked along her skin, causing the demon holding her to yelp and drop her hastily. She moved all the way down, rolling in a backwards somersault to come up on her feet again, an ability she hadn't been aware of before.

It was different from changing into the demon. This was an understanding from deep inside what to do with the energy, with the flame. She knew now how to shape it, how to throw it, so she did, tossing a hastily formed ball of fire at the demon in front of her. It spattered against his broad chest and the flames stuck, licked at its clothes. Surprised, his bellowing reaction shook the building.

She threw another fireball at him but missed, catching stacks of paper on fire. Rose knew fire, breathed it, lived it, became it until she felt herself breaking into pieces of flame, each one holding strength and destruction until the full horror of what she could do fell upon her and she came back to herself, shuddering, flames still licking at her palms. A bucket of water dumped on her from behind.

Shocked at the cold and wet, enraged, Rose put her

~ ☾ ~

burning hands out against her damp tee shirt and kicked out behind her, catching the fat proprietor right in the balls.

He groaned and fell to his knees just as his front door opened. Rose faced the newcomers with her hands fisted and her eyes filled with fire.

The blond walked with a feline grace that had Rose narrowing her eyes. His signature energy brushed up against hers, like rubbing velvet the wrong way. A were. She remembered the sensation from the club. Two more weres stood at his back. She struggled to find the flame inside her, but the water had effectively dowsed her ability.

"Well now, my sweet, sweet Rose Walters," said the newcomer, his voice a combination of amusement and respect. "Let's go for a ride, shall we?"

"Why should I go with you?" Rose coughed. Her throat felt like fire and tasted of smoke.

He raised his eyebrows. "You'd rather stay here, with these two?" Flames crackled behind him.

He had a point. Rose lifted her chin, ignoring the water dripping off her hair. "What's your name?"

"Chazz." He stepped forward, offered her his handkerchief. "Wipe yourself down. I don't want you dripping all over me as we go."

She took the handkerchief, wiped herself off as well as she could, wringing the water out of her hair. She dug into her jeans pocket, pulled out a band and tied her hair back. "Satisfied?"

"Not yet," he said with a leer, openly eyeing her damp shirt, her nipples poking through her bra. "But at least you're not dripping. Come with me."

Furiously discarding option after option, she nodded, her face carefully blank. "After you."

"Oh no," he said. "After you."

"Very well." As she passed the burning papers by the door, she made a gesture and the fire went out, returned to her with a brief shock through her palm. Fire once again was hers, the water now vapor on her body. Oh. So *that's* how it worked.

Chazz prodded her, and she realized she'd come to a

~ ☾ ~

standstill. "Get moving."

Rose obliged, her feet carrying her to the other two men in the doorway. They took her, one on each arm, and walked into the hot sunshine.

The sun brought fire back to her and she flamed. The weres holding her yelped and dropped her. Without hesitation, Rose took off down the street, a streak of flame in the morning sun. Did they think she was *stupid*? She reached out to Gabriel as she ran.

Hey. Whatcha doin'? Got time to come to my rescue?

Stunned at first, his tone quickly turned furious. *Rose? What the hell!*

Chazz is on my tail. Damn! A body slammed into her and brought her down, one arm guarding her face as they skidded on the sidewalk.

"Going somewhere?" Chazz stood and yanked her to her feet.

"Anywhere you aren't," she retorted. Her knees throbbed and she tasted blood from where she'd bit her cheek.

The motorcycle rumbled up to where they stood at the curb. Chazz lifted her bodily onto the bike, holding her easily despite her struggles as he switched places with the driver.

He looked at her. "Hang on to me, or you'll regret it."

The other were now slid on behind her, pressing her up against Chazz. Their heat surprised her. Her damp shirt dried swiftly between the two men.

He chuckled, and the sound went through her body. "Enjoy it."

She repressed the retort that wanted to come out and set her teeth when he started the bike.

Making the best of the worst, she wrapped her arms around Chazz. She'd take him down with her, she vowed, and laid her head against his back. She felt Chazz relax a bit as they slipped into traffic.

Still there? Rose clamped a hold on her emotions, not wanting Gabriel to know how scared she was. *I just went out for milk, I wasn't doing anything risky. I swear it.*

She could almost see Gabriel rolling his eyes at her.

~ ☾ ~

Where are you now?

I think we're heading to Twisted, but I'm not totally sure. I'm on a motorcycle.

She could feel the turmoil Gabriel was in, but didn't know how to soothe him.

Keep this link open. Tell me what's going on as much as you can. We'll try to meet up with you. I'm not going to let them hurt you, he added, his mental voice a touch softer.

Warmth that had nothing to do with fire filled her and she smiled. *I know.*

I've got to talk to the guys. Stay in the background, okay?

Yeah. Okay. Rose relaxed further. She'd done all she could.

* * *

Gabriel turned from where he'd braced his hands against the window and looked at the men at the table.

Justin spoke up. "Rose?"

"Yeah. They've got her. Found her outside of Maggie's place, going for milk. I should have stayed."

"*Damn* the witch. Who's got her?" Justin demanded.

"Chazz. Satine's were tiger is in the driver's seat." He turned to Danny. "They've got one of our women now. I'd like to get her back before they hit Twisted. Then we can concentrate on freeing the rest of your women while we're there. Does that sound fair?"

Danny tilted his head and looked at Gabriel. "She is your woman."

Gabriel didn't respond. Justin cursed all witches everywhere under his breath.

Danny's eyes warmed with laughter. "These women. Difficult, no?"

"Have you known any who aren't?" Justin asked wryly. He turned to Gabriel. "Where are they?"

Gabriel scanned Rose's mind and brushed the last crumbs of doughnut off his fingers. "Close enough. I say let's go."

Danny also stood. "This sounds good. I'll go with you. Sig, Favor, go with Justin and Kellan. A second wave is good for the surprise element. Bring the cars."

Sig scowled. All the men stood.

~ ☾ ~

"Let's go, then. Keep in touch."

"Wait." Justin held up a hand. "Let's meet again, tonight at ten. We'll take stock and go from there."

"Sounds good. Let's go." Gabriel led the way out the door, his gut roiling. Chazz, Satine's garbage disposal, had Rose. Gabriel clamped a hold on his emotions as his demon struggled to be free.

Danny was wrong. Rose wasn't his woman, but she didn't deserve whatever it was Chazz had in store for her.

* * *

Rose kept her eyes closed and her mind attuned to Gabriel. She'd picked up on their plan and felt some relief that Kellan would be there as back up. If they were too late...she shuddered and thrust the thought away.

The bike's rumbling changed tone and she opened her eyes, lifting her head from Chazz's back.

They'd slowed, turned south. If they went toward the ocean, she didn't have a clue as to where they might go. If they turned away from the ocean - Rose sighed with relief as they turned on Pico Boulevard. Away from the ocean. So, he was taking her to Twisted.

She relayed the information to Gabriel and held her breath.

Got it. Kellan and Justin are in place. The rest of us are on our way.

He shut down the communications between them before she could say anything else. So, wedged between the men as she was, she began to plot. If they took her inside the club, she was as good as dead. So it was up to her, she reasoned, to make sure the Caine boys found her—*outside*. If that meant she needed to play a bit with her borrowed abilities, then that's exactly what she'd do and damn the consequences. So what if she got a little dehydrated? There'd be time to drink water later.

She looked around and realized they were still about a mile away from Twisted. Perfect.

Rose closed her eyes and focused on her rage. Focused on the power of the flames, the voice of the fire as it fed her, as she fed it. Knew again the amazing surge of energy the fire

~ ☾ ~

had poured into her. Slowly, her body heat rose.

A simmer, she thought. Warm. She started to become uncomfortably warm, but not too hot. Sweat beaded her forehead with her efforts at control, and the man behind her shifted uneasily.

Abruptly she pulled the mental release on the heat level just as Chazz pulled into the back parking lot of Twisted. Energy consumed her thoughts, a drug more powerful than any she'd ever known. Her head snapped back and she stared at the sky, her eyes filled with flame and the power of the sun.

"Fuck me!" The were behind her jumped off the bike before Chazz could bring it to a full stop. "The chick is on fire! Chazz!"

But before Chazz could get away, Rose tightened her arms around him and whispered to the flame, told it where to lick, how to heat the metal of his zippers. He howled and leaped off with her still clinging to his back. He sent the bike careening from him to crash into the plate glass window facing the parking lot.

Grabbing her hands, he pulled them wide, spun her around and tossed her away from him. Rose flew, laughed as though he were guiding her through a dance. She landed lightly on the balls of her feet. There was nothing he could do to hurt her. She embodied fire—warmth, life, energy, ruin and death.

Demons poured out of the back of the club in response to the bike going through the window, at least a dozen of them. They hesitated at the sight of the Weres, and balked entirely at the flames licking along Rose's body.

Rose ignored the lesser demons and watched as Chazz batted the fire at his crotch. She hovered, not quite touching the ground, outlined by fire, emboldened by it, her mind consumed utterly with the rush. The excitement. No high had ever buzzed through her blood the way fire did. Rose tilted her head as the demons drew closer to her, circling her warily. What kind of demons were they? Were any of them fire demons, like she was? They certainly looked flammable. Things like concrete had a dark, dense look to them, but the demons were more of a papery hue.

~ ☾ ~

As an experiment, she tossed a fireball at one of them and he exploded in flame, his screams high-pitched and almost inaudible. Dogs in the neighborhood barked in surprise and kept barking. Rose pulled together another fireball and eyed the next demon. He backed up, bumped into his neighbor, turned, and ran down the alley, the rest of them scrambling to follow.

Rose just hovered a foot above the ground, watching as the demons parted for Gabriel and a stranger, flowed on by them. The newcomer with Gabriel gave a great leap and caught Chazz mid-back, took him down to the asphalt. Both men let out a snarl and Chazz flipped, grappled with the other man. Rose turned away to study the building, unconcerned now about her enemy.

*＊＊

Gabriel approached Rose with caution. This time he got a better look at her demon form, and he couldn't believe what he was seeing—she was beautiful, eerie, flame licking along her arms, forming between her hands, flickering in her summer-sky blue eyes. Fire danced along the strands of her coppery curls. Her skin had taken on fur, an orangey hue with golden spots. He could see the horns protruding from her forehead, the ears elongated and pointy. Behind her, tiny wings, useless in flight, fluttered between her shoulder blades.

His own demon uncurled inside him. It fought to be freed, violently attracted to this transformed Rose. He shook his head fiercely and his demon subsided, pouting, though he knew his eyes still whirled green.

"Rose? It's me, Gabriel. How can you...it is you?" His voice held his demon, a growl that would not be denied.

She glanced at him over her shoulder. Her eyes took a bit to focus, and it seemed to him she'd grown taller. "It's me. I've got a fire demon's powers, and look at me! I know you've seen me before, but look. Look at what I can do." Her smile was quick and endearing as she rolled a ball of fire.

Before she could launch it, Gabriel caught her arm. Amazed at how hot she felt. "No." He growled the command even as his inner demon struggled again to be free.

~ ☾ ~

"Why not?" A frown gathered between her eyes and she tossed the fireball from hand to hand. "We don't like that place. We can get rid of it. Easy. Just, poof!"

"There are people to save in there, Rose," he said. Sweat beaded on his face and he wondered how much longer he could hang onto her.

She tilted her head. "Then let's go in and save them. The demons are gone. Come on, Gabriel, let's go be big bad demons together."

Her hands squashed the fireball and she streaked to the open door of the club, as fast as any fire. Gabriel roared a challenge. She turned to him and grinned, did a little dance in the doorway. "Come on!"

Gabriel changed into his demon, his heart in his throat. He caught sight of Danny's eye on him. Focusing, he took the time to tell him the plan. "We go to save the weres." He moved to the back door of Twisted.

The place stank of vampire. Gabriel grumbled low in his throat as he followed Rose's scent of smoke and sunshine down the stairs, traceable among the heavier scent of vampire that clogged at the back of his throat. As a human, he had a difficult time with the stairwell. As a demon, he hated it—too enclosed, the steps too small for his feet, yet he followed her.

Found her. With her demon strength she broke open the locks. All the doors stood open on the floor, but only three of them had held prisoners. She stood now in front of one of the doors, her head cocked to one side, little flames licking along the edges of her hair. "It's okay," he heard her say. "You can come out. We're the good guys."

Gabriel gave off a rumble that might have been laughter. She turned his way and grinned as Danny came up behind them. He looked into the room where Rose stood and cried out.

The woman, thin, pregnant and naked, cringed against the back wall, blinking in Rose's light. Seeing Danny, she flung herself to the floor and crawled toward him, whimpering.

"No, Rebekah. Please. Let's just go. Let's go." Danny stripped off his tee shirt and gave it to the woman, who put it

~ ☾ ~

on gratefully.

They heard a clatter on the stairs and tensed. Gabriel tucked Rose behind him and Danny and Rebekah ducked back into the room, but only Kellan, Sig and Favor came into sight.

"Good to see you," rumbled Gabriel, and Danny and Rebekah came out. Favor, his eyes blazing, ran to the woman and hugged her, hard. He lifted her into his arms and took her outside. Sig and Danny went into the other two rooms, brought out equally disoriented and distraught females in varying stages of pregnancy.

The seven of them escaped up the stairs. Rose turned deeper into the building and Gabriel grabbed her arm, concerned at how thin her aura felt. She'd be running on adrenalin. He couldn't let her reach Satine, not now. He needed to get her to safety before she burned herself up. He drew her into his arms, careful his claws didn't scratch her.

"No."

She pouted at him over her shoulder. "But why not?"

"No time. The kill must be up close, personal." He bared his teeth and appealed to her demon senses. "They deserve nothing less." He pulled her along up the stairs and to the street, one arm circling her shoulders, the contact soothing both of them. "Besides, we need to get you to Doc Cavanaugh. The rest of us will handle it."

Artlessly, she tipped her head, her fiery orange eyes holding curiosity. "But I want to do it. I want to kill them. They are bad."

"You can't kill." His heart froze at the thought of it.

"I can, too." They burst into the sun, to the almost empty parking lot. "I'm as powerful as you are. Maybe more. You just don't want me to be strong, do you? No one ever wants me to be strong. I'm not stupid, you know. I'm not weak."

Gabriel glanced at her. "I never said that you were."

The others had left, and Chazz lay dead on the ground, parts of him smoking but with no actual flame anywhere to be seen. The neighborhood dogs still howled.

She staggered as her feet touched the ground again. The tears fell, quenching the flames in her eyes. "No one wants me

~ ☾ ~

to be strong and powerful. But I am. And the day will come when I will be on top, I promise you that." Rose turned to Gabriel, her face fierce. "I will force you to respect me. Then I will save you."

She changed shape as she spoke, the flames subsiding as she shed her demon skin for her human one.

"I do respect you, you have all my respect. You are amazing, and handling this whole thing with a lot of grace." Gabriel shifted to human as well, gritting his teeth at the usual aching of his head. "But it's time to get to safety." Gabriel gripped her shoulders, her body growing cold under his hands. "Rose." He shook her gently, startled at the dullness in her eyes. "Rose, stay with me. Rose, damn it! Don't you leave me now."

"You need me, Gabriel. Let me in. Please." She slumped into him. Gabriel swore under his breath and swung her up into his arms.

Sirens sounded in the distance. Swearing again, Gabriel took to the back alleyways on a demon-speed run. The last thing they needed at this point was to be stopped by the cops.

~ ☾ ~

Chapter Fourteen

Rose pressed her face to the glass and watched her body in the hospital bed below. "Déjà vu all over again," she said, and sighed. Only this time, Gabriel Caine held her hand. This time, someone cared.

She clenched her fists against the glass. "Damn it, I don't want to die."

"Then don't."

Rose whirled, eyes wide, to see who had spoken.

He wasn't as tall as the demons she'd grown used to. Rather he was thin and wiry, barely six feet. His naked torso, a reddish brown, rippled with muscles that disappeared intriguingly into a pair of loose black pants. His black hair was short and spiky and his eyes flickered orange. She stared at him, strangely attracted.

"Who are you?"

He smiled. "Mephisto. The demon on your belly."

She absorbed the punch of his sex appeal even as she recoiled in disbelief. "What do you want with me?"

"You are my first Soul Chalice." He gestured to her stomach. "The spiral is my home."

"Why?"

He sent her a quizzical look. "Why what?"

"Why me, why here, why are you doing all of this? Or am I just going nuts? That's it. I must be going crazy. I must be dreaming."

"I'm just lending you my power. I'm not taking you over," he said. "Though I must admit it's proven to be much more entertaining than the last time I inhabited a human. Your innocent delight in what I take for granted is...refreshing."

~ ☾ ~

"But why are we *here*?" Rose gestured around to the waiting area she recognized from her coma.

"It seemed to be the safest way to talk to you."

"So, I'm not about to die?"

"Not right now, no."

Too many questions trembled on her tongue. He was the source of her powers. He gave her the gift of fire. "How do we separate, you and me? I mean, how will you eventually move on to the next girl?"

Regret flashed across his face. "Usually the host dies."

"Does the host have to die?" Fear pooled in her stomach.

"No. Not always. It takes a strong mind and a pure heart to survive, though." He sent her a smoldering smile again. "People like that are kind of hard to find."

"But not impossible," said Rose. Her mind worked at a rapid pace. "You have knowledge. I need some answers. I need to kill a vampire. How should I do it?"

The demon shrugged, strolled over to the window to look at the hospital scene below. "Cut off the head. Cut out the heart. Burn the two."

Rose flinched. "I'm not that good with knives. What if we just went with fire?"

Mephisto turned to face her. "You could burn yourself out trying to kill a vampire. Are you sure you want to take that risk?"

"You'll be with me. If I burn myself out, would that also kill you, since the spiral will also get burned?"

Uncertainty crossed the demon's face. "I don't know."

"So." Rose tapped her fingers on the window ledge. "You are on my body for the duration, meaning until I die. But before I die, I have to save Gabriel's soul, and kill the vampire. If you don't want to die along with me, then I guess you'll either have to jump ship or help me kill the vampire." She looked at the demon. "What's it going to be?"

"That's the other part that continues to surprise me. You are here to save Gabriel Caine, and the last time I possessed a woman I did my best to kill him." He chuckled. "It's amusing, how the world turns."

~ ☾ ~

"Why did you try to kill him before?"

Mephisto looked at her with surprise. "If attacked, will you not defend yourself?"

"Yes. Of course."

"He attacked me. I responded. Simple."

"Not simple. You killed his girlfriend."

"No." Mephisto frowned. "The past holds little interest for me, but I will tell you that ultimately it was Marianne who killed Marianne. Tell me why you want to end this vampire so badly."

"I'm carrying a part of Gabriel's soul for him, but I've got to get the rest. The stupid vampire stole it from him and he's pissed off," she confided.

"I can see why." He shook his head. "So I am helping to save Gabriel Caine. Fate works in funny ways."

"I want to kill the vampire, but I'm guessing I'll need you to leave me first in order for you to help me. Two of us being stronger than one."

His eyes sharpened on her. "If I leave you, there's no guarantee I'll help you, and you won't have my fire abilities to kill the vampire." He raised an eyebrow. "Doesn't sound like a good battle plan to me."

"Ah, but that's if I were trying to get rid of you. You don't have to leave. I'd much rather you help me kill the vampire. Please?" Rose took a step forward, put her hand on his arm. "It means everything to me."

Mephisto stared at his arm where her fingers rested. "That's a first. No one has ever said *please* to me before." He moved away from her as a tiny frown gathered between his eyes. "Why do I get the feeling that you are going to be more trouble than I'd originally expected?"

Rose shrugged. "I haven't a clue," she said. "Tell me about Soul Chalices. What are they, what good are they? And can I stop being one if I want?"

* * *

Mephisto put aside his niggling doubts and crossed his legs, sitting on a cushion of air. "No, you can't stop being one. Soul Chalices are always paired with Soul Stealers. Sometimes the two are within the confines of a family, but they are always within the same continent. It's not unusual for them to target each other, if they figure it out."

"I was told the legends were lost in time. That no one remembers what a Soul Chalice or a Soul Stealer really is, other than tall tales for a stormy night."

Mephisto watched the pretty vessel. When he tried, he could see the partial soul of the one she loved. He searched for hers to no avail. The thought she might be missing her soul distracted him to the point he barely knew what he was saying. "A chalice is what?" If only he had his own soul. He'd been searching for millennia.

Rose pressed her lips together. "A chalice is a cup."

"Or to use an older word, a vessel. In your case, you are a vessel for needy souls. Sometimes the souls need a rest outside of their bodies; sometimes they need healing. At other times they need a hiding place while waiting for the right escort. You provide these functions. Soul Stealers, however, steal souls to gain power. They hang onto them until their own soul turns black. When a Soul Stealer dies, the souls they've collected just disappear. They don't go either to Hell or Heaven, or Purgatory. They are wiped away and can never be reincarnated. Unless a Soul Chalice, or another Soul Stealer, happens to be nearby."

"And when I die?"

Mephisto shook himself back to awareness. Rose's face was tight with panic. "When you die, the souls you may carry at the time all go to heaven, along with yours. Simple, really, the job you do. Except, my dear, your soul seems to be missing."

He watched as the knowledge acted like a punch to her heart. She gasped a little for breath, and took a couple staggered steps toward him. "My soul is missing?" She gripped his arm.

He shrugged apologetically. "It seems so."

"Satine. Damn her."

"I will tell you that if a Soul Stealer can steal a Soul Chalice's soul, it takes divine intervention for the Soul Chalice to be able to harbor souls. And from the looks of it, you've had that divine intervention." He patted her hand. "Soul Chalices cannot end up in Purgatory. I'm not entirely sure how you got there without a soul," he mused.

"What do I get from the whole thing? I don't understand."

"You get wisdom, and time. Your lifespan grows longer with every soul you hold, no matter for how long. Which is good, since you're bound to the tribred down there," he added, chuckling.

"But why would living a long time matter? And what do you mean, bound to him?" Rose pushed the hair out of her eyes. "Explain it to me. But slowly, because I'm still panicked about Satine having my soul."

Mephisto looked at her, and a small part of him fell in love. She had so much potential. "It's called the tribred effect. Tribreds live a long time, longer than your average human. You, as a Soul Chalice, will also live a long life. You don't have to have a soul to survive, but it makes life easier. That, by the way, was why you fell into drugs. You almost didn't have a choice.

"As for you and Gabriel, the two of you are well matched and you are not for me, more's the pity." He did a back flip and landed on his feet. "And now it's time to rejoin the living. Shall we?" He crooked his arm to her, wanting her touch.

Rose stepped back, alarm crossing her face. "Wait. Gabriel doesn't want me. And I'm not totally sure I want him, not in a bound-to-him way. That sounds, um, rather final."

Mephisto's heart clenched, a painful jolt as he remembered his own once-human life. "Oh, it is most definitely final. I advise you to go ahead and let yourself fall in love with him. It won't hurt you, as Gabriel is almost there himself. If a bound pair is separated before their time, the loss to them both is incalculable. I can't believe that will happen to you."

Rose sniffed. "That's easy for you to say. You've never had your heart broken."

"You think not?" Mephisto rubbed his chest absently. "My heart was broken a thousand times before your great-grandfather walked the earth." He let the pain swim through him and managed to give her a smile. "We really must leave.

~ ☾ ~

They're getting worried about you."

"You haven't told me whether or not you'll help me kill the vampire," she protested. "Or how I'm supposed to get my soul back."

Mephisto gave her another half-hearted smile. "We'll have to leave it to Fate," he said. "She seems to be firmly in your corner, though, so I wouldn't worry too much about it. Now it's time to get you back where you belong. Gabriel worries about you. Come.

* * *

Mephisto took Rose's hand and pointed toward the hospital bed. It seemed to Rose that they just floated through the walls and down into the room. She settled back into her body and sighed in relief. No pain this time around. She felt nothing but a nice floaty sensation.

Rose's floating came to an abrupt end.

There you are. I've been looking for you.

She frowned as Satine's voice eased into her consciousness. *I don't want to talk to you.*

I know. But here we are. You will bring the Caine clan to me. Satine's voice made Rose colder than ever. She shivered slightly. The scent of lilies wafted in the air, mingled with a faintly familiar antiseptic flavor.

The hell I will. Why would I do that?

Because I want you to. Because you want to please me. Because I will kill you, and them, if you don't. Reasons enough?

I suppose. Warmth stole through her hand, and she recognized it as Gabriel. Gabriel held it, kissed it, and slowly the warmth pushed away the chill of Satine. Rose reached a careful tendril of thought toward Gabriel, pulled him in.

Good. Bring the Caines to me tonight. I owe them for killing Chazz.

I'm in the hospital, Satine. Not sure I'll even be walking by tonight. Chazz wasn't exactly a saint. Rose opened her eyes, looked at Gabriel and tightened her hand in his as she waited for Satine's answer.

And now he's dead. You will pay for that. I'll contact you.

~ ☾ ~

Keep your mind open— or you will regret it. I'll make sure of it.

The contact broke off and Rose shuddered. She searched Gabriel's face. "Gabriel. I'm so cold." At the look on his face she let out an exasperated sigh. "I'm not asking to have your baby. I'm just asking you to warm me up."

Relief filled her as he climbed up into the bed and held her close to his chest.

"How did you do that?"

"What?" She pressed herself closer to him.

"How did you bring me in to hear the conversation between the two of you? That's not supposed to happen. And it didn't hurt."

Rose shrugged. "I don't know. I just thought I should. Figured it would save some time."

"Damn Satine for using you."

"There's more," she said, her teeth chattering. "Somehow, she stole my soul. That's why I got into the drugs. The sex. It was almost inevitable."

His arms tightened around her briefly. "It wasn't your fault. That must be comforting."

"Yes. I'm coming to terms with it." She breathed him in, snuggled deeper into his arms. "'With understanding comes forgiveness.' Who said that?"

"I'm not sure. You know, if I had resisted her at the beginning, you wouldn't be in this position." Regret laced his voice.

She smiled against his chest, inhaled the spicy scent that was his. "She is a Soul Stealer and I am a Soul Chalice. Our story started long ago. We were bound to meet again, bound to try to neutralize each other."

"I guess so. We'll have to write the manual."

"Ha ha. So when are you springing me from this place?"

"Soon. Oh, and I got you a present. A cell phone. To help you feel safe."

"Thanks." No one had ever cared about Rose's safety before. The surprise brought a wave of emotion with it. "I've never had a cell phone."

~ ☾ ~

"Oh please, don't cry," Gabriel said. "Tissue. Where's tissue?"

"On the tray I think." Rose wiped at her cheeks and laughed at the mild panic on Gabriel's face as he handed her a tissue. "It's okay. Happy tears."

He cleared his throat. "All our phone numbers are in there."

"That's good." She settled against him again and thrilled at the sound of his heartbeat, slow and steady beneath her ear. If they were truly bonded as Mephisto had said, that meant she had a future. What did being bonded mean, anyway? Was it a demon thing, or a Fae thing?

If they were bonded, could the two of them, wounded as they were, have a good life?

"Stop thinking. Start resting," he ordered.

"See if you can get me out of here, and I'll rest," she promised.

He sighed then, folded her against him and rocked her. "Just give me a moment, here. Just a moment."

Maybe she should take Mephisto's advice after all and just allow herself to fall in love with him. He cared, she knew that much. She could feel the care and concern pouring out of him, wrapping her as closely as his arms held her.

Gabriel's heart thudded against her cheek, a comforting sound. After a few minutes of silence, he sighed and shifted to look into her eyes. "When we leave here, I'll be taking you to the old homestead like we planned."

"The place you grew up?" Rose brightened at the thought. "I am glad."

"My mother used to plant these wonderful gardens, or so I'm told. Gideon tried to keep them alive but only managed in the orchard, and what he called the secret garden. I'll show it to you," he added. "If you'll agree to rest while you're there."

"I'll rest if you're nearby." She stirred, brushing the hair out of his face. She placed her hand on his scarred cheek. "Thank you. For everything. I'm glad you're here."

She saw the pain in his eyes as he moved her hand from his face and kissed her palm. "I know," he said, and drew her

~ ☾ ~

close again. "I'm glad to be here. But Rose," and he hesitated.

She shook her head, not wanting to hear it. "Gabriel. Let's just enjoy, okay? We need the physical connection right now, and there's a lot to do before we get to the future. So let's don't worry about it. I'm a big girl. Now, tell me what I looked like, when I was all demony."

He kissed the top of her head and cleared his throat. "You have wings."

"I do not." Delighted, she pushed away to look him in the eyes. "I can fly?"

"Nah. They're just little girly wings. And a couple of cute horns, too. And you've got sexy spots all over. Kind of like a leopard, only orangey and brownish."

Her eyes alight, she grinned. "Really? Do tell."

Gabriel spun a tale of her demon self that kept her laughing until her sides ached. She watched him with a smile in her heart. According to Mephisto, she and Gabriel made a good match. It remained to be seen if their match was strong enough to defeat Satine.

~ ☾ ~

Chapter Fifteen

Rose watched with wide eyes as the gate opened silently. Hedges on both sides turned the long driveway into an escape from the neighborhood around them.

The car followed the curve until the hedges dropped away and revealed a two-story yellow and white ranch house. To Rose's family-starved eyes, it looked like a home, with a wide front porch, windows open to the summer breeze, white curtains billowing. Two buildings winged out from the center of the house, giving it a sprawling, welcoming look. Elm trees planted nearby provided shade. Gabriel pulled up and parked next to a perfectly kept Mustang in a bright blue. Gabriel grunted.

"A '68 Mustang. Must be Kellan's."

Gabriel had pulled away from her, gotten distant the minute they'd left the hospital. The drive out had been quiet and Rose hadn't known how to make things easy again between them. Now though, the house consumed her thoughts.

"Oh, *Gabriel*." Rose put her hand on his arm, squeezed. "It's beautiful."

Gabriel looked at the unraked leaves, the peeling paint. "It has been. Kellan is waiting for us. Come on." They got out and Rose was hit with the scent of orange blossom. She felt the grin take over her face.

"Orange trees?"

"There's a citrus grove out back, a part of the original parcel of land. The whole San Fernando Valley used to be citrus groves and farms, way back when. My mother redesigned parts of the land long before I was born." Gabriel

~ ☾ ~

shrugged. "I think we have photos of the place before she got her hands on it, but I'm not sure."

Rose approached the front door with curiosity. This, then, is where the Caine matriarch reigned over her tribe. This is where she gave birth to Gabriel, and where she died. What of Maria Therese still lingered in this house?

As she crossed the threshold, she felt a warmth, a welcome, as though a loving spirit inhabited the house. Not that she believed Maria Therese herself was here. Rather, it was a house that had seen much love and harbored the expectation of more love and laughter, to come.

She turned to Gabriel, slipped her hand in his. "Gorgeous. Hardwood floors, hand painted borders—how long has this house been in your family?"

"The original burned down. This house was built in the nineteen twenties on the bones of the first one, and expanded through the years." He squeezed her hand, let her go and shoved both his hands into his pockets. "Justin would know more details. Caines have owned the land for a couple hundred years, if not longer. It's the largest parcel still left in the west Valley."

"Hey guys. Come on out and give me a hand," called Kellan.

"It sounds like Kel's in the back. After you," he said.

Rose found her way to the back door through the cheerful kitchen, fascinated with the painted vines and flowers that bordered the top of the wall. "Who did all the paint work? It's beautiful."

"I'm not sure. I'd forgotten about it," he added. "You know how you live with something and then just stop seeing it?" He shrugged. "It's like that for me, all the hand paint work." He opened the back door. "Come on."

A brick patio spread out in front of them with a patch of straggly grass beyond it. Further back sat the citrus grove, easily fifty trees filling the space between the patio and what looked like guesthouses or barns at the back of the property. "This is gorgeous." Rose turned in a circle, caught her balance. "Absolutely gorgeous."

~ ☾ ~

"It needs work. That part never seems to change." Kellan came toward them. Rose stifled a giggle. Straw hat, plaid shirt, battered jeans and work boots all turned him into a farm hand.

"You gonna plant the crops, Farmer Brown?" she said, letting loose her giggle.

Kellan grinned back. "Nope. And there aren't any cows to milk, either, but I do have livestock. Come see."

They followed him to one of the outbuildings. What had looked like a barn turned out to be a large, two-story storage shed crammed with boxes and furniture. Kellan led them to a corner where, burrowed into a covered couch, was a mama cat and her three scrawny babies.

"Oh! Oh, the poor thing," cooed Rose. She knelt beside the mama and let the cat sniff her hand. It gave her a weak lick and put her head down again.

"It needs food. And water. We should move them, too." Rose turned to the men with a hopeful smile. "Don't you think?"

"Ah, maybe not," Gabriel said. Rose wilted in disappointment.

"I've already made an appointment with a local vet."

"They're probably hopping with fleas." Gabriel kept well back from the cat and her kits. "I hate flea bites."

"One year, we had four dogs and Gideon didn't keep up on the flea stuff. Gabriel's dog had them worst and he was covered in the things. Had to have allergy shots because of it," Kellan confided to Rose.

"Kel," warned Gabriel.

"Which is why they can't come into the house until they've been de-fleaed," he continued.

Rose touched the kittens, played with their paws. "Look. Look! They have six toes! Can you *imagine?* These are magic cats!"

"Come on, Rose. Kellan has the cats handled, and you promised me you'd rest."

Reluctantly, Rose let Gabriel draw her away from the cats and back through the yard to the house.

~ ☾ ~

Kellan walked on her other side, putting a hand out as she swayed with tiredness. "I've got the perfect room for you," he said. He grinned at Gabriel. "Our room. It's perfect for her. Don't ask—you'll see."

They walked into the kitchen and Gabriel automatically took the back stairway to the second floor. Their room sat right at the top of the stairs.

Kellan ushered Rose into the room and gestured to the ceiling. "Look familiar?"

Rose stared. "It's a spiral. Oh! Beautiful." The words were written in English, the lettering a gothic style, the colors in soothing shades of blue and gray. "What does it say?"

"Lie on the bed and see if you can figure it out," he said.

Rose lay down and looked up. "So beautiful," she murmured, and yawned. "This is such a peaceful house." She relaxed into the mattress as sleep swept over her.

* * *

Gabriel closed the door to the bedroom and turned to Kellan. "Do you realize what that is?"

"Yeah. A sleep spell, or something. I told you I had the best night of sleep ever last night. Aunt Maria must have painted it. It still works. Neat, huh?"

He looked at his cousin thoughtfully. "This was the room you and I shared, until you left."

"Yeah." Kellan met Gabriel's eyes. "She painted it for you. For us, really, because I'd shown up on the scene before you were born, but she'd always planned for us to share."

"Do all the bedrooms have spirals on them?"

"Not just the bedrooms. They're *every*where."

Gabriel frowned. "I don't remember any spirals growing up."

"Neither do I, but that doesn't mean they weren't just there," said Kellan. "What we need is a witch. And before you say anything, I've already called Justin and Maggie. They should be here soon. But I will say, I don't think it's a coincidence that Rose has a spiral on her belly."

"So what do we do until the witch gets here?" Gabriel stuck his hands in his pockets and rocked back on his heels.

~ ☾ ~

"There's lots of work to be done outdoors. I've got garden gloves and trash bags ready on the back porch. Or, there's wood to chop. Should burn well after all the drying time it's had. If you're not above doing manual labor."

"After you, buddy. After you."

* * *

"You're gonna have to put your anger on hold, Magdalena. Tell me everything you know about Kendall Sorbis, and tell me right now." Justin downshifted as traffic slowed. He scowled at the witch in the seat next to him. She'd worn a jumpsuit of army green with a zipper down the middle, the rip-stop fabric outlining every part of her body. Justin did his best not to look.

"I don't have to tell you anything." Maggie's voice was like ice.

"Let me put it this way. The Weres said Kendall has opened a portal to the Chaos Plane. Maybe more than one portal, and is enticing demons this way. Do you really want to work for someone like that?"

He waited while she thought, trying not to breathe in her spicy scent. He sent his window down for a blast of hot air.

"I don't work for him. We used to be lovers, but that was years ago. I got thoroughly burned." Her words were quiet and edged with pain. "I picked up the phone in his office because I was there as a favor to his wife. Looking for any sign of his whereabouts. He's run off," she added. "He left his bride of two years high and dry."

Justin narrowed his eyes. "Why did you tell me he was on his anniversary trip?"

"Because that's what I was told to tell anyone who inquired."

"Any ideas about why he ran off?" Justin glanced at her. She'd bitten her bottom lip and her eyes were squeezed shut.

"He was wanted for questioning about a murder, but when the cops came to his door a couple of days ago, he'd already split. His young wife found a note protesting his innocence. He's apparently searching for the real murderer."

"What do you think?"

~ ☾ ~

"He's capable of it." The words were cool and without malice. "He's got a curiosity gene a mile wide. He likes to...experiment. Death—causing it, or seeing it—never bothered him."

"Some lover."

"Like you said. We all make mistakes. Such as the multitude of mistakes you've made recently."

"I still don't understand why you're pissed off." He bit the words off without looking at her.

"Rose disappeared from my house. I'm frantic with worry about her, but you don't respond to my phone calls. I call the office and you don't even have an assistant to tell me what's going on. Damn it all to hell, Justin. You left me in charge of Rose's safety, and then you don't tell me what happened to her. That, plus everything else that happened in the past twenty four hours that you just now told me about, gives me every reason to be angry. You ass." The look she flashed at him made Justin grateful she didn't turn him into one.

"I called you eventually," he pointed out, and winced when she let out a short scream of frustration. He heard her quick breathing, her struggle for control. When she finally spoke, her voice was tight.

"Justin, I know I'm not a Caine. I understand we have a hate/hate relationship. But I'm getting close to Rose and consider her a friend. I've been a part of this case almost since the beginning, and you're shutting me out. How would you feel if the shoe were on the other foot?" she demanded.

"Okay. I see your point. But it's not like we had time to give you a jingle. 'Hey Maggie, yeah, come on over, we're having a bar fight.' Be reasonable," he added.

"When you got home last night, you could have called. When you were at the hospital, you could have called. I would have called you," she said, and turned to face the side window. "In fact, I did call you. And boy was that a mistake."

"Look." Justin shifted gears, exiting the freeway at Victory Boulevard going west, and continued. "I'm sorry, okay? It's not that I thought you couldn't handle what was happening. It's just that everything happened so fast."

~ ☾ ~

"Yeah, pull my other leg," she scoffed.

Justin grimly kept his thoughts off her legs and her other luscious body parts. "I was trying to keep you safe," he bit out.

"And that made you happy," she shot back. "Obviously, since you're just bubbling over with joy."

"What does my being happy have to do with anything?" he said, bewildered.

She tossed her hands up in the air, barely missing his face, and looked away. "Apparently nothing, since you were so *un*happy about having to see me again."

"Oh, I get it. You're angry that I kissed you." Justin grinned. "Now it makes sense."

"What? That's not why I'm angry," she grumbled, and crossed her arms.

"Oh, that's right. You're not angry that I kissed you. You're angry that you kissed me back. Don't pout. It's not attractive," he advised and turned the car into the drive. The gates stood open, so he eased the Jag down the long drive.

"I'm not pouting. I'm thinking up ways to torture you slowly before I kill you."

Justin laughed. "Good luck with that." He pulled the car to a stop in front of the house. "We're here." He got out of the car and leaned against the hood, just looking at the place and remembering.

He heard Maggie get out and slam the door behind her. Justin turned to look at her and caught his breath again at her profile. She was too damned sexy for his peace of mind.

She wavered a little, put a hand out to steady herself against the car. Her eyes were glassy. Concerned, Justin moved to stand in front of her, breaking her view of the house. "Maggie? You okay?"

Maggie blinked, and a tear rolled down her cheek. "Justin."

"Hey." He wiped the tear away. "It's okay. The house hits some people like that." He leaned against the car next to her, studying the house that had been his home, giving her time to pull herself together.

"I used to come here on the anniversary of her death. After, I mean. After Dad left and we closed up the house." He sighed.

~ ☾ ~

"It always caught at me. The house looked like it was waiting. And I wasn't what it was waiting for."

She turned to face him, their bodies mere inches apart. "That must have hurt."

"Yeah." He shot her a crooked grin. ""Yeah, it did. But the inside—you've got to see the inside." He grabbed her hand and pulled her toward the front door. "It's the best."

The door stood open. As they stepped inside, a hint of incense seemed to welcome them.

Maggie looked around, her eyes wide. "Spells are everywhere. Did you ever notice? Everywhere I look, I see a spell of one sort or another. It's absolutely, breathtakingly beautiful."

"This way. This was my favorite room." Justin tugged her over to the hearth room, a huge room anchored by a fireplace at one end and three large windows to the front of the house.

The fireplace was big, in keeping with the rest of the room, clad in river rock with a black slate hearth and a thick, wide mantel of black oak polished to a shine.

Over it was painted a tree, rich in detail, thick with leaves. It looked alive, and for a moment Justin could swear he heard the rustle of the leaves in the summer breeze.

Maggie stepped closer to Justin. "This is amazing, absolutely amazing. Did those leaves just move?" She left his side to step up on the hearth and look at the painting.

Justin shook his shoulders and took a breath. "Maggie." She turned to look at him, and their eyes locked. Energy rose between them, hung in the air.

"Hi guys. Maggie, we need a witch. Come upstairs—there are a couple spirals I want you to look at."

Justin didn't know if he should hit Kellan or hug him. He turned from Maggie in relief.

"Kellan. The whole house has spells painted in it. Maybe we shouldn't be here. I'm not getting an overly friendly vibe from it."

"I know. It's waiting. Since Gabriel's back for a while at least, and I'll be in and out for a few months, we decided it was time to open the place up. But it's not like we're going to paint over anything. We need your opinion, your expertise. And your decoding abilities," he added. "Come on."

Maggie sent Justin a hot look before following Kellan upstairs. "The spells I've seen so far have been simple ones. Spells of love, faith in family, and protection, mostly."

"Why are they here?" The three of them stopped on the landing, with the two men looking to Maggie.

"I'm supposed to know?" Maggie gestured. "I'm thinking, okay?"

Kellan sighed. "Okay. Look in this room, up at the ceiling. And then I want to show you the one in the master bedroom."

Maggie looked into the room where Rose slept. Justin heard her swift intake of breath then she was out the door again. "A sleep spiral. A very strong one, I might add," she said, yawning. "Next?"

Kellan led the way down the hall to the end of the wing, where the door stood open. A huge bed, bare of sheets, dominated the large room. Right over the bed someone had painted a wreath of roses and ivy.

Justin looked closer; entwined there in the foliage were runes. The design looked older there, different somehow from the other paintings he'd seen. He frowned at Maggie, who looked at him with wide eyes. She licked her lips, and panic crossed her face.

She fled the room.

Kellan looked to Justin with raised eyebrows. "What was that about?"

"Don't know. Let's find out, shall we?" The two men left the room, but Maggie wasn't in the hallway.

Justin shook his head. "I'll find her. You go do whatever it is you were going to do."

Kellan grinned. "You got your eyes on that, then?"

"Do you?" Justin frowned.

"Nah. She's pretty, but no pushover. She's smart, plus, you know. A witch. I like my women a lot less complicated." Kellan clapped his brother on the back. "Enjoy yourself."

"Yeah. Whatever." Justin shook his head and went downstairs. He found Maggie standing in the great room,

~ ☾ ~

deep in thought.

"Well?"

Maggie jumped. "Well." She shook her head, focused. "Like I said, a strong sleep spiral on the ceiling in Rose's bedroom. It's mostly calming, protective, with reassurances of safety and happiness while encouraging sleep. The one in the master is different." She blew out a breath.

Justin looked at her quizzically. "Something wrong?"

Maggie grimaced. "It's—there's a strong sexual pull to that particular spiral," she said, and wiped her hands on her thighs. "Sex and fertility and deep, abiding love. I'm dead certain you don't want me yanking you in there for a hot and sweaty bout of sex. I mean, I don't want to yank you in there. I mean...damn it."

Justin grinned, and his grin got even wider when she flushed. "Never mind. I understand your meaning."

"Okay. When I walked through the kitchen, I found more spirals. Ones of blessings. Protection. Love of family, love of brothers. Respect. That kind of thing."

Justin frowned. "I never thought she manipulated us like this."

"It's not manipulation, exactly. It's more of a wish, a hope, or protection at its most basic."

"And the sleep spiral? Rose took a look at it and was out."

"That can happen. I'll study it closer. My guess is it depends upon the mood of the person who looks at it. Someone who needs sleep, needs to feel peaceful, will find what he needs in that room. Someone who isn't as needy won't be as affected by it. But that's all speculation at this point."

"Hmmm." Justin thought of the two men who had slept in that room as boys. One the product of rape; the other tossed out by his mother. The spiral in that room made sense.

Maggie brought out her cell phone. "I'd like to take photos of every painting. I'll need to get my good camera from home, but I don't want to waste time and they really should be documented. I can use my phone, if you don't mind?" Her brown eyes had cooled and only mild interest showed there

~ ☾ ~

now.

"Not at all. Feel free. I'll be outside when you're ready to go." Justin watched as she went toward the kitchen. He didn't know if he preferred her hot and angry, or distantly polite. Both made him itchy.

He headed outside, glancing at his watch. Three o'clock. He huffed out a breath and followed the sound of voices around to the back. Kellan raked dead leaves from the overgrown bed of roses while Gabriel took out his excess energy on a pile of logs that needed to be split for firewood.

The rhythmic thunk of the axe, plus the soothing sounds of the rake, took Justin back in time and he looked about absently, as if expecting to see his father there, directing the other two. He shook his head at the fantasy and leaned against a sycamore tree.

"Now there's good, productive work for your idle hands," he called. Kellan shot him a grin over his shoulder, while Gabriel hefted his axe.

"There's another axe here. Join me," he said. "We'll race," he added, chuckling.

Justin eyed his younger brother. "Considering you're bigger than me, I'll pass on that, thanks. So, I've been thinking."

"Ah. Something new. Good for you," applauded Kellan.

"Smartass. What I want to know is, why did the demons leave? Why didn't they fight?"

Gabriel thunked the axe deep into a log and came over to Justin. "Perhaps they were just waiting for Dorothy to click her heels so they could go home?"

"You're both smartasses." Justin shook his head and grinned from one to the other. "Danny called, changed the meeting to midnight tonight. Are you both still in?"

Kellan snorted. "Of course."

"Couldn't keep me away."

"What about Rose?"

Gabriel frowned. "We'll keep her here. The house has enough protection. She'll be fine."

"I want Maggie here with her. She can do research," Justin

~ ☾ ~

said.

"That works, if she doesn't mind."

"Maggie will have to pick up clothes, being a girl. She can pick up food and stuff, too. And once she's back, you can join us." Justin looked up at Gabriel who leaned against the house.

"You guys should know Satine contacted Rose today in the hospital. Rose couldn't keep her out."

Kellan sent a disgusted look toward Gabriel. "And you're just now telling us?"

"First opportunity. Rose is supposed to hand the three of us over to Satine tonight."

Justin snorted. "Hell. No way is that going to happen."

"Of course not. We'll carry on as planned." Kellan sent a dark look toward Gabriel.

"Just checking. I'll give Maggie a heads-up. Maybe she can put an obscuring spell or something on Rose while she's here, to make it harder for Satine to find her."

Justin held up a hand. "I'll deal with the witch. You guys keep taking your sexual frustrations out on the gardens. Luckily there's a lot to do out here."

"Sure is," Gabriel retorted. "You'll be taking your turn at it."

"Dream on." Justin turned and went into the house.

* * *

"I'm not done taking pictures," Maggie protested as Justin marched her out of the house. "I need a couple more hours."

"You'll get them." He opened the passenger door of his Jag. "Right now, I need to get you to your car and your laptop. I need you to shop for food for a few days, and I need you to drive back out here to take care of Rose tonight while my family and I meet up with Danny. So please. Get in the car."

With a suspicious glare, she got in. "Why don't you want me at the meeting with the weres?"

"They aren't big on witches," he said. "I'm doing you a favor. Trust me."

"You're being overprotective. I can take care of myself. Let me go with you, and leave Rose to Gabriel."

"I need Gabriel with me. I'm asking you to guard Rose."

~ ☾ ~

Maggie lifted an eyebrow. "Why do I get the sense of being railroaded?"

Justin turned to her and pinned her with a glare. "Look. Satine will try to use Rose to get to Gabriel. If I could be in two places at once, I'd be guarding Rose myself. I am asking you to do that for me. Would I do that if I didn't think you capable?" He stared her down.

"No," she allowed. "Okay. Got it."

He started the car. "Good. You can take as many pictures as you want, do all sorts of research while you're there. As far as I'm concerned, as soon as Gabriel arrives back to the place after the meeting, you can go." He pulled out and headed down the long drive.

"At least tell me where you'll be. What you're doing tonight."

Justin swung onto the 405 Freeway going south and merged into the slow-moving traffic. "We're meeting with the Weres at our office in Santa Monica at ten to discuss the, ah, disposal of Satine and Vlad."

"You're going in tonight?"

"Not necessarily," he said. "We're considering all the options."

"I hope you have Doc Cavanaugh on your speed dial. I have a feeling you're going to need her."

Justin pushed aside the thought. "We need you to keep alert. Try to stay with Rose, if at all possible. You two should be okay in the house tonight. It's not like the neighbors are so close they can see the house. No one will know you're there."

Maggie sniffed. "Just keep me informed. You did such a lousy job of it earlier."

Justin flashed a grin. "I could always dip into your mind." *Like this. Do you want me to message you* this *way?*

Maggie stiffened beside him. "No! Stay out of my head. Don't do that unless there's no option. Got it? Just text me, or something."

Justin turned onto the southbound freeway, satisfied.

* * *

Rose sat in a tree swing in the citrus grove. "It's so

beautiful here."

Maria Therese smiled. "This house is filled with love. You should stay here until you and Gabriel are ready for your own home."

"Gabriel is fighting me. Fighting what might be between us."

"He is fighting with himself, child. He hasn't yet learned to accept his entire heritage. Instead he picks and chooses." Maria Therese shrugged. "If he doesn't learn to use all of himself, he will fail."

"Die, you mean."

"Perhaps. There is more than one way to fail." Maria Therese reached out and took Rose's hands in her own. "You do matter to him. But he is afraid to love."

"He thinks he's incapable of love." Rose rested her head on Maria Therese's hands. "I am so angry at Satine, at my own part in Gabriel's problems. I'm afraid we'll lose."

"Dear child. Don't let fear stop you from doing what needs to be done." Maria Therese's voice filled with emotion. "You cannot stop events from unfolding. You both must move forward. Have faith in each other. Gabriel will remember who he is in the end."

"But are we going to win? Can you promise me that we win in the end?"

Maria Therese smiled. "I haven't been shown the end. But I do know that if you don't go into this battle, you will all lose more than you can know. None of you will be able to run from the fate that will await you, if you refuse to act. Gather your courage. Do what must be done." She moved as if to leave.

"Wait!" Rose left the swing to stand beside her. "Just tell me one thing. The demon on me—it seems to drain me too much to be useful. How do I get around that? How can I use it and push through the weakness that comes?"

The older woman looked at her steadily. "Mephisto is drawn to you. He will give you more than he will take, in the end. I know it's dangerous, but I deemed it necessary to use him. You need his strength, his power, to do what must be done."

~ ☾ ~

Rose reeled. "You put him on me?"

"A bit extreme," she admitted. "He didn't seem to mind at the time, and it seems to have been effective, so far. Now, trust yourself. You will have the strength you need, when you need it. Remember to call on him for help. Though he is no friend, he is not your enemy, either. Mephisto will make all the difference in the fight to come." Abruptly Maria Therese gathered Rose in a swift embrace. "Be strong." And she was gone.

Rose opened her eyes, the scent of the citrus orchard slowly fading as she looked around at Gabriel's childhood room. She could have sworn she'd been talking to Maria Therese, out there in the orchard.

Rose yawned and gazed up at the spiral on the ceiling. Pretty. What did it say? As she followed the words, once again she succumbed to the lure of sleep.

~ ☾ ~

Chapter Sixteen

Two Caines sat opposite the three weres of the Santa Monica Preserve.

"Where's Justin?" Danny shot an irritated look out the window where the sounds of nightlife were diminishing.

Gabriel followed his gaze and pushed down any worry. "He'll be here any second. So, what's the plan? Now that you have your women back," he added.

"You are right, we need to take out the club and all the vampires. Tonight." Danny Roush paced between the conference table and the door. "They need to pay for what they did to our women."

"We agree. We do. But we can't go anywhere near Twisted tonight." Gabriel put up his hands before the weres could protest. "It's not that we don't want to," he added. "Rose has also been compromised by Satine. She's under a compulsion to bring all of us to Satine tonight. So getting anywhere near the place is suicide for us."

"What we were figuring is to go in at sunrise tomorrow," Kellan said. "The vampires' powers will be weakening. And they lost a good dozen demons today. Unless they have more than we think they do, they'll be even more vulnerable at first light."

Danny studied him. "Do you think they'll bring in more demons?"

"That depends on where they got these. If, as rumor has it, they're bringing them through from the Chaos Plane, they won't have time to re-staff tonight. My guess is they'll flee. Find another playground." Gabriel shrugged. "But it's hard to say. Satine isn't the most stable vamp around."

~ ☾ ~

"Tell me about Rose," Danny said. "She's a fire demon? I was surprised to come around the corner and see her standing there, tossing fire."

"Hitchhiker from her time in Purgatory," said Gabriel. "Possibly up to three months ago."

Danny looked impressed. "She's held on for a long time, then. Will she be safe tonight?"

"Yes. She has a bodyguard. A witch," Kellan added, his voice dour.

Danny frowned. "I didn't know you worked with witches."

Gabriel sent a glance toward Kellan who shut up. "So far, she's been helpful."

A smile tugged at Danny's full lips as he looked from one to the other. "Your family is—most unusual. That you're willing to work with both witches and wolves is admirable."

"I suppose so. Kellan, give us our bomb options." Gabriel, uncomfortable, turned to Kellan. "When we do go in, it would be nice to blow the place to smithereens."

"If we set off four charges one level down, that should pretty much take the building down."

"Risking any people on the streets. But we have an alternative," blurted out Favor.

"Sig? What's your alternative?" Danny regarded his second with a raised brow.

"We go in. Satine doesn't know Favor or I. We go in, clear the place of humans, kill the vampires, and get out."

Gabriel steepled his fingers, shooting a glance at Danny. "Simple, to the point."

"And stupid," Kellan ground out. "Every vampire there will know you for what you are."

"Exactly," shouted Sig. He stood and punched the air with his fist. "We hide in plain sight. Doing anything else will get many killed."

Kellan gave a snort of disgust.

"Sig. Sit," ordered Danny.

"Kellan," Gabriel said, his voice quiet.

The two men bristled. Kellan turned away, went to sit on the far end of the conference table. Sig leaned against a wall

~ ☾ ~

and stared at the rest, his chin thrust into the air.

"So bombs aren't going to be viable," Gabriel concluded.

"They *are* viable," Kellan argued. "If we're going in during the day, it's all good. Going in at night is more difficult. We'd need to get the bombs in position and clear the place of humans." Kellan tapped his fingers on the polished table.

The sound reminded Gabriel of the passing time. Where was Justin?

Danny shrugged. "If we can get both Satine and Vlad out of the way?"

"Then we have a better chance of slipping in with little notice. We just need to figure out how to detain the two of them."

Kellan interrupted. "Wait. The lower we go, the less precise the bomb has to be. Or if we do several small charges, and add fire, I think it will do enough damage to destroy the building without taking the entire building down, or harming anyone on the surrounding streets. The sonics shouldn't cause that much damage. It may take out a few windows in the neighborhood." He shrugged.

Sig sighed. "What is the point, if we don't kill any vampires? We need a big enough bomb. I've had training," he added, eyeing Kellan. "I could help."

"Do we know *why* the J'aadt demons didn't defend their territory?" Kellan swiveled around on the table to look at Danny. Gabriel caught their surprised glances. "Remember? They all up and left. We practically waded through the lot of them to get to you guys."

Chagrined, Danny shook his head. "J'aadt demons can be bought. If they weren't paid, they'd walk."

"Perhaps a fire demon was more than they bargained for. J'aadts don't like fire. If Rose tossed a fireball at one of them and it went poof, the rest would clear out." Gabriel glanced to the door, expecting Justin.

"J'aadt demons don't like fire any more than vampires do. That is the most likely interpretation, I agree," Danny said.

"Where is Justin? He should have been here an hour ago." Kellan looked to Gabriel. "I can't reach him. Can you?"

~ ☾ ~

Justin? Where are you? At the lack of response, an icy shiver trickled down Gabriel's back. He shook his head and looked to Danny. "Have there been repercussions from the loss of the were tiger?"

"Not yet. Rumor has it he hooked up with Satine a few years ago after being kicked out of his own pack."

"So only Satine will be the injured party." Gabriel looked toward his brother. Alerted by the tension in his shoulders, Gabriel cleared his throat. "Kellan? What's up?"

"Vampires." He turned to his brother, his eyes whirling iridescent gold. "They've got Justin. There," he added, and looked out the window.

Gabriel could easily see across the shopping mall to the building opposite them. There, spread-eagled, two stories off the ground, was Justin.

His head lolled to one side. A vampire held his right arm and leg, another vamp had his left arm and leg. They hovered, grinning right at the group in the window.

Gabriel swore a quiet oath.

Kellan put a hand on his brother's shoulder in sympathy. "Open to her."

"No." His eyes blazing, he glared back. "You don't know what you're asking."

"It's the only way we'll find out what she wants."

"She wants Rose. I'm not sacrificing Rose for Justin. And I'm sure as hell not sacrificing Justin for Rose."

Let me in, Gabriel. Satine's words sliced deeper than usual in his mind. With a roar, Gabriel dropped into a chair and clutched his head.

"She wants in," he gasped.

His golden eyes gleaming, Danny looked at Kellan. "We could take down the club since she is here. She's here, and her demons are gone. I'm thinking we go boom, if..."

Kellan grinned. "I have some smaller bombs in the car. Just in case," he added. "My car is a '68 Mustang. Electric blue. Take the back stairs out of here. It empties out into the alley, which backs into garage number four. My car is on the second level, you can't miss it." He tossed Sig the keys. "Bring

~ ☾ ~

it back here when it's over. You can handle it?"

Sig jingled the keys and grinned. "I can handle both the bombs and the car. When you see fire in the sky, you'll know we've succeeded."

"Take the place down," Gabriel ground out.

"Go. Now!" Kellan moved to Gabriel's side as the weres swiftly left the room.

"Talk to her. I'm with you, Gabriel. I'll do what I can, just don't let her in. I'm not as good as Justin, but..." He put his hands on his brother's shoulders as Gabriel opened the connection up between him and Satine.

Satine. What are you going to do to Justin?

Nothing. If you cooperate. The tension in her mental voice added to the pain in Gabriel's head.

What do you want? The pain lessened, and Gabriel was grateful for Kellan. He took a breath, focused mentally on Satine and saw her pacing in front of their office door.

You know what I want. Your soul. Forever. Come to me, Gabriel, she said, and her voice turned seductive. The pain eased and pleasure filled him. *Be with me. Keep me safe.* Her voice lightened, and more and more she sounded like Rose. *Let me in, Gabriel, hold me. I need you. I love you,* she whispered in Rose's voice.

Rose? Yes. Come in. Come to me, he answered, desperate, and at Satine's crow of triumph, the spell she'd woven shattered.

He gripped his head. "She's coming. Damn bitch."

"Well." Kellan wiped the sweat from his forehead. "I caught some of that. She tricked you into thinking she was Rose. You didn't have much option."

"You can't stay." Gabriel dared his brother to contradict him.

"I know." Kellan sighed. "Ready to go out the window?"

"No. I've got to stay here. Try to detain her, give the weres their chance."

"Too bad," Kellan said and, opening the second story window, he perched there. "Don't be long." And he jumped.

The scent of lilies grew strong as Gabriel moved to the

~ ☾ ~

window.

"Gabriel," and he turned, his back to the opening.

Satine stood in the doorway, dressed in black leather, her dark red hair curling down below her waist. A whip curled in her hand. Her lips shone electric red.

"Satine," he said. "Always dressed like a cliché. Why do you have Justin?"

She blinked. "Insurance. I need him. I need you. I want you. Can't you feel how much I want you? You took everything from me. My tiger. My demons. Now I get you in return." Her need pulsed between them. He took a step backward, bumped into the wall when Rose's voice burbled in his brain.

Gabriel. Just checking in with you. I'm awake, and Maggie and I are going to eat junk food and watch episodes of NCIS until you get home. Gabriel?

Relief filled him, along with a sense of her energy. Refreshing. He took a breath in gratitude. *Rose, remind me to kiss you.* Gabriel looked Satine in the eye, took hold of the window frame.

"You don't need insurance, Satine. You need your head examined." He turned and dove out the window, doing a somersault in mid-air and landing on his feet.

Kellan was throwing rocks at the vampires holding Justin.

"How's it going down here?" Gabriel picked up a decorative rock from the planter at the side of the building, aimed, and hit a vampire right on the nose.

"Not bad. If we can get them both to let go of Justin, we can catch him when he drops."

"But we've got Satine on our tail," objected Gabriel. He threw another rock. A window shattered in the building opposite. "Oops."

"You have the Satine problem. I have the Justin problem. Whatever you do, don't let her get back to Twisted." Kellan threw two rocks, bam bam, and both vampires let go of Justin.

Surprised, Kellan watched as Justin fell, roused himself as Gabriel passed him. "Hurry up!"

They caught him, all three of them tumbling to the ground. Gabriel untangled himself from his brothers and stood ready

~ ☾ ~

to face Satine. The other two vampires had vanished the second they lost Justin.

Satine floated down from the window of their office. Her whip curled lazily in the air, a snap at the end warning the men that she knew how to use it.

Kellan, grab Justin and get the hell out of here. Go! Now! I'll be back, little brother. Kellan gathered up the smaller man and was soon out of sight.

Gabriel felt the adrenalin pound through his system, knew his eyes had turned to full demon. His vision grew sharper in the dark as he watched Satine saunter toward him.

The night around them was preternaturally still. Heat rose from the pavement. Gabriel's powers surged through him.

"Stop," he said, and the word reverberated through the air. Surprised, Satine tried to take another step but found her feet wouldn't move.

"Gabriel. You are my creature. Come to me," she said, lifting her chin in command. The whip, restless in her hand, licked out at him but did not touch him. "Do as I say, and I will leave your precious little Rose alone."

"Like I'm supposed to trust a vampire," he scoffed. "Right. Don't think so."

"And demons are so pure," she mocked.

"Ah, but I'm not only a demon. I've been reminded that I have the gifts of another heritage to claim, to use."

"You are mostly demon. You can't hide that from me," Satine snapped. "Is your family trying to tell you that you're not what you are? I know. I can see. You are demon. Your soul is black, as black as mine was before I left it behind. It is withering inside me, and with every death you cause, your soul dies a little more. Ask *her*. She knows."

Despite his efforts, the doubt she raised crept in. He narrowed his eyes. "Every word from your mouth is a lie."

"Is it? Your soul is almost lost, and then you really will be the monster you fear. And she won't love you, a soulless beast." She looked at him, pensive in the dim light. "But I need you. I crave you, with or without a soul. You are a part of me, and have been ever since you used me and discarded me

~ ☾ ~

in your shack in the middle of nowhere. You think that is a lie?"

"You weren't real to me then. You were never real until that last night when you stepped out of my dream."

"When you refused my gift."

"Yes."

"Remember the *hunger*." She flicked the whip at him. It grazed his stomach, and at the whip's bite he was flung back into that dirty shack by the freeway.

She floated, just above his reach, her breasts, barely screened by white lace, taunting him. Her scent arousing him. He had reached for her, flung her to his pallet and plunged into her body. Used her to forget.

"This is bullshit." Dragging himself out of her illusion, he caught her hand just before she touched him.

"Be with me. Stay with me. We will rule the city, you and I, her voice purred in his mind. *Can you see it?*

Gabriel could. They would rule the dark. It wouldn't matter if he killed, as he wouldn't have a soul any more. He could be the beast he was born to be, and have the world at his feet if he so desired.

A breeze brought the scent of the sea down the mall. *Gabriel? When are you coming back?* Rose, looking for him again, keeping in touch. Opening to him.

Gabriel's head cleared from Satine's illusion and revulsion had him throwing her away from him. She screeched in dismay and rose from a crumpled heap, stalking after him, licking her lips. "Was any of that a lie?"

"All of it," he grated, stepping back. "Do you really want to fight me? Here, now?" He could feel his demon energy striving to burst free. Struggling for control, his voice grew deeper, husky. "You would lose."

Satine took on a helpless look, tears trembling on her lashes. She fell to his feet and grasped him by the legs. "I don't want to fight you. I want to join with you. I want you, Gabriel, only you. Come to me, be with me, please," she begged, and blood tears stood in her eyes.

"No." Digging deep within, a long-forgotten lesson

returned. Cool green energy surged up from the ground through his feet and spread throughout his body.

"No? No?" she sputtered. "You released my demons, stole my werewolves and killed my were tiger. You are all I have left, and you will obey me." She came to her feet, all righteous fury.

Not the slightest hint of compulsion reached him. He stood taller. "No, Satine. I won't. Tribreds aren't meant to be a vampire's plaything."

"You think denying me is freedom. You are wrong. Rose will be mine before the full moon," she hissed, and her eyes burned red. Satine leapt up at him, her mouth open, teeth gleaming in the night. Gabriel grabbed her arm and shoulder and, using her momentum, swung her off her feet and sent her skittering, belly down, over the asphalt. With a squeal she bounded to her feet and was suddenly behind him, her teeth at his neck. Gabriel froze.

"Naughty boy," she panted, and struck. But her teeth only grazed his skin as he flipped her over his head, smashing her to the ground and flipping her face down. Gabriel planted a foot in her back and she growled, a more feral sound than even the weres could make, and struggled to shift him off her. Strength born of all living plant life surged through him.

A distant howling came to them on the night's breeze, part terror and part pure joy. Satine struggled harder, added her voice to the cries in the night. With one immense effort, she rose up, causing Gabriel to do a back flip in the night. He landed on the balls of his feet, ready for a fight, but she left him without a backward glance, gone from sight in an instant.

The night filled with howling and fire lit up the sky to the east. Jubilee danced on the air.

Gabriel went cold. With Twisted taken down, where would Satine go? She'd find Rose and take her revenge. Fear built inside him as he ran.

* * *

Justin sat on the edge of the hospital bed and glared at Doc Cavanaugh. "I'm fine. I'm leaving." He struggled to clear his double vision without drawing her attention.

~ ☾ ~

Absently, she made a note on his chart. "No, you're not. Fine, that is. You're going to stay here until Kellan gets back, and then I might let you leave." She looked up at him, determination clear in her whiskey-gold eyes. "Don't push me," she warned. "You're deeply bruised. You haven't lost blood on the outside, but I wouldn't be surprised if you aren't peeing blood soon with the size of the hematomas near your kidneys."

He glowered at her, crossed his arms gingerly and focused on her face. If he looked anywhere else, the damned room tended to slip to one side. "Since when did you get to be a pain in the ass?"

"Since you keep showing up here with demons that need fixing," she said tartly. "Besides, I got my doctorate in being a pain in the ass. Didn't you know?" Megan Cavanaugh turned aside, picked up a syringe. "Roll up your sleeve."

Justin eyed her while he complied. "What the hell is that?"

She swabbed his arm with alcohol and tossed the swab into the trash. "Something to help you deal with the dizziness and double vision you've been experiencing since you got here," she said, and popped the needle into his arm.

"Ouch! Hey, I didn't say anything about dizziness," he protested.

"Yeah, I know. The whites of your eyes gave you away. They've got a yellow tinge to them. If you'd been anyone else, I'd have said you were in liver distress—but since it's you, it must be from consorting with vampires." She wiped the injection spot, slapped a small bandage on it, and patted his hand. "You'll be fine, and in a shorter time than if you hadn't had the shot." She disposed of the needle in the sharps container and turned to face him.

"So. Activity in the Chaos plane is rising, forcing Demonic activity here. There's a rumor going around, about some big bad that has your family targeted. True? False?" She crossed her arms and raised her eyebrows.

Justin just looked at her. He really didn't want her involved.

Megan sighed. "Okay, fine. Just give me this much, then.

~ ☾ ~

How many more demons and Fae and such am I going to be treating? How many more people do I need to train to deal with demonic injuries?" She tapped her foot and met his gaze with a frown. "Because, frankly, just taking care of your friends and family is becoming a full time job for me. If you're going to have substantial casualties, I'm going to need assistance. A paycheck would be nice, too."

Justin frowned. Okay, so she's already involved at the deepest level. "I don't know what to tell you. We don't want a full-scale war."

The door opened and Kellan knocked as he poked his head in. "You done? Can I spring him, Doc?"

"Come in, please, Kellan. I need to talk to you." Megan smiled. Kellan leaned against the doorjamb, his eyebrows raised. "I've just been asking Justin how many more injuries to expect. It's becoming a full time job, handling you and your friends."

"According to the Doc, demonic activity is rising," Justin said. His body ached and he longed for the oblivion of sleep.

Kellan grimaced. "You're right. However many people you can train to handle what's coming, well then, bring 'em on. It's been too quiet for too long. Couple hundred years at this point, right? I'm thinking the wait is almost over."

"I agree." Wait, what had he agreed to? Justin frowned and refocused on his cousin.

Megan raised her eyebrows. "I only have the facility for three overnight beds. Just one surgery bay. If you want this place expanded, I'm going to need financial help."

The men exchanged a glance. Kellan gave up. "I'll see what we can do. You find the staff. Can he go now?"

Megan Cavanaugh made a note on his chart. "He should stay here for observation a full twenty-four. The vamps got rough with him before you carted him away. But," she added, her hand up to forestall their protests, "I'll let him go, as long as you promise to bring him back to me if he starts peeing blood." She glared up at Justin. "Do you hear me?"

"Yes ma'am," he said. "I promise ma'am." He slid off the examining table and gave her a swift kiss on the cheek. What

~ ☾ ~

had he promised her? "Thanks Doc," he added.

"The door's behind you, Justin."

"I knew that." Justin turned. The room whirled. He took a step and his knees buckled. Kellan grabbed him. "Oops. Shouldn't have had that last drink," Justin muttered.

"I've gotcha." Kellan looked to the doctor. "We owe you," he said to Megan. "Again."

"Don't worry. You'll be paying up. Go on, take him out of here."

Justin allowed Kellan to lead him to the car in the lot.

~ ☾ ~

Chapter Seventeen

Gabriel pulled up to the dark house and cut the engine. Taking off his helmet, he knew Rose wasn't in the house. She'd be in the yard on such a hot night. He pulled his leather coat off, tossed it over the seat, hooked the helmet on the bike, and followed the lines of the house to the back yard.

She sat in a swing with a fire flickering at her feet. Gabriel eased down on his heels next to her and reached for her hand, grateful for the quick soothing of his demon. It had become surprisingly natural, the two of them tethered together that way. He studied the fire, not knowing how to ask the question that burned inside. If his soul was truly dying, like Satine said, did he really want to know?

Rose broke the silence. "It's lovely out here, the scent of citrus blossoms."

Memories flooded him at her words. "It's one of my favorite places in the entire world." He looked up, gave her a smile. "But you shouldn't be out here. Let's get you inside, okay?"

Rose's eyes sharpened. She sniffed the air around him and wrinkled her nose. She poked at him, her eyes wary. "You stink of vampire. You let her touch you. What happened?"

"She captured Justin to get me to cooperate because she's running scared of Vlad. Does it bug you that he's got that stupid name?" Restless, he stood. "It really bugs me. Why aren't vampires ever named Al, or Bob, or Tom?"

"Gabriel," she reproved. "Justin's okay? You rescued him, right?"

"Yes. Kellan took him to Doc Cavanaugh. He's fine, it's just, hell." Gabriel rubbed his neck and wished desperately for a

~ ☾ ~

beer.

"What aren't you saying? What is it? You're scaring me now."

"Satine said my soul was almost all dead. That you knew it." He crouched next to her again, met her curious gaze head on. "Do you know? Can you feel my soul dying? You've got to tell me if you know."

"It's not withering, nor is it dead. It's a bit anxious about being in two places, but from what I can tell, it's holding on. But you know that," she reproved and lifted their twined hands. "By touching me, you know all that, don't you? Can't you feel it?"

Understanding flooded him, made him weak with relief. "Satine made me doubt myself." He kissed the hand he held and let it go.

"You're the one who told me she's good at illusion." Rose leaned back in the swing. "God, I love this place. Being here, napping, walking in the orchard, talking with Maggie, it's like I'm remembering who I was before Satine stole my soul. I was an amazing person, Gabriel. I loved art. I used to work in acrylics and watercolors, but I'd forgotten all about that. Can you believe it? I forgot all about it. I wonder whatever happened to my canvases."

His heart much lighter than it had been, he watched her, glowing in the night. She'd grown in the past few days. No longer the scared and shivering woman who had been calling to him through fog and mist. This woman held herself with strength and serenity. "You're an artist. I don't know why, but that makes sense."

She straightened up and smiled at him. "I'm recovering bits of myself here, pieces I'd forgotten about. It's rather amazing."

He held her gaze. "What about Mephisto?"

"He told me that only a person with a strong mind and a pure heart could force him out before he's ready to go. Ultimately I might have to bargain with him."

"You don't have a soul. That puts you in jeopardy. He could easily claim your body." Gabriel frowned. "I don't like it that he talked to you."

~ ☾ ~

"I don't think he'd like this body," she said on a laugh. "His own is pretty spectacular. Why move into a female when the male is so much stronger?"

"You are spectacular."

Her eyes glowed at his husky words. "Gabriel."

Every muscle in his body locked as she stood and moved to him, put a hand on his chest. Desire pumped through him. She rose on her toes, her hands sliding up to his shoulders as he caught her by the waist and lowered his head to hers. At the first touch of her mouth on his, he moaned. Need flowed between them and the passion they'd ignited early that morning on Maggie's balcony flamed again. Gabriel lost himself in her, in her taste, in the feel of her slender body pressed against him.

A hot wind blew through the trees and just as quickly died. The crickets and frogs fell silent and the night stilled around them. Gabriel broke their kiss and listened. Nothing moved. The hairs lifted on Gabriel's neck and fear swamped his desire.

"Inside. Now." Gabriel grabbed her around the waist and half-carried her toward the house despite her squeak of outrage. He took her all the way into the kitchen's back entry before he set her down on her feet again.

She stared at him. "What the hell was that about?"

He crossed his arms and thought frantically. How to explain the silence, the fear for her safety that now consumed him, without sounding like a lovesick idiot?

At his continued silence, Rose sniffed. "Talk about cavemen," she muttered, and stalked through the darkened kitchen, down the hall and to the main stairway.

Following her, Gabriel's lips twitched, his dread lessening. "Caveman? I think I missed part of the conversation."

Rose stopped three steps up the stairs and whirled around. She jabbed her finger at him. "You are the most frustrating and willfully ignorant man. Hard-headed and arrogant." At his blank look, she blew out a breath and flew up the stairs.

Gabriel watched her go. How in the world would he be able to walk away from her? At a cough behind him, he turned to

~ ☾ ~

see Maggie standing in the doorway to the hearth room.

"What did you do to make her angry?" She crossed her arms and leaned against the doorjamb.

"It felt like we were being watched. Out there." He shook his head. "Spooked me, I guess."

"You don't look like the type to get spooked easily."

"I didn't used to be. I just want to keep her safe, you know?" He looked up the stairs. "I should go."

"You'll walk away from all the sparks flying between you? That makes you an idiot." Maggie shook her head. "You Caine men. You're all more trouble than you're worth, as far as I'm concerned," she added tartly. "Go on. *Go* to her, or you'll regret it later."

Gabriel went. Eagerness had him taking the stairs three at a time, following her scent. At the end of the west wing, dim light shone from the master bedroom. He strode toward where he could feel her waiting.

"I can't stop being who I am." He pushed the door open as he spoke and fell silent at the seduction within. Fat candles had been set on the floor by the wall and the king-sized bed had been made with new linens, a welcome lake of pale blue. But the bed didn't hold his attention.

Rose stood in front of the window. She glowed in the waning moonlight, golden in a shower of silver light. Beautiful. Mesmerizing. She turned to him, purpose in every line of her body.

"Listen to me, Gabriel Caine. I want you. I want you like I haven't wanted anything, ever. You are the drug that itched beneath my skin, the high I longed for but never knew existed." Her voice, low, reached him, wrapped him up in need.

"No." Fear slammed through him. He didn't know tender. He couldn't give her tender, and that's what she deserved. Gabriel opened his mouth to tell her so and then she was there, taking his hand, her eyes so serious. She pulled him toward the bed, lifting up his tee shirt with one hand.

He took a deep breath and stepped back, grabbed both her hands in one of his. "Rose. No."

~ ☾ ~

She stilled, looked up at him, her face open and guileless. "You told me you cared for me. Was that a lie?"

"No. Not a lie." Out of options, Gabriel backed up and sat on the bed. Rose stepped between his knees.

"Then talk to me."

Gabriel sighed, brought her hands up to his mouth. Kissed each palm.

"I have killed those I loved. I'm not about to kill you, too. It's my biggest fear."

Rose frowned, but before she could argue with him, he released her hands. Slid his up to her face, cradled it gently. "I do want you. I do. But there is no future for us, Rose. There can't be. I can't risk you and live with myself."

"We're adults not children, and we're not unrealistic. Becoming lovers won't change anything. Stay. Be my lover. Be the first real love in my life."

"How am I supposed to deny you?"

"Tell me you don't want me." Her breath in his ear sent a shiver through him.

"This is a mistake," he said, hovering, drawing out the moment.

"Not if we both want it. We do both want it, Gabriel." Her hot hand went to his ruined cheek, held him.

He turned and pressed a kiss into her palm. "This is for now. Not for always. Right?"

Her smile reached her eyes and she leaned into him. "Just for tonight," she murmured, and pushed him flat onto the bed. "We'll argue about tomorrow later." She pressed tiny kisses along his ravaged cheek, skipped his lips and kissed his other cheek before moving on down to his throat.

He leaned his head back to give her mouth better access. His heart caught, tangled with emotion as she scrambled on top of him.

Gabriel sighed, drew her closer and nestled his face in the scented curve of her neck. His senses stretched out, rejoiced at the feel of her against him even as he grew hard against her.

"You've been a hunger in my soul that I never knew existed," he said, his voice low.

~ ☾ ~

She caught her breath. Framed his face in her hands and looked deep into his eyes. "Kiss me."

It wasn't their first kiss, and yet it resonated like one, she thought dimly. Slow, and sweet, causing shivers to chase across her skin. Lips and tongues and the meeting, parting and meeting again lengthened time to what felt like hours. He tasted like dark sin, deliciously spicy-sweet, and the thrust and dueling of their tongues took on a sensuality she craved.

They parted, taking a quick breath. The candles scented the air with vanilla. The night breeze, heavy with citrus blossom, drifted in through the open window. At his look of wonder, her heart took the last step into love.

On a sigh she dug her hands into his hair; the silky strands a spicy delight to her senses. She gasped for air when his lips left hers. He nipped at the juncture of throat and shoulder, and all her senses leaped in surprise.

"Gabriel," she moaned. She held his head to her, her senses swimming.

His hands skimmed her sides, lifted her shirt up and off. Rose, eager to follow his lead, tugged at his tee shirt until he stripped it away and his chest was at her fingertips.

He was all hard muscle and cool skin. She burned hot as flame against him as she trailed kisses across his chest, ran her hands down his arms. Rose looked deeply into smoky gray eyes, and smiled as she felt his hands go to the snap of her jeans. She did him the same favor, and after wrestling with denim, they were both naked on the huge bed.

Her body amazed him. Slender, limber, her small breasts with their tight pink nipples entranced him. The line of her body drew his eyes down to the copper curls between her long legs, and his mouth watered even as his hands stroked, teased, discovered.

She was fluid, hot in his arms, her summer-blue eyes mesmerizing as she flowed over him, touching, soothing, inciting everywhere they connected. Her eyes were alight with mischief. Her hand on his aching cock, her silky hair sweeping his belly and the feel of her hot, wet tongue there snapped his tight control.

~ ☾ ~

With a roar, he lifted her over him, brought her mouth to his, and rolled with her, trapping her beneath his body as he ravaged her mouth.

Had it ever been like this? Wild, soothing, a crescendo built inside him. More, he had to have more. He caught one taut nipple between his lips and tugged, suckled.

"Gabriel!" Rose held his head to her breast, gasping for breath. His mouth was hot where the rest of him remained cool. She shivered at the contrast, gasped again when he transferred his attentions to her other breast, sending sparks to ignite the heat between her legs. Her hands lifted his face to hers for a searing kiss. "Take me."

The look in his eyes, both hungry and agonized, made her thump him on the shoulder. "I'm burning for you. God, Gabriel. Put me out of my misery, for pity's sake."

"Are you sure? Rose. Are you absolutely sure?"

She kissed him fiercely. "Yes. Now. Please!"

His eyes changed, turned intent, the clear gray now molten silver as he put her under him and raised her knees up to her chest. Need roared through him and without thought for gentleness, he thrust into her, a wild joining of bodies and minds.

He reached for her mind and through their connection he knew her reaction to his hardness deep in her body, the melting and the new tension that gripped her. Knew when she felt him in her mind. Her eyes met his, wide with joy.

You are mine. Mine!

Her exultation filled him, warmed him like nothing else could as she held him close. For a few moments he didn't move, caught in the wonder of their coming together. He'd been afraid of *this*? He couldn't think why. He reached to her. *I am made for you.*

He reveled in the tight grip of her legs, the welcoming pulsations of her body hot around him as he slowly withdrew then plunged again into her. He kissed her, ravenous, as their pace accelerated, sweat sheening their bodies.

Rose remembered to breathe. He filled her, surrounded her, and possessed her in every way possible. She'd never felt

~ ☾ ~

more alive as she did beneath him. Her lungs filled with his scent, her mouth with his taste as they rolled across the big bed, grappling with their furious need. Rose stroked his hard body straining against hers as they climbed to impossible heights of sensation.

She tensed, crying out as her climax rocked her. Gabriel stiffened in her arms; she wrapped herself around him as he joined her in pleasure a fraction of a second later.

Gabriel collapsed to one side of her. Her legs slid down his as she relaxed deeper into the bed. Peace surrounded them. The cooing of the doves outside added to the sense of home, and Gabriel breathed in the scent of the two of them. His heart filled with a painful joy as his body pulled him down into sleep.

"Gabriel. I love you. I do. You probably think I'm just being female or something, and that's okay. You don't have to say a word." Her words were slurred with sleep.

He tensed. "You said making love wouldn't change anything between us."

She chuckled. "It hasn't." She stretched beneath him. "Hmmm. Except I feel wonderfully sleepy. Shhh. I'm going to sleep now, the best sleep ever."

Gabriel kissed her head and tucked her against him as he rolled to his side. "Sleep, then. Morning will come soon enough."

He laid a cheek against her head and stared into the dark, wide-awake after her revelation. This couldn't be anything other than temporary. Tonight Rose slept, warm and alive in his arms. He'd wring every drop of closeness with her that he could. He was selfish enough to do that. He'd deal with tomorrow when it came.

Out of the corner of his eye, he caught a peculiar light glinting in the darkness. Peering closer, he saw the shimmering strands of blue and purple Fae bonds wind around him and, for the first time ever in his memory, cling to another person.

Rose.

The meaning infiltrated his sex-and-fear-hazed brain.

~ ☾ ~

They'd been bonded. Their lives were now intertwined beyond death.

Gabriel held her close, refusing to panic even as his world changed to an unrecognizable shape. Once bonded, it couldn't be undone. Life for one who loses his mate is close to hell on earth, they'd seen that happen to Gideon and Maria Therese. He cursed softly under his breath, doing his best not to wake Rose. A Fae mating had *not* been a part of his plans.

* * *

Justin made his way unsteadily from the Jag where Kellan had left him fast asleep to the hearth room. Maggie was there, bending over to tend to the fire. Her curvy bottom, presented to him as she bent over, had his hands itching. He stopped a couple steps from her.

"Careful, there," he said, and gestured to her hair when she turned sharply at his words. "I'd hate to see all that hair burn up."

Her look of surprise turned sardonic. "As if you care. Back off, Casanova."

Justin took a couple careful steps back and spread his hands wide. "Satisfied?" He suppressed a yawn.

"Kellan gave me an update. You doing okay?" She narrowed her eyes at him.

"Ready to do the mattress mambo whenever you want." He leaned against a wing back chair for support and leered at her, knowing she half-expected it.

"Shut it down, Reggae Boy. You're useless after consorting with vampires." Maggie sniffed and moved back to settle on the couch.

"Then hit me with an update. What ya got?"

"Not a whole lot. There's nothing anywhere about the Soul twins. I did find a ton of sites about spirals, and something caught my eye but it's a very slim similarity. Nothing that exactly matches what we've got going on here." She put her chin on her hand and stared dolefully at her computer screen. "We're kind of where we started. And before you ask, there's been nothing on Kendall, either, except the cops have cancelled the APB on him."

~ ☾ ~

Justin frowned. "I thought you were good at this research stuff."

"I am. But there has to be something out there for me to find. I'm finding nothing. Zip. Zilch. Nada. If you think you could do better, you're welcome to try." She pushed the laptop across the coffee table to him.

"Testy."

"Failure tends to make me that way. But I've come up with a theory. Sit down before you fall down."

"And?" Justin settled on the edge of the couch and did his best to focus.

"Do you remember Doc Cavanaugh talking about the Soul Chalice and the Soul Stealer? How they balance each other out, and how they often destroy each other? I think maybe that means they can't live without the other one around."

"Just what are you saying?"

"I'm saying that if we kill Satine, maybe it's a binding of some sort and Rose will also die."

Justin stood abruptly. "Your theory sucks. What are you basing this on, anyway?"

Maggie shook her head impatiently. "Put the pieces together. Maria Therese felt guilty that she didn't live long enough to care for Gabriel. Rose was her way to save him. What better vessel than a Soul Chalice to rescue a soul from a Soul Stealer? And then, once the deed was done, Soul Chalice kills Soul Stealer, or they destroy each other, thus leaving her son to live a happy life."

"If Rose dies, Gabriel will live a life of hell. He doesn't deserve that."

"You don't know that. You're just being difficult."

"I do know that. They're Fae bonded, Magdalena. They've been *bonded*. I noticed it yesterday, but I don't think they know. I saw what happened to my Dad when Mom died before her time. I wouldn't wish that kind of agony on anyone, much less my brother." Grim satisfaction ripped through him at the surprise and remorse crossing her face.

Justin continued. "So everything you just said? It's wrong. You are completely, totally, and utterly wrong. About

~ ☾ ~

everything," he said. His every word stood out, chilly and distinct. In a rush of movement he left Magdalena and the fire and went out into the night.

Justin stalked unsteadily through the trees to the far end of the property. Orange and lemon blossom perfumed the night air, soothed him with their familiar fragrance.

He couldn't accept Magdalena's theory. If Rose died, his brother may as well be dead, too. Their family couldn't handle it if it happened again, and especially if it happened to Gabriel.

Justin reached the back of the property and turned to stare at the house in the distance. Doc Cavanaugh's voice came back to him. *"But wherever there's a Soul Stealer, you'll find a Soul Chalice, doing whatever she can to rescue the stolen souls. Balance. Good and evil. Yin and yang, if you wish. Usually the two Soul Entities end up killing each other."*

Maybe Magdalena was right after all. Damn it. She couldn't be. Could she?

Justin sighed and leaned against one of the old eucalyptus trees edging the property to the north. A hole in his life had been filled when Gabriel returned. Losing his brother again wasn't an option. He lifted his face to the stars, but found no answers there.

He sensed Magdalena the minute she stepped outside and turned her face to him. He didn't like her here. She muddled his thinking. But he didn't have much choice. He'd asked her for help. He couldn't just pat her on the head and thank her, sending her away. She wouldn't go, anyway. She had a stake in the outcome now. She'd befriended Rose, so she was there until the bitter end. He understood that.

He didn't have to like it. All he had to do was steer clear of her.

She came to him, her arms crossed protectively over her chest. He'd hurt her, he knew, but it wasn't his job to protect her.

Like hell it wasn't. He'd been raised to know better.

She stopped three feet away and looked straight at him, those chocolate brown eyes steady and straightforward. No

~ ☾ ~

tears, thank God. He should have known he wouldn't get tears from her.

"I'm sorry."

Her apology took him by surprise. "Nothing to be sorry about. You came up with a theory which is more than the rest of us have done," he said roughly.

"The theory sucks." Maggie looked down, rubbed the toe of her shoe in the dirt.

"It does, yes. But I didn't have to blame you for it."

"Understandable. What do we do now?"

"Let's go back to the house. I need to sleep horizontal. You should go home, get some sleep." They moved together, walking in the waning moonlight.

Maggie shook her head. "I'm not driving anywhere, I'm too tired. If there's a blanket around, I'll just sleep in the living room. You know we'll all do everything we can to fix this, to save them. We're not going to stand by and do nothing."

Before they walked in the front door, he stopped her, one hand on her shoulder. As tall as he was, she was tall enough to only tilt her head a little bit to see his eyes.

"What is it?"

"I still think you're wrong. About Rose having to die, I mean. But I do appreciate what you said, about all of us working together to save them."

"Rose may have to be point person on this. I'm not saying I like it. I'm not saying she will die, either. It's just that's the way it might have to go down. I'm sorry."

"She won't, not if I can help it," he vowed.

"Stop being such a man," snapped Maggie. She jerked open the front door. "You're not always going to get your way."

"No kidding," he said, and followed her into the living room where the flames still licked at the wood in the fireplace. "But I can do everything in my power to keep her safe."

Maggie frowned as she settled into her chair again. "You can try. Gabriel will have something to say about keeping her safe. And if you haven't noticed, Rose has a mind of her own."

"Yeah. Smart, stubborn, sexy." He shook his head and sighed. "I'm beginning to think it's the curse of the Caine

~ ☾ ~

men."

"What is?" Maggie looked at him, suspicious.

"Getting involved with smart, stubborn and sexy women." Maggie looked at him steadily. "Not even you would push a woman who said no."

Justin held her gaze for a moment, coldness stealing through his veins at her words. "Who said anything about *us* getting involved?" He left the room without a backward glance.

* * *

The sun shone in on them. Gabriel stirred first, stumbling out of bed to look for his clothes.

He heard Rose shift on the bed. She yawned. "Morning."

"I don't want you to take any risks today," Gabriel warned. He pulled on his shirt and jeans and studied the rumpled woman in the huge bed. He'd spent all night worried about her. His patience had worn thin.

"That's a fine way to start the day." Rose pulled the sheet from her face and gave him a lazy smile. "I won't if you won't. Stay here with me today. Let's play house." She stretched. "I feel fantastic."

"You look fantastic. Get dressed." He bent and picked up her tee shirt and tossed it to her.

She sat up and the sheet fell away, leaving her naked. She looked her question, one eyebrow raised.

Gabriel swallowed hard. "I can't."

"I disagree, you most certainly can. Come sit over here." She patted the bed beside her.

Gabriel took a couple steps towards the door. "No, really. I can't. Look, I'll never forget last night. Every part of it is emblazoned in my memory, and for that I am grateful. But we've got a job to do. We can't afford to get distracted by a personal attachment right now."

Rose's steady gaze made him uncomfortable. "Maybe later?"

"Maybe later." His relief at her understanding was short lived.

"Or maybe never. That's what you really mean, isn't it?

~ ☾ ~

Once you get your soul back, you won't need me to keep your demon in check. You'll be gone faster than a thought." Her eyes, her voice, remained cool, calm.

Gabriel's very heart shook. "You don't know that. Neither one of us can see into the future. We don't know how this will end."

Rose reached for her tee shirt and put it on. "We don't know, that's true. Could you pass me my underwear and my jeans? However, we have right now. And right now, I want you to know that I will fight for you, for us. I don't know how it will end. Neither one of us may survive, which makes right now even more important." She pulled on her panties, snapped up her jeans, and moved to where she'd left her shoes the night before.

"We've got a lot to do. We can't get distracted. We can probably take Satine out, but Vlad is older, trickier, scarier than Satine," he protested. "Mephisto almost killed me the last time we met. Can't you understand? Distraction is the enemy here. We've got to stay at the top of our game." Gabriel felt his reasoning waver under her narrow-eyed scrutiny. He was right. He had to be right, or the last ten years of his life weren't a sacrifice, a penance for Marianne's life. His last ten years meant nothing.

"I'm not going to stop loving you just because we have a lot to do," she said. "I'll do what I have to in order to survive. You'll do the same, because that's how you're made. But I'm telling you now. When we get through to the other side of this, then you'll have to deal with me because I won't just let you disappear."

Exasperated, he folded his arms across his chest and shook his head. "I don't like it. I don't like it one bit."

Rose rounded the bed, stood on tiptoe and kissed his cheek. "I know. But I'm done asking permission. You go check on Justin, and I'll help down in the kitchen."

"You're not going anywhere today, Rose," he called after her. "You're staying right here." She didn't bother to answer him.

~ ☾ ~

Gabriel stared out the window, feeling his heart, as well as part of his soul, now resided with Rose.

~ ☾ ~

Chapter Eighteen

Rose walked into the kitchen to find Maggie staring out the window over the sink, a bowl in one hand and a spoon in the other.

"Hey."

Maggie turned to Rose. "Hey. Want coffee? It's almost ready."

"Awesome. Looks like you've got food well in hand."

"I've got muffins coming up." Maggie hefted the bowl and gave the batter a few more strokes with the wooden spoon. "And there's a strata in the oven. It's good, you'll like it. Spinach, potatoes, cheese, eggs. Almost better than sex."

Rose grinned and stretched her hands above her head. "Nothing could be better than the sex I had last night. Absolutely nothing. Damn stupid tribred." She opened a cupboard to grab a mug.

Maggie snorted. "Those sentences don't go together, chica. Care to explain?"

"He wouldn't touch me this morning. Gave me a lot of mumbo about keeping our lives free of distractions, meaning any sort of relationship. The idiot." Rose poured coffee and sat at the counter, watching as Maggie moved with her usual economy of motion, filling the muffin cups.

"I know. That's just one of the downsides to getting involved."

"Coffee's good." The heat of the cup warmed her hands. Rose watched her friend for a few moments. "What's wrong?"

Maggie brushed a curling strand of hair over her ear and shook her head. "You got a few hours?" Finished, she slid the muffin tin onto the bottom shelf of the oven.

~ ☾ ~

"According to the cave troll upstairs, I'm sequestered here. I've got all day." Rose studied her as she set the table. "You look like hell, though. You've got dark circles under your eyes and a pinched look, as though your head hurts. Was the couch that uncomfortable? I think we have more beds coming today."

"Oh for Pete's sake." Maggie closed her eyes, muttered a few words, and lightly touched the skin beneath her eyes. She took a deep breath, expelled it, opened them again and turned to Rose, her head at a questioning angle. "Better?"

Now she looked fresh, rested, and ready for the day. Rose nodded admiringly. "Good work, sister. Can you teach me that spell? I'll bet it comes in handy."

"It's just a quick glamour. Sure, I'll pass it along. What's going on with you? Sex so good it was bad?"

Rose stifled a laugh. "He thinks he's going to kill me. I can't be too concerned about it, you know? I trust him not to kill me."

"Trust is important."

"I love him, Maggie. He says he can't let himself love me back. Which really sucks."

Maggie reached across the countertop and gave Rose's hand a squeeze of sympathy. "You're right. It really sucks."

"I shouldn't have dumped on you. But why is he pushing me away? Is it just because he's afraid I'll self-destruct or that he'll kill me?"

"He's a man. Who knows what makes him tick? But you're a Soul Chalice, too. I for one am not worried about what Mephisto or his fire demon powers could do to you. I think your Soul Chalice powers, whatever they are, will be more than a match for him."

A timer dinged and Maggie moved to the oven. "Strata's done. The muffins will need about ten more minutes. If the world is turning as it usually does, the men should be walking down the stairs any minute."

Rose's stomach rumbled. "It smells divine."

A clattering from the stairs had Rose grinning and Maggie rolling her eyes. "Right on time."

~ ☾ ~

They heard Gabriel's deep tones, Justin's more musical voice, and the soft hint of the bayou in Kellan's as the Caines gathered at the bottom of the stairs.

Maggie caught Rose's eye. "Before we're interrupted, just tell me this. Do you have any sort of plan? To get the rest of his soul back?"

"Sort of. I still have some parts to figure out, but I've got the basics. Not that he cares." Rose rested her forehead on the counter. "I don't know if I can do this, Maggie."

"We'll help. I swear we'll help you, Rose. Don't you dare believe that you're alone in this mess." She cleared her throat, turned and brought out plates. "Would you mind setting the table? I believe the hordes are about to descend."

* * *

Gabriel waited at the bottom of the stairway and watched Kellan and Justin come down the stairs, Justin moving slower than normal.

"So, you let a bunch of vampires jump you. Pansy," he said. "Lucky for you, someone's been cooking. Kel, what did the good doc say?"

"He should be all right, but if he starts pissing blood we're to take him back. Oh, and she's going to need to expand her operation if we keep getting our asses kicked."

Gabriel snorted at that. "Write the lady a check." They made their way into the kitchen. Gabriel's stomach growled.

"What's cooking?" Justin winked at Rose.

"Strata. Muffins. Coffee. Sit and eat and enjoy." Maggie shooed them all to the big, scarred table in the corner of the room. The pan sitting in the middle of the table steamed gently.

Silence fell as they all ate. Rose got up to refill coffee cups, including her own, aware of the unspoken messages flying behind her as she returned the pot to the counter.

"Stop worrying. I'm fine, really. I got lots of sleep, and the good doc gave me the green light." Rose smiled at everyone. "So there's no need to treat me like glass, okay? Justin's the one who tangled with vamps last night, not me."

"I'm fine."

~ ☾ ~

"Let me throw out what I found last night about spirals." Maggie's words drew all eyes to her. She held Justin's gaze for a moment before looking at Rose beside him.

"Go on."

Maggie folded her hands on the table. "I found the spirals, traced them to a small village in Mexico with deep roots in Santeria and the Catholic Church. They are blessings at the most basic form, as you can see here." She gestured to the spirals surrounding them. "Blessings, ease of sleep, love of family, these are basic, core values to be shared among family and friends."

"And all this time I just thought it was weird wallpaper," Kellan said.

"But, blessings." Gabriel looked encouraged. "That's good, right? A good thing."

"All the spirals in the house move counter to the spiral that contains the demon. The spirals here are giving. The one on Rose is a containment spiral, or a keeping spiral." She turned to Rose. "It's my belief that Maria Therese saw that a demon was hitching a ride on you. She forced it into the reverse spiral, the only thing she could do to save you from it taking you over immediately."

"Sorry," interrupted Rose. "But you're wrong about Maria Therese and Mephisto. She asked, he said yes. The spiral is there, but it's not to contain him on me. It's to prevent us from removing him. He can leave by his own free will, but nothing else will force him away."

Everyone at the table fell silent. Rose shrugged. "See, I had this weird dream yesterday. Maria Therese told me she sent the demon to me in order to give me the strength I would need to keep Gabriel's soul safe."

Maggie took a breath. "Okay, new information. I won't dispute what you've said, but the demon could also be the price you paid for returning to life. If you hadn't agreed, you might have died in the hospital for good." Maggie shrugged, apologetic.

Rose grew pensive. "Here's how I see it. I was slated to die a messy death. Then, on a beach north of here, Gabriel had his

~ ☾ ~

soul stolen. Kind of like a cold war spy, I get activated to go in and help out hey-presto, just in the nick of time." She looked at their faces as they sat around the table and spread her hands wide. "So here I am. Not who I was before I died, but not yet who I will be after this is done." She paused, took a breath.

"Look. I don't know what will happen when I confront Satine. I do know that I'm the only Soul Chalice around, the only one who can actually rescue Gabriel's soul, and my own I might add. Frankly? I'll be lucky to survive the fight with Satine long enough to give Gabriel's soul back to him.

"I'm not stupid. Maybe I didn't finish high school, but ever since I got dropped into this world of vampire-owned nightclubs and hunky tribreds, I've known I don't belong here any more than I belonged in my previous life. It's borrowed time. I'm working on being okay with that."

Justin cleared his throat. "It's hard to argue against your theory. Maggie had already come to the conclusion that you and Satine could end up destroying each other. But don't begin to think you're going up against the she-devil by yourself."

"I'm working on protective spells for all of us," put in Maggie. "I've got a few ingredients to get, but I should be ready to go by tonight."

"I'll be with you, Rose," promised Kellan, his eyes dark and full of retribution. "We'll all have your back."

"Damn it, what was my mother doing all those years? Hanging around in the waiting room for the opportunity to meddle around in my life?" demanded Gabriel.

Rose's smile at the show of support died. She faced Gabriel, her chin set. "I don't know. But I can tell you this. I'd give my very soul for a mother who cared so much for me that she was taking care of me from the other side. Now if you'll excuse me, I've had enough to eat. I'd like to be alone for a while. I'm going to take a walk in the orchard. I need to do some thinking, and I don't want company." She pushed back from the table and stood.

Gabriel moved as if to stand and she put a hand on his

~ ☾ ~

shoulder. "It's perfectly safe out there," she added.

Gabriel bit his lip and shoved his hands in his pockets.

They held silent until the slam of the screen door. Maggie put her head in her hands. "That went well."

"Way to support the girl, Gabriel. Way to go." Justin gave a disgusted snort.

Guilt rode him and he turned on his brother. "And just how do you suppose you're going to fight the vampires, huh? Gonna send them all on a little vacation, make them feel guilty for trying to kill you? At least Kellan and I can call up our demons to fight."

"Oh yeah, that's the way to do it. Taunt your brother." He stood and went toe to toe with Gabriel. "You're a little too amped up on the demon juice. You revel in the fight. Your control is worth shit. You think you have nothing to live for and you're ready to go down, or go full demon. What about Rose? Isn't she worth living for? Can't you see, you stupid ass, that she's already mated with you?"

Gabriel, his eyes blazing, gave Justin a short punch to the gut, got a slug to the jaw in return, and they were down on the ground, slugging and wrestling each other like they hadn't done in twenty years.

Maggie looked at them, appalled. She glanced at Kellan who edged his chair back and away from the two on the ground. "What should I do?"

"Let them blacken each other's eyes. They'll get over it. Better the two of them pound it out than not confront the issue." Kellan shrugged. "At least, that's what Gideon always used to say. Hey now, no turning, that's not playing fair," he shouted as both men's eyes whirled, demon-green.

"Guys, guys—come on. Stop it right now." Maggie stamped her foot but the two brothers ignored her. "You don't want me to put a whammy on you," she warned. They continued to tussle.

"Aw, go ahead and whammy 'em," said Kellan. He stretched out his legs as if to enjoy the show. "Before they start breaking the furniture," he added as a picture fell from the wall.

~ ☾ ~

Maggie focused, gathered her energy, and tossed it toward the two men. As if two invisible hands had pushed between them, they were shoved apart, beyond arm's reach, and lifted in the air off their feet. "Stop it, now." Maggie's voice deepened and grew huskier than ever with the power swirling inside her.

Justin and Gabriel both snarled at her and her energies shook them like puppies. She dropped them and they landed in a clatter of long limbs and cries of surprise.

As one, they rose to confront her. She stood tall, a wind ruffling her hair. "Go ahead. Try it." Her brown eyes were frosty with the challenge, her hands at the ready.

Justin slumped against the wall, touched his mouth, swollen from one of Gabriel's punches. "Trust a witch to stop the fun," he said, and fell to his knees. Coughed. "If I start peeing blood, I'm blaming you."

"So am I." Maggie glared at Gabriel.

Gabriel snarled, starting for Maggie.

"Please." She held up her hand and he stopped. "Do you even know why you are so angry? Maybe Justin's right and you are in danger of becoming your demon permanently. Well, don't take it out on him. You'd better do some serious thinking before you lose it all together. The woman loves you. Why don't you try being worthy of her love instead of whining about your blood?"

He hesitated, staring at her. Finally he turned away, slamming through the kitchen door to the outside.

Maggie sank down in the nearest chair and trembled in reaction.

"Way to go, dollface. Way to go." Justin sent her a look.

Kellan moved to Justin, helped him up. "Let's get you back to bed." Over his shoulder, he smiled at Maggie. "Don't worry about it. It's nothing you could have controlled." Justin shook off Kellan, snorted and made his way out to the stairs.

"So they pound on each other rather than the people who deserve it." Maggie shook her head in disgust. "That's pitiful."

"They're still finding their way." Kellan slumped back into his chair, exhausted. "We're all still finding our way. We

~ ☾ ~

haven't been together like this in years. The only person missing is the oldest, Gregor. Then it's really a party."

~ ☾ ~

Chapter Nineteen

Satine huddled below the rubble that had been Twisted, deeming it the safest place for her to hide with the summer sun overhead. Others were above her; not all had fled the destruction, though she couldn't find Vladimir. The space she'd poured herself into was compact, just a bit of the staircase near her office that hadn't yet collapsed. She had no other place to go, and didn't know how to find Vlad's daylight home.

She cursed her lack of forethought. A nice place in the mountains wasn't out of her reach, but did she think about investing? Of course not. She'd followed where Vlad led. He'd been so determined to take over from his sire. Once he got the club and all the Los Angeles vamps, he'd abandoned their real estate game. Too bad he didn't realize what an example he'd set for her.

With every drop of blood in her body, she wanted Vlad's power. She *deserved* Vlad's power. If only Gabriel's soul had surrendered to her! She'd be on top. Vlad would be dead. Caine and his brothers would also be dead, they wouldn't have thought of destroying the club.

They had gone too far. Overstepped their place. She'd have her revenge, though. She always did revenge well. With everything the Caines had done to her, revenge was completely justified. They scared her demons, freed her weres. They killed Chazz. When they ruined Twisted with a couple of well-placed bombs, she'd just been lucky to be away, trying to turn Gabriel. But even if he came to her on bended knee, begging to be her slave, she'd deny him now. Deny them all.

Her thoughts roved over the building, touching on other

~ ☾ ~

vampires where they rested, hiding until she needed them. She'd been lucky. Some had remained incredibly loyal to her. She'd definitely have to reward them for surviving, for staying with her through the apocalypse that had become her life.

The Caines had to be dealt with. Destroyed, except for Gabriel. She'd torture him before she killed him. All she needed was the dark. Once sundown hit, she'd take them all out.

Sara. The voice slid into her mind as if they'd done it thousands of times before. The vampire clenched her fists. *Rose. The name is Satine. What the hell do you want?*

I heard you want Vladimir destroyed. Do you have any ideas on how to go about that?

Satine bit her lip. *You still have all the Caines in your back pocket?*

There was silence. Satine tried reaching down the pathway to take her to Rose, but a smooth metal door barred her way. Frustration built inside her.

I am still with the Caines, came the cautious reply. *Look, if you don't want Vlad taken out, then fine. I'll leave you alone.*

No, wait! Satine had thought this through, several times. Her favorite bedtime fantasy. *He's like stone. He has few weaknesses. But even stone will crack open when you hit it at the right angle.*

So fire is out, mused Rose.

Fear skittered through Satine at the mention of fire, a vampire's worst nightmare. She pushed the thought away and focused on Vlad's demise. *Beheading works, but you need a blade sharp enough, and a hand strong enough to wield it. You bring the Caines tonight and I'll bring Vlad.* Satine put as much persuasion in her mental voice as she could. She felt Rose waver.

If we manage to free you from Vlad, then you'll leave us alone? All of us?

That's truly all I want.

We'll see.

Abruptly the sense of Rose drained out of Satine's mind. Elation filled her. Finally, she could see a way clear. Once she

~ ☾ ~

had the Caines in front of her, she'd use one against the other and take them all.

Kill them all.

First, of course, Rose. It was a fitting punishment for Gabriel, to see his love die...slowly. Then she'd rip him apart after making him beg for her. The other Caines, well. She'd have to see which of them were up to her weight, sexually. She might be persuaded to keep one of them.

As she planned the Caines' destruction, a part of her roving mind kept watch over the building she huddled in. Another part touched upon Vladimir. If he ever found out about her plans, he'd destroy her. Slowly.

Vlad hadn't spared her much time since they destroyed his sire. He rarely showed up at the club. He was always off on some adventure or errand without her, or spending time at his lair, a place she'd never been invited to. Yet he expected her to be there whenever he wanted, for whatever he wanted.

Fear ate at her rage and cunning. He was out there, somewhere, and he would be waiting to punish her for failing to keep the club safe. And this time, it wouldn't be a mere cat 'o nine tails wielded in his tireless hand.

No. It would be a thousand times worse. Not a satin-sheeted bed with velvet handcuffs. More likely, it would be an iron bound coffin tucked away in the bowels of the mountains north of the city or something similar that she couldn't escape from. A place where she would waste away, desiccated, bloodless, alone until he saw fit to release her.

She caught back a sob of pure panic. Nothing was worse for a vampire than the absence of their senses. Touching nothing, being suspended in the dark, was one of her nightmares from childhood. How ironic that, now she had become one of the world's most dangerous predators, that nightmare actually looked to come true.

He'd even told her so. As he'd whipped her that last time, he'd told her he suspected her of treason, of wanting his power. He'd told her she'd never get away from him, that she was his pet. His plaything, to use or ignore at his desire.

Satine's low growl in the dark caused a minor rumbling in

~ ☾ ~

the plaster and building materials above her head. Dust sifted around her as she caught her emotions. Footsteps reverberated from far above. She couldn't scent who it was, but she knew it wasn't night yet. That switch that all vampires had in their heads hadn't been triggered. It wouldn't be safe to rise now, not even to stop the intruder.

Satine.

A chill slid down her spine. She went still as stone there in the dark, her face pressed against her knees. If she kept her mind blank, empty, maybe Vlad wouldn't find her. Terror struck her bones, made them feel brittle and almost human in their delicacy.

Satine.

The compelling need to answer him grew stronger. Satine bit her lip hard and kept as blank as she could, blending into the wallboard beside her. Willing her mind to be stone. Cold, dark, numb. She had only a breath to prepare once she felt his mind touch hers.

He broke her image of stone wide apart. The pain came next. Her spine arched with it, her mouth opened wide but no sound came out. Her eyes strained to see in the dark that had become absolute. He'd caught her and she was no longer in her own mind, but in his. Satine was *his* now, to do with as he pleased.

With no sense of her body, her mind, terrified, fell into the abyss he'd prepared for her.

* * *

Gabriel came through the front door like a hurricane, bringing the heat of a Santa Ana wind with him. "Where is she?" he demanded, striding into the great room where Maggie sat working on her computer.

She looked up, bewildered. "Rose? She's outside. At least, we all saw her go."

"I've walked the entire orchard. Looked in the back storage sheds. I thought maybe she was with the kittens, but no. She's not out there, anywhere. I can't even feel her mind." Gabriel's hand went to the scar on his throat.

Kellan, slumped in a deep armchair, sat up. "What about

the cars? Would she have taken one of the cars?"

"If someone was stupid enough to leave the keys in the car, you betcha she'd take it," said Maggie. "That's opportunity knocking, right there."

Kellan paled. "The Jag."

The men scrambled for the front door, Gabriel getting there first. He yanked it open and stared. Maggie's purple van. Kellan's gleaming Mustang sat beside Gabriel's motorcycle, but no Jag. "Aw, hell. Justin's gonna kill you."

"Wait, here she comes."

Rose maneuvered the Jag down the long driveway and brought it to a careful stop beside Maggie's van.

A collective sigh of relief went through them, and then they were following Gabriel down the front steps to the Jag.

"What the hell did you think you were doing?" he exploded, yanking the driver door open. The sheer relief that she was back and safe fueled his fury. "Or were you even thinking? Do you remember the last time you were alone? This could have ended in a huge disaster. How thoughtless can you get?"

"Uh oh." Maggie retreated back to the house.

Rose got out of the car and faced Gabriel. "I paid a visit to Satine. I thought that maybe I could get her to tell us how to take this Vlad guy out."

Gabriel shared a brief glance with Kellan and Justin.

"I'm here, safe and sound, and so is your precious Jaguar," she added, thrusting the keys into Justin's hand and glaring at him. "If you didn't want it stolen, you shouldn't have left the keys in the ignition."

Rose moved to go around Gabriel, but when he kept blocking her way, she put her hands on her hips in frustration. "Now what? Want to insult me some more? Treat me like I don't matter?"

"No. Damn it, don't put words into my mouth."

"Stop trying to protect me," she flared back. Taking a step back, she evaded his reaching hands. "And don't touch me," she added icily. Stepping around him, she headed for the house, her head held high.

The three men stood looking at each other, each of them

~ ☾ ~

feeling helpless. "I really don't like this," said Kellan.

Justin snorted. "Women. Nothing but trouble."

Gabriel looked to the house and sighed. "Yeah."

"Glad I'm not the relationship type." Kellan followed his cousins into the house.

Justin snorted. "And Gabriel is? Puh-leeze."

"You'll get yours, boys," Gabriel declared. "You'll get yours."

* * *

Rose picked up the coffee Maggie set in front of her. "I think I got enough information to help at least. Please don't make me feel guiltier than I already do." That guilt sat like a ball of lead in her stomach.

Maggie patted her hand. "I understand why you had to go. I just wish you'd asked me to go with you."

She turned her hand and gripped Maggie's. "Thank you. For coming when I called, for being here now. I just...thank you."

Surprise crossed Maggie's face. "You're welcome."

They both looked up as the men came in, jostling each other until they stood silent, waiting. Even Gabriel looked at her expectantly, as though she should lead.

Rose took a deep breath. "I'm sorry. I should have trusted you to believe in my idea of talking to Satine, and I didn't. But I did learn a few things. First off, Vlad won't die easily. Apparently he's made of stone. Rock. Whatever, fire won't kill him and I'm not about to waste a blade on trying to make that work. So we might have to forget about him for now."

"You went to a vampire to figure out how to kill a vampire? Okay. That makes a twisted kind of sense."

"Thank you so much Justin," she said drily.

Unexpectedly, Maggie came to her rescue. "Satine shouldn't be a big problem. From my research, killing a young vampire isn't that hard. Coming out alive is the tricky part, especially since she's your opposite. The demon, however, will be a bit more difficult."

"I'll take anything I can get. You've got something I can use?" Rose turned to Maggie.

~ ☾ ~

"I don't know how much this will help, but you need to claim your personal power. Keep that knowledge of your power in the forefront of your will to live. Sometimes, a person's will to live keeps them alive beyond all reason." Maggie shrugged. "It's from an ancient Sumerian text."

"Sumerian text? Who reads Sumerian texts anymore?"

Rose sat as Maggie poked back at Justin. Kellan had bent to speak privately to Gabriel. Their voices filled the kitchen and her heart expanded. Love just filled her up. She *loved* these people. Though it had happened fast, the bonds from her to them were firm.

Yet each of them might die in the battle to come. If she could keep them out of the fight she would, she vowed. Gabriel's voice broke into her concentration. "Wait. What did you say?" She reached over and touched Gabriel's arm.

"We'll have to use me as bait," Gabriel repeated. "I've been thinking about it. Satine wants me, so we'll give her what she wants."

Rose nodded. His idea drew awfully close to hers, with one exception. *She* would be the bait, not Gabriel. Better that they believe his plan, rather than working to get their acceptance of hers. She cut across the voices arguing against Gabriel's decision. "Let's do it tonight. She's expecting us." Tonight, she thought, while she still had the courage.

Gabriel flashed her a smile. "I agree, tonight." He looked around the table. "Any takers?"

"I think you're nuts. Both of you. But I'll be there as your backup." Kellan, cradling the delicate, rose-painted cup between his big hands tickled Rose. She stifled a giggle. "Are you expecting Vlad to be there as well?"

"Mister made-of-rock?" Rose frowned. "She said he would be. I don't know how much we can trust her."

"I'm not comfortable with you waltzing into danger. Any of us, for that matter." Justin frowned from Rose to Gabriel.

Rose smiled. God but he was so sweet. "I know. I'm not comfortable with you being in danger, either. But we'll both just have to suck it up, won't we?"

"I'll work on some protective spells." Maggie slid on a pair

~ ☾ ~

of glasses. "I'll have to go shopping. But there are things I can do that will help."

"Thank you." Rose reached across, squeezed Maggie's hand. "I really appreciate it. So we strike tonight."

"The sooner the better, for my state of mind," declared Kellan. "All this togetherness is making me twitchy."

"He's a born loner," confirmed Justin.

"What about the weres? Think we should bring in Danny Roush's pack?" Kellan looked to Gabriel.

"Yeah. I'll give him a courtesy call. He should at least know what's going down. If I've read him right, he'll want to be there. Do I think we'll need him? Nah. My guess is her vamps will have scattered. She'll be there, though, pissed off and plotting. The only variable is Vlad. If he's there, then it'll be all hands on deck." Gabriel looked to Justin. "Sound good?"

"It's the way I would go," and Justin turned to Maggie. "Are you planning to join us? Or will you cast your spells from afar?" His voice turned taunting.

Maggie flushed. "Of course I'll be there. Some spells aren't effective unless they're cast at the last second." She scowled at Justin. "Don't worry, though. I won't let your irritating presence mar my concentration."

His eyes flashed. "Good."

"Rose, may I suggest, at the risk of acting bossy, that you get some rest? Drink lots of fluids. If you're planning to go all fire-demony tonight, you'll need the hydration. Another meal or two would probably be a good idea, as well."

Enthralled at the palpable tension in the room, Rose missed what had been said. Maggie and Justin? "What?" She flashed a look at Gabriel. "Oh, food. Got it. Sounds reasonable." Maggie and Justin. Interesting.

"Kellan, do some recon this afternoon. Suss out what the local law enforcement has to say about what happened at Twisted. We may need a badge tonight, so set it up."

"You got it. I'm gone, people. Gabriel, Justin, I'll call. Otherwise, don't look for me until tonight at the scene." Kellan moved in and gave Rose a hearty kiss on the lips. "For luck," he said, and gave her a grin.

~ ☾ ~

She grinned back. And there was another sweetie. Kellan was big, bad, mean...and soft as a marshmallow inside. "I'll take all I can get. Thanks."

Maggie cleared her throat after Kellan left. "What about me?"

Gabriel looked at her. "I'm pairing you with Justin. Get whatever you need for tonight but keep him with you. He'll have phone calls to make and such. I'm staying with Rose, but if Justin needs to get to Doc Cavanaugh's, he'll be closer if he's with you, and I won't have to leave Rose alone."

Justin popped Gabriel on the shoulder. "I'm fine, Gabriel. All clear from last night's vampy fun and games."

"Your kidneys are doing well?" Maggie gave Justin a stern look.

"Breakfast made a new man of me. Ladies, if you'll excuse us?" Justin motioned to Gabriel and the two of them went outside.

* * *

"What's going on?" Gabriel watched as Justin paced the wide front porch, the door closed behind them.

"I still don't trust Magdalena. Are you sure we should have her come? I can ditch her."

"Rose is attached to her. I believe Maggie is who she seems to be. You're not the only one who can use the Internet, you know." He watched Justin, surprised at his brother's unusual jumpiness. "If you're that concerned, stick close to her."

"Trust me, I will," he said grimly. "So what's on your schedule?"

"Demon drills. I want to be able to go demon on purpose and not just in reaction to emotions." He wanted to be ready to fight with all of himself.

"That'll come in handy. Don't wear yourself out on drills, though. You'll have fighting to do tonight, so take your own advice about extra meals. Although I understand your reasoning, we need to be prepared to handle other vampires."

"Yeah, I know. It's why I want to make the switch easier."

"Don't forget, you're part Fae, too. You should practice calling on your Fae heritage. You never know when you'll need it. I can stay with you and help if you like."

Understanding dawned, and Gabriel smiled. "You are so transparent. You're attracted, aren't you? She's got you scared, Magdalena does. Otherwise you wouldn't be shoving this down my throat."

"Not true. It's not my fault you weren't here, little brother. You're gonna be front line on protecting Rose, as well as the rest of us. You need to give your Fae blood a chance to help."

Maggie came through the front door, her head held high, eyes hidden by big sunglasses. She carried her purse and her computer bag. Both men turned to look at her. Justin leaned toward Gabriel. "Remember. You are more than demon. It's time you started acting like it. We're taking the Jag, Magdalena. Your van will be safe here."

Gabriel opened the passenger door for Maggie. He sent Justin a grin over the top of the Jag. "You guys take care," he said.

"Oh, a bit of advice. If you want Rose to sleep, keep her out of the master bedroom. Apparently there's a strong sexual prod on that spiral. Happy marriage and all that." Justin winked, slipped on his own shades and folded himself into the car.

Gabriel tapped the roof a couple of times and backed away, watched as the green Jag went down the long driveway. A sexual prod on the spiral in the master, huh? He stood in the drive and looked toward the house.

Rose appeared in the doorway, her red hair a riot across her shoulders. Her arms were crossed and suddenly Gabriel was able to see through the protection she'd gathered to the uncertain woman below. He wanted her. No spiral could force something that didn't otherwise exist.

He reached her in a breath, gathered her body into his arms. Buried his face in her hair and breathed in her essence.

"I'm not good with words," he rumbled. "But the thought of you getting hurt...it scares me."

Her body softened against his. She opened her arms and hugged him tightly, pressed her face against his chest. "The whole thing scares me," she confessed, pressing back against

~ ☾ ~

his arms to look at his face. She raised one hand to gently trace his scars.

"Come on. Let's go upstairs and take a power nap," he suggested. He tucked her under one arm and snugged her against his side.

"I want to remember this. Every moment with you."

He steered her to the smaller bedroom he'd grown up in. "I want you to sleep, so we'll bunk down here. In you go." If they went to the master bedroom, he'd seduce her again. Or she'd seduce him, and she really needed sleep.

Rose climbed onto the twin bed and moved to one side. Gabriel lay down next to her, pulling her into his arms.

"Rest now. Just rest."

"You think breakfast wore me out?" She chuckled sleepily. "Silly man."

"I think Satine wore you out. If you're not sleepy, don't sleep. I however could use a catnap."

He knew when she dropped into sleep and gathered her closer, resting her cheek against his heart.

How had this happened? How had she become the center of his world so quickly? He frowned, keeping his eyes off the spiral. It would be enough for him to see her through this safely. It would have to be enough.

Dread crawled along his shoulders. Whether he saved her or not, that night would see an ending. He set his jaw and closed his eyes, breathed in her sunny scent. He'd give himself fifteen minutes, then he'd go out and practice.

Fifteen more minutes to bask in her. That's all he needed.

~ ☾ ~

Chapter Twenty

"No. Noooo, nooo, noooo!"

Rose screamed and bolted up straight in her bed, panting and sweating. Late afternoon sunshine streamed in through the window and her racing heart calmed somewhat. A bellow sounded out in the garden and then the back door slammed open before she heard Gabriel's footsteps on the stairs.

He burst into her room, frantic, his demonic tail slowly disappearing as he moved.

"Are you okay? You screamed. What's the matter?" He sat on the bed and reached for her, cradled her against him.

Rose burrowed into his wide chest for comfort just until her heart rate slowed to normal and her breathing settled. It was all she could allow herself. She struggled out of his arms then, moved to the window, and pushed it wide. Feeling the sun on her skin, she sighed.

"It was a dream. It was only a dream." She turned to Gabriel. "I dreamed about tonight. About fighting with Satine, only—I couldn't go all fiery. There was something wrong with that part of me, and she won. She won the fight."

"What do you mean, she won the fight?"

"I mean, I bled out under a bunch of snacking vampires while you killed her and then another bunch of vampires started snacking on you." Impatient, she pushed the hair out of her eyes and moved to the door. "I need water. Are you coming, or not?" Rose headed down the stairs, satisfied when Gabriel followed her.

She filled a glass with water and leaned against the cool kitchen counter, Gabriel close behind her. "It's okay. I'm not going to fall apart again."

~ ☾ ~

Gabriel watched her. "You worried about tonight?"

"You mean, getting within grappling distance of Satine and not being able to get hot? Hell yeah I'm worried."

Gabriel sat. "Tell me everything you remember."

"Fighting. Lots of noise, nasty burnt smells, stuff," she said, purposely vague. "The part that really bugs me is I couldn't catch Satine on fire. She grabbed me, but I had nothing. No flame, no demon. Nada."

"What if you go in flaming? Or at least thinking flamey thoughts?"

She shot him a quick glance. "Do you think she hampered my ability to turn demon?"

Gabriel shrugged. "It makes sense. Fire kills her. Why wouldn't she have a defense against it?"

"So that means I can't kill her with my fire. Oh, that's great. Now we have no plan of attack," Rose stated, her face set.

"Hang on. That's not what I said. What about if you go in all hot to begin with, as the demon? You'd dry up any defense she had pretty quickly. After all, some vampires are extremely susceptible to fire. She probably is, too. It's just a matter of flaming before she touches you, so she can't dampen the fire."

Unwillingly, Rose thought about the possibilities. "Yeah. Okay, that might work."

Gabriel reached a hand out, pushed her hair aside. "I don't want you going in alone. That's just irresponsible. Promise me you won't."

She looked at him thoughtfully. "We'll have to see how it plays out. I mean, I'd much rather not go in alone. In my dream, after Satine had bitten me, other vampires came in, lots and lots of them, crawling out of the woodwork."

"And no one was in there to help you?" Gabriel shook his head. "That's so not going to happen."

"You did show up. The vampires, though, they overran you. You died. There in my vision, you died." Her throat closed up at the memory. "I think we should go in as a group. Maybe. If you think it's a good idea."

"Absolutely. We go in as a group."

"Good. That's good, I think." Restless, Rose stood and

~ ☾ ~

moved to the sink. She stared out the window and gnawed on her lower lip.

"Hey." Gabriel stood, too, and looked down at her.

"Yeah?" Rose tried, but she couldn't read his mood, his eyes guarded against her.

"After this is all over." He tucked a strand of hair behind her ear, touched her cheek gently. "I mean, when we've cleaned up this mess. I'll probably, you know."

"Stop." Rose's heart sank. "We're not having this conversation. There's no reason for you to run again. Your family needs you here. They certainly don't need me. So when you're thinking about the future, remember that this is your place. It's not mine. Not really." She turned away and refilled her water glass. She blinked furiously.

"You mean more to me, more than I thought possible. I just. I can't," he said. He turned away, punched the wall by the door and left a hole in the plaster. "I can't risk you," he growled. "It's too much for me."

She stopped him with an upheld hand. "Please. I understand, I do. Really. But we're done on this topic. You need to go away now, play with your demon side. I've got some work to do on my own." She looked at the clock on the oven and sighed again. "We don't have that much time, after all," she said.

Gabriel stuck his hands in his pockets. "I'll be just outside."

Rose turned to rinse her glass out in the sink. She couldn't watch him walk away, not today. Not when he'd soon be walking out of her life permanently.

Unexpectedly her vision blurred as she recognized the truth. He was it for her, the only man who would ever hold her heart, and he didn't want it. If he did, if he loved the way she loved, the danger wouldn't matter. They'd face it together, come what may.

Pain deeper than she'd ever lived through slashed her heart and she gasped for breath, gripping the edge of the sink until her fingertips turned white.

"This is hard, Maria Therese. Letting him go. It's hard." She rested her forehead against her hands and just breathed,

~ ☾ ~

ignoring the knives in her lungs. She had a job to do. Maria Therese was counting on her. She couldn't let this very personal, much unexpected connection derail her now. Saving Gabriel was the goal. Her own happy ever after? Not so much.

Rose slowly straightened, looked out the window with unseeing eyes at the citrus trees glowing green in the sunlight. Before she died, her life had been pitiful. Funny how death changed her perspective. Now she knew a wider, scarier and more wonderful world. Now she loved and soon she would gain, or lose, more than she'd ever known existed.

Then the rest of her life would begin, or end as the case may be. Rose took a shuddering breath and forced her fingers to release the counter. If she lived, at some point she'd have to figure out how to live without him.

Maybe dying again wasn't that bad an idea, after all, if it meant Gabriel got his soul back, and if she could take Satine with her. Maybe that would go a long way toward her redemption.

Maybe.

* * *

"Gabriel." Kellan leaned against the alley wall across from what was left of Twisted, his cell to his ear. The afternoon slipped toward evening but the heat held sway.

"Yeah. What's up?"

"The insurance people were through here, cleanup crews have started. The Fire Marshall can't figure out how the fire started, or what could have caused such an internal collapse while leaving the external structure still standing." Kellan winked at the insurance gal who walked by with a clipboard and an unfriendly look in her eye.

"You think Satine is lurking down there somewhere?"

"It's hard to tell. The fire stink is so bad, it's hard to scent vampire."

"What about other demons? Have you seen any around?"

"Not a one. I think they cleared out during the fight in the parking lot."

"And no overwhelming evidence of more vampires."

"Truthfully? There could be a hundred down there." Kellan

narrowed his eyes on the upper story. "From what I've overheard, they aren't worried about vandals. The place is unstable; the explosions plus the illegal underground development has the whole thing ready to fall."

"Great. We'll be battling the building as well as vampires."

"Looks like. You okay with it? With your girl going point on this, I mean?"

"Hell no. Would you be? Never mind. We'll meet you there at midnight."

* * *

Gabriel stuffed his cell into his pocket and stared at the citrus grove, unseeing. So it appeared Rose's dream would come true. His hands clenched into fists and released again. He would do everything in his power to keep her safe. If his mother had really talked to her, had really put her mark on Rose as it seemed, then he could do no less than keep her safe. And then walk away.

He laughed at himself, short and bitter. Yeah. As if it would be that easy. With a thought he bounded away, leaped the treetops, shifting into his demonic form as he jumped. The strength that flooded him also filled him with despair, and he roared his unhappiness to the sky.

Dogs for miles around began to howl in sympathy.

* * *

Rose watched him from the upstairs bedroom window. He flowed from human to demon, one step to the other without a pause.

She could probably do that. The few times she'd played with fire it had come so naturally. But practicing in the house just didn't feel like a good idea. The last thing the Caine family needed was a house fire.

Rose put her palm up to the window, covering Gabriel's distant human form. Anything, any sacrifice, she vowed. She would do anything to keep him safe.

Anything.

Her cell phone rang, disturbing her train of thought. Maggie. Huh.

"Hello."

~ ☾ ~

"Rose. We've just talked to Kellan, and I understand he just talked to Gabriel."

"Okay."

"We're meeting at the site at midnight. You'll need more rest, more fluids, and some protein for dinner, so have some leftover strata."

Rose rolled her eyes. "Yes, mom."

"Come on," Maggie chided. "I'm doing my best to keep you alive here."

"I know. I'm sorry. What else?"

"Well, I've got a sort of safety net I can toss around you, but I can't be positive it'll protect you from Vlad."

"The rock."

Maggie sighed. "Yeah. I don't have any strategy for dealing with him. There are too many unknown variables."

"Okay." Rose stared out the window where Gabriel continued to flash between human and demon.

"Are you okay with this? We can back off, you know. Do something else at a different time."

Rose shook her head. "No. I don't think we should put this off."

"If you say so," Maggie said doubtfully. "I'm still looking up ways for you to deal with the demon inside you. An exorcism won't work—too basic for what we're dealing with."

"I see." She sat on the edge of the bed before her legs gave out.

"It might come down to strength and trickery. I just don't know. I'm sorry."

The defeat in her friend's voice galvanized Rose. She injected a cheeriness into her voice that she didn't feel. "Don't worry. Everything will turn out fine. But I need you to promise me something."

"Sure."

"If, on the off-chance that I don't make it, you have to make sure Gabriel stays alive. Don't let anything happen to him, okay?" Urgency thrummed through her. "It's important."

"Sure." Maggie hesitated. "You sound demented, you know that?"

~ ☾ ~

"Please." Rose closed her eyes and lay back on the bed as a tiny pain worked its way through her forehead.

"Okay then, you got it. Protection for Gabriel. I can rig a type of safety net for him, as well. I've been able to practice on Justin, and it seems to work okay." Maggie's voice chilled slightly at the end.

"Hmmm. I sense tension in the air. How's it going with Justin, anyway?" Rose rolled over to her side.

"You mean the irritating, arrogant, know-it-all ass that is Justin? Fine."

Rose's lips twitched. "Yeah. Okay, subject closed. Stay cool, right?"

"Right. We'll see you in a few hours now. Get some sleep," Maggie ordered.

"Don't forget to rest your brain," Rose said. "Bye." She turned her phone off and rolled to her back again to stare up at the ceiling. After the morning she'd had, and the night she was anticipating, the sleep would do her good.

She studied the spiral, content to let herself get drowsy. A character in the spiral caught at her. Before she could examine it, the pull of sleep caught her and she succumbed, her eyes closing at last.

* * *

Resting after bounding around the orchard for a couple of hours, Gabriel lay flat on the ground under an old grapefruit tree, the sun dappling his face, and looked deep at his reluctance to use his Fae powers. It wasn't so much that he didn't want to use them. It was more that he wasn't sure he could fully believe in them.

A low chuckle brought him to a sitting position. There, cross-legged in jeans and a faded green tee shirt sat his mother, Maria Therese. Her dark hair, so like his own, had been pulled back into a ponytail.

"Mom." Shock strangled the word in his throat.

She smiled. "I've waited so long to hear you call me that."

"What are you doing here?" He looked around, scrubbed his face. "Am I dreaming?"

"Nope. It's really me. You are ready for what I can teach

you."

"Wait. I'm sorry," he said, and reached for her hand. He didn't think he'd ever held anything quite so precious. "I'm so sorry I killed you." Finally able to say the words lifted a burden off his heart.

Surprise lit her face. "Gabriel. You didn't kill me. None of us knew what would happen if I brought you to term, but I loved you. I wanted you, so much that I persuaded Gideon to let me try." *You were the only one to speak to me, mind to mind, while you were still in the womb. How could I not love you?*

"Really?"

"Really. The Fae bloodline is strong within you. There is much for you to learn and not much time."

Gabriel flushed. "Whenever Gideon gave us lessons, I didn't listen. I made him so mad."

"I know." She patted the hand that held hers. "The most important thing you need is the healing abilities. Yours are just as strong as Justin's. You tried as a newborn to save me, to heal me. I believe it was such a traumatic event for you that you blocked all memory of it, all knowledge."

Her gray eyes, so like his own, softened at the memory. "I loved you so much, and then I had to leave you."

"Mom. Please." Gabriel blinked at the moisture in his eyes. "Tell me what I need to know."

She released his hand and picked up a stick. "The Fae channel healing powers from every living and growing thing. Feel the earth beneath you, feel the life teeming there." In the dirt between them, she drew a spiral. "When you need to, use that life-force to heal. Lay it gently over burns, for instance, or use it like thread to sew up gaping wounds. The force you pull from the earth is grounded within your own life force, though. If you use it too freely, you could die."

"I've seen a bit of what Justin does. I know how it wears him out."

"It's there, Gabriel, inside you. You are just as much Fae as you are demon and human." Humor lit her face. "It wouldn't surprise me if all that ability isn't just waiting to be tapped."

~ ☾ ~

"Healing. Okay, got it. What else?"

Maria Therese sighed. "Too much. Let's see. You'll always be able to find your mate by using the bonding threads. You can travel them if you don't let yourself think too much, but only as a last resort, and only when all else fails. Food will help ground you, just as it does when you change in and out of demon-form."

Gabriel watched her as she spoke, her hands moving gracefully in the air, punctuating her words. He tried to memorize how she looked with the sun dancing in her dark hair and her face so alive.

"You're beautiful."

Maria Therese stopped in mid-sentence to give him a brilliant smile. "You are special, Gabriel, and not just because you are my son. I know you are already bonded, had hoped the two of you would find each other. Rose needs you as much as you need her. And now," she said, rising to her feet and dusting off her jeans, "I must go."

"What about Gregor? Justin? Kellan, too. What should I tell them?" Gabriel hastily stood, surprised at how small his mother was.

"Tell them what's in your heart. You have been alone for too long, Gabriel. They have needed you." Her hand reached up and stroked his cheek. "You have needed them."

"I love you. I have always loved you." Gabriel's vision blurred as tears gathered and fell.

"Dear boy." Smiling, she rose up on tiptoe, put her hands on his shoulders and kissed each cheek then backed away.

"Wait." Gabriel swung her up in a desperate hug. He could feel her delighted chuckle. "Don't leave. Please."

Her words whispered in his ear. "I must. Now live the life you were meant to live." The form in his arms faded into nothingness.

Gabriel sat back down with a thump, the pain a reassurance that yes, he was awake, and he'd really had a conversation with his mother.

His mother. Astonishment filled him. *Would anyone believe him if he told them?*

~ ☾ ~

***

"Hold still." Maggie scowled at Justin who fidgeted in front of her.

"This is ridiculous. It's not going to work." He shifted from foot to foot and wrinkled his nose. "Whatever you're using smells terrible."

"That's asafoetida," she said absently. "Look, you've got to stop breaking my concentration. If I mess this up and you, or anyone else on our team, dies, I am so gonna kill you."

Justin held himself still and watched as she went through her ritual of mumbling words and sketching designs in the air. A shower of herbal dust filtered down over his head and shoulders and she clapped three times.

He didn't move, just met her expectant gaze with one eyebrow raised.

"How do you feel?"

"Fine. How should I feel?"

Maggie sighed. "It'll work. It has to. I just was hoping for some, I don't know, physical or mental manifestation for the person being protected."

"Sorry."

"It's fine." She turned away and bagged the rest of the smelly powder. "I'll keep working, see if there's something better out there."

Justin looked around her tiny kitchen. All clean lines and cool greens, it made a nice contrast to the floral abundance in the living room. "I like this place."

"Thanks." Her voice was stiff.

Justin mentally shrugged. It was past time he took off for awhile. "Hey, if you don't need me as guinea pig any more, I'm heading out. I've got some work to do and I want to get some supplies of my own."

He caught the anxious glance she shot him. "Don't worry. I'll pick you up in time."

"Yeah, okay."

"Maggie."

She looked at him, really looked at him for the first time since they'd gotten to her house hours ago. Justin felt that

~ ☾ ~

look down to his bones.

"Yeah?"

"Please don't worry. We're going to knock those vampires on their ass." He gave her a grin. "Our might plus your protection? We've got it in the bag."

She sniffed. "What kind of supplies are you getting?"

"I'm dropping by Sol's place, Alexandria Books." Justin shrugged. "I just thought maybe he'd have some words of wisdom for us. Maybe some weapons."

Chagrin crossed Maggie's face. "Damn it. I should have thought of Sol."

"Yeah, well. Being all the way out in Pasadena, it's not like he's within walking distance. So, I'll be back around eleven tonight. Unless you want to have dinner with me?"

Justin watched as her brown eyes frosted over. "Yeah. Didn't think so. Bye." He sauntered out through the floral living room, very much aware that he'd rather spend the next few hours needling her than running out to see Sol, magical bookstore notwithstanding.

~ ☾ ~

Chapter Twenty One

A construction fence had been put around the burnt-out building to keep the kids and the criminal element out. Gabriel and Rose were the first to arrive. They approached as they had that first time, going around on foot to the alley in the back.

"How long will it take, do you think?" Rose hugged herself as they waited in the dark. Nerves had her stiff with tension, and she was aware of a burning pain on her belly. Surreptitiously she rubbed where Mephisto coiled, waiting.

Gabriel squeezed her hand. "It won't be long before the others are here."

"No, I meant...never mind." How long would it take for a vampire to burn into ash? How long would she have to keep up the flame? Rose's nerves ratcheted up as she went over all the possibilities.

She'd changed her mind on the way to the club about going in as a group. The best thing would be to go in alone. Keep the rest of them out of it for as long as possible. All she'd need would be a brief period when no one was watching her - when no one would notice if she leaped the fence.

"Maggie and Justin are near."

Rose's tension eased slightly as she remembered Maggie's plans for more protection for the others. "Good. That's good." They both looked up at a slight noise. Kellan dropped down beside Gabriel.

"Hey." He dusted his hands off on his jeans.

Gabriel rolled his eyes. "Show off."

Kellan shrugged. "I like the heights, what can I say?" He gestured up to the high block wall behind Rose. "I was up

~ ☾ ~

there."

"Oh." She sent him an uncertain smile. If they would just get involved in discussing strategy, she might have a chance to go in first. Rose took a few steps away from the men, staring at the fencing in front of them. She heard them talking in hushed voices behind her.

"Anything to report?"

"I haven't seen, heard, smelled or felt so much as a twitch from the building, and I've been here nonstop since the cleanup crew left. The smoke has just about killed my nose."

"Damn."

"I don't know how lucky we'll get, finding her here," added Kellan.

"And if we do find her here - could that be a trap?" Gabriel wondered.

"Yeah. That thought had crossed my mind."

Maggie and Justin came around the corner. "We're here with smelly stuff and sparkly stuff to keep us all safe," Justin said with a grin for Rose, who gave him a wan smile. "Hey now. What's this? Are you doubting us Caines?" He slung an arm around her and walked her back to the other two.

Rose pressed her lips together tightly to keep from groaning. She'd have to start over again to get away from them.

Maggie grunted. "Yeah. Why doubt? You know, they've never actually put away a vampire. Gabriel and Kellan remember each other as children, and Justin prefers to surf rather than train to kill. A bunch of misfits like us? No problem, we'll get the job done. Yeah, right." She snorted.

"Don't listen to Ms. Doom n' Gloom, Rose. Everything is going to work out. Okay?"

Rose looked from him to Maggie with wide eyes. "Maggie?" Panic had her by the throat, her pulse beating in rapid time. All her senses seemed to go on high alert. It was almost time. She needed to get in there. Soon. Soon. She could feel it. The demon on her belly writhed. He knew, too.

Regret flashed across Maggie's face. "I'm sorry. We'll be fine. I shouldn't have brought that to the fight." She moved to

~ ☾ ~

Rose's side, gripped her hand. "We'll be fine. Gods, your hands are freezing."

"Not for long." But Rose nodded, licked her lips. "We'll be fine. Of course we will."

"Anger is always good," Kellan murmured, looking at Maggie with speculation.

"Words, words, words," Gabriel said. "Let's get this show on the road." His nervous energy spread through the others and raised tensions.

"We can't just waltz in there without preparation," snapped Maggie. She pulled the small backpack off her back and squatted to get what she needed. "None of us are going in there unprotected."

"She's worked hard. The shields work for a majority of things. If the building collapses on you, you'll have a bubble of air. That sort of thing. And it sure smells better than the first concoction she made up," Justin added.

"Direct magics," continued Maggie, "will rip right through these protections. Not that I'm expecting anyone with direct magics in there. But I'm thinking the protection should give you time at least to call up your inner demons. Get them working before anything is thrown at you and you should be fine."

"Someone's coming." Kellan hopped back up onto the wall, looked in both directions. When he hit the ground again, a wide grin split his face. "We've got help."

Justin's face lightened. "Danny?"

"Good show." Kellan exchanged a glance with Justin and Gabriel.

Rose grimaced and sent a quick glance to Maggie. "It'll be okay?"

Maggie shrugged. "I'm not a fan. But if this pack has allied with us, I'm not going to complain. Just let me finish." She stood in front of Rose, her sharp green eyes meeting Rose's summer blue. "Do you agree to this protection I'm about to bestow?"

"Hell yeah."

"Okay then." Maggie worked quickly. A light sheen of sweat

~ ☾ ~

covered her face when she finished. With a fistful of dust, she blew it over Rose. The scent of amethyst, rosemary, and sage lingered in the air.

"Done. Next?" Maggie looked to Gabriel, then Justin, then to the man standing beyond them. "Oh. Sorry."

Justin came to Maggie's side. "Maggie. This is Daniel Roush, of the Santa Monica Preserve wolf pack. Danny, Magdalena de la Cruz." He slid an arm around her waist.

Maggie smiled. "Thanks for being here."

Danny bowed his head slightly. "It is the least we could do. You are a witch?"

Maggie tilted her head to one side. "Yes. It's in my blood. As the wolf is in yours."

Gabriel came up and put a hand on Rose's shoulder. "And you've sort of met Rose."

She'd tensed when Gabriel touched her but gave the newcomer a half-smile. "You were on the perimeter of my vision at that point though. Thanks for coming to my rescue."

"Which you didn't need." Danny smiled.

"Hopefully we won't need you tonight," Maggie said.

Justin gave her a warning look before turning to the others. "Okay. Let's take all sides, partner up. Maggie and I, Gabriel and Rose, Kellan you go in after Rose. Danny, why don't you and your boys hang out just inside the perimeter to mop up anything that gets away?"

"Sounds good. I'll keep in touch." He disappeared around the corner. Rose noticed everyone watched him go. She took the moment to sidle over to Maggie.

"Graceful, isn't he?" she murmured to Maggie. Maggie merely raised her eyebrows.

"Of course. He's a were. Comes with the territory." She shrugged and moved to Justin. Tapped him on the shoulder. "Ready?"

"Do your mojo," he agreed. "Thank God you came up with something better smelling."

Rose edged away from them again, walked to the fence and peeked through a hole in the black fabric.

A hulking gray mass streaked with black sat where the boxy

~ ☾ ~

white building had been. Two big garbage bins stood near by. The closer she got to the place, the more she could smell the fire. The scent called to her. She could feel Mephisto wanting to get in there too, wanting to fight. Rose agreed. She called upon him, grateful even as his warmth filled her from the inside.

She knew fire. She knew its strength. Before thinking about it too hard, she was up and over the fencing without a flame or a sound. She couldn't think about those she left on the other side. She had the best chance of finding Satine and rescuing Gabriel's soul before a huge fight started. If it were just the two of them, Rose stood a chance of success and survival. The way she figured it, if any other vamp were around, her chances of both dropped to almost zero.

Rose took a step and burst into flame. She didn't know if she held her shape or not as she moved, but she felt alive and aware, energy filling her, fire gorging her veins.

Her eyes saw beyond her humanity as she picked her way through the bones of the building. Surprisingly, she was able to pick up on the different smells. The fire smell she dismissed as easily as she did in her dream. Demon smell made her nose wrinkle, though. Full demons were nowhere near as amiable as the part demons she'd grown so used to. Gabriel smelled delicious, but this scent—it bothered her.

Rose followed it to a stairwell, where she picked up another scent, vampire, with a healthy dash of lilies and Eternity - Satine's perfume. Rose remembered it from the last time she was here. A bloody haze rose in her eyes and she moved down the stairwell as fast as a thought. Walls had partially collapsed in places but she flowed over the debris, no obstacle in her hunt.

Nothing living lurked down here. She felt herself expand, let her fiery fingers touch the walls to learn as she moved downward, deeper into the earth, her mind tuned to one thing. A whisper, a whimper hung on the air and she followed the thread of sound. Breaking away from the stairwell she pushed through a hole in the wall and jumped to the floor below. The corridor shrank into itself at the far end, but she

~ ☾ ~

went there anyway.

The scent of Eternity was stronger down here, mingled with fear and disappeared into the rubble in front of her. Opening her mind, Rose let all constraints dissolve and became fire, flickering through tiny, impossible passages, searching.

Movement behind her had her pulling herself back into her body. She whirled around, her eyes wide at the unforgotten scent of malice.

Vlad stood in front of her, his blond hair and dark suit impeccable in the dusty corridor, his eyes almost black. He stared at her in curiosity. "Why have you come?"

"To destroy." The voice that came from her sounded more like Mephisto than her own. Rose blinked in confusion.

Vlad lifted an eyebrow. "Your friends have already destroyed this place."

"Not the place. Satine. She's mine." Rose fragmented into fire again.

"Wait."

She pulled herself together. "Why?"

"Why indeed." The vampire circled her. Rose stood absolutely still, her awareness at its peak with his every footstep.

"You left them all outside. That's arrogance."

"No, that's confidence," she retorted as he came around to face her again.

"If you think so." He chuckled, a dark sound that slithered down her spine and chilled her. Mephisto flared brightly again inside her, but the fear remained.

"Why are you even here? Are you so enamored of Satine that you have to protect her?" Rose tipped her head to one side. "Because I don't see it. You're not weak."

Vladimir nodded approvingly. "Satine is not one to inspire loyalty," he agreed. "I imagine as a human she was infuriating."

"So becoming a vampire doesn't change your personality?" She asked, her hand touching the scar on her throat.

"Ah yes. You were bitten." He smiled as her hand dropped

~ ☾ ~

from the wound. "Unfortunately, you are very much as you ever were when you become a vampire. Only the individual's capacity for change becomes limited. It is a rare person, indeed, who willingly becomes a vampire."

"Are you going to kill me?"

Vlad laughed, surprised. "I'm not sure."

"We don't have any argument with you, per se," she said. "But I owe Satine, don't you think?"

"You would let me leave?" The vampire leaned against the wall. "How very amusing."

"We both know I can't take you down, so we're not talking overwhelming generosity on my part. Sure, leave. I've got nothing against you personally. But I'm very afraid the others will be coming soon, and if you don't want a fight you should go. I'm sure they could take you apart, working together."

Vlad gave her a look she couldn't interpret. "I can see that you need to do something with all that energy amassing in your body. You are vibrating with it."

Rose knew it. It felt almost impossible to keep her skin on, so to speak. She lifted her chin. "Well, either go or stay. I've got a vampire to kill."

She turned to the rubble in front of her and started to pull chunks of wallboard out of the mass.

Rose heard a sigh behind her. "You could have been my perfect distraction. I am quite sure you would have captivated me for at least a couple of centuries. Alas, the demon has first claim on you." He gave a weary chuckle. "And you are heart-deep there, as well. I would give you one piece of advice," he added, as his voice grew more distant.

"And that would be?" Rose asked, her mind only partly on Vlad. If she became fire, could she find a way between the floors...?

"Take care to not be alone with me again. I won't promise not to take you for myself. You are...most unusual." The advice floated in the air around her, menacing.

Rose whirled about, but the hallway was empty. "Okay. Consider me warned," she said, before turning back to the pile of debris where the vampire scent was the strongest. Without

~ ☾ ~

thinking, she dove into the debris, her body splintering into bits of fire as she went.

* * *

Maggie completed her protection of Gabriel and Kellan. "Okay, let's round up and go in."

Justin came running down the alley from his last minute discussion with Danny. He looked around at their group. "Where's Rose?"

Gabriel grew cold with fear. "Damn it, not again." He twisted around to look for her.

Justin turned back to him, frustration etched on his face. "I can't find her. After Maggie did her mojo on me, I turned to look for her but she was gone. So I went to talk to the weres, thinking maybe she'd walked around the corner, but – nothing. She's not there with them. She's not with us. She's just gone."

Gabriel paled. "Gone?"

"I checked with Danny—he hadn't seen anything. They won't go in until we do. He said he'd know when we did." Justin shrugged. "He didn't say anything about Rose."

"How long are we talking?"

"Five minutes? Maybe ten?" Justin shook his head. "I'm not sure."

"She's gone in." Gabriel's despair hung in the air.

Maggie let out a cry. "No!"

"Yes. She had a dream this afternoon—said that she'd gone in alone, and vampires covered her. Killed her." On the last word, Gabriel jumped the fence in front of him, leaving the others cursing behind.

He was already halfway to the opening when the others made the jump, his demon strides even longer than his human ones. His tail twitched in the night, and his growl filled the air.

Gabriel inhaled deeply, catching Rose's scent, the ocean mingled with woodsmoke. As he followed it through the destroyed building, another scent overlaid the first.

"Vampire," he rumbled, and with a leap and a grasp, he caught Vlad by the throat and shoved him against the wall.

~ ☾ ~

The building shook with the force of the hit. He looked into the vampire's bloodred eyes and snarled. "What have you done to her?"

The vampire grinned, sending a cold finger of fear down Gabriel's spine. "Wouldn't you like to know?" he taunted.

Gabriel slammed him against the wall again. Plaster rained down.

"This is a good way to bury her, though. Carry on. You and I will get through this just fine, but will your precious Rose? Once the demon in her has worn her completely out, drained her of her energy and the water in her body, will she be able to claw her way to the surface?"

Gabriel's fingers bit deeper into the rock of Vlad's neck. "What did you do to her?"

"Absolutely nothing. Scout's honor," smirked Vlad. "She let me go, if I promised to let her attack Satine. Ah, that got your heart rate going, didn't it?" Vlad licked his lips. "I wonder if your blood is as sweet in demon form as it is in human form."

Gabriel roared and punched him in the nose, the crunch under his hand extremely satisfying. Vlad's head flew back and hit the wall. More plaster tumbled down on them.

Vlad grinned, his teeth glistening in the dark. "Oh yes. Do spend more time with me while your cute little fire demon grapples with Satine."

With a roar, Gabriel threw the vampire down the hallway and away from Rose's scent. Seeing his brothers in the shadows, he turned away, the vampire forgotten, and raced to find Rose.

His heart stuttered when he got to the pile of debris, the place where the building had shrugged in on itself.

"Rose!"

His heartbroken roar echoed throughout the ruins. Justin and Kellan looked at each other in despair. "Go," urged Justin. He felt Maggie behind them. "We'll take care of this," he added, gesturing to the vampire chuckling at their feet.

"Oh, no you won't," he said, gasping with glee. "Nothing will help her now. She's got to finish it on her own. That's just how quests are made. Didn't you know?"

~ ☾ ~

With a roar of his own, Justin lunged at him, but the vamp wasn't there.

Vlad stopped at the opening to the building, a hundred feet away. "This will be one for the history books," he mused. "Satine. It's time to wake up," he murmured. "Enjoy, young Rose," he said with mild regret. "Expect burns when you play with fire."

Justin turned to follow, but the vampire was gone. He turned back to Maggie, who stood, her hand over her nose and her eyes streaming. "You okay?"

She shook her head and raced out of the building. Torn, Justin looked from her to where his brothers had disappeared and, cursing, followed the witch, leaving his brothers to deal with what was inside.

* * *

Kellan followed the scent of his brother, his body lithe and strong in its demon form. He was used to it, had made the shift more often than his brothers and so moved with ease through the human-sized corridor.

He dropped through a hole in the floor and landed hard enough to make the building tremble.

Kellan stopped abruptly at the sight of Gabriel on his knees in front of a pile of rubble. The whole hallway seemed to shrink in on itself, making standing upright impossible. He bent to Gabriel, putting his hand on his shoulder.

"Gabriel."

"She's down there. She's there." Dread and panic hung in the air.

Kellan shook his head in regret. "I'm so sorry, dude."

Gabriel turned on his brother with a roar. "I'm not letting her die. Not after—not now. I love her, damn it. She's *mine*."

Kellan backed off, his hands up. "Okay. Okay." He looked at their surroundings before he moved to kneel beside his brother. "Let's start digging." With his huge hands, he shoveled aside debris. After a moment, Gabriel helped. Dust rose with their movement, and the ceiling seemed to come closer to their heads as they worked.

Every effort brought more rumbling toward them from

beneath and above. They kept at it, though, blinking their demon eyes and breathing as little as possible. Minutes passed without any obvious success.

Finally Kellan pulled back, as they were showered again with plaster and ceiling tile. "Okay. This isn't working." As if underscoring that, the building groaned around them.

Gabriel didn't seem to notice. He kept shoveling out the sheet rock and plaster, his lips moving in a frantic chant.

Kellan tapped his brother's shoulder to get his attention, but Gabriel didn't budge, just kept muttering and shoveling. Finally Kellan grabbed him around the waist and dragged him back just as more of the building came down in that corner.

Gabriel snarled and threw a punch that didn't land. Kellan, his demonic muscles bunching, kept his arms around him and dragged him out of the hallway into a bigger room that didn't show much physical damage.

"No! I need her, I need to get to her," shouted Gabriel.

Kellan let him go and swung him around to punch him in the jaw. Gabriel ducked and would have gone by him but Kellan was too fast. "You can't. Damn it Gabriel. You can't go in there. The place is about to fall apart on us."

Gabriel turned anguished eyes toward his brother. "I can't let her die."

"No. Of course not." Kellan could see the blue and purple mate-threads glimmering softly in the night, leading away to the pile of rubble they'd left behind. If she died, it would be almost impossible to keep Gabriel alive. He hauled in a breath and thought fast.

"We can't go in physically. But can you reach her mind? Can you keep an eye on her that way, help her out mentally?"

Hope trickled into Gabriel's whirling green eyes. "Let's try." Abruptly he sat down in the middle of the scorched room and closed his eyes. "Rose," he whispered. "Where are you?"

He searched, but found only the hiss and crackle of fire gone out of control. His voice rose in a roar of denial and despair.

Kellan turned at a sound. "Gabriel. We've got company, and they're looking hungry."

~ ☾ ~

Gabriel turned unseeing eyes toward Kellan, who motioned to the doorway. Vampires stood there with more of them filling up the spaces.

"Let's clear the place. Make it safer for Rose. Let's fight, Gabriel."

Gabriel took a breath. "I can get behind that." He got to his feet and sent a cold grin to their visitors.

"Show time," and Kellan grinned as the first one charged, its eyes whirling scarlet with bloodlust.

* * *

Justin strode into the darkness, looking for Maggie. This was not the time for the witch to go solo and, obscurely, he felt obligated to help. The lights of the parking lot had died and the moon hid behind the clouds. But he found her, heaving into the dirt next to the building.

He took in the situation as he strode her way. Kneeling beside her, he put one hand on her forehead, helping to support her, and kept a knee to her back for the same reason.

Maggie retched a couple more times but nothing came up. "I'm sorry, I'm so sorry," she gabbled, and swiped her wrist across her mouth. "I'm so sorry."

"It's okay. Maggie, look at me." Justin was kind, but firm. Maggie turned to look at him, misery in her brown eyes. "Is it the smell?"

"Vampire and smoke and demon all mingled up and gods!" She turned and heaved again, with no visible result. "No one in their right mind could survive that."

Justin's lips twitched. "Are you scared?"

"Hell no," she fired back. "I just don't want the smell of ashtray and moldy socks in my nose for the next decade."

He laughed at that. "You're right, that is what it smells like. So do me a favor, and let me help you. I can put a block on your sense of smell so that you won't notice it."

Maggie looked up at him with suspicion. "Why would you?"

"Because you're one of the strongest women I've ever met, and if I left you out here hiding from a smell, you'd regret it tomorrow. The fighting has begun, Maggie. Our side is down two." He nodded to the building beside them, reverberating

~ ☾ ~

with battle cries. "We're needed."

"I don't know," she demurred. "I don't want to go back in there."

"No sane person wants to fight," Justin murmured, and brushed the bangs out of her eyes. He lifted her chin and looked into her eyes. "Trust me. I'm not going to hurt you. I'm just going to put a block on your sense of smell. No tricks, no hidden suggestions, nothing, I swear it."

She pulled in a deep breath of clean air. "You swear it?"

"I swear," he said, and held out his right pinky finger. "I pinky swear it."

"Oh, well then, that makes it okay," she said, confused, and linked pinky fingers with him.

Justin smiled. "Just look into my eyes," he murmured. "I don't have a lot of time, and I'll need your cooperation. Keep yourself open and look into my eyes." Justin sent into her mind the suggestion that she not smell anything and that every breath she took felt like clean, pure air, giving her energy. He also gave her the suggestion that her sense of smell would return to normal at the rising of the sun.

When the pain in her eyes eased, he smiled. "There. All done. Now, let's go in there and kick some vampire ass."

She jumped up, looking refreshed. "Ready when you are."

The two went back into the building.

Vampires were everywhere. "Can you conjure fire?" Justin shouted to Maggie. She smiled.

"First lesson I ever learned."

"Then get to it, woman. Vamp on your left." He watched as she turned, pulled a fireball out of nowhere, and threw it at the middle of the strike zone as if she were pitching for the Dodgers.

The vamp brushed at the fire with a comical look of disgust just before it went up in smoke. Young, and not too bright, mused Justin as he pulled his blades from the holster on his back. He moved to Maggie's back and swiftly dealt with the two young girls approaching him, blood in their eyes.

Soon Justin was too busy with vampires of his own to destroy to keep more than an occasional eye on her.

~ ☾ ~

Chapter Twenty Two

Rose pulled herself together after her foray through the rubble. Her hand brushed over her head, reminding herself that she was in demon form, complete with tiny horns on either side of her forehead.

How bizarre. She craned a look over her shoulder and saw the tiny wings that Gabriel had told her about. He was right, useless for flying, but yeah - cute. Even as she was cataloguing all the changes her body had gone through - yep, spots and fur - ugh, hooves? - another part of her mind checked out where she'd appeared.

It was colder down here, the scent of fire more distant, as if it hadn't had time to penetrate this far before it had been put out. The space was tiny, too—not much room to even turn about at the end of a stairwell. But there, at her right hand, huddled Satine, her head on her knees, pale arms wrapped around her bare legs.

Her mouth flooded with fiery satisfaction. "Satine."

But the vampire didn't move. Rose frowned. Bent to touch her shoulder. "Satine." Rose shook her, tilted her head back. Her eyes were open, but blank.

Puzzled, Rose took a step back. "Well, hell. Are you dead? No, I can't believe that. A dead vampire doesn't have a head, I think. Hmm." She could feel Mephisto in her head, chuckling at her thoughts.

"Oh, shut up. I'm doing the best I can," she growled. "I can't just burn her up while she's—whatever is wrong with her," complained Rose. "That just isn't fair."

Since when is killing a vampire based on fairness?

"She is my cousin," Rose pointed out.

~ ☾ ~

She stole your soul. Don't ever forget what she put you through.

Trust me, it's something I'll never forget.

Mephisto chuckled. *Plus, she'd love to drink your blood. Why give her any chance? Family blood is the closest to their own and so provides them with their greatest strength.*

"Now you tell me." Rose pulled her thoughts together. "I'd better grab Gabriel's soul while I have the chance." Rose shed her fire demon and knelt in front of Satine. Her stomach roiled with the change. Stubbornly, she swallowed and ignored the nausea. "Here goes nothing." Rose closed her eyes, reached out and touched Satine's chest.

"Gabriel Caine," she whispered. "Where are you?"

A howling filled her mind. Faces of people she'd never met flipped by like an old-fashioned movie even as their souls streamed into her easily, quietly. She waded through them, a salmon swimming upstream, anxious to reach Gabriel's soul.

Individual stories battered her mind, pushed against her, desperate for her attention. Stubbornly, she kept only one name in her mind. One face in front of her.

As she drew nearer to Gabriel's soul, it glowed golden. Rose could feel a smile break out on her face as she beckoned it. The glow came toward her, flowed into her as so many others had in the past few seconds. This time was different. Her chest tightened and her heart labored as the pieces of Gabriel's soul rejoined.

Another soul, blindingly white and tasting of cool water, slipped into her and Rose gasped. What had been a waiting, even when she had Gabriel's soul in her, became whole again. She had her soul back, and all of her memories.

Before Rose could pull away, even more souls flooded into her, eager to escape Satine. They rushed inside her, to the place made for them, and their stories were told in disjointed pictures as they came. Her vision blurred as she tried to keep track of them all.

The flood slowed, had almost stopped when she felt still another, partial, soul slide into her. This one had a silvery glow with dead spots and a metallic aftertaste. Rose gasped,

~ ☾ ~

arched at the pain as she absorbed the battered and damaged soul.

Rose stumbled away from her cousin, her pulse beating frantically. Her limbs felt filled with lead. How in the world was she supposed to handle such agony? She could feel her white soul surrounding the silvery one, burnishing up the dead spots. Her blood pounded in her ears and she dropped to her knees.

Rose. The demon's voice snapped her back to her surroundings. *You'd better change back now. You'll be stronger when you do.*

I am tired, she admitted. Staring at Satine, she sighed and called the demon. As fire filled her, his borrowed strength returned, flooding her limbs with energy.

You're getting good at that, said Mephisto. *Let's make a bargain. I like being with you. So how about I leave part of my powers with you, as long as I can always have a home on you when I need one?*

If you leave a part of yourself within me, I'll be yours to command. Right? Rose shook her head. *No.* She'd had enough of other people pulling her strings.

It's not that big a deal. Have I been demanding? Do you really want to be normal?

Rose made a face. Being normal wasn't on her top ten ideas of a good time, not when she was surrounded by tribred demons and witches and Weres. "I'm not normal, though. I'm a Soul Chalice." Satisfaction rang through her voice.

Satine's eyes sharpened and her face snapped to Rose. "Who the hell are you talking to?" Satine looked the fire demon up and down. She frowned. "Who the hell are you?"

Rose grinned. "Hey, cousin Sara. I'm here to kill you." Her body flamed. She sent a couple scout flames down her arm and they jumped from her hand to Satine's arm.

Satine screamed, patted it out. Her eyes whirled red. "You make my mouth water. It has been years since I've drunk," she added piteously. In a flash she went from huddled on the stairs to wrapping her arms around Rose, sinking her teeth into her shoulder. Fire flared, danced along the slick coldness

~ ☾ ~

of the vampire.

Rose gasped with pain. Poured everything she had into the flame, shimmered with it. She tried to turn into pure flame but Satine's mouth held her to her demon shape.

Satine pulled away. "You want to play, cousin? I do." Giddy with Rose's blood, she spun Rose away from her and into a wall, head first.

Rose burst into flame again. She shook her head, groggy, and came toward Satine, who merely grinned. Rose's blood darkened her lips.

"Come on. Come to me. I'm not finished with you yet. I want to feel your heart thunder under my hand, feel it fail. I want to drink all your memories and give you some of mine."

Rose, dizzy from heat and blood loss, couldn't keep her eyes on Satine and before she knew it, Satine had caught her again, her teeth sinking into the same place.

This time, Satine took her deep. The pain, the scent of smoke all fell away and Rose was there, her boss David in front of her, his eyes like fire as he gazed hungrily at her. The small convenience store was just as it had been, smelling of hotdogs and coffee. But it wasn't her, she realized. It was Satine who had dressed like her. Rose recognized Sara's shorts and the tattered Hendrix concert tee shirt.

It was Satine who begged her boss to kiss her before pulling away with a promising pout when they were interrupted. It was Satine who had set up her rape later that evening. As Rose relived that event, saw again her virginity stolen from her and her subsequent fall from grace, saw Satine steal her soul, a rage built inside. The fire on her outside grew even as Satine drew hard on her blood.

Rose shook herself out of the past and screamed. The vampire's bite burned, more like acid in her veins than fire. Rose felt her vision fade. *She's getting stronger. Help me! Mephisto, help, give me more oh please God!* If I don't make it back to Gabriel, all is lost...

I'll help you...

"Hurry!" she shrieked.

*As you so desir*e. And the demon Mephisto chuckled.

~ ☾ ~

Rose's internal body temperature shot up, her blood almost boiling inside her. Satine pulled her mouth away from the suddenly hot blood, fascinated. Thinner than water, it flowed down Rose's arm.

Satine stroked the orange and yellow spotted fur in amazement. "You are magnificent," she murmured.

A pain caught Rose in the belly and she sagged in Satine's arms, her eyes wide and her mouth open, unable to get any sound out. All the air was just gone from her lungs and her heart labored, struggled to beat in the silence between them.

A ripping sound caught them by surprise. Rose screamed once, finally, her lungs moving fast as her heart raced to catch up.

Mephisto looked at her over Satine's shoulder, his handsome face smiling at her. "Rose, my love. Let's get the job done, shall we? Though I will spare you as much as I can."

"What will I owe you?" she gasped.

Mischief broke through the sadness in his eyes. "I don't know. A soul like yours – even if just returned - would be quite a coup."

Mephisto stepped up right behind Satine, wrapped his arms around them both. With his touch, the blood flowing down Rose's arm stopped. His curious eyes seemed to dismiss the vampire struggling between them, as though she were already ash. Satine's screams went higher than normal human hearing but Rose didn't notice.

Rose was caught in Mephisto's heat. His touch reignited her flame. "Look into my eyes, Rose. Just focus on my eyes." The orange flame she saw there fascinated her. She pressed closer, feeling the cold body of the vampire between them as only a barrier to something she needed. Between the two of them, flame engulfed Satine, her struggles and screams unnoticed.

The two fire demons, their eyes only on each other, burned the vampire between them almost without realizing it. Once the barrier of her body fell to the ground as ash, Rose sagged in Mephisto's arms. The wound in her shoulder reopened and blood poured down over the soft fur that covered her tawny

~ ☾ ~

skin.

***

Mephisto hesitated. He'd enjoyed his time on her body, had dreamed about holding her in his arms even while she dreamed about the tribred. Leaving her now to die wasn't his first choice. Taking her soul was even less appealing; a first for him.

Sighing, he knelt down on top of the vampire ash and drew Rose down with him. He put his mouth over the wound in her shoulder, tasted her blood. The vampire had been right. She tasted amazing. Though why that surprised him when her soul also had the most incredible scent and flavor...He drew in a breath, then with all the power available to him, instead of taking her blood, he sent his life and flame into her body.

The healing fire scorched her on the inside and her body arched as she screamed. Mephisto watched, fascinated. He'd never actually tried this before. He pulled away from her shoulder and eyed her anxiously. He needed her to live, but not at the expense of his own life. He watched her eyes flutter open.

"Rose. You need to go back to your lover. Go to Gabriel." With a lingering look, he vanished in front of her eyes.

***

Rose panted as her heart struggled to return to normal, shuddered at the loss of his heat. She pulled herself up off the floor, leaned weakly against one wall. Satine was nothing more than ash. She did it.

Euphoria caught her, and she grinned up into the darkness. She was free. She was alive. She saved Gabriel. She did it!

Fine dust, followed by slightly bigger chunks of debris, filtered down through the clogged portion of the stairwell and her true situation settled over her as quickly as the dust.

Urgency thrummed through her. Her only chance was to get through the debris the same way she did the first time. Then, rage and protectiveness had given her the impetus she needed. Now?

Her mouth was dry. Her eyes burned and her lips felt cracked. The battle wasn't done, but she was wiped out

~ ☾ ~

completely. Rose stood, stumbled and would have fallen, but Maria Therese stood there.

"Are you so ready to give up, to let my son lose his soul?"

"No. No! Of course not Maria Therese," Rose cried out, but her vision had faded. "Of course not," she mumbled, and her eyes ached for the tears she could not shed. She blinked, her lids like sandpaper against her eyes. "Onward and upward." She looked up at the debris clogging the way out and felt her wings flutter uselessly on her back.

"Come on, Mephisto," she implored, but the demon remained silent. "Okay then, the hard way." She filled her head with every memory of fire she could find. The way it looked, the way it felt to hold it, a fireball spattering against the ground where she'd dropped it. The sun and its fiery rays burning her as a child. Marking her? It didn't matter. Fire was hers. She was fire.

She let the images fill her head, looked up again to where she knew Gabriel waited for her. "Go, Rose. Go now," she whispered to herself, and without another thought launched herself to the ceiling above. But her head never got close.

She fell back to the ground, and in despair felt herself scatter as flame.

* * *

Gabriel ripped the head off the vampire in front of him and tossed it across the room. He staggered when something like a sonic wave hit his chest. That part of him tied to Satine just evaporated. *Rose?* No answer. Gabriel waited for his soul to return, but nothing else happened.

Plaster dust and ash swirled in the building, adding to the dark chaos and battle cries. Danny's wolves were fighting alongside Kellan and Gabriel. Fireballs lit up the area where Maggie and Justin worked. Slowly the eight of them prevailed against the newest vampires in the city and quiet returned.

A pile of body parts had been stacked in a corner farthest from where Rose had gone. Kellan flicked a cigarette lighter on and caught the hair of one vamp on fire. Quickly it spread.

Gabriel turned back to the hallway to make sure no other vamps were hiding out, relieved when he cleared the area. He went once more to where Rose's scent was strongest. Out of the corner of his eye, he caught sight of the purple and blue light, twisting away from him and into and down through the pile of rubble.

His mother's voice came back to him. *You will always be able to find your mate through the bonding threads binding you. You can even travel them, if you don't think about it too much.* Gabriel changed shape abruptly, staggered in the hallway in his human form. He touched the soul mate threads tentatively. They were cool, tensile under his fingertips. Unbreakable? Gabriel shook his head. There was only one way to find out.

Putting all his trust into the Fae heritage he knew nothing about, Gabriel grabbed onto the soul mate threads and willed himself to Rose. His vision shifted, grew better by several magnitudes. His body cooled, and then he lost all sense of who he was. Keeping his focus on Rose kept the world from tumbling by as he traveled through impossible cracks, down, down into the earth. He felt the cool surround him, felt the air expand to accept him.

Gabriel's hand touched Rose's chest and his awareness of his body sprang to the forefront of his mind. His breath whooshed out of his lungs as his eyes adjusted to the deeper dark. Rose lay awkwardly, partly on a staircase leading up to rubble, her naked human form cool to the touch.

"Rose. Damn you," Gabriel choked. He gathered her up in his arms very carefully and stood. He had her now, but how the hell were they to get out of there?

Don't think too much about it. His mother's voice drifted in the air. Gabriel could see the mate-threads binding Rose to him; he let himself remember how he'd ridden the threads.

Back. He needed to go back, needed to ride the threads that had been there, but weren't any longer. Trusting again to a heritage he knew little about, he felt his vision narrow, felt how, still carrying Rose, they slipped their way through openings too minute for the human eye to see as they zipped between floors. Up, up to safety.

The fresh air was his cue. Once again his breath whooshed

~ ☾ ~

out as his feet settled on the floor. He staggered as Rose became solid once more in his arms. He whirled, desperate to get her out of danger. Eyes wild, he didn't see the fire bars that had been erected between them and freedom until he walked into them.

Surprised, he sprang back, but the flame had done its job.

Rose jolted awake, tongues of fire flickering from her fingertips as she changed again to demon in Gabriel's arms. She blinked her orange eyes up at Gabriel and smiled.

"Hey. Your eyes are purple and silver. Very cool."

Gabriel crushed her to him. His breath came hard, each one filled with pain and relief.

"You can let me down now," Rose said. She coughed and a little bit of smoke came out of her mouth. "Brilliant," she sighed. Wiggling a bit, she smiled again. "No, really. Please put me down."

Gabriel lowered her feet to the floor and steadied her, one hand on her waist. "Are you - I couldn't follow you. I couldn't hear your mind. I just about went crazy while you were down there and I don't want that to ever happen again, do you understand me?"

Rose slipped out of his hold. "Satine is gone."

"I know. I felt the connection dissolve. Thank you," he said.

She looked around at the room they were in, the doorway blocked with bars of fire. "We're trapped in here."

"Currently, yes," began Gabriel. "But the others are out there. They'll help us as soon as they can."

Rose shrugged. "I never thought I'd survive this. Having come this far is kinda neat. Which reminds me, I have something for you." She moved in to him and put her hands on his chest. She smiled up at him. "Close your purple eyes. Wow, you've got to tell me what you've been doing."

"I won't close them." Gabriel's voice broke. "Not when I've needed the sight of you."

She closed her eyes. A glow surrounded her that had nothing to do with fire and everything to do with her.

He thought receiving his soul would hurt as much as having it taken from him had. Instead, his heart expanded

~ ☾ ~

with wonder as, unbidden, the three parts of himself; human, demon, and Fae separated in front of his eyes, clear and distinct, before swirling together, stronger than ever, and disappearing inside him. Gabriel felt whole, perhaps for the very first time.

"Thank you. Again." His voice was hoarse, but she heard him and stepped away.

"What is it about your eyes? Some sort of demon thing?" She tilted her head up to his.

"Fae, not demon." He eyed her warily. Should he tell her they were mated?

The air shimmered at the edges of Gabriel's vision. He shifted slightly, watched as another fire demon came into being. He wasn't that much bigger than Rose. His skin reflected Rose's light, turning it redder than it might have. His black hair gleamed. Gabriel's muscles tensed and he phased into his demon form, grateful now for the practice. He noted with pleasure that he stood almost twice the other demon's size.

Mephisto.

Gabriel put Rose behind him.

The newcomer winked at Gabriel and gave him a short bow. "Gabriel Caine."

"Yes."

"I have been watching you from my vantage point on Rose. What a fascinating experience." Mephisto folded his legs and sat on the air.

"You're free," said Gabriel. "Not constrained in any way."

"Observant. Yes, I am. But she's not," and he smiled at Rose. "You see, she bargained with me. But she didn't know she was bargaining, so we've got that bit of business to finish before we can move forward."

Quicker than thought, Gabriel's hand shot out and punched Mephisto in the nose. Mephisto careened backwards in surprise but Gabriel plucked him out of the air and shook him, one big paw dwarfing the other demon. Rose cried out, but both demons ignored her.

"That's for Marianne, you bastard," he growled, and

~ ☾ ~

punched him again. "Give me one good reason to spare your life."

Awareness flickered in Mephisto's black eyes. "She wanted me," bit out Mephisto. "Marianne's soul was black. Taking it was too easy. You wasted your time with her." Blood flowed from his nose but he made no effort to staunch it. Gabe's fist plowed into Mephisto's abdomen, causing the demon's eyes to bug out.

Flame flickered along the demon's arms as he caught Gabriel's hand. "Burn again, if you must," gasped the demon. "Rose will die if you do."

Gabriel's tail whipped around Mephisto's waist, holding him in mid-air. Gabe stepped back, slapped at the fire that had danced along his forearm, and prepared to hit the demon again.

"Wait!" Rose was there, pressing herself up against him. "Don't hurt him."

Gabriel turned to her in disbelief. "What?"

"Please. He saved my life. Can't you tell he's exhausted? He can barely fight you. He hasn't taken a swing, has he? Let him go," she insisted, pressing kisses across his chest. "Please, Gabriel."

Reluctantly, Gabriel's tail unwound itself from the demon.

Mephisto dropped lightly to the ground, his eyebrows high as he glared disapprovingly at Rose. "What are you doing?"

Rose put herself between the two demons and lifted her head high. "We made a bargain down there?"

"Yes," admitted Mephisto, wary.

"You gave me a part of yourself. That's why I'm still a demon, yes?

"Yes. It's temporary. The bars of fire called it out of you so you wouldn't burn."

"I'm going to give you something that you desperately need." She glowed, shades of gold and silver sparking a web around her demon form.

Mephisto paled, his face going gray as he grasped her meaning. "How?"

Rose shrugged a shoulder. "Found it in Satine. I don't

know how she got it, but I thought you might want it back. It's not much, there are pieces missing."

"I'll take it." The words rushed out of his mouth. He bowed his head in supplication. "If you please." Rose stretched a hand out to Mephisto and took a step toward him.

"Wait," commanded Gabriel. He turned to Rose, beyond exasperated. "What are you thinking? You're giving a demon back his soul? Wait. Do full demons even have souls?"

Rose turned to Gabriel. "He gave me a part of himself. Right now, I have strength. I don't know how long I'll have it, but the fight's not over. So let me do this, okay?"

"I don't like it."

"You don't have to." She eyed him. "I'm giving his back, just like I gave you yours back. Is that a problem? Satine had it. When I took yours back from her, I got mine back and Mephisto's came, too, as well as all the others she'd amassed through the years." She cupped Gabriel's cheek with one hand, her eyes steady on his face. "He just saved my life, Gabriel, and now I have his soul. I'm not about to withhold his soul from him."

"Okay, okay. But we'll do it my way." He turned Rose toward Mephisto, and held her back to his front, one big arm across her body protectively. "First," he said, addressing Mephisto, "if she does this for you, then you leave the greater Los Angeles area. If I catch even a whiff of your stench on the air, I will find you and crush the life out of you."

"Agreed," Mephisto said, his eyes not leaving Rose.

"Second. Release all claim on her soul."

He rolled his eyes. "Fine. I release my claim on her soul." He waved a hand and the bars of fire melted away, leaving a slightly sulfurous scent behind. "Not that I really had a claim there, so that one was easy."

Gabriel kept tight rein on his temper, wanting nothing more than to hit him again. "Third. If we ever need you, you come."

Startled, Mephisto looked up at Gabriel, wary. "Why would you want help from me?"

Gabriel shrugged. "I've heard about the rumblings from the

~ ☾ ~

Chaos Plane. You could come in handy if it ever comes down to a fight between Chaos and humanity."

The demon's eyebrows rose. "Interesting. Agreed. Now, dear Rose." Expectantly, Mephisto turned his charm toward her. "Whenever you're ready."

Rose patted the arm across her body. "Gabriel?"

Reluctantly, he released her and took a half step backwards. "I'm here if you need me," he grumbled.

She flashed a grin at him over her shoulder. "I know."

Turning back to Mephisto, she smiled. "You've had a tough time of it. Hopefully, this will bring you a measure of peace. I did what I could to heal it, but I don't know much and there was little time."

She reached out and put her hand onto his bare chest.

At her touch, Mephisto's body arched and a look of pained surprise crossed his face. Gabriel could almost see the demon's soul pass through Rose and into Mephisto's chest, a silvery, glittery, jagged burst of light, surprisingly small, that spread through him.

Mephisto sank to his knees, agony contorting his features.

Rose snatched her hand away and stepped back, alarmed. Gabriel's arms came around her protectively. "Gabriel! What did I do wrong?"

They watched as Mephisto, his face bloody, bowed his head to the floor and howled. Flame burst along his arms and streamed down his hair. He flung his head back, caught Rose's hand in his and pressed a kiss on the back of it. His flame didn't touch her. "Thank you," and his eyes glistened with moisture. "It has been too long housed in others," he gasped. "My body is making room again."

"I understand now. Blessings, Mephisto," she murmured.

The demon cringed. His flame flared high and both Rose and Gabriel blinked at the brightness. When they could see again, Mephisto had vanished.

Kellan appeared, backlit by firelight. "We've gotta get out of here. The building's gonna go."

Rose turned to look at Gabriel, her face paling. "Mephisto. He's leaving me. I mean, I know he left, but he's leaving me,"

~ ☾ ~

she whispered, agonized.

Gabriel lifted her. "Stay with me, Rose. Stay with me." Her body had grown very cold, a last flush of heat on her cheeks slowly paling.

"I'm here," Rose whispered, clutching at his shirt. "I'm not leaving you. Not now."

As he held her, her fire demon form wavered and vanished, leaving the human Rose in his arms. "I'm just plain me again," she sighed, and a tear rolled down one cheek. Her head lolled back over his arm.

The building rumbled beneath his feet as his fear and anger surged. He held her tighter to him and ran for safety through the scent of hellfire and smoke.

He emerged into the night and ran to the far edge of the parking lot where his brothers and Maggie had gathered. A rumbling behind them had them moving again into the alley.

"Quickly," said Kellan, and waved Gabriel through the hole in the fence. "Get her to Doc Cavanaugh. We'll follow."

"No. Get my clothes, and a coat, a blanket, or something to cover her up," Gabriel ordered. As the others hesitated, he growled. "Now!"

"Blanket, coming up," promised Maggie. She flew through the darkness out of sight.

Justin tossed him a bag. "Your clothes. Well, my clothes, but you're welcome to them."

Gabriel held Rose close to his heart, feeling her strength slowly slip away. Fear, unlike any he'd ever known before, set his heart sprinting. He rocked her. "Stay with me, baby. Stay with me. Come on, you can do it."

Maggie came panting up, a blanket in her arms. Once it was spread out on the ground, Gabriel laid Rose down. The others stood guard.

The heat of the day still lingered in the ground. Gabriel called upon the life force deep in the earth, felt his vision shift again. There on Rose's left shoulder, unseen by his demon eyes, a barely-healed vampire bite shone pink and silver in the moonlight. "Don't think, don't think," he said to himself, before fastening his mouth over the same spot on her

~ ☾ ~

shoulder. Gabriel heard Maggie gasp and Justin whisper low, but he quickly forgot his audience.

Gabriel breathed the life force of the earth into Rose as it flowed into him, careful not to lose himself. He could taste Mephisto on her, knew that the fire demon had breathed a part of him into Rose to save her life. It grated, but Gabriel found a moment to give the demon grudging thanks. He could taste Satine there, too, but her influence waned as his breath pushed earthly life into Rose.

Finally, she stirred in his arms, her body growing warm again. Not demon hot, just human warm. With a last kiss on her shoulder, he lifted his head and searched her face. "You okay?"

Rose looked up, blinked. "Yeah. I think. Help me stand. We won, right?"

Gabriel grabbed a tee shirt from the bag near him and dropped it over her head. It was long enough to cover her half way down her thighs. "Right. The vamps are toasted. Mephisto is gone and Satine, well. You know better than we do about Satine." He found sweatpants in the bag and pulled them on.

"Satine's ash on my back." Rose sent a wry smile to her friends. "You guys don't know how lucky you are to have family that you can love."

"You sure you can walk? I could carry you."

"I think I'm done being carried. Just don't go too fast, and I'll be fine." Rose stretched her arms over her head. "Man, what a night."

Gabriel turned to his brothers and Maggie. "Thanks, for everything. You guys okay?

"A few scrapes, teeth marks, bruises," and Justin shrugged. "I'll give everyone a check after we get back to the house, do any triage necessary. Maggie, you're coming too." His voice left her no room for argument.

"Okay." Maggie bent and picked up the blanket, and they all turned and started walking to their cars.

The night still held heat. Gabriel looked up at the stars, dimly glinting in the city sky, one arm wrapped around Rose.

~ ☾ ~

"I don't know how to say this."

"Don't talk about leaving. I'm too tired to argue with you, and my heart is too sore right now." Rose rubbed her chest.

"What the hell were you thinking, going inside that place by yourself?" he demanded. He stopped her in the middle of the street and gripped her shoulders. "Didn't we talk about that? Didn't we say we'd go together? You know how things fall apart when we're not together. Damn it, Rose."

"How were you going to get your soul from Satine? Tell me that, big guy," she demanded. "Do not push me around. I've got a good brain. I enjoy using it. So accept me the way I am, because I've gone through more changes than I care to remember in the past few days. I'm done changing. Done."

"How do you think I felt, knowing you were where I couldn't reach you, where I couldn't protect you?" He pulled her into him and held her tightly, his heart hammering hard in his chest. "I can't, I won't live without you. I'm done being alone, because alone? It really sucks."

Astonished, she lifted her head off his chest and stared up at him. "You don't want to leave?"

"I've never been more serious in my life. I don't want you to feel like you have to stay with me just because I changed my mind. And it's not really that I changed my mind, it's that I finally started listening to my heart. Rose, I need you in my life. I love you." He felt her melt into him then, her hands stroking his back. "And I will push you around when it comes to your safety."

Rose sighed and snuggled closer. "I think I was born loving you, missing you. Needing you."

Her aura grew shiny-golden in the night. Gabriel had never seen anything so beautiful in his life as the ash-covered redhead with the golden glow. "You take my breath away, I love you so." Gabriel thrilled to feel the steady beat of her heart against him. He pressed a hard kiss to the top of her head and leaned back to see her face. "I'm not letting you go, not ever again."

She studied the clear gray of his eyes, saw the love filling him, and her heart sang. "You'd better not. You've given me

~ ☾ ~

more than I knew to want. I'll need some time to pay back the favor." She lifted her face for his kiss.

Footsteps pounded down the street toward them. "Ah, good. Welcome to the family, Rose." Justin bent and kissed her cheek before catching Gabriel's eye. "I need some help. Fast. Maggie collapsed before we got to the car. Kellan's with her, but I need you." Urgency pulsed off him.

"I'm there." Gabriel turned to Rose. "I'll carry you."

"No." Laughing, she held her hands up and backed away. "Go on, I'll just walk at a normal pace, thank you. It'll give me a chance to work out the kinks."

Justin zipped off, faster than Rose's eyes could track. His voice floated back to them. "Hurry, Gabriel!"

"They're just around the corner. Half a block." Gabriel took a step forward, not wanting to leave Rose.

"I'll be right there. Go, Maggie needs you." She blew him a kiss, her eyes shining with love.

"I'll hold you to that promise," he growled, having snatched her kiss from the air. Then he was gone, and the wide street empty but for her.

"How things change," she murmured to herself. Deepest night was edging to dawn. A couple more hours and the sun would pour down over her new life. Rose walked slowly, cataloguing everything that had happened in the night.

Mephisto. She would miss him. It was stupid to pretend otherwise. His soul was so badly damaged, and she didn't have it long enough to figure out what to do with it. She could only hope that he'd heal, over time. Though the debt between them had been cancelled out, she still felt she owed him. He'd given her the precious gift of his powers, and she'd known what it was like to be different. Strong. Losing that had been such a shock to her system. She couldn't cope until Gabriel had stepped in, brought her back to life.

But if she had to lose Mephisto, she had hit the jackpot with Gabriel. She shook her head in disbelief. Not only Gabriel, but through him, the entire extended Caine clan. And now she had Maggie, her first real girlfriend since childhood. Plus she had her soul back, where it belonged.

~ ☾ ~

Her life, so empty before she died, had miraculously been filled with wonder and delight and love. Above all, love.

Rose sighed, full up with happiness, and yawned. "I could sleep. I could really enjoy sleep." Realizing that she'd stopped in the middle of the street, she hugged herself and laughed. To look forward to sleep seemed like such a luxury, and yet it was now hers.

"If I have my way, you will sleep in my arms every day of eternity."

The voice sent a cold stream of dread down her spine. She spun around to find Vlad behind her. "I did warn you." He stood a yard away, striking in his dark suit, his hair a blond nimbus, a mockery of an angelic halo.

Rose blinked. "I forgot." *Gabriel!* Her mind shrieked his name, over and over, a ghastly repetition from just a few days earlier.

He examined his fingernails. "You...forgot. That's insulting. You forgot me, gave a demon his soul back, oh wait. You gave *two* demons their souls back. And you utterly destroyed my favorite toy." Vlad looked at her and she felt his ice-blue eyes pierce her soul. "Satine was a Soul Stealer," he continued. "You are a Soul Chalice. It seems a fair trade, you in her place. Come to me."

The command in his voice went deeper than she'd ever known. Before she could stop herself she'd taken three steps toward him. "No. No!" Desperately she stopped her forward progress and called upon the one part of her she'd never tried to manipulate before. Power she'd never known, not even as a fire demon, burst through her, filling her with a light that illuminated the neighborhood.

Exhilaration streamed through her. Wings beat on her back, surprisingly heavy, bigger than the little demon ones. She heard shouts behind her but didn't dare turn to look, keeping her focus steady on Vlad. "You can't touch me."

Curiosity crossed the perfection of his face. "Watch me." A gesture from him had a blanket of black coming down over her, smothering her light, disorienting her. It swept her up and wrapped her tight. *Gabriel!*

~ ☾ ~

* * *

Gabriel came around the corner at demon speed to find Rose bursting with light, large, angelic wings protruding from her back. Shock had him stopping to stare in awe even as blackness came down and shrouded her completely. Suddenly Rose was nowhere to be seen.

Vlad stood there, his arms crossed, not a hair out of place or a wrinkle on his suit.

Raw, human fury edged with fear possessed Gabriel. Without a thought he launched himself at Vlad, caught the vampire's arm as he tried to spin away. "Oh, no you don't," he growled, and using the other man's momentum, he slammed the vampire face down into the asphalt, once, twice before it could squirm free. The ground shuddered beneath the assault.

"You cannot defeat me." But the vampire breathed hard as his body struggled to heal. He sidestepped Gabriel's next assault.

"You touched Rose. I did warn you. Dance all you want, but you won't be able to dance forever. You've never met the likes of me," said Gabriel. He gauged his enemy, dodging first one way, then the other. *Justin. I need your swords.*

Coming, bro.

Quietly. Don't spook the vamp.

Got it.

Gabriel felt the connection with Justin fade. Rose was still there, quiet in the corner of his mind. *You okay?*

Get it done.

Her words loosened the knots in his gut. Gabriel did a running flip over the vampire, ending up closer to the corner where Justin waited.

Vlad spun around to keep him in sight. "The likes of you are a dime a dozen. You're not even hard to kill." His contemptuous dismissal crawled under Gabriel's skin. He flicked a hand and cuts appeared on Gabriel's arms. Blood flowed freely.

Gabriel brought healing power, lay it like a cloth over the wounds on his arms without taking his eyes off Vlad. The bleeding stopped, and he raised a brow toward Vlad. "Gee. Is that the best you can do? You haven't killed me yet," he taunted. Other cuts appeared on his body but he refused to give them power.

The two men swayed in the street, searching out the other's weaknesses. Ten feet separated them, an easy leap for both. Vlad tossed his golden mane. "You're just a demon. I've killed thousands of demons in my time. I've lived longer than you could dream of living."

"That makes you an expert at living?" Gabriel felt Justin fit the swords into his hands as he held them behind his back.

Vlad sighed, world-weary. "I'm an expert in survival. I'm real tired of you always riding to the rescue, though. I suppose I should just kill you outright, rather than turning you. Mmm. Pity." With a flick of his hand, two more cuts appeared on Gabriel's thighs, tearing into his jeans.

"Yeah. Good luck with that." Gabriel brought the blades into the open and gave them an experimental twirl. "These have great balance. They've killed a lot of vampires tonight. I'm thinking, though, that you'll be the last one they kill before dawn."

With demonic speed and Fae grace, Gabriel went airborne, knowing exactly where each blade needed to be placed as he moved. The swords flashed in the waning moonlight as he spun around the vampire, making ribbons of the suit he wore. Blood appeared.

Vlad gestured furiously and Gabriel's leather coat was soon in tatters. A few of the vampire's cuts had made it to his skin, and they were both dripping with blood.

"Stand still, damn it." Vlad wiped at a slash on his cheek. "I'll kill you." Vengeance burned in his eyes and he grabbed for a sword as it flashed toward him.

"Oh yeah, grab the weapon, that's bright," scoffed Gabriel, and with an upwards yank, the vampire's thumb was cut clean off even as the other slashed at his neck. Vlad, shocked, opened his mouth but whatever else he would have said gurgled into nothing.

Gabriel swung the other sword and that blow took the head clean off. It flew several yards before coming to a stop beside a

~ ☾ ~

sewer.

Gabriel dropped the swords and ran toward Rose, who lay face down in the middle of the street. Whatever had hidden her from sight had vanished. "Rose! Damn it, you'd better be alive."

She rolled over, her eyes wide. "Gabriel!" She reached for him just as he got to her side. "You're hurt."

He shook his head. "It's nothing."

Rose looked beyond him and shrieked. "Gabriel! Fire, for God's sake!"

Vlad's headless corpse had risen to all fours. It crawled, searching for its head. Gabriel and Rose scrambled to their feet, Rose backing away as Gabriel advanced. He swept up one of the discarded swords and impaled the body, jamming the sword into the asphalt below.

"That should hold you for a bit." Rummaging around in his pockets, he brought out matches and lit the once-fancy suit in several places. The fire spread quickly. Gabriel retrieved the head from where it had rolled and placed it in the middle of the back, eyes down. The golden hair caught, frizzled up and disappeared, leaving the skin of the head to blacken in the flame.

A car came around the corner. Rose hid behind Gabriel, who tensed up. How to explain this to a human?

Kellan got out of the Jag's driver's seat and they both relaxed. "You guys, go. I'll stand watch, make sure there's nothing left. Justin wants you at the house, and hey, put a towel down on the seat. If even a drop of blood gets anywhere inside that car, you're cleaning it."

Gabriel grinned. "Thanks, man. Come home as soon as you can."

"Yeah." Kellan watched them drive away, the love between them tangible and glowing. Sighing, Kellan turned back to the burning vampire and settled in for what was left of the night.

~ ☾ ~

Chapter Twenty Three

Gabriel looked around the main room of the Caine family home. Cleaned and put to rights with a fire in the fireplace despite the summer heat, it was warm, inviting and currently filled with people. Justin stood scowling behind the chair occupied by Maggie. Kellan had sprawled across one large sofa.

A week since their alliance with the wolves against the vampires, they'd healed and talked the entire thing out from one side to another, though they still weren't sure what to make of Rose's new manifestation.

He sat on the other couch with Rose curled up against him, marveling at the strange and wonderful turn his life had taken. Rose snuggled against him and yawned.

"I'm thinking pizza for dinner." As everyone groaned, Gabriel shrugged. "Okay. Justin, you pick."

"He's gonna pick Chinese," Kellan complained. "Justin always picks Chinese."

"Actually, I was thinking Thai," Justin countered.

"I like both." Maggie kept her gaze on the fireplace.

"Well, somebody had better order something soon, because I'm starving," Rose declared.

"Will you accept a bucket of chicken?" The voice came from the doorway, and everyone turned to look at the newcomer. "I dropped it off in the kitchen."

"Gregor!" Justin went to welcome his brother. "Good to see you, bro. Healed and healthy. You look well."

Rose looked to Gabriel. "Who?"

Gabriel's eyes met hers. "My oldest brother, Gregor."

Gabriel stood, uncertain, and looked to Kellan who also stood.

~ ☾ ~

They waited for Gregor to walk over to them.

Justin spoke rapidly into Gregor's ear as they made their way slowly across the room to the fireplace. Gabriel waited, nerves thrumming through him. All he wanted, all he'd ever wanted, he realized, was his family's approval. Something he thought he'd never be able to get after Marianne's death. And Gregor...he'd never truly forgiven him their mother's death.

Gregor finally stood there in front of his brothers. His blue-black skin shone in the firelight, his suit immaculate even after traveling all day. Gabriel stifled a smile.

"Well, well. Look what the cat dragged in," drawled Kellan. He shoved his hands in his pockets and rocked back on his heels. "You would arrive after the fight." The room fell silent. Justin took a few steps back, out of the action.

Gregor raised an eyebrow. "Cousin. I understand you're leaving soon."

Kellan's eyes flashed. "I'm gone in thirty seconds, just say the word."

"Gregor, that's not necessary," Gabriel began, but when Gregor's steel blue eyes cut his way, Gabriel's voice dried up.

"You. Were you too busy to write? To call? To let us know where the hell you were?" Gregor's voice chilled the air between the men. "Family isn't for convenience. We're forever. You need us, call. We'll be there. That's how it works. And you," and he turned back to Kellan, "the same goes. I don't care how footloose you are. You keep us informed. Do you hear me?"

Gabriel blinked. "Damn it, Gregor. I didn't want to see the disappointment in your eyes. In Gideon's eyes. I fucked up, real bad."

Gregor put a hand on Gabriel's shoulder and shook him slightly. "The only disappointment was in thinking you didn't trust us enough to tell us what happened." He put his other hand on Kellan's shoulder and looked from one man to the other. "Damn it, I should knock your heads together. But you'd just gang up on me. So I only have one thing to say."

"What's that?"

"It's about time you came home. Did anyone bring beer?"

~ ☾ ~

"I'll make it up to you, I swear."

Gregor's fingers flexed hard enough to hit bone. Gabriel winced. "That's in the past. You're here now. That's what matters." He turned to Kellan, his eyebrows raised. "Well?"

Kellan shifted from one foot to the other. "We never were the hugging kind, you and me, if that's what you're waiting for."

Gregor stifled a sigh. "What are your plans?"

"Don't know. Hadn't thought too far ahead." He shrugged. "Didn't think you'd care much." He lifted his chin in defiance.

"You stubborn son of a bitch. You're family. Of course we care. Of course I care."

"Then I guess I'll stay for a little bit."

"Okay then. Okay." Something that might have been relief flickered across Gregor's face.

"Did someone say beer?" Justin broke in.

"I want some chicken." Kellan moved to the kitchen.

Rose stood, annoyed. "Hey now. Isn't anyone going to introduce me?"

Gabriel reached for Rose's hand and drew her to his side. "Gregor, this is Rose. We're going to get married at some point. Oh, and she's a Soul Chalice," he added, and grinned down at his love.

Gregor, coming toward her with a hand out, stopped in surprise. He dropped to one knee, took Rose's hand, and kissed the back of it. "Welcome, Healer of Souls," he said, and his eyes shone brightly. "Angelkind are always welcome on this side of the veil."

Maggie whistled. "I *knew* it!"

Rose's eyes widened. "Oh, but I'm not a – what?"

Gregor's eyes twinkled. "You are mainly human, yes, but Angelic blood runs in your veins as well. Otherwise, you would not be a Soul Chalice." He looked from Gabriel to Rose. "You are well mated," he said, and smiled when Gabriel slid his arm around Rose.

"Let's go get some food, shall we? Before Kellan eats all the chicken." Justin grinned at Gregor. "I'm starving."

"You're always starving," said Gregor.

~ ☾ ~

"True," Justin agreed, and they headed toward the kitchen, Maggie falling in behind them.

Gabriel kept his eyes on Rose's face, her cheeks lightly flushed with surprise. "How about that. You're part angel!"

Rose shook her head and tightened her grip on Gabriel's waist. "Alice's adventure in Wonderland is nothing compared to my life. Absolutely nothing."

Gabriel brought her around to face him, and lifted her up for his kiss. "Don't worry, Rose. I'm here. I'll help you through your Wonderland, if you let me."

Rose kissed him, and pulled back to look him in the eyes. "I'd rather it were you than anyone else."

"Have you thought about kids? Like, how many we should have?" Gabriel nuzzled the fading silver scar on her neck, planted a few quick kisses up to her ear.

"Kids? Rabbit hole," Rose warned, her eyes wide. "I'm falling."

Gabriel grinned and swept her off her feet. "I've got you. No worries."

<<<<>>>>

~ ☾ ~

ACKNOWLEDGEMENTS

Many thanks to Jenn Reese, my very first critique partner from years back who always encouraged me to keep on writing. We've come a long way, girlfriend! Thanks also to the Los Angeles Romance Authors and FF&P chapters of RWA. Your help and support has been vast.

Huge thanks to my brother Greg Cunningham, who a few years ago gave me an unused Mac G4 – that gift gave mobility to my writing. Thanks also to the crew at my local Coffee Bean and Tea Leaf, where most of DEMON SOUL was written.

Most of all, thanks from the bottom of my heart to Heather Howland, Crescent Moon Press Acquisitions Editor, who saw beyond my terrible three-line pitch to the shiny 100 first words of the manuscript and requested to see more. Your faith in me has bolstered my own.

And to Liz Pelletier, writer and Editor Extraordinaire, who does more in 24 hours than seems possible for one woman. Because of your hard work, this is a much better book than it was six months ago – thank you, thank you, thank you!

About the Author

Christine Ashworth is a native of Southern California. The daughter of a writer and a psych major, she fell asleep to the sound of her father's Royal manual typewriter for years. In a very real way, being a writer is in her blood-her father sold his first novel before he turned forty; her brother sold his first book before he turned twenty-five.

At the tender age of seventeen, Christine fell in love with a man she met while dancing in a ballet company. She married the brilliant actor/dancer/painter/music man, and they now have two tall sons who are as brilliant as their parents, which keeps the dinner conversation lively.

Christine's two dogs rule the outside, defending her vegetable garden from the squirrels, while a polydactyl rescue cat named Zaphod holds court inside the house. Everything else is in a state of flux, leaving her home life a cross between an improv class and a think-tank for the defense of humans against zombies and demons.

Please drop by and visit Christine at her website at
www.christine-ashworth.com.

CPSIA information can be obtained at www.ICGtesting.com
Printed in the USA
LVOW081824140213

320154LV00001B/66/P

9 780984 180592